THE
BOOK
OF
NORMAN

D1572256

THE
BOOK
OF
NORMAN

A Novel

ALLAN APPEL

Mandel Vilar Press

This book is typeset in Adobe Garamond. The paper used in this book meets the minimum requirements of ANSI/NISO Z39.48-1992 (R1997). ∞

Cover image ©iStock.com/Matt_Gibson/RedBarnStudio

Cover design by Sophie Appel

Publisher's Cataloging-in-Publication Data

Names: Appel, Allan.

Title: The book of Norman : a novel / Allan Appel.

Description: Simsbury, Connecticut : Mandel Vilar Press, [2017]

Identifiers: ISBN 978-1-942134-31-2 | ISBN 978-1-942134-32-9 (ebook)

Subjects: LCSH: Brothers—California—History—20th century—Fiction. | Judaism—Relations—Mormon Church—Fiction. | Camp counselors—California—History—20th century—Fiction. | Fathers—Death—Religious aspects—Fiction. | Angels—Fiction. | Nineteen sixties—Fiction. | Jewish fiction.

Classification: LCC PS3551.P55 B66 2017 (print) | LCC PS3551.P55 (ebook) | DDC 813/.54—dc23

Printed in the United States of America

16 17 18 19 20 21 22 23 24   9 8 7 6 5 4 3 2 1

Mandel Vilar Press
19 Oxford Court, Simsbury, Connecticut 06070
www.americasforconservation.org | www.mvpress.org

*In memory of Allan Kornblum and Peter Minichiello,
dear ones, who have gone, and in celebration of
our grandson, Samuel Peter Appel-Metz,
who has arrived.*

In heaven an angel is nobody in particular.

GEORGE BERNARD SHAW, *Man and Superman*

The Angels of Wind and Fire
Chant only one hymn, and expire
With the song's irresistible stress. . . .

HENRY WADSWORTH LONGFELLOW, "Sandalphon"

For He shall have His angels watch over you on every path you take. In their hands they'll carry you so you'll not even stub your toe on a stone.

PSALM 91

You who are free
Rescue the dead.

DAVID IGNATOW, "Rescue the Dead"

Profound thanks, as always, for the friendship, wisdom, support, and good cheer of Janet Abramowicz, Paul Bass, Stanley Cohen, Marc Kaminsky, Stuart Kramer, Sandy Lieberson, Mark Oppenheimer, and James Ponet; and for the love of my wife, Suzanne Boorsch, our children, Sophia and Nathaniel, our son-in-law, Geoffery Metz, and my brother, Joseph, and his family.

THE
BOOK
OF
NORMAN

|

AFTER I walked rapidly down Broadway and across Eighty-Sixth Street, all the way from the Jewish Theological Seminary up on 122nd—this was back in 1967—on a bright, surprisingly cool afternoon on the day before Passover to be precise (which is also the arcane Jewish fast of *Ta'anit Bechorim* that I once in my previous zeal had observed), I made my way beneath a brilliant blue sky to the northern end of the grassy oval in Central Park.

I approached the gray metal trash can at the center of the gathered crowd. I ceremonially withdrew my ragged draft card from my pocket. I extended it above the smoldering flames.

Like a shopper racing down the aisles of memory, I ransacked all the *brachot,* the long roster of brief Hebrew prayers that mark everything from rainbows to new babies, in order to locate an appropriate one to mark the red-letter moment in my life that was about to unfold:

In short, what's the blessing for offering your Selective Service ID to the fire?

I stared at the small orange flames that leaped through the space of three glowing sticks and the pile of embers and ashen burned papers at the bottom of the trash can.

I paused; I considered. Strange religious thoughts floated through my mind: A sacrifice? A burned offering?

Just the year before, I'd studied the detailed instructions for the offerings at the ancient temple in Jerusalem; the preparation and consummation of the sacrifices; and how the officiants had to be scrupulous that certain of the young lambs be wholly consumed by flames, had to become a "holocaust," as

3

the explicit Hebrew terminology commanded. Otherwise, the priestly obligation on behalf of the nation is not fulfilled.

Now here I was, in the throes of the anti-Vietnam War movement, weirdly trying to make those esoteric studies relevant. Just what obligation—national, moral, or you name it—was I fulfilling by this act?

I fingered my card. I had always liked having it in my wallet. Oddly, it connected me to, well, something larger than my puny, confused self.

Yet as I stood there and faltered, what fully consumed me was only indecision, as I continued to hold the draft card above the fire, and my fingertips began to grow uncomfortably hot.

There were no cops or other uniformed people in the circle of students, protesters, and passersby.

"Do it. Let it go, man," an anonymous man's voice clamored. As usual, I was looking for a way to do it and yet not to do it at the same time.

I smelled the smoky air. I lowered the card a little more. I flipped over my ID as if I were a fry cook and my arm the spatula. I let the card become singed at one corner, and then on the other, seared, like a burger, just the way I liked them.

Then when it was too hot to hold any longer, I let it go.

The card floated down and settled on an outside ember. As it began to curl and burn, I reached in to grab it, but the intense heat drove my hand away.

As I watched it become ash, a couple of people gathered around the trash can, put their arms lightly on my shoulders, and watched the burning with me in a companionable silence, as if we were indeed sharing a rite at an altar.

Another anonymous hand slapped my back and a gravelly voice said, "Right on, brother."

"You did a beautiful thing," crooned another voice, this time a woman's. "Really, really beautiful."

Her words were brief and receding, but her tone was so sweetly articulated, long and so stirring, I imagined the voice had to belong to a young, beautiful creature, perhaps a singer, a soloist, perhaps a gorgeous ingenue new to New York from a wholesome place like Kansas and specializing in auditioning for virginal female heroines—maybe Joan of Arc or an angel.

I nodded, I smiled, I turned, and as I walked away I searched the dispersing crowd for the owner of that voice, for just a glance of a face, a chiseled nose, a mysterious nostril rapidly viewed through a half-pulled-back hood of a red sweatshirt, strands of hair that flickered golden in the firelight.

She might have been beautiful. I wondered if I had seemed brave in her eyes, and if so and if she were free tonight, maybe we could meet up at the West End Bar for a sandwich and a beer? No, not beer, wine.

Yet I didn't see her in the slowly dispersing throng; I saw only a middle-aged couple, salt-and-pepper-haired and earnest in the smiles they sent my way, who seemed to look at me and send along the V sign for peace with their two raised fingers.

This occasion called for wine to celebrate and to toast to peace, to brotherhood and to sisterhood, to beauty, to . . . I felt there had to be something more.

I turned back toward the trash can and lingered, staring so long at the expiring fire that when I finally glanced over my shoulder, every last bystander had drifted away. I was alone, and felt no longer even the modest, momentary hero I had become for a brief instant in my own eyes.

In fact, quite the opposite. I was already in my mind composing an exculpatory note to the Selective Service: Dear Honored Gentlemen of the Draft Board: I recently lost my card. Would you kindly send a replacement to the following address, care of . . .

That's the way I was, before the angels arrived.

IN A kind of ceremonial daze at what had happened, I walked alone all the way back up to Tom's Restaurant, on 111th Street and Broadway. I could have taken the bus or subway of course, but I treated the occasion and what had transpired as if it were a kind of holy day and I was not allowed to use transportation other than my two sneakered feet.

At Tom's I slid into a window-side booth. The usually busy place was fairly empty. I did a census of the scattered diners. There were nine. I was the tenth, just enough to make a quorum for prayers.

Feeling secure in my tangle of contradictions that at the moment felt like a cozy nest, I calmly ordered.

Soon I was methodically tracing, with the tip of my knife, a chunky trail of tangerine-flecked Russian dressing across my first and, some fifteen minutes later, my second bacon cheeseburger of the afternoon.

For those of you not up on all your minor Jewish fast days, that fast day on which I had burned my draft card and then consumed the first two cheese-burgers of my life, is called *Ta'anit Bechorim.* It is observed only by firstborn Jewish males, such as your narrator, commemorating how we were saved from the plague of the death of the firstborn in Egypt.

For all the Passover seders I have ever participated in, as a child or as a so-called adult (for we are always called not the adults but the *children* of Israel, and for a reason), the death of the innocent firstborn boys of Egypt has always deeply disturbed me. And that is compounded by the painful drowning death of so many Egyptian soldiers and charioteers as we fled from them across the Red Sea. Sure, they wanted to kill or re-enslave us, and God hurled them, their very best captains, deep into the sea like a stone.

We recount this every day in morning prayers. The question I had been asking myself for years: Might there not have been another way?

AFTER YEARS of struggling to live a religious life, I was in my third year at the seminary and had miserably faltered in my effort to fulfill even a respectable fraction of our 613 annually mandated commandments.

So, on that long-ago day, which that year also coincided with my late father Paul's birthday, and that no mere coincidence either, I in my mind had wiped the slate clean.

In those two linked gestures—burning the draft card and consuming the forbidden mix of milk and meat in those delectable burgers as a reward—I had solved my Vietnam Problem and my Jewish Problem.

Or so I thought.

For at the center of my little heresies and profound unease was also a Father Problem I didn't even know I had until the miraculous summer that was about to unfold.

In using the term *miraculous,* I don't want to be taken metaphorically.

For I intend this memoir to be a testament to the real and living presence of souls and of Jewish angels in our lives who help us attend to them; and these angels are powerful, visible, and mysteriously among us.

I believe they embody the forces—all right, call them impulses or newly turned pages—that help us say words that are essential and yet have never been said before; or to act in a manner that is unlikely or even undreamed of, but is ultimately indispensable to our well-being. The results can indeed be miraculous.

Had I not been touched by angels and by the presence of souls long ago, in 1967, to be precise, when I was a very young man, I would not be the person I am.

But remember, angels have minds of their own. Especially Jewish angels.

I was touched not by a single presence but by two angels, one named Tali and the other Aviva, the first tall and fair, regal and serene as the Sabbath Queen herself, but also with shoulders like a power forward in basketball; the second her opposite, for Aviva was compact and small but with the muscles and spring of a gravity-defying gymnast.

Both had recently been discharged from the Israel Defense Forces after their victory over, yes, those pesky Egyptians once again, this time in June 1967.

We met the angels, my brother, Jonathan, and I, when we were working summer jobs in Los Angeles at Camp Tikvah, which, most appropriately, means "Camp Hope."

You will meet them soon.

But to back up a bit, on that long-ago Fast of the Firstborn in 1967, that I was marking at Tom's Restaurant, on precisely the same day, it turned out, on the other side of the continent, Mormon missionaries were knocking on Jon's door.

Younger than me by one and a half years and a gifted natural athlete the way I was a nerd and a young scholar, Jon had recently dropped out of UCLA.

He had made that decision shortly after he'd heard Timothy Leary lecture there on the joys of LSD. When I first learned of the next chapter in his wanderings, which was Jon's serious embrace of LDS, the Church of Jesus Christ of Latter-day Saints, I had the extreme bad taste to suggest to him that this error in his ways may well have been merely a consequence of a bad high compounded by dyslexia.

Understood that way, couldn't it be easily fixed from LDS back to LSD?

Jon did not think much of my suggestion, and who could blame him?

Not long before his transformation he had written me that since nuclear weapons were recently banned in space, it was altogether wrong for the powers that be to ban acid that would deny kids enjoyment of all that newly liberated cosmos.

However—thus I paraphrase the enthusiastic style of his letter and several that had followed—he no longer needed LSD or even the beautiful pot he occasionally grew.

Why?

Jon said he now had all the deep space of Mormon theology, including all of its vast starry systems that included the Planet Kolob, where Heavenly Mother and Heavenly Father conjugated, created, and launched us all, each and every soul, of all faiths, sizes, and persuasions. He was beginning to understand that we are little discrete human souls buffeted by the Mormon intergalactic winds to vector our way to earth, here to live our lives as a test of our moral character and to earn a trip back to our heavenly birth planet.

I don't think this sarcastic assessment—reader, please be warned as my tone often slips into the terribly mixed feelings of that summer!—does adequate justice to Jon's quality of yearning, or to his hallucinogenic arguments for the doper's life he had been pursuing.

For Jon had the true spiritual person's hunger, and he believed that the doors of perception through which we experience life are only opened a crack; one's task on earth must be to widen them.

I didn't give him credit for this, of course. Yet I still do not think the Mormons ever gave Jon the right hammers and screwdrivers to do the job.

Yet I could not say that to him, not really, until Tali and Aviva entered our lives.

He had dropped out of UCLA shortly after the Prophet of Acid's sermon in front of a hugely stoned crowd that thronged the steps of Royce Hall at the university.

Then during those several months of my exit from organized Jewish life (so I thought) in New York, while I was forgoing studying for my Talmud exams by hanging out at the War Resisters' League on Bond Street . . . in short while I cheeseburgered and agonized my way out of the seminary and out of my plans for a professional Jewish life, my brother in his time off from driving a cab was beginning to attend his own seminary, a Mormon one, in LA.

In those initial months of studying Joseph Smith and Brigham Young, Jonathan Gould was very often, I believe, still quite ripped while he drove the dangerous night shift, but with the *Book of Mormon* now resting on the passenger seat beside him.

"Protection, brother," is how he described his companion.

Other cabbies were being robbed at gun- and knifepoint, he wrote. But not him.

Who was I to say that this was not an improvement over how he had been hanging out at head shops? Or sitting cross-legged on a red blanket spread out at Hilgard and Leconte and other fly-by-night hallucinogenic street-corner drug markets out by UCLA?

There he had been stringing small red clay beads onto a fishing line, creating bracelets that he sold here and there around LA and sometimes also from the front seat of the cab. I don't think business was very brisk.

I believe Jon had not only torn up his Selective Service card, but had also smoked it. That is, he dropped the torn pieces into joints that he had soaked in a rich, murky gallon jug of Cucamonga red that he used to keep stashed in a corner of the garage of our duplex on Orange Grove Drive.

Jon had always been exceptionally inventive about his personal drug use. He had created these wine-dark joints on wrinkled Egyptian paper that he rolled and prepared as lovingly as a scribe might work on a papyrus. Then he dried and stored them in a Fig Newton tin, brushed them with cinnamon, and perhaps with just the tiniest sprinkle of acid crystals for that extra spiritual insight.

Well, whether there were shards of draft cards in them or not, these were as tasty as they were potent.

Had marijuana become legal over the next decade or two, my brother by now may well have become the CEO of the new pot products division of Nabisco.

"What did I do with that immoral war?" he asked me years later. His answer: "I smoked it, man."

Before the Mormons made their beachhead in his life, Jon had had two near-accidents in the cab. That was shortly before I arrived home to LA. And both occurred way downtown in the most derelict sections where our dad used to hang out. And that was no coincidence.

Yet the accidents hadn't stopped his driving. In fact, he talked about those vehicular brushes with death as hardly more than taking a turn a bit fast. In hindsight I believe they were also serious games he was playing to test his new beliefs. I believe he was trying to gauge the power of the Mormons' doctrines and to locate and to communicate with our dad's soul.

It took me a long time, and my dates with the angels, to find out that was what he was always moving toward after all.

At that time, most Jews and especially yours truly could not even have approximated such specific geographies of the routes of souls transiting toward heaven, whereas the Mormons had mapped these out with as much celestial detail as the auto club.

During that fraught period, I could tell you exactly on which six corners of Manhattan Island each of the Hamburger Heaven outlets stood. But of Jewish Heaven? Please!

What I'd learned at the synagogue, at the seminary, and in our religiously confused childhood home, gave me little guidance in Jewish celestial matters, not even a road map or blueprint. And, believe me, you need to be equipped because in this regard the Mormons are daunting.

That's why I needed the angels to intercede where I alone would have failed miserably.

But I get ahead of myself.

Jon kept driving that old yellow Checker, mainly at night. He was one of a small number of white drivers at his garage who would stop for Negro passengers after the Congress on Racial Equality and other civil rights demonstrations broke up out at UCLA and to a lesser extent at USC. Many cabbies just waited for their fares at the train station, but Jon knew that there would always be a handful of students and organizers who'd need a ride home to South Central or to Watts where few other cabbies dared to go.

To and from these calls, he also spent time transporting the missionaries who had befriended him; but he was also cruising the produce market, Skid Row, Pershing Square, and other threadbare districts of downtown LA.

That's where Paul Gould's *neshama* and his *ibbur*—Hebrew words for two of the several forms or emanations of his wandering, unsettled Jewish soul—may also have hung out. Maybe Paul was inhabiting the next guy in a flashy suit leaning shakily against a lamppost as Jon cruised slowly by.

A *neshama* is closest to the physical breath, the invisible fluid or stream, as it were, that carries the spiritual identity. After death Jewish souls then need cozy bodies of the human and the living to inhabit—at which stage they are *ibburs*—so we can locate them and assist them as they take care of unfinished business.

Jon never used those terms, and I didn't either, not until the angels' arrival taught me.

Yet souls don't care what you call them, only that you catch them. Like a penny on the sidewalk or your misplaced glasses, make no mistake about it: a Jewish soul wants to be found.

SO, BY my best calculation, on or about that spring day in New York while I was enjoying my bacon cheeseburger at Tom's, two Mormon missionaries were calling on Jon.

One of them was a tall, lanky thirty-year-old named Western Oaks. Everyone called him Wes. Although I have always believed a person deserves all their syllables, I eventually called him Wes as well.

After my brother flung open his door, Wes politely inquired if they might enter and, to use their lingo, share a little of their treasure with him.

"Hell, I'll take any treasure I can get," Jon had answered.

Still in his boxers, and likely still brandishing his morning can of Budweiser to take the edge off the night's questing, Jon yanked open his screen door and added to his expansive reply: "Enter, brothers, and pray your righteous hearts out."

When they had found a cleared spot to stand amid his socks and his sneakers, his *Playboys*, *Sports Illustrated*s, his old marked-up UCLA course catalog, a quiver of incense sticks from his dalliance with the Hare Krishna folks, his well-worn copies of *UFO Monthly*, the cigar box where he kept his hacking cash, rolling paper, roach clips, and his other materials that newspaper reports of the time used to refer to as "psychedelic paraphernalia," Jon, so the story now goes, apparently teetered, eyes half-closed, and politely inquired, "Now, say again: What religion are you folks?"

"LDS. Mormons. The Church of Jesus Christ of Latter-day Saints," said Western Oaks.

"Damn, I love the Mormons. I really do."

When Jon was high, especially in the half hour or so before he drifted into unconsciousness, he had a wonderfully generous spirit. "I got absolutely nothing against the Mormons. Pray away, brothers."

Wes and the other brother, or elder, as they ID-ed themselves, promptly took my brother's hands. They asked him how he was and if there were problems or concerns he'd like to share with them.

Jon surely must have mentioned Paul because Wes was almost immediately telling him of the Mormon doctrine of the three levels of heaven: How the dead, even the non-Mormon dead, are just up there in a great kind of waiting room full of spirits. It's not that different from the doctor's or the dentist's office, just waiting for the score to be tallied and determination made as to which one of heaven's several levels you are designated to enter.

And, yes, in one of those fine and golden next precincts Jon would definitely see Paul again.

Whether Budweiser and lysergic acid were in my brother's bloodstream at the time or not, or whether just such a promise proffered was exactly the one he had been simply waiting for all his young life, it elicited a powerful response.

Wes and the other elder intoned a Mormon prayer that must have been not only righteous, as we used to say in 1967, but also very potent. For Jon's life from that instant on began to change drastically.

As mine was doing at just about the identical interval of time. Only a coincidence?

After I left those Vietnam War protesters in Central Park and devoured the forbidden foods at Tom's, I picked up three empty vodka boxes from in front of College Liquors on Broadway. Then I proceeded to begin packing up my books. Over the next month I sold my entire Jewish library. With the proceeds I bought the airline ticket back to LA. Cost: ninety dollars, which is exactly five times the Jewish magical number eighteen, and nearly exactly what I had raised from my book sale.

BY THAT time, Jon had taken a turn as dramatic as my own, if not more so.

He had fully given up his doper's apartment down by a rank canal near Venice, he had closed down the red clay bead business and moved home to live with our mom, Paulene, and our grandmother, Ida, whom we called the Relic because of her ancientness. The house was a duplex on Orange Grove, paid off just six months before Paul died. It was not far from the Temple Beth Ami synagogue on La Cienega Boulevard, where we had grown up.

Jon had another reason for moving home, apart from the good rent.

Home was also easy walking distance from the Mormon ward building, or meeting house, on Gregory Way behind La Cienega Park. Although it was not far from the world of our childhood, Lido Theater, Kentucky Boys Restaurant, and St. Mary Magdalene's Catholic Church, and of course our temple, who knew that the Mormons had been there all along?

Unlike Jehovah's Witnesses and numerous other proselytizing Christian sects, they had never come to our house.

And there was more: Jon got his great mop of curly hair neatly cut for the first time in years. He now looked like a marine recruit. He had woken up from his forbidden substances haze and was doing so, alas, just as I was eager to dive right into it, and to spend the summer, with his guidance, along with a fistful of those wine-soaked joints, as we walked together fraternally zonked along the beach at Santa Monica.

To use one of Paul's favorite poker terms, the kicker was that Jon was already also seriously thinking of getting himself baptized into the Mormon Church.

YET WHEN I arrived home in the second week of June, Jon no more knew that I was a seminary dropout than I knew he was an LDS convert-in-training and on the precipice of his formal religious dunking; I thought it simply another dalliance he'd soon lose interest in.

Of course from the second we eyed each other at the airport there were indications, the first being that I hardly recognized the neat-looking guy in pressed blue jeans and a short-sleeved white shirt who appeared by the baggage claim Number 7 at LAX.

Unlike him, I always wear long-sleeved shirts; I'm embarrassed by my skinny arms. But Jon was naturally powerful and looked that way in all his limbs. Without working out, his muscles expressed themselves, not in bulges of knots, but in a kind of natural, graceful shape of strength.

With those arms, by the baggage conveyor belt, he suprised me from behind and nearly lifted me off the ground in an embrace.

His eyes were clear and his smile broad, and I noticed that tucked in behind a rubber band that circled the outside of his blue LA Dodgers baseball cap was his yellow chauffeur's ID.

"The rabbi has returned!"

"Put me the hell down, man," I said, very unrabbinically.

Before I left, Paulene had written with consternation that Jon was still driving the cab and she was intending to do something about it. She hadn't written what.

As I slipped into the front seat, I sniffed the air for the pot I was expecting, hoping, craving, to find.

As we drove toward home, I fiddled with the radio, trying to reacquaint myself with KFWB and with other stations I had enjoyed listening to.

Otherwise we were as quiet as a taxi driver and his passenger, each surreptitiously taking the measure of the other. At Sepulveda Boulevard Jon reached across and into the glove compartment. He asked if I minded if he smoked.

Aha, I thought. Finally! But what I said was, "Why would I mind?"

"I'm really trying to quit. Not there yet."

"What a joker you are."

Oh, we ignored very well.

As we cruised along Century Boulevard, Centinella, and then through Westwood, we cycled through brotherly small talk, but slowly, turning over each prosaic tidbit, like popcorn from a bag we were sharing and both did not want to empty.

Because what then would follow? A confession?

Finally, I asked him if he was interested in driving up to the big concert of rock and rollers, including Peter, Paul, and Mary, the Moody Blues, and The Mamas and the Papas, being planned in Monterey a few days later. Jon had always enjoyed driving to concerts in the foothills, in the desert, even up to the Angeles Crest Mountains, anywhere, half a state away no problem, and at a moment's notice. Yet he declined my invitation by silence.

That should have been another clue.

Next we talked about the Six-Day War that had recently rocked Israel and the Middle East. "They really whupped the Arabs," he said. "You seminary guys must have gone nuts."

"Oh, sure."

An LA Police Department motorcycle cop in jodphurs and shades sped by in the opposite direction just as the familiar smell of Lucky Strikes—Paul's brand—filled up the cab.

"Not to worry. The cab's clean, man. All the joints are behind me," Jon answered my unasked question. "Tobacco only."

"You get busted?"

"No, no. I just stopped."

"No more gorgeous joints soaked in, what was it? Cranberry juice, brown sugar, and brandy?"

"Cranberry juice, brown sugar, brandy, and anise. Don't forget the anise. All behind me, brother."

"And the sun's not going to rise tomorrow."

With an earnest calm, he answered, "Believe it."

Boy, did that plant the seed of disappointment. After all, I was newly freed—or thought I was—from the dietary laws and from the dozens of other religious strictures, which, as I then had seen them, had held me in their unhappy, rule-obeying, life-limiting thrall.

Now we turned off Olympic, sped south past Temple Beth Ami on La Cienega, then west onto Pico for a few blocks, where Jon skillfully maneuvered the big taxi onto Orange Grove, then into our driveway.

There it was: the duplex with white stuccoed walls that we shared with our grandmother, she in the downstairs apartment, and we upstairs. I was home.

Here at least there appeared to be no surprises, at first.

Everything seemed normal and unchanged: a hibiscus bush with large, flaming red flowers in front, stout jade plants on both sides of the walk. Same off-white paint on the walls, and the bright orange terra-cotta roof tiles over the porch; the two with cracks at the southern edge of the roof appeared no more serious than when I had left.

As we moved my stuff in, I noticed Ida's slider on the downstairs porch with its pile of old *Life* magazines.

As I carried a bag in, I paused over them. I may have been wrong, but here was the precise one I remembered from my visit ten months ago when I was last home to officiate, as a rabbi-in-training, at Paul's funeral. It was the 1961 issue marking the centennial of the Civil War with a cover photo of a former Union drummer boy. He was now—or in 1961—115 years old.

"She's asleep, inside," Jon reported the grandmother news. "Like always," he said as we climbed the stairs to our apartment. "She's like this Olympic champion, of sleep. Anywhere, anytime, she does it well."

Although I felt an impulse to let loose *my* secret, I didn't speak a word of what had happened to me in New York.

There were certainly opportunities, but each time something told me to shut up, to wait for a better moment. Then when I thought that moment for my big revelation had arrived, well, it somehow got derailed.

For those first awkward hours together we were in effect the don't-ask-don't-tell brothers.

I dropped my heavy green duffel onto the second of the twin beds in our childhood bedroom. Even though there was still some fading sunlight outside, the venetian blinds were three-quarters closed and the place was shaded.

Except for my infrequent visits home during college and during the few days I had been here for Paul's funeral—before I fled all the grief and all the "what a fine rabbi you will be" comments—I had not shared a bedroom with Jon since I'd left home seven years before.

This all felt therefore doubly unnerving, as if the lingering coziness of the past were making a half-hearted effort to muscle out a much more disturbing present that neither of us was yet ready to acknowledge.

Still we were both accidental detectives, attentive to new clues. I found my first piece of physical evidence when Jon went back downstairs to fetch my remaining luggage.

Giving in to a craven impulse, I reached toward the small mahogany nightstand that separated our beds. It had three drawers. The top had always been mine, the second Jon's; the third we shared.

Now I pulled open the third. I saw only a few handkerchiefs neatly folded and some balled up pairs of white sweat socks. I unpacked a little and tossed some T-shirts into my drawer.

I closed the third drawer, but then reopened it, wider.

That's when I saw it for the first time: at the back, a black book, whose mottled but glistening cover beckoned in the half-light.

The small silvery letters on the spine clearly spelled out *Book of Mormon*.

I picked up the volume to assess it.

At first I did not even open it. I just held it like a loaf of bread or a half pound of lox they hand you at the deli, where the idea is that you make your judgment by heft and feel. Initial impression of the volume: its hundreds of thin, onionskin pages of small black print made the book feel heavy and ungainly for its size. It felt droopy in the hand. It also gave off a well-worn smell of an old wallet, or of wet leaves.

I heard the trunk of the cab slam shut, and I accelerated my examination of the book. There was gilding at the edges of the pages, but the book didn't seem to be very well thumbed.

When I heard the screen door downstairs slam shut, I quickly replaced the book in the drawer in the exact spot where it had reposed. I lifted up another few pairs of socks nearby and noticed lying there Ayn Rand's *The Fountainhead* and a rumpled copy of *UFO Monthly*.

Cool, I remember saying to myself, with a touch of relief. Very cool. No problem. This is just another dalliance, a new chapter in the questing life of the Jon I know and love. No big deal.

I suddenly remembered Paulene's leafing through *UFO Monthly* one red-letter night maybe a decade earlier. The Foot, as we called Mr. Footlick, the temple's executive director, had just tossed Jon out of Hebrew school. His violation: smuggling in a large order of lard-soaked fries from Ships Restaurant across the street from Temple Beth Ami.

"How is it that I have one son who reads this flying saucer dreck and now also eats it, while the other is a genius already studying the Talmud! Go figure kids. Apples and oranges," Paulene said.

"Hey, man," Jon said now as he bounced into the bedroom with my bag on his shoulder, and drew me back into the present. "Hey, man, forgot to tell you: Mom's not going to be back till later tonight. Out with the Foot on a date or working late or both."

"You're kidding."

"Nope."

"The Foot? That's bad."

"That's the way it is. She's packed the fridge with the usual stuff if you're hungry. Forgot to tell you."

"Double shift for her?"

"She felt bad she couldn't come to the airport."

"The work's good for her."

"Yes, it is. Keeps her busy. Very busy."

"She's okay, right? How do you find her?"

"Oh, fine."

"And yourself?"

"All right. Terrific, really." Then without letting me go on with my tentative interrogation, he said, "I've got to go down and look in on the old lady. Getting over a cold."

"Oh, I'll go."

"No. She's probably snoozing. Best to let her sleep. You can play ball with her later. I'll tuck her in. What do you think of the neighborhood?"

"Doesn't seem changed that much."

"A few houses sold. Nelson next door desperate to sell but he keeps turning down buyers because they're Negro."

"Very nice! I'm not surprised."

"And you?"

"Me what?"

"You changed much?"

Jon paused and then said, "How's about after I check on her, we go for a walk? Around the old block?"

"I don't know."

"Sure you do."

"What's on your mind?"

"I told you: a walk. It's easy. You just put one foot in front of the other. If you forgot, I'll show you how. Come on."

2

AS the sun was dipping into the Pacific some five miles west at Santa Monica Beach, we checked that the Relic was sleeping securely downstairs—the snoring was the telltale sign—clicked the screen door shut, and began our promenade.

We walked south along Orange Grove past the many small houses and two-family duplexes like ours that had displaced the farming bungalows that were originally here along the margins of the orange groves that abounded in the area in the 1920s and 1930s.

What remained now were only vestiges of that agricultural beginning: here and there small, decorative citrus trees, mostly young ones bearing miniature lemons and oranges and a painfully thin trunk rising out of a disc of dirt the size of a pitcher's mound. These dotted many of the front lawns Jon and I now passed.

I was almost beginning to relax, when the first revelation hit.

And it wasn't even about the Mormons. Not them. Not yet.

"Got a news bulletin for you, Norman. Mom's dating the Foot." He said it almost casually as we walked.

"So you said."

"But it's big time. Serious."

"No way!"

"Very."

"Oh, man!"

"Exactly."

"The evil Mr. Footlick!"

"Takes a little getting used to, right?"

"Wow!"

How strange it was to talk about your mother this way. Jon didn't appear to have a girlfriend. I certainly didn't. Your father just dead and your mother has a . . . boyfriend? Things were out of order, out of time, out of whack. And worse. Paul had really hated the Foot, the guy who had dunned him for dues and for "capital assessments," always for money Paul never had.

And Dad was not yet cold in the . . .

That's right. That phrase, "not yet cold in the ground," was the cliché that had announced itself in my head as we walked on in nervous silence.

"I don't know how long they've been seeing each other, but, yes, flowers and candy arrive pretty regularly."

"Incredible!"

"Sees Candies, the large sampler."

We were now almost at the next corner. I slowed down, and Jon matched his gait to mine. I tried to analyze why I was so upset. It wasn't only that the Foot was the man in our local Jewish world whom Paul had made fun of the most. He was also the guy who had suspended Jon from Hebrew school for his French-fry smuggling and for other infractions, and more than once. He was over-cologned, stocky, a glib fundraiser who categorized people as prospects either for a major gift or a minor one, or just financially insecure or too insignificant to consider. That last was Paul. Yet he obviously had been interested in Paul's wife. In short, the Foot was Paul's Jewish Nemesis.

And then it was staring at me. It was not just the Foot; it was the timing.

I made a quick calculation. Paul was dead only ten months and a few days. By the generally accepted tradition, a minimum of eleven months is required, sometimes even a little more, before a widow is permitted, according to Jewish law and custom, to resume, well, a dating life.

But hadn't I just left the seminary? Who cared about Jewish rules and customs anymore! Hypocrite! I silently accused myself.

We walked on past where maybe a dozen years ago a set of triplets had been born that brought together our whole block for a few weeks. That family had moved on, Jon said, and their front lawn needed cutting and the bushes by the porch were overgrown.

Now we walked past 1138 Orange Grove where Carmen Nadler had once enticed me in when I was fourteen and showed me her breasts.

I felt suddenly like sprinting, but to get away from whom?

I couldn't get it out of my head. Our family was one for whom Judaism had always been a kind of make-up-your-own-rules-as-you-go game. So almost a year had gone by since Paul's death. So what! What was the problem with Paulene and the Foot?

I hated the way I was responding, like Dr. Strangelove's leather-gloved hand pumping the air in the automatic salute of obedience. To whom had I any longer a need to be obedient?

Let it be, I told myself as we walked another half block down Orange Grove. Look at Jon, almost sauntering like James Arness down the main street in *Gunsmoke*. Not a care in the world. Be cool. Cool like Jon. Follow his lead, I told myself.

But he had only begun with the late afternoon news flashes. "It's not going to be a slacker summer either, pal. She got us jobs."

"At the restaurant?"

"Mom would never do that. At the camp."

"What camp?"

"The temple camp, of course. Where else?"

"You've got to be kidding."

"I'll be teaching swimming, and I'm proud to be walking beside the Jewish drama counselor."

"Jesus!"

This was absolutely no way to begin my Big Non-Jewish Summer.

"Don't tell me. Footlick. She made the arrangements through him?"

"I'm sure."

"Dad's turning in his grave."

There, another obituary cliché. Suddenly my head was full of them, always a sign of trouble.

"She signed the contracts in our names."

"That's illegal."

"You going to sue her? Anyway, we could use the money."

Then I said it again, in a different way: "I'm glad Dad isn't alive to see this. This would kill him again if he knew."

"Maybe he does know."

"Huh?"

"I said maybe Dad does know. You can't be sure. Maybe he's okay with it, so calm down."

I was suddenly in an angry, baby brother-squashing mood.

"He's dead, Jon. D-E-A-D."

"Yes, I can spell. Anyway, a body's in a grave. A body is only a body. Not a soul. His soul lives."

"Oh, sure."

"His *soul's* not there, man."

"Oh, no? Where is it? In Utah? I saw your *Book of Mormon* in the bedroom. And I'm none too happy about that either."

"Dial it down. Don't shout so the whole neighborhood can hear you. I'm not hiding anything from you, although I wish you wouldn't go through my things."

"I didn't 'go through your things.'"

"Just walk."

I did but now with guilt in my gait, across Airdrome and past the brown, stuccoed building of Louis Pasteur Junior High School that we had attended.

"I need to think."

"Think away, drama counselor."

In fact, as we walked, I didn't have a thought worthy of the name, just unsettling images: my mother and the Foot holding hands; now Paulene popping candies and tossing the wrappers in the air; Paulene opening a picnic basket full of corned beef sandwiches and pickles from Canter's Deli, and handing them to the Foot who consumes each one in a single bite; now they're dancing on the plot of grass beneath which Paul was buried up at Mt. Eden Cemetery out in the valley.

It was all crazy!

In my rampaging hubris I was also thinking that I, the former star of the LA Jewish Diaspora, yes, I should be the one rolling out the banner family news of this summer. It was to have been *my* dropping out of the Jews, not Jon's dropping into the Saints, or Paulene's dating that little putz, Irving Foot-lick.

Yet, look where we had landed!

Compared to everything that was happening to my brother and to my mother, my break with the Jews seemed like dull news, and profoundly poorly timed. All the clichés inside my head beat themselves into an embarrassing, shameful silence.

The whole of the previous year as I had prepared student sermons at the seminary, I'd had nightmares that as I stepped up to our practice podium in the seminary basement, beside our often flickering Eternal Light, I'd lose my ability to speak. Some part of me really wanted it that way, a kind of rabbinic sports injury that would sideline me, maybe even end my career, like the struggling pianist not sure if he's good enough for a career on stage who gets his hand sliced off in his garage tool shop. Career over and done with before it began.

I was a pusillanimous fellow, and I longed for external factors to force decisions.

Aphasia. That was a solution of sorts, and I was open to it.

No wonder I found angels.

Now a kind of movie theater opened up inside my head, with vintage images of our parents and of the life we had lived together; it was my own unasked-for matinee. Here was a Damon Runyonesque gambling dad and a smart-talking waitress for a mom. Oh, perfectly-named Paul and Paulene, great dancers, both of whom Jon and I had often watched, as little spies hiding behind the secondhand furniture in the corner, as Dad and Mom swerved and swayed following the linoleum dance footprints on the garage floor.

There they played "Do the Bossa Nova" on our scratchy record player and practiced their other routines.

What beautiful Arthur Murray moments, with Paul twirling Paulene, her blouse sleeves flying like wings until she collapses—no, until she elegantly settles, queen-like—onto the green sofa just as in the movies. Now he's bowing to her on one knee before the sofa, Paulene's throne, Mr. Debonaire Gambler Without a Cent in His Pocket, but handsome with that pencil-line mustache, our parents like a working-class Fred and Ginger.

Amid the general threadbareness that clung to our lives, I realize now that right then and there might have been where the ground was laid for believing in what only *seems* impossible.

Paul was always bringing home his enthusiasm for a new horse or for a ticket with just the right numbers, which guaranteed that it would pay off. He used to joke that, yes, it may be taking just a little longer than hoped for, but when the Family Gould finally hits it big, it would not be merely one lousy leaking ship but a whole goddam fleet, and laden with a king's ransom in gold that will be coming in.

You can count on it.

Our mother was the most beautiful waitress who had ever worked up at Canter's Deli on Fairfax, Paul said, and he was proud of her. Her nightly haul in tips also regularly cushioned his weekly losses at the track or at poker.

A customer of Paulene's once left ten silver dollars as a tip.

"Why only ten?" Paul had asked jokingly. "That's an insult, boys. Your mom is worth what? At least ten times ten. How much is that?"

We dutifully did the multiplication.

"No! Ten times ten times ten."

I often wondered why Paul always carried on this way when her tips came up. Paul's style rarely fooled me. Beneath his act I began to detect, even as a little kid, my dad's low-key desperation. It was always there, grinding away nervously at every moment, and it scared me. Yet there was also a feeling—all right maybe love is not the word for it—that while it never went by a fancy name somehow it was also always there somewhere in the mix and filtering up from his wisecracks as well.

Because how could you say he was abandoning us for the track when he always bet on nags that had the letters N-O-R-M-A-N or J-O-N in their names, with the letters in any order? Norman and Jon indeed. They—we—never crossed the finish line first for Paul. Yet what had our dad's gesture meant?

Such questions formed our—or at least my—version of family life.

Walking now in silence, Jon and I arrived at the next corner. This was the Nelsons' brown house with its broken cedar fence, where Paul occasionally had played long night games of stud and draw poker as a substitute for his all-nighters at the parlors or the private games downtown. Suddenly I remembered how one night Paulene had yelled at him with barely a note or hint of child-protecting humor or irony: "I hate when you go to that Silver Dollar place. It's not even a casino. Just cards and watery coffee and lousy waitresses who spill it on you. Stay home, and I'll serve you coffee!"

He had just stood in the doorway and listened. Then, as he made his move to leave, she delivered her Barbara Stanwyck lines: "In case you haven't noticed, you have two growing boys. Stay home for a while. Go to Nelson's for an hour if you have to. For chrissakes, Paul, keep it in the neighborhood."

"There's no game at Nelson's tonight," he had said and then out the door he went to the Silver Dollar Casino, and I raced back into bed lest I be caught at my surveillance yet again.

And that's where, thirteen years later, Paul Gould had died: at the Silver Dollar Casino, a card parlor in a crappy building off Pershing Square. Drawing the kicker to an inside straight; getting the wrong card, and dying, not at the home of Nelson, who had been a combat medic in the war and who might have saved him, but at the seven-card-stud table, a dollar the minimum bet; they had been playing all night.

Our hard-luck dad.

That's how it had happened. Jon had reported it to me when his call reached me in New York. I was cutting some morning rabbinic homiletics class. So they had to track me down. I was sitting in the library, that august space with floor-to-ceiling tomes by the rabbis, surrounded by Akiba and Hillel, by Maimonides of Spain and Philo of Alexandria.

I was at the table in the far back of the room, in the corner at the base of the steps leading up to the rare books, reading a copy of *People* magazine when the librarian came up to me and said there was a call: Jon said it had happened at the seven-card-stud table, where he was sitting with a big glazed doughnut and barely-sipped coffee with Cremora packets squeezed between the thumb and index finger of his right hand. He had been wearing the gold Star of David cufflinks that Paulene had bought for him, discounted at the temple gift shop; he had conceded to wear them, yet often slipped them off as soon as he left the duplex, but not that night.

That night he had raised one hand, as if to bet or bluff, and then clutched his chest; Jon had reported what he found out from the other gamblers and from the cops. A couple of Paul's so-called poker friends at the table thought he was joking with that trembling upraised hand—he was always joking—faking an attack as if to say the cards he'd been dealt, yes, that bad. They will kill you.

Well, they had.

It all came back, as Jon and I arrived now at Venice Boulevard and I stood staring at the long traffic light as wave after wave of cars surged by, their white and red flickering lights the color of poker chips: Our father at the stud table, his jaw growing tighter in the paralysis of life's exiting seconds; his eyes dimming, but no one noticing.

Irony is, he had a straight flush to the joker and would have won the hand, Jon said. That was the mystery of Paul Gould.

Somehow I had woven that story into my junior rabbi's junior eulogy at the funeral, giving it, God knows how, a legit angle because gamblers, by Talmudic law, are considered so unreliable, they cannot be witnesses in court. Well, at least not as pertains to capital cases.

"You're a million miles away."

"Lot going on here, Jon. Thinking a lot about Dad."

"Yup. Me too. That's why I'm awful glad you're back home."

We now angled across Venice toward the opposite sidewalk for the return trip.

"You think he . . . loves her? The Foot."

"He sends over presents. Like I said, Sees Candies."

"Dad used to bring her those."

"Yeah, the smallest box they sell. These are top-of-the-line creamy, three layers of them and big as golf balls. Believe me, I'm the first to grab one of them. You want to know something else?"

"Actually I'm not so sure I do."

"He signs the notes: 'With esteem, respect, and affection, Irving.'"

"'Irving'?"

"Cute, huh?"

"Very."

"Got a question for you, man."

"Oh?"

"Did Mom and Dad ever use the word love? Saying I love you, Paul. I love you, Paulene."

"That wasn't their way."

"On one of their wedding anniversaries, I forget which, we had to *force* them to kiss each other. You remember? It was you who told him he couldn't leave without planting one on her cheek. Right?"

"Can't say I remember."

"I do."

"Where are you going with this?" I glanced up and caught Jon staring off into the distance. I wondered if he were spotting some golden or silver apparition over the Culver City rooftops. Then why would I even think of *that,* which confused and unnerved me further?

"Candy and kissing don't add up to love," I then said, "and you don't have to say the word for it to exist."

"I guess that's true," he conceded.

"Love. Love. Love. I feel you're about to break into song."

"It's just that I never really heard Jewish people talk about it. Love. That your experience at the seminary? In New York?"

"Love in New York? 'I love New York!' That's our motto. You love New York. He, she, and it love New York. We love it. Jon, everybody loves each other in New York."

"I'm trying to explain something, Norman."

"Who's stopping you!"

"You're so sarcastic; you don't make it easy."

I couldn't dispute that.

We walked another quarter block, up the slight incline. The weight of unsaid declarations made it feel like half a mile up a mountain. Then he said it. "The Mormons. These people. I feel they . . . love me. They accept me . . . no conditions . . ."

"Stop already! Just stop with that stuff."

"They love me for who I am, for . . ."

"And we love you for what? For who you're not? Because you're really Ho Chi Minh? Clark Kent?"

"Norman."

"There's a phone booth. Pop in."

As we recrossed Airdrome and then Saturn Street, to my surprise, I felt my pulse quicken as Jon talked for another minute, maybe two, at first haltingly, and then his voice rising into a higher register as if he were trying to convince not only me but himself as well about Jesus's unconditional love and about the Mormons' new revelation feeling to him like cool water on his tongue. He actually said that and, well, that was about enough.

All my defensive retrorockets began to fire. I was lifted, way off the pad.

So much for aphasia.

Instead of shutting up to let Jon go on and explain himself, as I should have done, words poured out of me in a nervous volley: "This is just crazy. This is all plain crazy. I just hope you're not going to say Judaism is about the crusty, dusty old law and here comes Christianity and Jesus all about love. And you've suddenly made this great discovery. Because it's the world's creakiest argument, a false dichotomy, a Christian canard for centuries that's just not true. So you got your hair cut and you stopped smoking dope. Congratulations. That's fine and good. I thought you were onto something much more interesting when you were running with the Hare Krishnas. Tell me everything you've said up to now, about the Angel Moroni and the Mormons and about Mom and the Foot, and love, love, love; tell me none of it is true. Tell me I'm dreaming."

"You done, man?"

"Maybe I am; maybe I'm not."

We had never had such a conversation. I felt in the midst of a kind of pissed-off daze and wouldn't relent.

"It really is not the end of the world. Try to be cool."

"I'll show you cool. How's about, 'And you shall love your brother as yourself'?" That's the golden rule. Brother and friend, with the same root in Hebrew, in this context not meaning you, blood brother, but every flaming fellow human being. Big democratic friendship and love among the biped mammals with speech. The golden rule of Judaism, pal, and pretty frigging lovey-dovey."

"All right, Norman."

Here was another traffic light, a great circle of black dots backlit red. We stopped, my body did, although my tongue, I'm sure, kept walking, and waving. I can't recall what I said, and it's better that way. I stared at the light. I took a deep breath; I counted and watched, making believe it was my count that caused the red to flicker to green.

That's when I felt a nudge from Jon's arm at the small of my back, and his whispered words, "It's going to be okay."

In the block and a half that remained before we got back to the duplex, more came out. He'd been meeting with Western Oaks and another missionary and other Mormon folks for about six weeks. He was just reading and talking with the Mormons at this point. Yet it was serious reading and serious talking. Nevertheless, the LDS church, to use his phrase, had already become "this new *anchor*."

"But you haven't, uh, signed on the dotted line?"

"You mean baptism, Norman? Can't say the word?"

"Screw you, Jon."

My heart was suddenly thumping in my chest. He also seemed to see through me—or was it *into* me—with a clarity I found not only new, but deeply unsettling. In the few yards that remained before we got home, I must have pulled away from him.

But he caught up with me, draped a strong arm over my shoulder, and said, "I'm really sorry for upsetting you, man. I really am. And on your first day back. I guess I couldn't wait. Real bad form!"

"I'm sorry for popping off," I said. I guess I needed him to be who he had been more than I knew. I needed him to be that way, at least for a little longer.

"Baptism's Jewish, you know. In its origins."

When I heard that, I believe all that came out of my mouth was an anguished *Oy vey*!

"Oh, I know; I know," Jon said. Now it was his turn to run on, a trait that, well, runs in the family. "*Mikvah*, ritual bath." Does that make it better? Less foreign? I'm down with that. So maybe the way you should think about is that I won't be baptized, just, you know, I'll be *mikvah*-ed."

"But that's for women only in Jewish tradition. The *mikvah*. I know you're going through lots of changes, but I take it you haven't begun to menstruate."

He gave me a long-suffering stare.

"It's in the works, isn't it?"

"Menstruation?"

"Conversion."

"You wouldn't want me to lie."

"I don't know," I said as we approached home. "Lying has its place."

Now we had arrived at the driveway. He separated himself from me, and went to lean against the fluted column of the lamppost by the curb. The dull bulb cast a whitish wash of light down over him. I had come home expecting one thing and had stumbled into another, my life feeling like a kind of play with one unexpected turn after another. Maybe that's why Jon looked to me almost theatrical, standing there, his hands tucked into the front change pockets of his Levis, his eyes peering up for stars in the smoggy sky, like a Southern California Hamlet about to unburden himself.

And then he did.

With an enthusiasm that threatened the little moment of partial safe harbor that we had somehow established, he confessed that he couldn't get enough of this Mormon stuff. Western Oaks was not only a terrific explainer, but he barbecued a mean spare rib, and the Mormons also had great pick-up basketball out at Sorrento Beach by Santa Monica, an ongoing game all summer long, and they were always friendly and fun to be with. He felt so welcomed, so warm. The ideas were great; the people were great. It was important that I listen, and understand.

Well, I listened, or thought I did. What emerged from my mouth, almost in a tone of flabby apologetic complaint, was simply: "But we're Jewish."

My declaration sounded so remarkably strange, even to my own ears. It was as if it had, well, just fallen out of me, like a last, sad coin shaken from my pocket.

"The new revelations are big enough to love and to embrace everyone. Forever and all time. Jews and Gentiles. The entire human family. I'm telling you, Norman, it's the greatest."

"The greatest? Like Muhammad Ali?"

"Absolutely."

"Only the Mormons don't accept Ali and the Negroes, do they? Small problem? I think. No Negroes in their priesthood, last I checked."

"I think that's being worked on. Anyway, they can still come on in, just not into what they call the Melchizedek Priesthood."

"I really can't believe this."

"Doesn't Jewish law change? Over time and place. Same thing. Wes tells me they're waiting on a new word of prophecy about the Negroes."

"I'm sure the Negroes will be glad to hear that."

We had by now meandered up the narrow walkway that bisected our duplex's lawn and led to the porch, and then inside.

A tiny brown snail was making its way along the margin of the sidewalk at the walkway's beginning. In the driveway Jon's taxi was still giving off an uncertain engine tick or two from the drive home from the airport. Beneath the furthest rays of light cast by the lamppost I just made out a faint trail like silvery spit on the pavement left by the little mollusk.

When we were kids, I used to be up early before school to play what had to be my very first theological game: making believe I was omnipotent, a giver of life, a deliverer of death. Up and down our little path, which had seemed far larger then, I would stride. I'd pick a snail entirely at random, one day one bigger or smaller or slower as I played at being God.

And you know what I did next.

I will not describe it, except to say how that shell snapped underfoot with a disintegrating crack I remember to this day.

I had that same angry impulse now. I don't know if Jon read my mind, but here he was now taking me into a big bear hug and telling me he loved me. Then he added, "And I love the Jews . More than you know. Believe it, man."

"Well, that's just spectacular to hear. Speaking on behalf of the Entire Jewish People, let me say the Jews love you right back, and then some. They see your Mormon love and raise it with some Big Jewish Love."

"I'm your brother, Norman. Don't treat me like an enemy."

3

AS I looked away from Jon and from that snail's glistening trail, suddenly my mood lifted because there was my redoubtable grandmother, Ida, waving to me from behind the porch window.

Here was Paul's still mostly Yiddish-speaking mom by now nearing the ninety mark, and well deserving of the name we often called her, the Relic. None of us could be sure exactly how old she was because she was, as we say now, undocumented.

I skipped up to the window and did a few goofy dance steps and waved.

"Better get in there before she breaks the glass," said Jon.

We had helped babysit Ida from as long ago as I could remember, maybe from when we were as little as about ten years old; apart from natural affection and curiosity, the real draw was that she had a television before we did.

When we watched TV with the Relic it gave Paul and Paulene more time to go out to dance downtown, or to play cards, or to go to the track without guilt, I guess. We watched a lot of baseball together, the Relic and I, although Jon mainly read his comics. She was this repository of our family history along with European history and she let out her secrets every now and then like how she had seen Emperor Franz Joseph of Austria-Hungary parade through her village.

It was worth all the babysitting to hear those tidbits.

Here was Ida now holding the drapes open with one thin arm waving and smiling through the porch window as she sat in her wheelchair. Her other hand was lost inside my funky little boy's baseball glove that she was brandishing at me. I'd given it to her when I tried, with some success, to teach her the rules of baseball in my broken Yiddish.

Now she was pressing the glove impatiently against the pane.

"Go on in, man."

Yet I hesitated.

"What's up?"

"Just taking it all in."

I don't know if it was just Ida's remarkably unlined face refracted through the glass, but she seemed to have, well, an expression completely new to me : she was smiling and you'd have to call it close to radiant. That was a real departure from the Relic I remembered, a person whom Paulene used to describe as being able to speak only in one language yet to complain in a dozen.

What in the world did this betoken? Had she become a smiling Bahai? The world's oldest convert to Jehovah's Witnesses? They were active missionaries on Orange Grove too. After all, this was LA, and I seemed to be afraid of finding change now, everywhere I looked.

Ida began tapping on the window with her glove; *shashoo, shashoo,* the leather made its sound, like a big winged insect trapped and working its way across the pane. Now she was motioning to me, as if to say, what the hell is wrong with you, grandson! Get in here this instant and toss the ball.

"It's either you go in there or she'll break it and we'll have to replace the glass, man. Oh, and by the way, I told her."

"You told her? What?"

"Just go. Go in."

And so I went in to give my grandma a hug.

Ida smelled of camphor and soap and I also detected a note or two of the crispy grilled cheese sandwiches she had cooked for us, almost always timed for the seventh inning stretch of games we watched with her on the weekends.

Now she pulled out from the pocket of her perennial apron the bald green tennis ball, almost as old as the glove. I knew my duty. I took the ball and I popped it into the glove a few times.

"Bilko," she said happily. "Bilko."

Bilko, and I knew I was home.

Steve Bilko was the boom-and-bust first baseman for the Pacific Coast League LA Angels. As Jon and I, our noses to Ida's old Muntz TV, had oohed and aahed about his big home runs, especially during the 1956 and 1957 seasons, or about his many big whiffs, Ida picked up that to "Bilko" was, well, just what baseball was all about.

I wheeled her out to the porch where Jon was stretched languidly on the steps just as an old Chevy going up Orange Grove toward Pico Boulevard backfired.

"Whoa, Bilko, Grandma. Is that a Bilko or what!"

But Ida, who by now knew our tricks well and was no fool about false Bilkos, dismissed our characterization with a dismissive wave of her hand.

Jon reached up and gave Ida a slow-motion high five and then said, with just enough irony, "She's the *only* one in the family who knows."

"You explained your . . . you explained in English?"

"And some Yiddish too. Just like baseball. You know."

"Why'd you do that?"

"I had to talk to someone in the family and you weren't here yet. She gets it too."

"No way!"

"The baseball prepared her, Norman. No kidding."

"What a goof! Like what? No, how'd you tell her you're now . . . coming round to a religion that believes in, what is it you said, the celestial, telestial, the terrestrial, not one place, but three, the trifecta, man, the three levels of heaven? Did you explain that to her in Yiddish?"

"I did, yes. That's easy. Drei Himmel."

"Vos?" said Ida.

"You see! That's right, Grandma. Drei Himmel," Jon repeated, smiling broadly at the Relic and pointing up toward the darkening sky as if the Mormons' three-tiered heaven could be viewed there, just above the lamppost, beyond smoggy Perseus, if you just scrunched your eyes up enough.

"Drei? Vos Himmel?" She was shaking her head in a gesture that was decidedly skeptical.

I was with her, 110 percent. Jews don't think much about heaven. Often when we babysat her, Ida would doze and in the midst of sleep call out, with a deep sigh, *Gott in himmel*, "God in heaven"; it was just, well, a form of kvetching, not belief in a zone that actually existed somewhere.

But Jon wasn't buying that any more either.

"Grandma, *himmlen*. There." Jon pointed skyward again. "*Himmlach*," he tried again. "*Himmelfen,*" he said as he invented various plurals of "heaven" in Yiddish or in German, or in any neologistic formulation that sounded as if it might grab her.

Now he illustrated with three fingers aimed at the sky near Ida's face. "Bilko."

"She thinks it's not three heavens but three innings, man. Or the infield fly rule. Or three strikes against Bilko. Why don't you leave her alone?"

"What's the harm? She's my grandmother."

JON'S WORDS hung heavily in the air. He had only begun.

"You don't understand, do you?"

"Indulge me."

"Because of your, you know, your own religious training, I thought you of all people would really understand, and be interested, man! You would be the best at it. And you could really explain it to Mom and to the others so they would understand. As a rabbi. As a person of faith."

"Holy shit."

"Well, that's not quite what I was expecting to hear from you."

As Jon and I talked, Ida was gently pounding the pocket of the glove with the tennis ball as we had instructed her and mumbling, "homer" and "Bilko" and, well, rather enjoying herself with us in a companionable kind of way for a deaf hundred-year-old, I supposed.

"Isn't she beautiful!" he said. "I love this old lady. And I love you, and I know—."

"Oh, shut up already with how you love me! How about some *reason* here. Just give me clearly, concisely . . . why are you doing this!"

"But I already told you. I've been telling you and telling you."

"Tell me again."

"I love folks so much I don't want to lose them. It's that simple. And with the Mormons I won't. I won't ever."

"And you really believe that?"

"You know what hell is to the Mormons?"

"I'm about to learn."

"Hell is the removal of love. And heaven is a love so big that no one is lost, not ever. I'll see Dad again inside all that love, and Ida here when her time comes too. I believe I'll see them all. In celestial heaven. So I hope and pray. Although it's going to take some work. I'll tell you all about it."

"Oh, I'm sure you will."

Jon was by now sitting on the step beside me. It was as if his enthusiasm had a physical reflection inching himself closer and closer. His big frame was touching me and again his powerful swimmer's arm was draped uncomfortably around my shoulders.

But where was he in his mind? It was scary how much I suddenly did not know now or recognize about my own flesh and blood.

Mormons revel in visions of gauzy perfection, as I came to understand that summer, and Jon was already traveling on the wings of one that was bearing him swiftly away.

Although I had been stuffed like derma with Jewish erudition, yet what I knew of concepts of heaven was so disturbingly thin and scattershot I could not debate my brother. I felt ignorant and unprepared. I did not know even where to begin on the civilized side of sarcasm.

Oh, he was so right. All I knew of a Jewish heaven or Jewish souls in transit were remnants of lessons I had vaguely absorbed during intervals of Jewish study when I was not nodding off or wondering what in the world I was doing at a seminary beneath a skullcap with an ancient professor trying to interest me in an impossible-to-decipher Aramaic text, when I should have been at an anti-war demonstration at Columbia or on the bus from the Port Authority heading south to register voters.

Now those moments were coming home to roost, and all my education availed me little. I blathered on, but I was really speechless in the meaningful sense. I was kaput, Bilkoed, lost as can be about heaven and about the afterlife, suddenly in a game out of my league.

I hope you see why I was in dire need of Jewish angels to lend an assist. They had not quite arrived, although, fortunately, they were near.

"And I can't tell you," Jon went cheerily on, "how I've been waiting for you to get here. I mean I've never checked the calendar so much."

"But it's not like that."

"Everyone knows what Judaism means to you. So you can get what this means to me."

"Come on, Jon."

"But it's true. A faith. A headquarters. I never knew. How it shapes you and, you know, fills your very being."

"My 'very being'? Where the hell is that! Please."

"No, Norman. I'm your brother, man. I know your joking ways, and yet how many times when we were kids did I see you standing and praying by the closet right up there, man, in our bedroom. Facing east, you explained. Toward Jerusalem. What a goof, I thought then. But now I understand. How many years did you do that? I saw. Rocking back and forth toward Jerusalem and *baruch atah Adonai*, praying away . . ."

"That was a while ago," I interrupted him again.

Yet Jon couldn't or wouldn't stop.

"So you've changed what? Your style. So you're maybe not so religious, with the details. That's okay. But not the heart of it. The living Judaism, man. That's what I'm talking about. How it organizes your hours with daily prayer at appointed times and how you see the world through it. That's what it feels like when it comes over me."

"But you sound like a song is coming on, or pneumonia. You sound like you're making fun of yourself."

"That's what you're hearing maybe, and I can understand what a shock it is, but it's serious as sin. I need you, man. I really do. I don't know how to talk to Paulene about this. I mean even how to begin. And the Foot! The way she's suddenly, through him, so involved with the synagogue, you think that's made it any easier! She's been inviting me to all this temple stuff that I have to say no to her over and over again. In my opinion they need to be told, and the right way. I'll do anything you advise to break it to them slowly, the right way so they understand."

"What if they don't?"

"Oh, I know you can help them understand. Or at least pave the way. I really mean it, Norman. You're going to be my emissary because coming from you, a serious religious guy, it'll, you know, go down smoother."

" 'Go down smoother'?"

"Uh huh."

"You might start by *really* explaining it to me so *I* understand. So I really get it, because I don't."

"Sure."

"Because I have some news for you."

Then it all spilled out.

My confession of what had happened in New York, my skipping so many classes, my hating to pray in the basement synagogue of the seminary, which was like a bunker in wartime, dank, windowless, with a *ner tamid*, an eternal light that made eternity seem about as exciting as the inside of an old refrigerator with a flickering fifteen watts of gloom. How as I cut class, the rabbis cut the scholarship, how I sold my books, how I . . .

Unburdening myself, I would disqualify myself as Jon's emissary. So I told it all, how I struggled to hold in the tears as I stood in front of that tribunal of three stern graybeards, the rabbis Leifman, Leibman, and Schneur, like a law firm that had adjudicated my case and had decided, even before I walked into that book-lined office, I was no longer worth Judaism's investment of scholarship money; that maybe I had even been embezzling on the time and effort they had expended on me already. Yes, I had been a here-today-gone-tomorrow young scholar. I was a bar mitzvah bust.

I told Jon the whole thing, the whole story of my Jewish disenchantment and with details, not excluding all the surreptitiously consumed cheeseburgers, topped by bacon, avocado, and a touch of pineapple. I told Jon about the guilty euphoria of cutting class to attend a demonstration somewhere, but my real destinations were the best greasy spoons in the five boroughs, and how, if he dropped this Mormon nonsense, we could go to New York and have a spectacular time together.

It came out by turns inspired and as relentless as a ticker tape, as matter-of-fact as a news report of damage after disaster, as passionate as a confession.

Yet Jon never heard a word of it, because it echoed only inside my head.

"What is it, man? Are you going to break it to them or not?"

"Let me think on it."

"Sure."

"Because I just don't know if the timing is right."

"Totally understood. You want a few days to get used to it yourself."

"That's it."

"Yeah, you adjust to it first. I understand. I'm cool with that," he said. "For now."

"We've got to be more than cool. We've got to keep our mouths shut."

"Why are you shouting?"

I apologized as we wheeled Ida back into her apartment. I said I'm sorry two or three more times while I maneuvered the wheelchair, and I had no idea if I was apologizing in advance to a still-absent Paulene or to Ida, or maybe I was sending general apologies out to the North Vietnamese and to the Negroes, to the draft board or once again to Leifman, Leibman, and Schneur, and to the New York Board of Rabbis.

I just kept on saying, "I'm sorry, I'm sorry."

That's when Jon put his index finger over my lips and said, "Shhh. Shhh. Enough."

"Jet lag."

"Absolutely. You're home now, Norman. Take a load off."

I thanked him again for picking me up. Yet I wondered if I had made a huge mistake and should never have come home, because I knew this Mormon business had been percolating, no matter how much I tried to deny it.

I knew it was different. But not like this!

Yes, I should have made a connection at LAX for a flight to Hawaii, three thousand miles across the sea. There absolutely no one knew me.

And what in the world had Jon meant by being cool *for now*?

4

IT was going to be difficult, but Jon and I both had, sad to admit, just the right stuff to continue to flimflam and to conceal, especially from our mother.

After all, we were a gambler's sons and charged by Paulene even when we were young, on all those father-absent, window-watching evenings, to avoid following in Paul's footsteps. So of course we watched those very footsteps very carefully.

Still, it's no wonder that neither Jon nor I turned out to be carbon copies of Paul, who, though often a loser at the games at which he professed proficiency, nevertheless had a wicked memory for cards and for adding up numbers, a basic arithmetic so electrically fast, he could always best both Jon and me.

We turned out to be only B minus players at poker, or at blackjack, or at picking horses. Also as out-and-out liars, we were completely unaccomplished.

Although we could avoid and evade with the best of them, and at general bluffing and fakery we had natural talent, even if Paul winked, Paulene would catch us, eventually.

That's because she, as an attractive waitress over the years had, as she put it, "seen it all." She prided herself on an accumulated knowledge of human nature in all its ridiculousness. That acumen extended big time into her sons' natures, and, as she often said, "I have your number."

In short, I was always afraid she could see right through me.

That's why I had been planning on telling her pretty soon after my arrival about what had happened in New York.

Now I had not one, but two secrets to manage.

Fortunately on the night I came home, she was not only working a double shift, but afterward, so Jon reported, she had gone to a sisterhood meeting at the temple.

Jon said she was being given an award for helping dish out danishes or some such service on the hospitality committee. Paul had always made fun of this kind of activity. Wasn't it enough she schlepped dishes at Canter's? Now she had to be the Queen of Hospitality at Temple Beth Ami?

I could almost hear his voice in the house calling out, "You serve everyone, absolutely everyone, but *me*!"

As we waited for Paulene to return, a small clearing seemed to have surfaced in the thick jungle of all that suppressed emotion between my brother and me, but then just as mysteriously it closed.

We now settled into a strategic silence with each other as we fooled around and ministered to Ida.

When she didn't seem interested in watching TV, Jon suddenly announced he was going upstairs to read. This was not like him, but as I came to understand that summer, it was not toward the newspaper or to the comics or to *UFO Monthly* he was energetically heading, three steps at a time.

He was going up to read several chapters a night, making his way through the battles and revelations, travails and journeys of the Nephites and the Lamanites in the very long *Book of Mormon*.

It calmed him before sleep, he would later tell me, because all the reiterative "And it came to pass,"-es, with which that book was written to echo a biblical style, were also much more effective than the now-forbidden two beers a night that Jon had previously consumed to chase away insomnia.

While I continued to wait—with not a little dread—for Paulene's return, Ida had me wheel her into the kitchen. There she had the good sense to set me to work as her assistant. Her eyes indicated the cabinet by the stove, second shelf from the top.

Here I knew my place, and there was wisdom in my following the familiar orders. I reached up and retrieved the paprika. I took the floppy loaf of Wonder Bread from the red and white plastic bin. I placed a white splotch of Crisco as big as a golf ball in Ida's cast-iron frying pan that I was certain she had hauled with her all the way from Austria-Hungary.

Next I turned on a burner and scratched a Diamond Safety Match out of the box she handed to me. It wasn't a cheeseburger coming my way, I knew, but something else pretty, well, special.

I followed her set of mumbled yet to me instantly clear directions and soon our collaboration yielded a redolence of garlic, oil, and slightly seared cheese that began to fill up the kitchen. Ida still had powerful wrists, and even from the wheelchair she managed to slide and to clatter the heavy pan this way and that over the fire. She would have made a good pitcher who could have heaved a wicked slider, had there been girls playing baseball in Poland in the 1890s.

As I watched her motion and checked out her profile, I suddenly saw something that shocked me, both because I had never seen it before with such clarity and also because it was unmistakable. I saw my father's face in hers: the long, curious nose, the big ears with the droopy lobes longer than they proportionally should have been, the mouth downturned in impatience, hovering on the precipice of bitterness at the world—just how Paul's face might have looked had he lived to be old.

Ida took my hand now in hers. Her fingers were gnarled and her palms rough with the knife lines of a life spent peeling and grating, chopping and dicing. Together we found the box of Sun-Maid Raisins and sprinkled these into the pan. I held the two slices of Wonder Bread out before her like an offering, each face up in my palm. Now she spread a dollop of butter on each slice, flopped squares of Velveeta on each, and then we tucked more raisins in the airy, doughy pockets. When the sandwich was assembled, I lowered it onto the shining black pan.

At the first sizzle I took a step back. From this slightly different vantage and through a little plume of cooking smoke I beheld Ida and saw in her yet another image of Paul: this time he as a much younger man, escorted by two female forms, the curving, moving outlines of which were barely distinguishable from the plumes arising from the sautéing butter, raisins, bread, and cheese in the frying pan.

In the interval that could not have been more than five seconds, Paul and the two female forms came in and out of focus in the smoking image above the fire.

If all this sounds barely credible or a distortion occasioned by what happens when high tension collides with jet lag, well, I apologize. But I saw it.

And—full disclosure of what was to become a habit of that summer—I had found one of Jon's old joints and had indulged in a few tokes in the bathroom before the cooking had started.

Nevertheless, time- and explanation-defying moments do occur, and angels thrive in them. Angels are also no fools. Although they require far less than a living person, while on duty fulfilling their mission, they do require some modest sustenance. So why not appear where the eating's good, such as in Ida Gould's kitchen?

Then I heard my grandmother's command: "Eat, eat," and, of course, I obeyed.

IT WAS 9:30. Jon was still upstairs studying Mormon texts the way I had once pored over the writings of the Jews. The whole apartment was tangy with the aroma of grilled cheese and garlic, I had had another few tokes, all was well, and still Paulene was not home.

We Bilkoed around a bit more, Ida and I, but I could see the cooking had been an exertion. She was getting tired, but I somehow did not want to wheel her to her bed yet; I did not want to be alone.

We stopped in front of the credenza where pictures of the relatives were displayed: old sepia photos of Ida's parents in that rigid nineteenth-century formal pose, the men with square skullcaps and the women puffing out their immense bosoms beneath their formal ankle-length dresses. Here they were, all the granduncles and grandaunts, the ancestors from a faraway Europe, whose names I never knew, arrayed in small, gilded ornate frames like a small army of memory in formation across the doily-covered dresser top.

Jon had always been far more interested in these long-dead ancestors than I had ever been. Years ago when he'd been obsessed with astrology he'd gotten Ida to talk about them and about any birthdays she could remember—when she still had talk in her.

She identified one as a cousin who had been a baker whose Sabbath *challah* the whole town lined up to buy Friday afternoons, another too religious for his own good. Each one was *tot*, dead.

"*Tot*," she had said when he pointed to the first one. "*Tot*," the second one. So the third, the fourth. All *tot*, thanks to Hitler, and then she mock-spit, at the mention of the mass murderer's name.

As the events of this Mormon summer played out, as you will see, Jon drew closer than ever to our Family *Tot*.

Ida and I lingered in front of one photo that showed Paul and his oldest brother, Dan, who had died in the war. They were wearing prayer shawls, and the snapshot captured them with the tassels being blown by the wind as they stood in front of a tall palm tree whose fronds swayed above them. Handwritten across the bottom of the photo was "Pearl Harbor, 1944."

Ida made some sort of grunting, dismissive noise.

"All gone, huh, Grandma?"

"*Tot*," she said in a whispered mumble. "*Tot, tot, tot*."

Now she leaned forward in her wheelchair and pulled open the top drawer of the credenza. Here was a little textile museum of dainty, tiny napkins, frilly doilies, and antimacassars. Ida knew my habits just as well as I knew hers. She carefully fingered her way through the layers of cloth and eventually found what she'd been looking for, unasked by me: a blue and white tin. When she lifted off the top, there was the collection of miniature Nestle's Crunch Bars.

Silently she handed it to me, and I took three.

I wheeled her out into the living room and positioned her chair beside the big La-Z-Boy recliner. I sat on the green hassock nearby, ate my candy, and held her hand.

In approximately this same position years before, right here, Ida and I had sat, with Paul and Jon over on the sofa, all watching Don Larson pitch to Dale Mitchell, his last batter in the 1956 perfect World Series game. "You remember, Ida? He whiffed. Struck out!"

"Bilko," she said.

"Bilko is right."

Maybe it was the buzz of the pot mixing with the methylxanthine in the chocolate, but again I had the eerie feeling it wasn't just she, but someone else peering at me through her. The sensation lasted a second—no, a tenth of a second—and I dismissed it as another effect of flying and fatigue and the little help I was getting from my chemical friends. But was there something— as the argot of the era then had it—something slightly psychedelic about Grandma? Or just my nonsense?

Now she took the bald tennis ball out of her apron pocket, where it bulged, and underhanded it to me.

"You're out!"

"Safe!"

"Out!"

"Safe, you nincompoop."

"Never argue with the umpire, Grandma."

"Bilko!"

After a few minutes of such play-by-play make-believe Ida's eyes began to close and her head drooped to the left so that it almost rested on her shoulder like a rag doll's.

That's when I heard the sound of an engine in the driveway and a car door click open.

I stood up, and braced for Paulene.

5

COME, listen to what the rabbis say about the laws relating to conning your own mother.

Ta ushema: Come and listen, as the rabbis used to quote us the formula employed by our two-thousand-year-old forebears as they introduced a lesson to us at the seminary.

Ta ushema: Come this way, you young and—so the commanding tone of the curt imperative implies—you insufferably arrogant and naive one who has the audacity to think you know the answer when you really don't know jack, you downy-cheeked pipsqueak.

Ta ushema: Come and listen to a question and to its answer, which will not be so obvious as you think.

In the process be humble and learn.

So.

Question: what is there to fear from your mother if the last time you saw her you presided as a young rabbi-to-be over the funeral of her husband, your father? And you watched her fill with pride at all the erudition you deployed, like a poker player bluffing with his bets, to disguise such a difficult, stressed-out family life.

That was ten months ago, and while the official mourning period is still ongoing Mom has begun dating another man, and not just any man, but Irving Footlick whose guts you hate, as did your father of blessed memory.

Oh, and Mom also assumes you are no more than a year and a course or two more away from being ordained as a full-fledged rabbi. She hasn't a clue of the new circumstances, of the truth: that what you really crave is, finally, to have nothing to do with the Jews for a while, to take a blessed vacation from

Abraham, Isaac, Jacob, Sarah, Rachel, Leah, the whole yammering tempestuous tribe.

That's why you have become a dropout big time. Yet at this moment when you are about to see Paulene again to negotiate this delicate business, Jon is upstairs surreptitiously studying "Two Nephi" or "Alma Six" or other chapters in the *Book of Mormon*. Or perhaps he has already moved on to that other Mormon treasure, *Pearl of Great Price*? No matter. You know that whatever his text, he is no casual reader this time; that there's no denying he's studying the way you once were riveted on tractates Baba Kama and Sodot and Nashim, the latter the Babylonian Talmud's rules pertaining to ritual purity. Just how will such riveting and relevant info help you now, pal, because you are definitely Jewish AWOL? You're supposed to explain all *that* to your mom?

On the other hand, she's the person in whose body you reposed and grew . . . and she will always but always love you, no matter what. Really? Yet just maybe there is a limit to a Jewish mother's love, especially if she is an exhausted waitress whom the customers have been, as usual, torturing at Canter's.

In short, what is there then to fear from your own mother?

Answer: nothing.

On second thought: everything.

THEN THERE she suddenly is: Paulene walks through the doorway, her arrival as always preceded by her verdant perfume. As she enters, my mother's small red purse with a golden clasp dangles over her right elbow and almost flies off when she opens her arms wide for an embrace.

"Well, smile, honey. Aren't you happy to see your old mom?"

She takes off her short coat and folds it neatly over the back of the chair.

I just stood there, astonished. The woman I had last seen had a face wracked by mourning, with sleepless baggy eyes, cheeks over-rouged and powdered, and a forehead lined by the burden of death and grieving. Now here she was, well, transformed and as effervescent as Donna Reed.

Paulene was even prettier than I remembered. A starlet's smile and even a touch of Loretta Young's sweep-you-away glamour embraced me. I just stared. Her face seemed lit up with hardly a trace of the long-sufferingness I had always noticed between the glints of her eyes—a ray or two of desperation that she always tried to conceal from us for how much she had to put up with in our father.

All that gone with . . . the winds of death.

That's how I saw her, and believe me I was an expert in the ups and downs of my mother's beauty and her fleeting postures. I had observed her many times through the front window where I often waited in the car, cruising the radio for songs that might transport me away from my pick-up duties at the end of her shift at Canter's.

Because most mothers in Southern California by then had begun to drive—but not Paulene—all this picking her up had made me uncomfortable. Maybe that's why on such assignments I used to imagine myself in *The Big Sleep*, or like a shamus in some noir film.

And yet it was hard to sustain that story line because I was, well, staking out my own mother.

Even though she'd not come straight from the restaurant tonight but had been hanging out with Mr. Footlick, by the position of her body I could tell not everything was well. When I used to pick her up at Canter's, if her hip was pushed against the corner of the booth's table, I knew she was at the end of her awesome supply of daily energy.

That's the way she was tonight, tired and maybe a little more Ida Lupino than Donna Reed as she is about to fall on the divan in romantic exhaustion.

Paulene knew all the stars and therefore so did we, her bright boys, whom she always instructed in which Jewish-born stars of stage and screen—they were always changing their names—had come into Canter's that day. Kirk Douglas, John Garfield, and once or twice Tony Curtis, born Bernie Schwartz.

"It's me! Stop staring, honey, and tell me all about yourself."

"Well, there's nothing much to tell."

"*That* I don't believe. Let me look at you, skinny! Don't they feed you at the seminary?"

"Oh, sure."

"Well, not enough. Sit down beside me."

I did.

"Now dish."

"Stop it."

"Come on, Norman. How can there be no news with such a smart and handsome boy! Are you still dating . . . what's her name?"

"I don't know who you mean by 'what's her name.'"

"Oh, that girl with the curly hair that you wrote about. The daughter of, what was it, the chief rabbi of Scotland? Who even knew that Scotland had chief rabbis to have daughters to date? Who even knew they have Jews in Scotland?"

"Oh, they do, I assure you. And all I heard about was how the chief rabbi of Scotland doesn't get along with the chief rabbi of Wales. And they both have serious ritual issues with the chief rabbi of Ireland who, they say, should have stayed in Australia. I was worried they were going to set me up with his daughter . My goal last year was to cover the United Kingdom and the former colonies."

"You joker. You must be thinking at least a little about a wife. Rabbis without wives are . . ."

". . . are what, Mom?"

"Oh, I don't know. Are not what a congregation is looking for. Am I right?"

"I don't know. Are you?"

"I assure you our Rabbi Joel without his wife and kids would simply not be Rabbi Joel. That's as clear as the nose on your face. I'm just a mother who wants her boys to be happy. So?"

"So what?"

"So what was wrong with the daughter of the chief rabbi of Wales?"

"Scotland, Mom. Scotland. Or maybe they came from the New Hebrides. I really don't remember anything except her hair. I wrote you, didn't I? That was just a kind of . . . courtesy to some of the rabbis. To accompany her to something. The Purim Ball."

"A ball? Jews going to balls like in the movies; doesn't that just get you? Tell me all about it."

"Oh, I didn't have a very good time."

"No! What was your costume?"

"I think I came as the donkey."

"She was Queen Esther, I bet. Fabulous."

"I can't remember."

"Yes you do. Tell."

As we talked, and I amplified on the little I recollected just to please her, and of course I filled her in about this huge globe of frizzy hair the girl had.

Paulene took it all in, giving me encouraging smiles while she fussed with Ida's apron or brushed her hair back while the old lady remained solidly dozing.

While I watched, I became astonished at how far Paulene had come during this past year of mourning, now just one, perhaps two, months shy of its traditional Jewish terminus. No wearing black or muted colors or abstaining from her lipstick or Maybelline for Paulene Gould.

During that year of mourning your mother is not supposed to get even more beautiful, is she? Plenty of other things can happen, of course, usually in the other direction.

Yet, that's precisely what had occurred. The mourning seemed to have liberated her.

"You really didn't go as the donkey?"

"All right."

"You joker."

"I think I was the devil. I wore a tuxedo and horns."

"Oh, you'd make a good devil, I'll tell you that. You ask her out on another date?"

I was silent.

"Nothing came of it?"

"Mom! I'm not getting married."

"Well, not yet. Did your brother tell you about the jobs? At the camp?"

"He sure did."

"Now don't sound that way. Everyone's looking forward to having you around the temple again."

"That's nice."

"I know you'd rather be doing something more exciting, but you didn't write that you had anything else lined up."

"No, I didn't."

"In fact, after that girl you didn't write much at all. So I said to Mr. Footlick, maybe he's gone off and eloped. I wouldn't have minded. Worse things have happened! You'll never guess what Mr. Footlick said: rabbis don't elope. I told him there's always a first. No?"

"No. You're being a nudge."

"You were busy, doing those tryout sermons at congregations that might hire you. I understand. You're busy. I'll bet you did great."

I gave Paulene a kind of camouflaged nod that was neither yes nor no.

"And I know you love little kids, and you can be such a little ham yourself, so I signed you for the drama job. If I hadn't, Esther Samuelson's son was interested, mind you."

"Sure, it'll be fine, Mom. It really will. Thanks."

"Where's your brother?"

"Upstairs."

"Isn't it great that he's moved back home? You're lucky you never saw that dump where he was living down in Venice. Practically under water. It should have been condemned by the health department. I knew he would come around, and so did Mr. Footlick and the rabbi. I hope you're encouraging him to follow in your footsteps. What do you think?"

"That's a terrible idea."

"No, silly. To go back and finish college. Not rabbinic school. UCLA."

I sat down on the green hassock as she swooped around the room picking up after Ida and me.

"Oh, absolutely. I'm encouraging him."

"Liar! What did he tell you? I think at least he's finally found a girl he's serious about. And not a moment too soon if you ask me. He's cleaned up and he's happier than I've seen him in a long time. And he's finally looking for a real job. What do you think?"

"I think . . . it's great."

"Well, we'll see. I'm so happy you came home for the summer. Both boys, just like the old days."

"Better than that, I hope."

"That's my wise guy. How do you find the old place? Not much different, right?"

"You're different . . ."

". . . I'm what? Oh, the hair. Just changed my coloring a little. You like the highlights?"

Suddenly there was the staccato tap of a car horn from outside.

"Oh, gosh. That's Mr. Footlick. He drove me home. Would you mind going outside and saying a quick hello?"

"Do I have to?"

"Go on. Bury the hatchet."

"I'm pretty tired, Mom."

"Norman?"

"You're really dating him? Jon told me. I mean dating, as in dating?"

"We don't sit around eating dates if that's what you mean. Of course we 'go out.'"

The horn squawked again.

"Now, go on out there. It'll take all of ten seconds. He's a very nice man."

"I'm not in the mood, Mom. Maybe he can call later tonight, and ask us for a payment on the temple dues."

"For your information, Mr. Smart Aleck, our temple dues are all paid up. Not only this year but next. And Mr. Footlick is not the ogre you two make him out to be. Never was when your father was alive, and he's not now either. He's outside because he didn't want to come in and get in between us on the night of your homecoming. Now isn't that thoughtful? He was kind enough to give me a ride home from the temple. He often does. That's all. He has excellent judgment."

"That's just great."

"Look," she then said, scrutinizing me one more time, "it's not a big deal. Come on."

She took my hand and yanked me up from the hassock where my body seemed to have folded in on itself, like a catcher after being hit by a foul tip.

Paulene was very strong, like Jon, and up I stretched. I followed her as she went to the door. Holding it open for me was a kind of courtesy that was also a command. We stepped out onto the porch. I noticed how girlishly she leaned against the railing and lifted up on her toes as she waved to the shiny black Lincoln Town Car parked on Orange Grove at the end of the walkway. I was surprised at how irritated I felt when a white-cuffed hand raised up and out through the window on the driver's side. A gleam of what had to be a cufflink caught the light of the lamppost as the Foot waved wordlessly back.

The engine turned over. The long vehicle that my father had dubbed the "rabbimobile" angled slowly away into the darkness toward Pico Boulevard. A modest tap of the horn marked Paulene's final wave and the departure of Mr. Footlick for the night. I went back in, and my mother followed.

"Let's not let it become a big deal."

"Agreed."

She went up to Ida who had been sleeping heavily in the La-Z-Boy recliner. "Play catch with your grandmother?"

"Always."

Then she withdrew a handkerchief from the high pocket on her skirt and wiped some spittle from the corner of the Relic's mouth, a detail that I had overlooked.

"She's been so excited that you're home. You remember how she always gets her spit up when she gets excited."

"Like a pitcher on the mound. I remember, Mom."

Then Paulene strode across the room and extracted her Lucky Strikes from her purse. She retrieved Paul's lighter from on top of Ida's dresser. I noticed now how it had lain beside a picture of our father in one of his big-lapeled jackets from right after the war. As she lit up and blew two immense smoke rings across the room, we sat there silently while the rings formed, settled between us, and then dissolved into shapelessness.

"Here today, gone tomorrow."

"You got that right."

"Got to seize it while you can. Life is what I'm talking about, son. What's troubling you?"

"Oh, nothing."

"There now. You're saved from the attack of the terrible Mr. Footlick. Really. Talk to me."

When I didn't, or couldn't, she came back up to me and took my face in her cool, lotioned hands that smelled like lavender. "And how's my favorite New York customer?"

"Just fine, Mom. Happy to see you."

"Really? I'm looking deep into your big brown eyes."

"Happy for you. Really."

"Well, thank you for trying. That's more than I've gotten out of your brother."

"He's happy for you."

"Hey, I guess everyone's happy then."

I took one of her Luckys myself and lit up. We stared at each other. We just sat there exchanging floating, dueling smoke rings. Trying to blow the biggest smoke rings was one of the ways she and Paul had tried to entertain us when we were little.

As the wreaths of smoke formed and dissolved, I thought of what Jon had said to me, not two hours before, about Paul's soul, because he had said a lot.

How, for instance, according to the Mormons, a soul is not to be seen as something like smoke, wispy or weak or plumey or ghostly like in a movie. To the contrary, a soul is a fully formed little sprite of a thing, Jon had said. An invisible tiny munchkin, a homunculus. It makes its way to earth and then lives in our bodies to survive all of the moral tests of life. Then it returns home after death, solid and victorious. That's the word he had used: victorious.

I remembered thinking: victorious! How foreign, how hymn-like, how Christian that sounds.

Just how was I going to be the explainer of such stuff to Paulene?

I wondered if she was at least remembering Paul, as I was, then, the way he blew rings, so slowly, so expertly, like a real craftsman, as if he might keep a cloud of smoke forming in his lungs and mouth forever. And how dramatic when they silently emerged, there a long snake, there a fox, a whole carnival of smoke animals he had been able to produce. Paul Gould may not have provided well for his family, but at this he was a magician, and no one blew better smoke!

As my face fell into the dumps, as she often put it, Paulene humored me and said, "Whatever's on your mind, honey, you can't get blood from a turnip."

I nodded or gave her a thumbs up, acknowledging her wisdom, but, truth be told, I often never quite knew what she meant when she talked this way.

I really saw her as an original, but one who also could spout all this clichéd nonsense. Yet coming out of her bright, lipsticked mouth, even clichés seemed okay, as if she were speaking something hard-earned and true, the truth of a night waitress at a Jewish deli on Fairfax.

I was very tired, and she sensed it. I felt my eyes closing. All I knew is that I loved watching my mother smoke, and I had loved watching my father do the same. They fought like Alice and Ralph Kramden in *The Honeymooners*. Yet how amicably they smoked together.

WHEN I had returned to New York after Paul's funeral, I already knew that something about his death and my presiding over his grave had changed everything. Oh, did grief ever become me and did I ever use Paul's passing as well to explain to Leifman, Leibman, and Schneur my aloofness from seminary activities that now ensued.

My three-times-a-day prayer dwindled to two, then one, then none. Then instead of joining the daily *minyan*, I pulled Ecclesiastes off my shelf to try to find some relief in poetical Jewish stoicism. I tried some Philo of Alexandria, whose skepticism had always appealed to me, but what did I care now about reconciling God with Aristotle? There was a sentence or two in there about transmigration of souls, the great *gilgul*, but it was a footnote, and one of those Greek things our teachers considered primitive, polytheistic, and lacking any real religious imagination; we had skipped over it entirely in philosophy class.

What did any of this have to do with my dead father? I kept an unsmoked pack of Lucky Strikes beside my hard metal bed in the seminary dorm because Paul had taught me my letters by holding up his pack of Luckys with the bright black and red target: *LSMFT:* Lucky Strike Means Fine Tobacco. Now *that* had meant something.

"You're floating off again on me, Norman."

"No, I'm not," I lied to my mother.

"That's okay. We're both tired, and oh are my dogs ever barking, honey. It doesn't get any easier. You'll come by the restaurant tomorrow?"

"Sure."

"You can practically walk over from camp, you know. A short hop from the park."

"Don't worry, Mom. I'll visit everyone, even Paul."

"Excuse me?"

"I guess I was thinking of him. At the cemetery. I'll of course come by Canter's is what I meant."

"Well, that will be very nice. I still get compliments there, and especially from the women at temple about what you said at your father's funeral. Such a beautiful speech."

Had we been at the same funeral? What had I really said at the funeral? Although only ten months had passed, to me it seemed as far back in Jewish time as the burial of Moses himself. Denied entrance to the Promised Land, though he got to see it from afar. Boy, did that ever seem nasty on God's part.

Yes, I'd relied on that story. I had likely hit all the pastoral points they'd taught us in intermediate homiletics. I'd explained the blessing you're supposed to recite, the formal formulation, statement of faith, that you're obliged to declare on hearing of the death for a first time: *Baruch dayan emet.* Blessed is the true judge.

I hadn't believed a word of my little graveside sermon and had acted the whole thing out. The wonder of it was that my hypocrisy apparently had not been noticed, only my clever wordplay. I think I must have been unconsciously thanking Paul for the career-reappraisal moment his death was providing, as if saying to him, Thanks, Dad. You see how easy it is to put one over on them! If that's what being a rabbi is about, maybe it's time for a reconsideration.

For me the best part was after they all had hugged me and Jon and Paulene and we were walking up the grassy hummock for the *kiddush*, the wine and cheese reception, in Mt. Eden Cemetery's little bungalow—we of course had selected the low-cost 250-dollar option—I broke away from my family for what I told them was to be a private moment.

I walked back down to where the little excavation machine stood, and three cemetery workers had picked up the shovels we had used to drop dirt on Paul's pine box.

He would have given each of them a ten-dollar bill had he been able to stick his arm out of the box. I upped the ante and gave each of the gravediggers a crisp twenty.

The smoke floated about the room, Ida stirred, and Paulene said, "Let's get Grandma to bed, and then you."

So we began our routine: I cradled Ida, one arm under her shoulders, the other under her legs, and carried her into the bedroom. Paulene pulled back the old knitted brown comforter and I centered the Relic on the mattress; she looked so tiny. Then I left the room so Paulene could undress her and put on her nightgown, and position a walker beside the bed.

Mom was very quick.

Then we methodically turned off all of the lights downstairs, except for the paced series of nightlights that led from the bedroom down the short hall to the bathroom, which Ida, if necessary, could still manage.

When we were done, we moved down the hall quietly in what felt almost like a weird ceremony, and out the door. On the way up to our place, we paused on the porch, where the night air had some citrus in it that suddenly revived me, or at least yanked me back from my ruminations on flesh, bone, decay, and the irritating unknowability of all things postmortem.

The perfume on Paulene's clothes as we slowly climbed up the steps to our place in the upper unit of the duplex was still strong; it seemed to mix with all of that cigarette smoke and with the aroma of the oranges, lemons, and the bougainvillea vines and their small pink flowers growing lush in the driveway beside the house.

On the landing just after I pulled the screen door open wide for the two of us to enter, she gave a sudden tickle to my ribs. I was surprised at how peeved, even angry, I suddenly felt at the playfulness.

Inside she shouted hello to Jon. He shouted back to her, but he didn't bestir himself from behind the closed bedroom door.

She occasionally barged right in—Paul had *always* done that—but not this time.

"Love you, younger son," she called back to him. "What are you doing in there? Top-secret stuff?"

"Nope. Performing evil deeds."

"Nothing I wouldn't do, right?"

"Love you, Mom. Take a load off," Jon called back.

While it all sounded the same, it also was so different, as if I were hearing the mundane exchanges like responsive readings that suddenly were not conveying the real meaning of what was floating through the duplex, and through our family life.

Now Paulene walked to the far end of the hall, where she paused in front of her bedroom. This cul de sac always collected the outside aromas of the flowers, Paulene's powders and perfumes, and the Canoe cologne that Paul used to buy at the discount counter at Thrifty's Drugstore, and it all was particularly concentrated this night.

Before turning in she said, "You're getting to look more and more like a handsome young rabbi."

"How's that?"

"Your brow is furrowed as if you're weighing some mighty decision. My little Solomon."

"Solomon was a king, not a rabbi."

"King, rabbi, I'll take either one. You just listen to me, young man: I'm so proud of you, and Mr. Footlick is. The whole temple family in fact."

The detective of Paulene's susceptibility to clichés, I particularly cringed at this one: *temple family* indeed. Still she went right on, not noticing, ticking off her points as if she were telling a customer the three kinds of soup Canter's is offering this night.

Where she landed, however, really caught me off guard. "But, honestly, you boys have to keep an open mind. I don't want you making Mr. Footlick nervous."

"What's the problem? I waved to him, didn't I?"

"I don't want to feel I have to negotiate every little common human courtesy with you boys. Just don't forget who got you your scholarships. And now the camp jobs as counselors."

"I know, I know."

"Jobs don't just appear out of thin air. You prefer to bus tables again? You were pretty good, Norman. You only dropped three platters that whole summer. You want me to arrange for that? Rabbis don't clean tables."

"I don't know why not. But drama? I haven't been in a play since high school."

"Yes, and what a wonderful Nathan Detroit you were. The best *Guys and Dolls* ever! You'll do fine. You know how I know that? Because you're a born faker."

Paulene leaned wearily against the door jamb to her bedroom. "The Jewish people need young men like you. You have no idea what joy it brings me to have both my sons working together at Camp Tikvah."

"It's just summer camp, Mom. It's not Mt. Sinai or the Golan Heights."

"Oh, no? Mr. Footlick tells me he's arranged with the Jewish Agency for two counselors who just served with the army in Israel. In the war. Girls, talented and very, very pretty, he says. Young heroes, pioneers. And they know how to shoot. So watch yourself."

"Really?"

"Yes, commandos."

"Great. Girl commandos."

"You don't think I would have accepted any old job on your behalf, do you? I know how to check out the perks. Only Mr. Footlick—"

"Enough already, Mom, with Mr. Footlick and with camp. You've made the sale already. Several times over."

"Fine, son. I just want to clear the air."

"You have."

"And stop staring. You want me to bring you a glass of milk like the old days?"

"Sure. That would be great."

SHE WENT into the kitchen, and I knocked on our bedroom door and entered. There was Jon stretched out in his pajama bottoms and a white T-shirt. He was reading intently. He raised a hand in a silent hello.

"You heard?"

"No one's thickened the walls since you left. I heard."

"So it's good. We're camp counselors with girl commandos, and if we don't behave they get us with their bayonets. What a summer this is turning out to be, and it hasn't even begun."

"Has for me," he replied distractedly, without interrupting his reading.

I maneuvered around his big sweat-socked feet that dangled over the side of the bed near the passage by our childhood desks. The matching desks with silly golden pen holders and gray blotters hadn't changed much, it seemed, except for the peeling veneer since we were doing sixth-grade homework on them. The bedroom was small and, of course with all my bags from New York now crowding in, it seemed even smaller and more constrained.

Tonight it felt minuscule.

As I got into my pajamas, Jon seemed instinctively to curl his body around his reading matter as if to conceal a *Playboy* magazine, the way we had when Paul had barged into the room. (Paulene's way was far politer.) More often than not, Paul was looking to grab the *Playboy* for himself.

I knew what Jon was poring over, of course, and he knew I knew that it wasn't Hugh Hefner's monthly. I was weary of contending. All I felt was an urge to flight, to go off some place where people didn't want me to be a drama counselor or an emissary, a religious explainer, a rabbi, or a future leader of my people Israel.

It's, by the way, just at such times—so I was soon to learn—when the cerebral systems are fatigued and stalled, and then lock, that we begin to open ourselves up to recognizing angelic forces forming up near us.

To some extent, of course, they are of our own making. That is why it's required to say a blessing of gratitude, a *shehechiyanu*, which is the blessing to mark a first, such as the arrival of an annual holiday, a wedding, or a newborn.

It's especially propitious to recite the blessing, and really nail it if you can, when you sense your first angel might be near.

As Paulene whistled some tune from *Oklahoma* that drifted in from the kitchen, and Jon was on his bed reading his Mormon *mishagas* silently beside me, I lay down and believe I mumbled such a blessing.

At the time I had no idea why.

Blessed sleep finally began to weigh down my eyelids when, absolutely glowing, and in a satin bathrobe, Paulene knocked and entered bearing the snack.

Under his sheet went Jon's *Book of Mormon*.

There suddenly was Paulene like a colossus bestriding the aisle between our two beds, like a model on a runway. Her hair was turbaned in a white towel, and her arms extended as she offered two tall glasses of cold milk that glistened in the half-light on the Relic's old silver platter.

"I don't care how big you two boys get, I'm always going to do this for you. And, Norman, you don't have to worry about the cookies. They're only Fig Newtons knockoffs and don't taste top of the line, but, I assure you, they are strictly kosher. See the little U on the box?"

"I see, I see," I mumbled.

She placed the tray with the two glasses, white and shimmering in the semidarkness, on the nightstand between us. Then she kissed us each goodnight and clicked the door closed behind her.

6

I DRANK the milk and then sought sleep even while Jon continued to read beside me.

I stretched out my fingers toward the crisscross of shadows falling in from the window and along the stuccoed ceiling and then along the wall. I felt as if I were inhaling not only the air in the room but some of the leftover oxygen of childhood.

As a kid, when sleep hadn't come I'd called out and, more often than not, Paulene, lying in her bedroom alone reading, smoking, and angrily waiting for Paul, would shout out, "Count your sheep. I'll give you a nickel for each one that makes it over the fence."

I had tried then, I really had, mainly for those nickels to supplement our $1.25 a week allowance, but I'd never been successful.

The sheep I'd conjured this time were jumping one by one over a rustic wall, leaning against which were an old paint can, two broken blue folding chairs, and an old tricycle with a bent wheel. It was an ensemble of detritus remarkably like the one at the base of the hedge in our backyard behind the duplex that Paul had never gotten around to cleaning up.

Now comes the weird part. As the sheep land, they transform into shapes unlike anything in our backyard or that I'd ever seen before, except maybe hinted at in a Busby Berkeley extravagantly choreographed dance number in the movies: the sheep are turning into angels—great rustling winged creatures who, in midflight over our fence, begin to shed wool, and to don sleek gowns as they morph into a human form, landing, elegantly reassembling themselves into a kind of heavenly chorus of exquisite female singers.

They help each other very politely to tuck their wings flat in back so their line looks smooth, and pretty soon the wings are invisible beneath white robes as they begin to chant in Hebrew, "*Kadosh, kadosh, kadosh, Adonai tzevaot m'loh kol ha-eretz kvodo.*"

That's the line from the daily prayer that you're supposed to chant while standing on your toes, elevating toward heaven. This variety of angels are called *ophanim*, which comes from the word *ophan*, meaning circle.

They are well named because their main job, over and over again, like crazy animals going around in a maze, is to sing and to praise God with continual choruses of holy, holy, holy in which they try to outdo each other.

What a dream to have my first night home!

Nobody bothered at school to ask why an all-powerful God, without human traits, would be so vain as to require continual singing of words of adulation. Maybe He just enjoyed good music.

I was asking that question in my dream state, I think, when I heard Jon's deep voice interrupting. "Yo, Norman. You all right?"

"Sure."

"Norman? You're mumbling in your sleep."

"What?"

" 'Holy, holy, holy.'"

"Holy, holy . . . oh boy."

"What you got going there, brother?"

"What?"

"I knew it."

"What do you know!"

"Things are changing. All around us."

"Will you stop it! I was dreaming. A dumb dream."

"Don't think so. You won't tell me what it was?"

"Why should I?"

"You don't believe in dreams?"

"Will you cut this crap out. Leave me alone."

Now Jon folded up his book, and pushed up against the headboard of his bed in a way that suggested anything but repose.

He waited with this infuriating newfound patience of his—or was it an indulgence—until it was safer to go on.

Then, with his back straight and legs crossed in a kind of lotus position, he sat up in bed. He struck me more as a Buddhist meditator than an incipient Mormon.

"What did she say to you? About me."

"Who?"

"Mom."

"I thought you heard."

"Come on, man."

"Well, she thinks you have a girlfriend and that you just haven't told her yet. That your girlfriend got you to shave and to get a buzz cut and to leave the man cave."

"You don't believe that, do you?"

"Oh, I don't know."

"I think you know it's right for me, girl or no girl."

"I know no such thing. Maybe you've got me wrong. Maybe I haven't started working on you yet."

"Norman."

"Did I say I would talk to her? I don't remember that I did."

"Didn't say you wouldn't."

"Hey, just don't leave those calling cards around! And, for god's sake don't have them, the Mormon missionaries or whoever, come by."

"Listen to you. Like it's the Russians are coming. Relax. They're really nice people. And they do these great barbecues every week out at Santa Monica. You should drop by."

"Salt of the earth."

Another silence.

And then Jon spoke again, and maybe it's what I brought to my flawed listening—a prejudiced view can feel as truthful as the truth, I'm sad to report—but he sounded to me not like the brother I knew, but as if someone had prepared a series of bullet points for him: here's what you say to a mother, to a father, to a brother, to a cousin; here's what you say to a family member when they have grown uncomfortable since you're a new conscript in the faith's zealous embrace.

And he was right. That's the way I felt. Mea culpa.

"Norman?"

"Is there anyone else in the room?"

"Can I give you another example?"

"Of what?

"Of how to talk to her?"

"Well, if you know, why don't you just do it yourself?"

Then, without waiting for my assent, he laid it right out: "Take baptism."

"You told me."

"I'm reminding you. So I know it's a dirty word, so don't use it. Like I said, tell her, you know, *mikvah*. Or maybe . . . start with the revelation that Moses got on Mount Sinai, the Ten Commandments. Have you seen the pile of Mount Sinai calendars she's got collected! She's into those. Only maybe don't call it revelation, but I mean, why shouldn't there be, after two thousand years, a new revelation, and the Mormons have been tapped for it this time, like the Jews were way back then? You get where I'm coming from? They like us because, well, they're the new Jews. And as to baptism, like I said, it's just a *mikvah*, the Jewish ritual bath. That's what I mean. She'll understand that. Points of tangency, sister faiths. If I get baptized, it'll just be like a big *mikvah*. You with me, bro?"

Oh, I was with him all right. "Are you nuts! That's just not right. Because after you're dunked, you pop up cleansed not of the grime on your epidermis, man, but of your Jewish identity. Some *mikvah*."

"You'll make her understand the right way then."

"Not if I don't understand myself."

"Look, the point is, I'm still going to be Jewish."

"How's that?"

"I mean I'm not going to wipe away my Jewish education, for example. It's not a lobotomy! I'm still going to know how to read Hebrew. Not like you, of course. Mine's pretty primitive and all that, but the Mormons really prize it, I'll have you know."

"Oh, I'm sure they do."

"You probably think next I'm going to go and *un*circumcize my dingus. But no way, José."

"Thank you for that profoundly moving statement of faith. Score *mikvah* for the Mormons, dingus for the Jews."

"A couple of times I have thought about telling her myself. Yet each time I couldn't figure out quite how to begin. I kept on rehearsing the words in my head, but none sounded right. I've been praying to Heavenly Father for an answer, for the perfect words, for how to do it, a way to tell her that's honest to me but won't pain her. They haven't come."

"Because maybe there aren't any."

"I suppose that's possible. But if it can be done, you can do it, man. I know you can. That's why He sent you home this summer. And I thank Him for it."

"Who?"

"Heavenly Father."

"Heavenly Father didn't send me here. United Airlines did. And I paid for the ticket. Come on, Jon, clear out your head."

"Oh, believe me, I have."

"When you say Heavenly Father, you mean God, right?"

"Sure. God. Let's not get stuck on the nomenclature. God is God."

"Then why convert?"

"Fine, fine," he said, and then we fell into another of those silences where I felt my heart about to leap out of my chest and into the pocket of my pajama top that lay over it.

I took a deep breath or two or three. I tried to calm down. I vowed to do better.

I didn't get very far.

Only perfunctory empathy came out of me, then disappeared like a passing cloud. When that drifted off, I took the all-familiar road that you will soon recognize: I became a Jewish cliché and I all but shouted in the deafening silence that followed: how could you do this *to me*! How could any brother of mine accept the Latter-day Saints' thanatopsis with its elaborate, silly, infantile architecture of salvation? Such primitive nonsense!

While I recognized this rampaging egotistical tone in myself, I didn't work very hard against it, didn't really catch it and send it away.

On the contrary, my sophistry was such that the very recognition, so went my puny philosophy, somehow gave me the illusory notion that I wasn't acting out of knee-jerk prejudice when I was already deep in its thrall. Can't you see it, Jon? It's for your own good that I refuse to be your personal ambassador of religious bullshit.

And, moreover, wasn't I, by refusing, also trying to protect Paulene?

As I lay there in the bedroom with my brother, and this passed between us, one wave of emotion after another back and forth over the abyss between our beds, hammering him, then me, well, it was as if the path I was about to follow through these waters that summer—until the angels finally came to my rescue—was already being fashioned: despite myself, I was being transformed into a monstrous Jewish John Wayne.

No, better a Kirk Douglas. Like Kirk in *The Indian Fighter*, I must circle the wagons, that is, the arks of Torah, family, faith, and even the Temple Beth Ami "family" including Mr. Footlick and this ridiculous Camp Tikvah summer that loomed, all for the purpose of warding off this surprise attack by the Mormons on my mother and on my family.

And the defense had to be strong because the attack was of the most brazen and potentially virulent variety: heretical, fraternal, and from deep within our very midst.

I turned angrily on my side, faced Jon, and spoke with a tone far more combative and accusatory than I expected: "But why of all the loonies in the world, the Mormons, man? Just because they happened to knock on your door?"

Jon seemed to catch these repeated questions like lozenges on his tongue that he would taste fully before answering.

He rolled back my way and his eyes sought mine in the semidarkness. With a deliberateness that gave his face, now latticed by slats of shadow from the streetlight, an eerie cast as if we were in a sci-fi film, he just stared at me, through me.

He seemed on the verge of speech, so I waited. But he didn't speak. So I waited some more. And with each hesitation my fury built.

That moment, which I see now these many years later in vivid memory, was perhaps another turning point.

"All you're telling me over and over is how silly the Mormons seem to you. You haven't told me one good thing about the Jews."

"No?"

"No. Sell the Jews to me. Go on."

"They're not a product. They're—"

"—Just tell me: *why* should I stay?"

That last remark gripped me with a sudden panic: I don't think I fully understood then it was not so much that Jon might be leaving the Jews that was eating away at me but a fear even greater: that he had found something wonderful, some superior set of symbols, rituals, language; a channel for transcendence that I, if I were honest with myself, might still be seeking, though no longer through the dumb old seminary. But being honest with myself was not something I specialized in that summer.

I looked away.

I heard Jon take a long breath. Then his sheets and blankets rustled. Now there he was lying even closer to me than before, his head propped on his hand at the edge of the bed, just two feet away from me, his eyes intense with a light fraternal and genial, but also relentless.

"Norman, the Mormons are very very good people, like I say. Warm, wonderful people."

"Warm? So maybe there *is* a girl?"

"Oh, man."

His forbearance shamed me, although it didn't shut me up. In fact, it seemed only to make the clichés and the stereotypes fall more and more out of me like autumn leaves from a shaken tree.

"In that case, very cool. More than one babe? Two or three at a time? Plural marriage? Sign me up, man. Today. Where's the paperwork?"

Jon just stared and waited.

"Okay. *Is* there some cute missionary?"

"No."

I simply refused to believe Jon on the merits, and his equanimity seemed to grow in inverse relation to what a jerk I was being.

"I just feel comfortable with them the way I never did in, you know, the temple, *our* temple. You don't feel comfortable there either, do you?"

"That's not the point. You don't go . . . change temples, religions, gods; you don't go from . . . *Adonai Elohenu* to Heavenly Father like you do from Coke to Pepsi. You have to have a *reason*. 'Good people' is not a real reason. 'Warm and comfortable' is not a reason."

"Why not? All right, if you insist on something else, I do have another reason."

"Finally. Okay. Let's have at it."

"I'm looking at the reason right now. You. And another reason's down the hall in her bedroom. Paulene. And Ida downstairs. And the fourth reason is up at the Mt. Eden Cemetery. Well, his body is there anyway."

AND THEN Jon explained it to me yet again and in more detail: life after death, eternal celestial life according to Joseph Smith, how through the Mormon faith he was going to remain with his nuclear family, sealed, linked, joined, welded together for all time.

When I pointed out that Jon didn't yet have a nuclear family of his own to remain with—a remark both sarcastic and typical, I fear—to his credit my brother once again let it pass in suffering silence.

When I told him I hated the phrase "nuclear family" because it implied to me not closeness but that sooner or later everything was going to blow up, he ignored that .

He meant, he patiently repeated, that all of *us* would remain together, a large, extended celestial family, in eternal life after death. Paulene, Paul, Norman, Jon, Ida the Relic, the uncles, aunts, and cousins, most of whom we hadn't seen for years because we were no longer on speaking terms with several, the whole team, even the Family *Tot*, the distant unknown relatives of Ida, the dead in the Holocaust.

They would join us in happy, happy communal, picnicking-and-barbecuing eternal life. Not *individual* life after death. Oh, no. A notion even bigger and better than the original Christian message of individual salvation. If faith were a toothpaste, this would indeed be labeled a "new and improved" product. Not individual salvation, but *family* life after death, on and on and on and on. That was the Mormon gift the missionaries had shared with Jon and that he wanted to share with me.

"Whoa! Our family life is not exactly *Ozzie and Harriet*. In fact it's a disaster. You want *that*, I mean *this*, to be eternal?"

"It's easy to joke. It's hard to believe. What do you believe, Norman?"

"I believe that we just let each other alone, try to be nice, tell a few jokes, have a few tokes, and we stumble along as best we can."

"And after we die? It's what? Just over?"

"Yes."

"You pay your check, you go out the door."

"You don't forget to tip. But yes, out the door. With luck you close it quietly."

"Drift off into the sunset. Like that? Adios, partner?"

"Pretty much."

"That's what you've concluded from being at the seminary? From all your Jewish studies is *adios*?"

"Yes, that's about it. I'd say not *adios* but '*shalom,* pardner.' "

"Got to be more, Norman. What do the Jews believe about life after death?"

"Oh, I don't know. Screw the Jews and screw the Mormons. And most of all, screw the afterlife."

"Whoa. You do go to the Jewish Theological Seminary?"

"Did go. Past tense."

"What?"

"I mean . . . I'm taking a break from all that . . . struggling. I'm off duty. You know. I've vowed not to read another Jewish book. For the summer."

"A person of faith is never 'off duty.' "

"That's what you think."

"No, tell me."

"Don't press and maybe I will."

"The Jews are not so good on the afterlife, are they?"

"No, we're not."

When I heard that "we" issue from my mouth, I felt something sag within, some tremor I'd never had before and did not recognize. It was as if I didn't know the person who had uttered it, or I didn't want to know him.

Hadn't I just left the "we" behind? Make that three thousand miles between New York and LA. Make that two thousand years of Jewish literature and traditions and beliefs. By my calculations that added up to five thousand good reasons I no longer needed the Jews with their brilliant, tortured commentaries on impossible questions like life after death. Nobody knew anything, and at least the Jews had the good sense and humility, more so than other religions, to be reticent, to shut their mouths most when it came to the unknowable. I was going to be a drama counselor; that was bad enough. Let's leave philosophy out.

I began to think more and more about Jon's stash of old joints. I didn't need the Jews and they didn't need me. That was to be the point of the summer, and my life beyond. Now all I was suddenly thinking about was the marijuana. Were the joints still in the Nabisco Fig Newton tin? Who had just said, "No, *we're* not"? Just who the hell was this "we"?

Jon swung his legs out of bed. A small flashlight flicked on. Jon now shined it on the *Book of Mormon* that he was extending toward me. "Would you mind if I read you just one passage?"

"Are you nuts?"

"No, I'm not nuts."

"I'm sorry, man. I apologize. It's just that now's not the time for that."

"Okay. But you sure need something."

"I was thinking of aspirin."

He tapped his book. "Stuff in here is much more powerful than acetyl-salicylic acid, man. Shall I show you?"

As he enthusiastically flipped through the pages of his new book, I felt a crazy fury rise inside of me. He was trying to proselytize? Me! Right here. Now? In bed! My own brother.

I put my hand on his forearm and pushed the book away.

"Ratchet it down, Norman."

"You ratchet it down."

"I'm not the one who's yelling. You'll wake up Paulene."

"Shut the darn book."

We paused. We were like boxers suddenly in a clinch.

"Okay. Okay," he said as he lowered the black cover over the pages, but then drew the book toward his chest, pressed it to his heart like some damn holy thing. He may as well have read me a thousand pages; that gesture hurt so much.

Then Jon stood in the aisle between the beds. He lifted up one of my blankets that had fallen three-quarters over the foot of the bed onto the carpet and tossed it over me. Then he walked the few paces toward the closed bedroom door.

A sense of panic struck me. For some reason I just didn't want him to leave the room. My heart raced; I felt a film of sweat on my forehead. A moment ago we were going to be together in heaven for all time. Now, already, here on earth, in this bedroom, it felt as if he were abandoning me; we were miles apart.

"Where you going?"

"You said you needed some aspirin. Relax."

When he went out, I flopped back down on the bed and studied, as I had when I was little, the patterns of the little dimples of painted white plaster on the ceiling above. By counting them I tried to calm myself.

I heard a quiet shuffling of bottles in the medicine cabinet down the short hall. Then the light went off. I closed my eyes. Suddenly there he was.

"Open your hand."

When I did, he placed the two small white pills on my palm.

I looked at them with the magical hope they would cure me. Of what I wasn't sure, except that I needed curing. I washed them down with what remained of the milk Paulene had brought.

Then Jon said a simple, "Sleep well."

That's how we drifted into sleep that first night home: two brothers, one a zealous apostate-in-training and one a defector from the faith become its sudden and reluctant defender.

Maybe.

7

EARLY Monday morning the alarm behind the box of Kleenex on the night-stand *bbbriinngged.* Like a character in a cartoon, I bolted up. I found the clock, and lowered the lever to stop the noise. My eyes were still vaguely glued closed. As I slowly allowed myself to wake, it felt like many Sundays of our growing up, when Paul had not returned from a night's gambling in Gardena or at the track at Santa Anita. He had the car, so there would be nothing to do and nowhere to go the whole day except that Jon would wander off to play pick-up games of basketball at the park, and I'd pack up my books to travel by bus for three hours of Bible, S. Y. Agnon and the early Hebrew novel, and the history of Zionism up at the University of Judaism on Sunset.

While Jon still slept, I made my way into the bathroom and then to the breakfast alcove off the kitchen.

There I found a note, as Paulene always wrote them, on the back of one of her Canter's Deli checks, addressed to "my favorite customers."

"There's Frosted Flakes in the Kellogg's Variety Pack you like. Welcome home! And don't forget you're due at camp for orientation at eight-thirty. Don't be late. Mr. Footlick is counting on you. Love ya!"

In a PS she also said she set the clock early because we needed to walk to camp; Footlick's car was in the shop and they needed our old oil-leaker of a Nash Rambler for some errands later in the day.

I got Jon up and, in pretty much early morning slow motion and silence, as if the Mormons had been only a dream we both had miraculously shared, we dressed in jeans and our Camp Tikvah T-shirts with their blue Star of David logo. These had mysteriously appeared hanging over the bedroom doorknob during the night.

That was Paulene. If only to please her I ate half a bowl of Sugar Pops.

Jon wanted to have a second bowl, but I urged him to save some room. I'd explain on the walk in.

On the lined side of the check I wrote, "Thank you, Mom. Great service; wish my favorite waitress were on duty here," and left my own mother a quarter tip.

That was the way we did it in our family. I asked if we should look in on Ida.

"We've got the schedule down. No need to worry," he said.

We clicked the brown front door shut and pulled the screen door behind and began the seven- or eight-block walk to Camp Tikvah.

As we walked I pondered the word *tikvah*, which, as mentioned, means hope in modern Hebrew; and it was on this, the first day of Camp Hope, as it turned out, that we met the angels.

I had by now developed the New York City quickstep, but Jon's longer loping stride, while stylistically way out of sync with mine, still kept us side by side as we traversed the long blocks toward camp.

It's always strange to be a pedestrian in car-centric LA, but this morning more so than ever. As we moved down Pico Boulevard, wave after wave of cars raced by, and that feeling that I always got—a kind of guilt-by-walking—seemed stronger than ever, as if it were shadowing me. What was that baseball-capped driver doing? What did he mean giving me a glance as we waited at the light? What was he thinking? That we had been up partying all night? That we were a couple of young guys new in town, still unable to afford a car? Lost and meandering our way out to Santa Monica to live the hippie, beachcomber, bum's life?

Was anyone whizzing by able to read the Camp Tikvah on our T-shirts? Take in the Star of David emblazoned on our breasts? Maybe one of the cars would slow, pull over, and out of it scramble racists with baseball bats bound for breaking up a civil rights rally at UCLA; on the way why not teach a lesson to a couple of uppity young Jews? Kick the liberal shit out of them before it multiplies. That used to happen. Paul said it happened to him once, in Chicago or maybe it was in Indianapolis, where he once worked as an organizer for the furriers' union before the gambling bug bit him. That was long, long ago.

We crossed Fairfax and the next major intersection, Crescent Heights

Boulevard. While we waited for that light to change, Jon raised his right arm and pointed north and west toward La Cienega.

Without quite looking me in the eye, he said, "Up there at Gregory Way behind the park is the meeting house for our stake. You can get to it from here."

"Your what?"

"That's what the Mormons call it. Stake. They don't use the temple up on Santa Monica except for special occasions. Stake, Norman. Stake. Think *shul*. The Mormon *shul* is the stake, or the ward. I bet you didn't know either that it was there when we were growing up. "

"Guess not."

"That close to home," he added, as if there were some symbolism I was missing.

"Mmmm. I'm getting hungry."

"S-T-A-K-E. I'd like to take you over there one of these days."

"For what?"

"Just to show you around."

"Sure."

"You don't sound so enthusiastic."

"Well you're not exactly inviting me to a Stones' concert."

"How do you know?"

"I know."

"Might just blow your mind even more."

We left it there and when the light cycled to green, we resumed walking.

AFTER A few more blocks we turned the corner at La Cienega Boulevard and headed up toward the temple, where my step quickened.

I then beheld it, a red and blue prow, the sign protruding over the sidewalk in the near distance—the painted beacon of Ships Restaurant—across from the synagogue.

I had been thinking about this particular vista and the treat to come ever since I'd slipped into the booth at Tom's Restaurant back in New York. If that had been the launch of my dietary violations big time, and in public, I was now bringing the show home, to a theater near me!

While Jon stood next to me with that scrutinizing gaze of his—what I mean to say is that as he indulged me—I just looked up at the overflowing marquee: half a bark or schooner gaudily painted a ketchup red and laden with all its forbidden fries and other fabulous nonkosher fare. As I now caught the aromas of bacon and hash browns from the kitchen inside, I felt like some kind of culinary captain of extremely low but enthusiastic rank finally returning to a shore he had just glimpsed but never had time to explore.

As I climbed the entryway steps, I reached up for the prow and for its mermaidish figurehead, with a crispy onion ring for her diadem, hanging over the sidewalk. Falling out in an abundant cornucopia from her decolletage were potential foods on my list to indulge in: rosy lobster claws, mussels, scallops, and various other shellfish, along with a cheeseburger big as a hula hoop dripping moisture, crispy ribbons of bacon, and a light, golden-brown chicken drumstick that could rival a Louisville Slugger.

Ships was considerably recessed from the corner yet directly facing Temple Beth Ami across La Cienega Boulevard. The ship was right on a collision course with the synagogue.

I made an adolescent leap up to touch a breast near the overhanging lobster claw, and landed awkwardly almost turning my ankle on the steps. I was so excited I might have toppled but Jon held me up from below.

"What are you doing?"

"Come on, we're early."

Whatever he thought of my antics, he just shrugged and, saying, "We just ate," he indulged me once again. Like a silly butler, I ceremoniously held open the restaurant door for him, and we entered.

Ships was a cavernous place with the kitchen smack in the middle like a ship's galley where cooks wearing US-Navy-style white caps at a jaunty angle and uniformed waitresses swirled about. We slid into one of the big red-cushioned booths with a full view of Temple Beth Ami across the boulevard.

A waitress in a tangerine uniform eyed us, but did not immediately approach.

We'd of course both been here before as kids with Paul and Paulene, usually after temple events that I'd excelled in—like being Mordecai's donkey in the Purim Pageant or Judah Maccabee in the Hanukkah play. And of course as to the fastest Hebrew speed reader ever at Temple Beth Ami, I was the gold-medal winner in that three years running.

Our usual reward then had been a malted milk, a peanut butter and jelly sandwich, or perhaps the scoop of celery-flecked tuna on the lonesome pale green bed of lettuce followed by the bouncing jello ball and rabbinically approved Reddi-wip, an extra portion please.

That was then.

Now in this new world of public pork eating that I was embracing this morning, I found myself having to choose between the Galleon Special—three sausages in the shape of a cannon on a boat of toast—and Eggs Benedict with Canadian ham.

The prospect of all that food and all that manageable transgression to come made me feel positively expansive. And as I was soon to confirm, these hopeful moments before appetite is satisfied in a meal can be a very treacherous time.

As we checked out the large shiny menus, I apologized to Jon for having lost my temper and for my stupid unbound irony that I'd loosed on him. I told him that I knew zilch about the Mormon path he was apparently going down. I did repeat that I thought it wrongheaded, that Joseph Smith had nothing on Joseph and his brothers in Egypt in *our* Book of Exodus, but, bottom line, I respected Jon's right to choose his own way.

It was a pretty speech. Never mind that I didn't believe most of it. Then I crossed my fingers, puerile me at my best, and added, "I'll even visit your stake or ward or whatever it is."

"That's great," he replied, with a glance at his watch, "as long as you behave yourself."

"Don't I always?"

"If you did, I wouldn't need to mention it."

With glee I pointed out to Jon the photo of the Eggs on a Rope—the rope being strips of bacon ingeniously twined into a nautical pattern—in the big laminated menu. That's just when I noticed him peering through the plate glass window.

I followed his gaze across the boulevard out to where Temple Beth Ami's side door had just been flung open, its metallic panel catching some reflections of the morning light. That was our destination for the orientation, but *after* my long-planned repast.

"You know what you want?"

He ignored me and just kept looking.

"What are you going to have?"

While my business was all appetite and to devour all things porcine in sight, and that was a lot, my brother seemed suddenly so fixed on some spectacle outside that I now tried to locate and to assess what he was following so carefully with his eyes.

At first I made out only a handful of counselors identifiable by the same blue and white Camp Tikvah T-shirts of the kind we had on this morning. They were trickling in through the temple's door that we had noticed earlier. We had plenty of time, so what was the big deal?

I returned to checking out the further inventive ways Ships had conjoined a ziggurat of tiny hash brown cannon balls, for example, piled up like ammunition beside a sausage cannon, whose disappearing wheels were balls of melting butter.

What kind of sight could be more gripping than that? Yet Jon had found one outside. He seemed, well, transfixed. It was him I watched first, as the menu slowly slipped away from his hands.

In retrospect I see that meant he likely saw the angels first.

Then I did.

My first view of our girls—our angels—of that summer was a wild group portrait: four extraordinarily shapely and tanned legs slow-loping down the sidewalk, visible between the cars passing on La Cienega Boulevard. They were like young antelopes somehow loosed on the streets of LA, moving with long and powerful strides, a gait that seemed, well, more than unusual, not only graceful and strong, but as if in a category all its own.

The shorter girl trailed the taller, and each time she strode to catch up, she seemed to elevate her feet off the sidewalk, both at the same time, remaining in the air with easy grace just as long as she wanted.

Of course this was possibly a kind of optical distortion caused by our viewing it all through a thick window, from across the boulevard, and all its busy traffic getting in the way of our gawking.

Yet I don't think so.

They were really, well, more than girls, at whom we now unabashedly stared from behind the cover of the menus, window, and distance. Even from across the boulevard you could see they were both beautifully tanned, bronzed, as the Coppertone Suntan Lotion ads used to say, but also different: as if the sun had reached them and lit them up from both outside and in.

One was tall and the other considerably shorter, but even from our safe lookout both young women emanated this remarkable gait or canter or quality I then—and now—cannot accurately describe.

They were athletic and choreographic at the same time, that is, they moved with a spring, a stride unlike any of the other counselors-to-be we had noticed entering the side door of the temple.

All right, I'll say it: they simply didn't seem like the rest of us who are bound by gravity and by the other laws of the earth.

The tall one was very fair-skinned, although you could see she was also deeply tanned in her own way. Yes, I know, a contradiction, yet only the first of a long list we were to discover that summer.

It was the tall one's hair that was most remarkable, red as a hibiscus flower, and it flowed behind her like one of the Graces in that famous Botticelli painting.

The shorter one had brown hair in bangs and a bouncy ponytail, but again it was the movement that conveyed the most amazing quality, a fluid liveliness as if every sequence of steps also had the vertical spring of a gymnast's bouncing across the mat.

From our vantage in Ships's booth we watched until the temple's side door took them in.

As randy young guys, we normally would have expostulated, "Look at those legs! Check out the rack on that one! Perfect boobs stacked beneath the Camp Tikvah medallion on her tight T-shirt."

Yet not a crass, vulgar, or profane word fell from our lips.

The terms you use in religion courses to describe such moments of completely unexpected and mysterious intensity that evoke reactions that run counter to normal experience, taking everything else away and transporting you, however briefly, outside of yourself, include *awe*, or *epiphany*, or *radical amazement*.

Maybe.

You're thinking, dear reader: Is he overdoing it again?

Still I think Jon and I both knew we had been privy to a remarkable sight.

It's entirely possible that Jon's reaction also was due to his newfound cleaner living and improved daily decorum, courtesy of the Mormons.

Yet what then kept yours truly from acting like a callow grossout?

No, we were both already in their thrall.

The waitress then appeared, as if yanking us back to earth.

"Gentlemen?"

This one had a pleasant if pudgy face that reminded me of Shelley Winters as Sue Lyons's jealous mom in *Lolita*. There was a pencil steeply angled behind her ear, I believe in her bun. The top of the pencil sported a little white sailor's cap for an eraser.

I decided against the Eggs Benedict and also to forego the Rope and the Galleon and the other multiple-yoked and pork extravaganzas. Instead I ordered only two eggs. I asked for them prepared sunny-side up.

I was instantly aware that Paul used to like that Depression-era song about keeping your sunny-side up, and his eggs that way . Or, as he said one night when I was with him at Ships after picking the right horse at Santa Anita, "I'll have mine with the eggs 'lookin' at me.'"

Jon lowered his menu to the table and politely ordered a bran muffin.

Suddenly I began to see other ship-themed details I hadn't noticed before: the cut of the waitress's uniform was sailor square; even the wavy ribbing at the neck was in keeping with a nautical style. The sign above the bathrooms— The Head—was lit by a small bulb in the shape of a life preserver. In all the years we'd come here I hadn't noticed that. Had those two girls entering the synagogue seconds before opened our pupils wider to all kinds of things?

"May I also have a double order of sausage, Miss, well done, and coffee?"

"You can have anything you want, hon. Long as you pay for it."

Jon requested extra jelly for his muffin.

"Make it a double order of bacon with the double sausage. And please," I added, "very, very crispy on the piggies."

"I love men with appetites."

This woman seemed not quite to carry herself with the quality that truly great and theatrical waitresses like Paulene possessed—namely, the unspoken knowledge of her work in the scheme of the world: that she brings us what sustains life.

Still, in all, this woman's departing remark had redeemed her in my eyes. "Waitress Hall of Fame?"

"No way," said Jon.

"Second level?"

"I'd say only first."

"We'll see," I said, finishing off our little routine by which no waitress ever could approach our mother's pedestalled spot.

We spoke nothing of what we had just seen out the window, but the angels were with us.

The waitress soon reappeared bearing an urn of coffee, with two white porcelain mugs. I took mine and added milk and sugar. Then, as I brought the cup to my lips, I noticed Jon staring at me. His index finger was raised as if requesting me to pause in my headlong consumption. I suddenly understood he was not drinking coffee.

"Since when?"

"Oh, about three weeks now. Never felt better in my life. Sleeping like a log."

"Good for you."

"No more stimulants, says Joseph Smith."

"Well, good for Joe Smith. You don't mind if . . ."

"Of course not."

"You want me to hold it under your nose? Does inhaling count?"

"I thought it was going to be difficult but not so. Smokes are next."

I drained a first cup in three theatrical gulps and sloshed another from the urn into my mug.

"You sure?"

"The body's the temple of the soul," Jon quoted somebody. "So I've gotten the good old Mormon janitors in here to start cleaning this temple out."

"Very impressive. You notice those girls?"

"Beautiful."

"Very."

And that's all we spoke of them, for now.

Yet the coffee had never tasted so rich, nor was the feel of the mug, which I raised to my cheek, ever so warm and comforting.

As my glasses began to fog up with the steam, an aroma of oniony cheeseburger drifted by. Let Jon become an ascetic. I'd match each of his acts of self-denial with one of self-indulgence. That way we'd maintain the equilibrium of desire in the world. Or some such ridiculous thought crossed my mind, which was now consumed by so much pleasant appetite. My taste buds suddenly popped up their little heads like daffodils in April. It was as if nothing but a giant tongue existed between my ears.

When camp started, I calculated that I could sneak in for a burger right after the kids went home. That would go for roughly five days a week for all Camp Tikvah's eight weeks. That was approximately forty cheeseburgers to look forward to.

Maybe it wouldn't be such a bad summer after all.

When I emerged from this aromatic reverie, I noticed Jon clasping and unclasping his large hands beside the dome-shaped tabletop jukebox that sat, with the salt- and pepper-shakers and napkin holder beside it, at the far end of the table and flush with the window of our booth.

He seemed nervous, and finally let out what was still troubling him.

"You have to tell Mom. Norman, I mean it. I've been thinking about it."

That again. He would not let up!

I put down my coffee. I felt a deep urge to shut him up by really confessing what had happened in New York. Happened not to him, but to me. Yes, this fat bag of appetite sitting across from him was weathering a life-changing crisis.

Instead these words came out: "You think she'll be able to keep it from the Foot? What you're doing. Mormons! You have got to be kidding! A flaming zealous Mormon, the swimming counselor at a Jewish camp? You'll lose your job before you swim a lap, man, and you think mine won't be far behind? Through my relationship to you, I'll be contaminating the kids as well. It can happen, you know. It can. That's what you want?"

"I don't think that will happen."

"How do you know it won't?"

"You're being ridiculous."

"I don't think so."

"But I can't be there under false circumstances."

"Cut out what you're doing, and the circumstances won't be false any more. I just solved your problem."

He averted his eyes.

"On the other hand maybe you're right. Maybe your secret would be safe with her because she'll be so goddamn embarrassed, so ashamed, she won't breathe a word to the Foot, or to anyone else."

"There's nothing to be ashamed of."

"Okay then."

"Okay what?"

"If there's nothing to be ashamed of, why don't you tell her yourself! You don't need me."

"I told you."

"You've got the wrong person. Didn't you see what I ordered for breakfast, man? Isn't it clear?"

"Isn't what clear?"

"My Jewish credibility is not what it used to be."

So then I told it. This time I really did. I confessed. How I was through with a rabbinic career, the whole sad tale.

Jon listened without interrupting. I hadn't been planning on revealing what happened. Not then. I guess it just had to come out. That's what happens sometimes in the optimistic interval before a tasty meal is served or after angels have appeared; it's a very dangerous time.

"So that's it."

"Whoa."

I dropped five sugars into my third cup and said, "Whoa! You got that right."

I had a long sip. And then another, and another. I could have been an advertisement for Maxwell House Coffee, or whatever brew they had served me. Never had I loved coffee more.

Jon just stared at me. I had no idea what he was thinking.

I said, "So I'll make you a deal. I'll tell Paulene you're considering becoming a Mormon if you tell her that her great dream to be the mother of Rabbi Norman is now history. I confess for you. You confess for me. What do you say?"

"Real bad timing, man. Real bad."

And that was the truest thing that had been said between us since I'd returned.

We sat in the booth, and there was nothing more to say.

We stared out the window across the traffic at the temple, up and down the boulevard. Everything was draped in a deep quiet like in the aftermath of a street crime but in the first few seconds before the first passerby notices and screams.

The silence was also a kind of tide on which I was floating away from Jon, and maybe he felt he was floating away from me.

I'm a very garrulous guy and it has taken me a long time to appreciate the value of the absence of talk as a kind of soil in which things more truthful than words can convey will emerge. The angels helped that summer, to be sure.

Yet then, at that first Ships breakfast, before their aura began to envelop us, I couldn't tolerate the silence for long.

It felt dangerous, so thoughtlessly I broke it: "You remember the Marranos?"

"Who? Yes, sure."

"Okay. That's the plan then, for now. We'll be the Marrano Brothers. In reverse. Yes, the Reverse Marrano Brothers."

"Sounds like a band, but not one I'd go see."

"Reverse Marrano Brothers. RMB. We'll brilliantly fake an interest in Judaism and be superb role models for the rich little kids from Beverly Hills. All the while we'll both be secret *non*-Jews. Each in his own way. We'll be playing a game, just like Dad always played a game. What do you say, man?"

Jon picked up his butter knife from his place setting and moved it back and forth between us like a metronome. Its message was: no, no, and more no.

If he hadn't been auditioning to become a Mormon, he might have articulated a little more clearly what I took his gesture really to mean: shut the fuck up!

Yet none of this, remarkably, seemed to dull my hunger. For when appetite collides with high anxiety inside a Jewish stomach, the feeling can be very scary and must be assuaged.

Jon just kept staring at me as if *I* were the strange case, me and not him, with his Mormon antics. His scrutiny was now making me edgy but not self-reflective enough to retreat. "So? What do you say, Reverse Mormon Brother? Deal?"

Jon was recalibrating. He slowly shook his head. If we'd been playing poker, I'd just shown him that I had, well, at least three of a kind. Should he fold, see me, or raise?

Mormon-to-be or not, Jon was good at the game. We were locked in.

Then, fortunately, breakfast arrived.

Thanks to the glory of Ships, here finally was not only a much-needed hiatus from our dueling, but also my long-awaited haul of forbidden food. I took immediate inventory: six strips of bacon, three sausages, two thin disks of hash browns nicely crisped in lard, and three pieces of rye toast cut into six halves and forming a kind of barrier protecting the two sunny-side-up eggs looking at me.

Beside Jon's modest Mormon muffin sat my dazzling cargo of pork, crisped to perfection.

For all this mighty moat of meat was piled magnificently high on a Ships plate that was shaped like some sort of nineteenth-century sailing vessel. It was a sloop, perhaps, long and trim at bow and stern, stern being where two half globes of butter, the size of golf balls, had begun their melting descent down, down, inexorably down toward the porcine-laden lower decks. A double-length toothpick leaned at a jaunty angle out of the uppermost slice of toast, and from it flew, like a maritime pennant, a wedge of orange cut to the shape of an S.

I smiled at my incipient Mormon brother, as if to say, I see your sin, Jonathan Gould, and raise it by this tasty haul.

"That's a whole lot of *treyf* all at once."

"And that's some good Yiddish for an apostate-in-training."

Then I raised my fork like a new devotee. Not sure before which altar to prostrate myself first, I decided to dive right into it all.

But the revelations continued, this time between mouthfuls.

As I in every sense of the verb pigged out, I sneaked looks at Jon. His eyes were closed, his appetite completely subordinated to new promptings, his head bowed, and he was apparently mumbling words of a prayer before he took the first bite of the muffin. It had to have been a Mormon *hamotzi,* the blessing over breaking bread, because beneath my loud chewing sounds as I crunched my sausage's carbonized casing, I heard what he was saying.

Yes, at least he only whispered the words, which I give him credit for, and he rushed them along to be out of my range. Yet he failed because they were not so hushed that I couldn't make them out: "And thank you, Lord, for bringing Norman on his long journey safely from New York. We thank you, in the name of Jesus Christ, amen."

We finished the meal without speaking further.

We rose silently, tipped generously, as we had been trained to do by Paulene no matter the level of service. Then, tucking our Camp Tikvah T-shirts neatly into our jeans, we headed across the street for our first day of work, and to meet our angels.

I wasn't sure about my brother, but I was ripe for some intercession.

8

BEARING what felt like the remains of an entire pig farm in my gut, I fairly rolled behind punctual, athletic Jon as we crossed La Cienega Boulevard in traffic, approached Temple Beth Ami's shining brass banisters and steep steps up to the sanctuary, but didn't ascend.

It was exactly 8:31.

We right-angled around to the side door where we were not surprised to encounter Mr. Footlick.

"Just the handsome young men we've been waiting for!"

The morning sun reflected off the dome of the Foot's pate and high forehead, both shinier than I remembered. He seemed very eager to greet us.

He moved to hug me, but I returned his gesture like a statue trying to unfreeze and to recoil; he backstepped awkwardly and settled for a manly, two-handed shake.

Mr. Irving Footlick was wearing the official Camp Tikvah T-shirt, but it was none too flattering. He was a stocky man with a rotund middle, and Jon and I both could have fit within his waistband's circumference. He also wore his khaki bermuda shorts high on his abdomen, like a sporty Humpty Dumpty. Instead of Keds hightops, which we of course were wearing, the Foot had on shiny black leather loafers with tassels and matching black socks.

"*Shalom*, boys. I'm so glad to see you!"

We both of us hoisted up our hopeful Camp Tikvah smiles.

"*Shalom* to you, Mr. Footlick," Jon replied.

A few other counselors straggled in and around us; with a brief greeting he handed them the orientation folders he'd given us. But he did not break off his tête-à-tête with the sons of Paulene. The Foot apologized for not coming in to say hello to us when he had dropped our mother off. Then he said conventional words of condolence again about Paul, even though our dad had died ten months before. Then he asked us how we found Paulene.

The more the Foot spoke, the more awkward I felt. All right, he was dating Paulene, and not me, not us. Not yet.

Words of outrage were forming up and felt as if they were about to march right out of my mouth and run the Foot down on the spot. Somehow Jon must have sensed it because that's when he, animated perhaps by his new-found Christian charity or just plain, native decency, interceded.

"Oh, Mom's great, Mr. Footlick."

"Well, she's a woman of true valor."

"What do you mean?" I shot back at him, ready to parse my way into as bad a first impression and argument as I could muster. But he would have none of it.

"It's so hard to lose your . . . partner in life. Believe me I know. But there's nothing to worry about. Your brother can tell you, Norman, that the temple family has taken good care of her since her, your, great loss."

"That's right," Jon said.

Now I really felt like slugging the *gonef.* That's the Yiddish term for "lowly thief," for that's how Paul had always characterized the Foot, the local king of temple fundraising, and it was exactly the word that echoed in my head.

He went on about our assignments: the use of the Olympic-size pool, big enough for Jon to teach butterfly to the older kids and to teach the little ones how to tread water, both at the same time; and the half dozen big puppets left over from some Purim ball that I might be able to use in my drama group; yes, indeed, the whole fascinating schedule for camp. Top of the line! Cutting edge! State of the art!

Was this guy capable of a thought of his own? An original phrase or even a word? Cutting edge? State of the art? For godsake, a swimming pool was a pool, and if I needed puppets, I'd just ask Mr. Footlick to volunteer.

Everything about the Foot, from his diction to his forehead to his socks, set me off this morning. I felt somehow ambushed by this new life I was being thrust into.

How could she go for this guy? Our mother! Then *that* other thought came into my head this morning. The thought I had no business thinking any longer. *That* one really ambushed me once again as it was about to for the whole run of the summer: namely, how could she date a new man before the required mourning period for Paul had ended? It was only ten months. She was one month shy.

In retrospect I think that was probably why I didn't just freak out then and there. My outrage was a kind of Jewish Outrage, and as a fresh dropout from Jewish life, I no longer felt that I was entitled to express it. Yet I *felt* it, big time.

Under Jon's ameliorating glance I managed to murmur, "Thank you, Mr. Footlick. We're both grateful."

"Irving. Call me Irving."

"Irving."

"You're both looking very handsome. All set to teach swimming? Theater?"

"Absolutely," said Jon. "Australian crawl, water polo, water ballet, you name it!"

"From *Hamlet* to *The Dybbuk*," I chimed in, surprisingly inspired by my brother's mischievousness. "I actually thought I'd do a nautical play, something with Jon's swimmers. Maybe on a water theme, from the Bible, of course."

"Oh? Like what?" Jon asked.

Of course, we hadn't discussed a word of this. He was putting me on the spot. He was goofing with me. We were like accidental stand-up comics riffing off each other, with the Foot as straight man and audience all rolled into one.

"Weren't we talking about maybe retelling Noah's Ark at the pool?"

"Right, right. We were, exactly."

"With a new twist."

"What kind of twist?" the Foot asked.

"Oh, I was trying to imagine what might have happened if the ark had an accident during the flood. You know. Noah meets the *Titanic*."

"Fantastic," said Mr. Footlick. "You're a very amusing young man."

Then the Foot turned squarely to me and said, "Your mother and I . . . I mean your teachers, Rabbi Joel, the whole temple family . . . we're so proud of your commitment to Jewish life."

"Right."

Another parade of words all formed up into biting invective were about to march out of the hectic Grand Central of my brain independent of me, and would launch a surprise attack when I was most unaware and vulnerable.

And I wanted to shout at him: If you want the truth, actually the last two years have been the worst of my life! All the scholarships over the years, which I'm sure your influence helped to obtain for me, just like these stupid jobs, have only prolonged my indecision and torture.

And here—I visualized myself reaching into my pocket and finding a few quarters which I would throw on the floor before him: Keep the rest of it, the scholarship, the jobs, the camp stipend. We'll get along without the summer income. I'm done with the Jews and I'm done with you, pal. I don't want to be working at a Jewish camp. And by the way keep your pudgy little fingers off my mother!

After all my admonishing Jon to keep our sins under our hat, why was it *I* who could barely restrain an urge to wild, public confession and freak-out?

It's not for nothing, I guess, that I had been selected camp drama counselor. Suddenly I was this version of James Dean from *Rebel Without a Cause*, this ridiculous young paladin, a flamboyant I-can-say-screw-you-to-anybody-anytime kind of guy, a ridiculous Jewish gunfighter, but in my imagination only. Oh, I was certainly my father's son in my little self-defeating heroic scenes written by, produced by, and starring myself.

Jon stoically crossed his arms over his chest and watched to see if I would self-destruct now, or in a few minutes from now.

"I trust you had an . . . interesting year at the seminary," the Foot's question reached me as if it had just curved in from the other side of the moon.

"Well . . ." I began.

This time it was not Jon but Mr. Footlick who saved me—and it wouldn't be the last time—from putting my footlick, I mean my own big foot, in my mouth.

"Well," he continued as I fumbled for some lying, well, diplomatic reply that somehow would keep everything for now from blowing. Yet what I came up with was only erring-and-uhhing, as I stepped into a pothole of aphasia, so the Foot finished my sentence for me: ". . . well, yes, it's that way sometimes. Norman, I know a thing or two about rabbis. What a difficult calling it is. Having worked in synagogues most of my adult life. There are emotional ups and downs, spiritually speaking. We'll talk about it later."

"We will?"

"Yes we will. But now's time for you and your brother to go on in there and meet the other counselors. This year we have two gorgeous Israeli girls with us for the first time."

Jon and I exchanged a glance as the Foot escorted us down the hall and into the largest of the temple school's classrooms, which was being used for orientation.

Sprawled among the large green and blue canvas bags of sporting equipment were unmistakably the two Israelis. One was on her knees digging through a backpack and the other bending over to tie a boot lace, both set apart from the other counselors, near the cooler. They were indeed like a couple of gazelles lapping up refreshment at the pond. Their Hebrew names: Tali and Aviva. Translation: "Dew" and "Springtime."

These were indeed the two rushing, athletic-looking girls who had so fleetingly but powerfully caught our attention during breakfast.

Tali was the redhead, statuesque, with lightly tanned skin and that fabulous forest-thick hair cut in dramatic bangs in a perfect straight line across her forehead. I mean not a strand long or short. As she tilted back her head and drank from a Dixie Cup, I noticed her long neck tapering into powerful shoulders so that she struck me as a redheaded Jewish Cleopatra who might also have been a strong power forward in basketball.

Aviva, the springy one, was her physical opposite. Small, lithe, and compact, she knelt in front of the water cooler now doing something else with her gear but also making such a candid surveillance of the room, including of Jon and me as we had entered, that I had to smile directly at her. And she smiled back, with a slight turn of her head and a coltish bounce of hair that, I swear, made my heart rate double.

In short order we learned from the Foot that Aviva was to be the Israeli folk dance counselor and also to work with me on the drama stuff. No surprise, she was also a gymnast. Tali, who indeed the Foot described as able to throw any ball, leap any barrier, and whack any birdie—he had said the girls' badminton games at his apartment complex, where they were staying for now, had already gotten the attention of all of the neighbors whom Tali beat handily, men and women alike. Well, she was to assist Jon at the pool and to be a general sports counselor, giving our pampered Beverly Hills camper clientele a duo of proud, athletic, Israeli role models.

What was most remarkable, I realized as the Foot made further remarks and introductions—and all I seemed to be able to do was to stare at the girls—was how out-and-out beautiful they both were. Just perfect, as in a movie, but one we had not yet seen. They both had dark smoldering eyes and skin made healthy by the air of the Judean and Sinai deserts, where they had served—a fairer version of tan for Tali and a deep bronze for Aviva.

Immediately I noticed how Tali and Aviva both wore glistening Jewish stars around their necks. Tali's rested at the base of her long throat, and, with Aviva, her *magen david* lay in the gorgeous fossa, uncentered, to the left and just above the clavicle, where I also thought I detected, later, during the safety spiel at orientation, the pulse of her lovely beating heart.

Both of the girls wore at the ends of their shapely legs combat boots around pale olive-green socks neatly folded over smooth, muscular calves. On their heads they wore tipped-back floppy camouflage hats with genuine patches from the Israeli Defense Forces.

In his speech the Foot had described them as the real thing: two genuine Israeli commandos, highly trained former soldiers having just served on the Egyptian front in the Six-Day War who were visiting us on a special exchange program.

"And because the draft is universal in Israel, they're girls, as you can see," he added.

Did we ever! Tali and Aviva were, well, genuine bombshells of the Sophia Loren, Raquel Welch, Brigitte Bardot caliber of sexy loveliness. How were such combinations possible on this side of heaven? Who even knew the admittedly egalitarian Israeli army went so far as to have girl commandos? Where did they find such picture-perfect females who could also run, shoot, blow up bridges and tanks, and survive on cactus milk and thistles in the desert? How they seemed to have slid off a pin-up calendar of the elite brigades of the Israeli Defense Forces right into Camp Tikvah just amazed me. Or as we used to say in 1967, it blew my mind.

Yet the best part was to come: they seemed there just for us.

Suddenly I was becoming aware of a newly discovered advantage—make that two of them—for my having delayed a public rupture, at least here in LA, from My People Israel.

As we all went about the awkward business of introducing ourselves that first day and doing a few of the Foot's role-playing exercises, I threw my brother more than one eye-rolling-aren't-we-lucky-guys glances. I wondered if Jon was feeling the same way about these extraordinary babes.

Yet his new LDS-inspired manner seemed to have eliminated gestures I used to pick up in such circumstances: no quick tongue thrust of carnality, no silent "wow" formed by his lips. Instead there was a kind of decorous reticence that made it very hard for me to read him.

With our squarish black glasses, which we had both worn since the sixth grade, and our unruly and curly hair—well, only *my* hair, as Jon's scalp had recently become practically US-Marine-and-LDS bare—we were both okay-looking guys. My point is we were far from the most handsome or coolest of young men even among the camp's counseling staff gathered in the orientation room that day.

Tali and Aviva, on the other hand, were startling in their good looks. So I just kept expecting them to be polite and then to walk away from us or to turn their smoldering gazes elsewhere and as time went on to pair up with the two best-looking guys, a couple of already-tan Jewish surfer dudes who somehow were affiliated with a universalist synagogue for Jewish TV and movie stars in Malibu. Wasn't that the way it always worked—the good-looking with the good-lookers, the movie stars with the stars, the ugly with the ugly, and for the rest of us, the in-betweeners with the in-betweeners?

Yet that's not what happened.

Everywhere we went that first day, touring La Cienega Park's pool, ballfields, track, the emerald-green putting oval, and other locations where the campers would play and convene, there the Israelis seemed always near to Jon and to me, always close by amid the throng of other staffers. Tali and Aviva could have had the pick of the male counselor litter, but it was obvious by the end of that first day of orientation that they seemed almost assigned to us.

When they smiled at us or brushed our shoulders as we lined up and did some getting-to-know-you, breaking-the-ice activities, or even shook our hands, they made us feel strong, proud, chosen. Their very presence seemed to carry the élan and bravado, female version, of the entire Jewish state that had recently triumphed over millions of Arabs in the Six-Day War.

Tali paired off with Jon to plan the swimming and sports activities, and Aviva with me to devise the drama schedule.

Did Aviva think the ark in the lunatic Noah play I had dreamed up on the spot should spring a leak and animal pairs would compete to help fix it? Or would a better plot be to let the vessel just sink like a giant brick to the bottom of the sea? That "sea" could be by the five-six foot mark in Jon's pool right below his lifeguard stand.

"But the animals were all so innocent," she said after I made my ridiculous presentation. "The humans failed, not the creatures of the land and the sea and the air."

I couldn't quite believe what I was hearing. Gorgeous, athletic, *and* a philosopher with a poetic flair!

All I could think of saying was, "Would you mind repeating that?"

"Creatures of the land and the sea and the air."

"I love the way you talk."

"You do? We'll see," she said.

It was amazing to me that not only had she taken my off-the-cuff theater suggestions seriously enough to ponder them, she was so cute the way she did it, the tilting of her head as she seemed to weigh my ridiculous notions with a kind of coy, cogitating beauty; well, she made me feel as if my ideas actually had some merit.

And there was more: her voice! There was birdsong in it. Her voice had all of the promise of early mornings and late nights, and secret lingerings and whispering and cooing in the hidden places beneath the ponderosa pines and eucalyptus groves in La Cienega Park. In my mind I was making out with her like mad when in reality I had barely shaken her hand.

But the most fabulous memory I have of our meeting is that when Aviva spoke that simple sentence to me—"We'll see"—she extended her lovely index finger ever so lightly to the corner of my eye, the organ of sight.

I still feel that touch today.

I was Camp Tikvah's luckiest guy.

All of a sudden neither my heresy nor Jon's apostasy-in-progress could hold a candle to the excitement of these Israeli bombshells. I mean, who needed Ships or the Mormon Angel Moroni if two real live Jewish angels would share the kids' milk and cookies with us every day for the next two months?

And the wonder of it was that after that first morning, it only got easier to fall in love with them.

9

FOR me, that whole first week was a kind of Southern California Jewish dreamin' come true. I can still hear the quiet thrumming of The Mamas and the Papas and Bob Dylan's "Tambourine Man" and his other thrillingly ambiguous anthems that meant everything deep and nothing in particular. Tap me on the shoulder now and I'll still hum; I'll practically march along to the stirring martial lyrics of the "Song of the Palmach" that the angels occasionally whispered in Hebrew as we corralled the campers from activity to activity.

The eucalyptus- and pine-filled La Cienega Park quickly got reinvented in my mind as a little garden of, if not Eden, then unexpected delights. My nostrils expand at the memory of the herbal aroma of the angels' shampoo and conditioner and the briskness of their powerful sunscreen, a secret product they said was devised during the recent war by brilliant Jewish scientists in Israeli army intelligence for combat in the desert. I can still see the angels' bikinis, the three dots of Aviva's little red one and Tali's stunning yellow.

Ah, well.

The weather remained a smogless seventy-eight degrees, and even the large number of our campers who hailed from the film community in Hollywood and Beverly Hills turned out to be not so spoiled as I had feared. Despite my formal dropping out from the seminary, which I still had breathed to no one except Jon, I was even enjoying picking up some new Hebrew vocabulary from Aviva, who seemed always to be with me, my new girlfriend and sidekick.

Then there was Tali. She was a living, leggy *Playboy* centerfold in her yellow bikini as she strode about the La Cienega Park pool deck, where Jon perched atop his lifeguard stand and beneath his Dodgers cap and with his nose smeared with white cream.

Yet I immediately noticed how he always seemed to check some camp documents, or reposition the pile of life preservers beneath him each and every time Tali neared. She was such a looker; was he just nervous? I completely understood. Yet as it turned out, that was not the case at all.

Shifting in his seat as she unconsciously assumed all kinds of fabulous positions coaching the kids in the pool, he always seemed to be averting his eyes. What was crazy is that it reminded me of strategies of some of the Orthodox kids I had met in New York in my first years at the seminary. Then I had been wrapping myself in the throes of life-denying observance. I had played the game of avoiding temptation by fingering the tassels of my prayer shawl and by gazing downward at all those lines in the concrete as a beautiful girl approached on the sidewalk as we walked down Broadway to or from class.

With this self-imposed torture I lasted perhaps six months.

So why wasn't Jon just flipping over Tali as I was over Aviva? In general it's hard to talk about who's hot to your own brother, but his complete indifference was creating an especially awkward barrier between us.

At first I tried to ignore it until, gradually, I began to see that his Mormonesque behavior with Tali was threatening to my prospects with Aviva; that was because it also became clear early in that summer that the Israelis were inseparable. They seemed to be interested in us together, or not at all.

Although I might be falling in love, or at least be in the thrall of the lustful jejune form of it, which was the limit of what I was capable of at that time, Jon was clearly not. My brother's eyes were on, well, a different kind of love, one that I did not even want to acknowledge or to give him credit for, until I was pushed.

Which happened soon enough.

It turned out that these spectacular girls had arrived a week or so before the start of camp and were staying in the extra bedroom the Foot had at his apartment near Roxbury Park in Beverly Hills. That was how Paulene had gotten to know them a bit before my arrival home. We learned from her that both hailed from Sfad, the holy city north of Jerusalem known for its mysticism and for its strange rituals, including spiritual ablutions in the cool waters of the purifying streams that ran through the nearby Judean hills.

That made perfect sense to me. Bring on the ablutions, in bikinis, if possible. Now. Please!

This background helped me make sense of the stunning aura and unusual style the girls presented, and so I will be forgiven for calling them angels, in the vernacular sense, but also, I came increasingly to believe, in the theological as well.

I'm speaking now of something beyond and deeper than perfectly symmetrical features and physical beauty, but the unique physical aura they presented. They were always fresh, as if just right out of the shower or emerged from a mountain stream; clean like new porcelain, with roseate ears and skin that almost shined like a beacon, a lighthouse. This was especially the case with Tali, who towered above the kids, they who couldn't get enough of her light, like little ships passing by a coast and she a colossus of a beacon on the shoreline.

Count me among those seeking her light. By the second or third day of work it was also clear the angels were as exquisite in their helpfulness with the campers as they were in their beauty and attention to us.

Now here was something especially peculiar: after the last of the campers were picked up by their parents or babysitters, the angels often went right home with the Foot, or if he was busy and had to remain at the temple, they took the bus down Olympic Boulevard on their own. They almost always, mysteriously, refused a ride from us, or our company, or my standing offer of sweet milkshakes at Ships.

At first I thought Ships, even for shakes, might violate some rule or not be kosher enough for these girls from Israel. Yet it was far more than that: it turned out that angels don't require much sustenance, and my praising the glories of a black-and-white shake only made them look at me as if I were half crazy, and maybe I was.

Of course, my runs to Ships, which had begun as soon as camp started, simply continued. Although Aviva hadn't joined me, yet, she knew all about them and never turned up her nose, and she never snitched.

Soon enough there emerged from me, as if it had a life of its own that needed to be embodied, all this puerile acting out that soon characterized my style of camp counseling, or non-counseling.

These antics included moving ahead on my upside-down Noah's Ark tale in which the animals, led by a large anaconda played by the fattest and most difficult-to-manage boy in our group, mutiny against Captain Noah and his whole family.

This kid, whom I'd chosen, was so obnoxious that I decided to let him organize the revolt of the other animal pairs. Their goal: to eat Noah and his family alive while they slept, and in the subsequent mayhem the ark sinks.

Hey, if these were Hollywood and Beverly Hills producers' kids, I'd give them a Hollywood Noah's Ark that would seem pretty normal to their parents; maybe I'd even get a movie contract out of it.

The brat loved it, and I confess I wasn't surprised at all; in him I had found a bird of a feather.

"If you do that with the story, if the ark is lost, how will the children understand where the race of human beings comes from?" Aviva asked on the Tuesday of our second week working the drama group together.

As she said this, she hitched and arched her back in the most peculiar way, as if she had an itch between the shoulder blades she was trying to scratch, but without using her hands.

"What's that about?" I asked.

"Adjusting my wings," she said very matter-of-factly.

"You're joking."

"Maybe I am, and maybe I'm not."

Her smile was so fetching, so sensual, my skepticism was half disarmed. Then she returned to our camp business and asked again about the ark.

That was a reasonable question, and she asked it as always with her strange and utterly charming way of speaking—about "the race of human beings." It was as if she did not quite number herself among them, or perhaps it was just a question of translation from her native Hebrew.

"How did the human race get here?"

"Details, details," I replied.

HARD TO explain, but in those first days of drama counseling, with Aviva as my exquisite sidekick, I felt, even at a Jewish camp, liberated. Gone out of my nose entirely was the seminary's ancient mustiness, its strictures, and Old World ways. Darned if I wasn't having fun.

It was the effect of the Israelis, who never had to figure out which Jewish rules to follow and which to ignore in order to qualify as Jews. They were,

ALLAN APPEL

well, Jews without trying to be. They seemed to make religion and identity easy and effortless, and that was my kind of religion.

Their impact on me was such that I even gave some thought to going to Israel when the summer was over. Maybe Aviva would fly me to meet her family in Sfad. Maybe Tali would cruise along beside us, I happily saddled on her back nestled between her fabulous winged shoulders.

Oh, well.

On the other hand, where might I get a good burger with melted Gouda and fried onions in the Holy Land?

While I was determined to have my fun, I was not so obtuse as not to realize that these adolescent heresies were outlets for my irritations with the institutional Jewish life and all rabbis and all executive temple directors like Footlick everywhere on the planet who, by my dumb calculus, had been oppressing me with their expectations all my life.

Yet it was odd how everyone gave me a wide berth.

And so I decided to return the favor, especially to my brother.

The next opportunity came one day after camp when we were racing with the girls to the corner stop at La Cienega and Olympic. The lumbering Number 5 blue bus had just pulled into its stop. As usual the girls hopped on and proceeded toward the back. As the bus pulled away, I ran after it, doing my silly antics, running beside it, carrying on.

Through the rear window they waved and even threw us both a thrilling little, teasing, final good-bye kiss. It was so much fun and mock-fun, so friendly, mysterious and inexplicable, magnetic, and alluring all at the same time.

After the bus pulled out into traffic I was utterly astonished by how unmoved Jon appeared to be by the prospects of this whole fabulous sexy extravaganza that had fallen into our laps and that seemed to be opening before us.

This was the conversation I began as I calmed down and together we started to walk home: "How come I never see you put your arm around Tali?"

"What do you mean?"

"I mean what I mean: not even once?"

"You checking up on me?"

"You bet your ass I am!"

"Look, we're not supposed to. Camp regulations."

"No one follows those. How can you resist?"

"Well, I can. And I guess I am."

"What a waste."

"I don't think so."

Then we shut up for a half a block or so as we walked east on Olympic toward Orange Grove, because even to self-centered me it was clear he really had something more on his mind than Tali's spectacular little waist and, below it, her great curving pelvis.

"I've been thinking about what you said."

"About?"

"About not telling Mom. About the Mormons."

"Oh?"

"Well, I'm sorry but I don't think it's a good idea to keep putting it off any longer. It's going to come out. You said so yourself."

"Yes . . . but," and then I suggested that the summer loomed so full of deliciousness—beautiful babes and burgers as far as the eye could see—well, why ruin it with any bad news?

"It's not bad news for me."

So I tried a different tack. "Okay, but if we keep it under wraps it'll give me a chance to work on you."

"Meaning?"

"Maybe I'll try to reel you back in."

"You'd be wasting your time, rabbi. I don't seem to be headed in that direction."

I felt expansive, the recipient of so much attention from the girls—I mean bombshells, I risk repeating, young women who could have had roles with Paul Newman in *Exodus*—what could be bad in the entire universe?

If Jon wanted my blessing, or whatever it was, to embrace the Mormons, today was his day. Why not give it? Heavenly Father? Adonai? God, Schmod. What was the difference! I didn't care.

"Hey, go for it, I guess."

"So you really don't mind?"

"Did I say that? I said, Live and let live."

It seemed to me that I really didn't know what I had just said, or what I meant, but there it was. The words put out there by me. Could they be sounds without meaning? The words must have meant something.

After we had walked another block in what was to me a rising tide of uncomfortable silence, suddenly Jon said, "Since you brought it up, I really do think it's you who's acting weird."

"What are you talking about?"

"You're overdoing it with her, big time, with Aviva. Way overdoing it. You've just met her."

"Feels as if I've been waiting a thousand years for her, for both of them. I just don't see how you can resist the tall one. I could go for her. She is one magnificent female creature."

"Creature?"

"Oh, stop it, will you! They're beautiful. What do the Mormons have against beautiful?"

"Nothing."

"Then?"

"Other things on my mind."

"Well, I'll pick up the slack for you. I've got an erection for the two of us."

"I don't like talk like that any more, man."

"That doesn't change the erection. I'm telling you, boners are erupting all over the place just seeing them, thinking about them."

I was really obnoxious.

By now we had arrived at the corner of Crescent Heights Boulevard, half-way between the temple and home.

I remembered where we were, what Jon had pointed out on our first morning walking to work together.

As we paused at the light, Jon moved his feet in that oh-gosh way he could and stared off over my shoulder. He was somehow all hesitation and all ear-nestness rolled into one moment of feeling. Then he said, "I have another idea. If you aren't comfortable yet talking to Mom about the situation . . ."

"The 'situation'?"

"Me, Norman. Me and the Mormons. It's not going to just go away."

"That's bad."

Then he stepped toward me, on that busy corner, and said that as I was a perpetual student or some such, would it be easier if I learned a little more about the Mormons first before talking to Paulene?

"You'll get some context, firsthand."

"You mean me *talk* to them?"

"It's been known to happen. They don't have a disease. I know you know how to talk. In fact I've noticed you talk particularly well, especially . . . when you're not stoned."

"Whoa, whoa. You want me to talk to one of your . . . missionaries?"

"Wes is not exactly a missionary any more, although of course he was. They don't bite. He's one of the guys I meet with. He's an elder. That's what the men are called."

"Hey, man, I'm an elder. I'm in fact your *real* elder."

"Come on, Norman."

"Talk about what?"

"Talk about Judaism and Mormonism. Talk about . . . the weather. Talk about how you're all warping out on Noah's Ark. Talk about those strange girls. About whatever you want."

"I think it's a terrible idea."

"No, you don't. I know you, man. In fact I think you're itching to meet the Mormons. To throw down the gauntlet. To have at them."

"You trust me?"

"I wouldn't have asked otherwise. Come on, it's a short walk."

AND THAT'S how I met Western Oaks.

We turned off Crescent Heights onto Gregory Way, which was a street with older houses, expanded bungalows really, but with porches of stone pillars and even some large green awnings whose fringes were flapping in the breeze. I wanted the street to be familiar, but it was not: a park-like setting unfolded on one side as small outbuildings from a long-ago, falling-apart hacienda might have once stood here in the early Spanish days.

As we walked I ransacked my memories of riding my bike around the neighborhood for so many years, but I couldn't recall this particular block. It was amazing that I could have missed it as a kid because I had ridden my red Schwinn everywhere, like a little stamp collector of blocks. As Jon and I promenaded, I was certain I had been right here before. Then suddenly I was not so certain. The block seemed new and old at the same time, like a stage set; Joseph Smith and Brigham Young could be lurking behind the Spanish bayonet. I would not have been surprised to see Zorro or the Lone Ranger and Tonto gallop across our path.

We stopped in front of a corner building, a big stucco rectangle with several formidable bushes of sharply pointed succulents on either side of the entryway. There was a slanting roof with rounded brown tiles like those on the old missions, and the grass was cut as short as the putting green at the park where we assembled with the campers in the morning.

Suddenly the shaggy canopy of trees that rose behind the buildings looked familiar.

"Are we on the other side? Directly behind?"

"You got it. It backs into the park, that area beyond the pool and baseball field. Convenient, huh?"

"For what?"

"I can get to camp quick popping over a fence, cutting through the park. After the seminary."

"After what?"

"I don't do it every day, but you're not the only one taking a break from camp now and then. But mostly it's before."

"Excuse me. 'Seminary'?"

"Early morning instruction, man. Where do you think I was at six-thirty yesterday? It's called 'seminary.' That's what they call it. For us newbies to get to know the faith."

"Like a school?"

"Yup."

"Been going on how long?"

"Just starting up. More or less."

"You want a seminary, I could talk about religious stuff with you, Jon. You wouldn't have to get up at dawn."

"You used to, to get your morning prayers done in time and not be late for school. Remember?"

"I was thirteen years old, and dumb as a log. You're old enough to know better."

"That's right. I do."

"I thought I owed it to everybody for the bar mitzvah party and the cocktail hotdogs. I prayed, I did all the stuff, but it was just payback."

"You liked it."

"Wrong."

"If it was all so dumb, mind telling me why you stuck with it?"

Hadn't the rabbis in New York been enough to deal with? Now to be interrogated by my baby brother!

Did I ever crave another joint, and to smoke it oh slowly as Paul did his Luckys, to draw the intoxicant deep into my lungs, and after that go have a Galleon Burger and a malted! I did not want to talk about seminary education of either the Jewish or Mormon variety.

Suddenly I regretted my decision to be here with Jon.

"Screw Judaism. Just stop it! Stop ascribing to me stuff you know nothing about. Look, you're an honest guy, Jon, so why not be honest with yourself: forget this and don't even get started. It'll be just like the Hare Krishnas were for you. Save yourself time and heartache, man. I'll be erudition on call. I'll answer your deep questions. I'll be all the seminary you need. I mean it, man."

"There's just one problem."

"Yes."

"This just *feels* right. For the first time the Mormons feel right."

That again. And yet across all the long decades and the elaborate conversations and arguments before and since, that simple statement might be the heart of it, the arrow in the bullseye of why you believe what you believe, or don't.

It just felt right to him, and at a time when absolutely nothing felt right to me except a two-cheeseburger meal, a malted, and my hand on the small of my angel's back.

My leaving the Jews didn't feel right, my outrage at him did not feel right, and my defending the Jews sure didn't feel right.

We walked on silently, because what more was there then to say?

Now here it was: beneath a large eucalyptus with smooth, peeling bark stood a nondescript building. It had a shiny black stone foundation, and narrow columns of glass brick that did not permit you to see inside. It struck me as a professional office, a long rambling suite of offices where a group of dentists might be inside filling cavities.

But this was the Mormon stake, the ward headquarters, Jon's destination.

I thought of the angels playing badminton in the backyard at Mr. Footlick's condo or off shopping in Beverly Hills, or in Century City, which they had recently discovered. Wherever they were, I wished they were here with me instead. I felt a little panicky.

"Mormons, Mormons everywhere," I muttered as Jon settled his fingers on the entry bar of the glass door, and paused.

"You see?" He was pointing to the door jamb just below the horizontal crossing, where a cartouche-shaped outline was visible in the brown painted wood.

"Used to be a *mezuzah* here. Nice, huh?"

"I'm at home already."

Yet I was a ridiculous ex-rabbinic student with a paunch full of bacon in an even more ridiculous Camp Hope T-shirt entering a Mormon precinct.

"You sure this is allowed?"

"Only the temple up on Santa Monica has restrictions, even for us . . . I mean for Mormons. There you have to be pure, and worthy. This isn't a temple. Here anyone can enter."

"Even me?"

"Even scary, skeptical, profane you."

I read aloud from the shining brass plaque: Property of the Church of Jesus Christ of Latter-day Saints.

Then Jon pushed the door wide open and my feet moved forward.

I WAS disarmed immediately.

Temple or not, I guess I was still expecting to find great racks of hanging black choir robes or golden statues of prophets and facsimiles of tablets, or those dioramas of families strolling in their Mormon togas, expressions of heavenly bliss plastered all over their faces, as images recalled from the Mormon leaflets and from TV ads floated through my mind.

However, as we passed through the lobby and walked down a short hallway, here were only classrooms with doors ajar. I peered inside. Plain gray folding chairs and movable blackboards and other details cascaded into a recollected feeling both institutional but also unpretentiously cozy. The place seemed amazingly like the set of classrooms in which we had grown up over at Temple Beth Ami. Just substitute the *Book of Mormon* for the *Five Books of Moses*.

In no rush to meet the great Western Oaks, I detoured into one of the classrooms we passed. Its door was wide open, and I took that as invitation. I was half expecting to see a black-and-white-and-blue collection of skullcaps, shawls, and Jewish prayer books nearby on a chair. Instead, here on the teacher's desk were Mormon tomes: *Pearl of Great Price, Discourses*, the autobiography of Oliver Cowdery, and various lives of Joseph Smith.

"Told you," Jon said, as if he had read my mind.

But when I wheeled around the blackboard on which there were drawings, words and other marks left behind from a recent lesson, a different story emerged: no *aleph-bet*, but elaborate diagrams and written above them, "Heavenly Father," "Heavenly Mother," "The Planet Kolob," "Terrestrial Heaven," and "Telestial Heaven." These were decidedly not notations you would find in Hebrew school.

With a quick glance at his watch Jon escorted me out and down another corridor. This one had a wide runner of thick-pile industrial carpeting that smelled as if it had just been unwrapped and tacked down. The hall led to two swinging doors that we now passed through.

As they opened we were greeted by the aroma of cooking oil similar to the Crisco aroma I recognized from the Relic's grilled cheese sandwiches. Boy, was I hard at work trying to anchor all of these foreign sights and smells to things I knew.

Above us two large ceiling fans were suspended, their blades slowly rotating.

I was in the Mormon kitchen, and from behind a large battered-looking metal table at the far end of the room, Western Oaks looked up to greet us.

He had an angular face and short cropped brown hair that rose above a squarish forehead into a kind of brown hedge.

He had on a white shirt whose sleeves flopped down to the elbows of thin arms. Seeing us, he laid down a pencil and gave one more crank to an old-fashioned adding machine that sat at an angle on the desk.

I got the impression our visit had interrupted his paperwork, or some calculation that had to do with the containers of succotash, corn, beans, and other brightly labeled goods in large, gallon-size cans piled high up a steel shelving unit that reached from the floor to the ceiling behind him. Picture a venerable library, only instead of row after row of books, see cans of stewed beans, tomatoes, corn, succotash, all of the vegetables of the world.

"Looks like you could feed the whole Mormon Tabernacle Choir out of this place," I said with my usual mouthy, nervousness-fueled arrogant first gambit.

"Easily," he replied.

Then Wes stood, or rather, as it seemed to me, he unfolded himself, going up, up, and up, until with all his angles straightened out he was fully standing, an ungainly six-feet-five, or six. He seemed awkward yet as endearing as Henry Fonda galumphing his way through the streets of Springfield in *Young Mr. Lincoln.*

For reasons that maybe are clear now but certainly weren't then, I liked people who seemed uncomfortable with themselves, and I liked Wes immediately.

"Hello, Jonathan."

"Elder Oaks, I brought my brother over." Jon introduced us.

We shook hands. I said, "I hope we're not disturbing you."

"On the contrary. Nice to meet you, Norman."

Then he added, leaning down toward me with a smile full of well-cared-for teeth, "I've been expecting you."

"Really? Why is that?"

"Your interest, you know, in issues of faith. I knew you'd be curious. Very, very nice to match the face with the legend."

"Legend?"

"Jon's very proud of you."

"Well, that's nice to hear."

"I hope you're proud of him."

They were both staring at me. All I could think to say was, "I've never seen so many canned goods all together in my life."

"We like to be prepared," said Wes.

"For what? Famine?"

Wes and Jon exchanged another look that I was certain carried some unflattering message about my penchant for sarcasm, stupid irony, and, well, all my deeply non-Mormon character traits. Frankly, who could blame them?

"Well, you never know."

"You never do."

At least we had the apocalypse in common.

Wes then stepped out from behind the kitchen table and gave me a long penetrating stare as if there were something about *me* that summer that invited scrutiny.

Because I was so nervous I launched into talking and talking. I told Wes how as a kid, a young twelve- or thirteen-year-old seeker, I had the notion that if you were a tall person, like him, then you obviously have the good luck to spend your life brushing up closer to heaven, closer to the realm of God, who's obviously looking down and checking on us, and that makes you, well, more spiritual, or certainly more worried about judgment. Shorter people including dwarfs and midgets possessed more the qualities of Mother Earth, so my theories went. I was a very strange bar mitzvah boy, as I said.

In retrospect, I guess I couldn't blame either of them for how they responded: stunned silence.

"So how is it up there?" I just kept on, but Wes took none of my bait.

"Oh, fine. The air's great," he said.

"Okay, so what's the big draw?"

When Wes was good and ready, he said, "Your brother's interest in the church must come to you as something of a shock."

"He's been through lots of fads."

"Not this time," said Jon.

Now Wes half-seated himself on the edge of his table. He was like a lawyer preparing to make his case before a jury. I guess the jury was me. He seemed very relaxed, which made me, well, uncomfortable.

"For Jon, Mormonism is the farthest thing from a fad imaginable."

"I don't think so."

"It's about your dad."

"Not a fad but dad?"

"Yes," Jon said.

"Not a fad but dad. Dad, no fad," I idiotically repeated like a bad spontaneous imitation of an Allen Ginsberg mantra."

"Dad's soul, Norman. I've been trying to tell you, but somehow . . ."

"Somehow what?"

"Somehow you always interrupt. You send me a signal that I'm an idiot to care."

"I do not."

"You do."

"I don't."

"What do you think you're doing now?"

"Guys, guys, guys," said Western Oaks.

I think Jon was tearing up, or about to, and I felt terrible. Shut up, I heard myself lecturing to myself. No matter what they say, just shut up!

"Look, Norman," Jon said when he finally recovered. "What I've wanted to say is that Dad is entitled to . . ."

Then his voice broke off, and he turned away again.

"To what?"

Wes finished Jon's thought. "Your father, Paul Gould, he's entitled to eternal life."

Now a surprising emotion rose in me. I turned toward my brother, or maybe it was, yes, mea culpa, *on* him. "You asked me to come talk to Wes about *you*. That's what you said. I agreed to that. Now you're blindsiding me. You're you and I'm me and Dad was Dad, and we're not joined at the hip."

"Oh, but we are," said Jon.

"We weren't when he was alive. We're certainly not now that he's dead. I don't want to talk about Paul. Especially with a stranger."

"Today you're the stranger."

"Then I may as well go now."

"Please stay," said Western Oaks.

"Then leave our father out of it."

"I can't," said Jon.

"Well, you could begin by talking about . . . many other things with your brother," Wes said, a teacher's encouraging intervention, so that we, for the moment, bypassed the big hole into which we were falling.

And so we talked—or they did—about Mormon teachings picking up the true thread of Christianity that was lost by the fathers of the early church after Jesus, and all that stuff: Mormon ideas of the afterlife being superior and truer, an improvement through rediscovery of the original over the current corrupted mainline Christian notions, and . . .

I listened to them, and then I listened to my own self-imposed warning broadcast, and it was so quiet, it died away, and I was my snide self once again.

"Tide detergent also says it's new and improved and offers to clean all of the stains from my pants, but if you've ever tried it—have you, Wes?—the product just isn't quite as advertised. None of them is. There is no proof, no evidence . . . whatsoever."

"Religion is not a product to be sold."

"Really, Wes?"

"Really, my friend."

"Well, I happen to think that all your missionaries are just the sales force. What would you call them?"

"They're sharers of the treasure we have. Why keep it hidden?"

And so it went, on and on. Yet what emerged and what in the end couldn't be avoided was Jon's need somehow to reunite with Paul.

That was the theme beneath all of the sparring between Wes and me, and then, when Jon repeated it, I, well, I finally just exploded: "I'm his son as much as you are. And, frankly, I don't plan on 'seeing' him again. Because he's D-E-A-D."

"Don't you find that terribly sad?" said Wes.

"Isn't sadness a big part of life? Some days I'd estimate 60, maybe 75 percent."

"Doesn't have to be," said Wes. "Not if you have life everlasting. Then death is no end but a glorious continuation."

This was precisely the kind of argument I didn't want to have with Jon or with a Mormon elder, or younger, or anyone, ever again. It was a waste of time and a waste of words. For confused afterlife theology, without a shred of the empirical, I could have stayed with the Jews.

Wes smiled a straight-line-of-teeth smile, which was neither gracious nor grimacing, maybe a little long-suffering. Mormons know what we non-Mormons, we whom they call the Gentiles, often think of their ideas. They are well schooled and well rehearsed in how to catch the ball of our doubt and even disdain, to give it a positive spin, and to continue the game.

"Well, we also love to cook. Maybe you'll come out to one of our beach picnics," said Wes.

"I've heard about them."

"To eat and not to debate."

"That's right."

"You boys think you have my number."

"The beach, you know, land's end, is a fine place to clear the mind."

"My mind's pretty clear."

"I don't think so," said my brother.

Wes now joined Jon, and suddenly I was sandwiched between them. I felt myself in some weird tennis match. Paul's soul was the not-so-invisible ball we were batting back and forth.

Still, amid all that, I sensed in Wes a calmness, as if he could elucidate important things and not get his back up at all my bad jokes and eye-rolling objections to their half-baked theology. What began to scare me, what was planted in me now, was a sense that this man actually believed all of the nonsense he was saying. And not only that, he wanted not to foist it on Jon, but, to use their favorite proselytizing verb, to share it. Was it possible there was something to this "sharing"?

At the seminary I'd had one or two teachers who also had this quality— this talent only for selling you a product—all right, passionately explaining an idea—so that it seemed they would only sell those ideas they would buy or subscribe to themselves. That made them believable and effective teachers. It gave people like Western Oaks a quiet charisma.

I could see why Jon was drawn to him.

As we continued to talk, I tried to suppress that thought. Instead I became aware of smaller things: for example, the way Jon now used the word *gosh* all the time instead of *damn* or *shit* or other harmless expletives.

These changes were small but still disturbing. It was as if Jon were imbibing not just theology and crazy notions of visiting Paul in the eternity of this Mormon afterlife, but also these Mormonesque mannerisms of language that were never in the lexicon we grew up with.

What was happening to my neurotic, joint-rolling, cussing, wild brother? Had all that been slipping away during the years I'd been in New York and I just never noticed? Or was Wes and company, in exchange for a theologically whacky bill of goods, suddenly hijacking my brother's *neshama*, his "essence," that he was somehow transforming, evolving, moulting into something *other* right before my eyes?

I suddenly wanted it to end. Here and now.

Yet there I was, lingering in the Mormon kitchen, suddenly quiet, as if my feared aphasia had struck this time for real. And into the space I vacated with my hesitations they rushed in during the days and weeks ahead with offers of beach parties, burgers, and barbecues.

"If you give me some advance warning, I can even promise you kosher hot dogs and burgers and even set aside a special grill for you," Wes said.

What had Jon *shared* with Wes about my recent bad habits?

"Oh, no thanks."

"Norman's a very . . . relaxed kind of Jew these days," said Jon.

"Well, you're not a true Mormon unless you respect another religion's food restrictions. In this ward you'd be surprised how well we understand the Jewish dietary laws."

"Oh, I'm sure. But kosher barbecuing for me at the beach? Way over the top. That won't be necessary."

"We like to accommodate."

"I bet you do."

I wanted to end my first visit to the ward, but I guess I wanted to stay . So I split the difference; I was paralyzed.

Now came that glance between them, the third or fourth one I'd noted. I sensed something bad was coming, and then it came.

"Norman, your brother is grieving deeply, as you must be, about your dad. I've lost my father, by the way. I know what you're going through. He wants me to explain how proxy baptism for the dead works in our church. In some detail. It's a source of great"—and here Wes hesitated as he searched for the perfect Mormon *mot juste*—"a source of great comfort. Will you hear me out?"

I said nothing.

"*Proxy baptism*. That's the formal, operative term. It's often misunderstood. It's the ritual for baptism for the dead, which is what we're talking about for Paul, your father . . ."

Then I did speak, but it was hard to describe; it felt almost not like my own voice: "Oh, you don't have to tell me who Paul is! I'll tell you who he is, who he was: a guy who barely had a pot to piss in, but it was his own pot. A very proud independent guy! He's someone who never liked stuff forced on him. A Jew."

"I thought you were going to try to listen."

"Nothing is ever 'forced' upon a waiting spirit," Wes went on. Then he spoke about someplace he described as the anteroom of heaven, a waiting area, quiet, not contentious. "Through the proxy baptism, the Gospel is simply *offered* to Paul there, to his waiting spirit. He can embrace it as we hope he will, or not," Wes said.

"Oh, really? How will you determine the answer? With a ouija board?"

The glance again, a fifth edition of it, and I felt really riled this time. Waiting spirit! Anteroom of heaven! Were they kidding? The so-called casual talk began to feel as if the two of them had planned a kind of Mormon ambush. I felt this deep force within me, which I'd not noticed before, a kind of fount pushing words out of me. I kept them from exiting, and maybe that turned my face into a scowl. Who knew, but I wasn't going to let these guys get away with it.

"Just listen, will you, man," said Jon. "For a change, take it in; listen without snapping back, without exploding."

Wes paused, and waited. Yes, I was ready to unload or to bolt, but why give them the satisfaction of my extreme behavior?

"All right, go on. But I can't stay all day."

So Wes did go on. Clasping his long-fingered hands across his abdomen, he said, "With Paul's proxy baptism we have a little problem in that our church baptism can be performed only by members who are in good standing for at least a full year."

"And I haven't even quite joined."

"Let's hope you won't."

"But there's a solution."

"I'm sorry to hear that."

"The solution is that a member of our ward can offer Paul the gospel instead, on behalf of Jon."

"And I take it I'm looking at him?" I said.

"It would be an honor. Because it's also one of our fundamental religious duties that I want you to know I take very seriously," said Wes.

"It's a gesture of . . . love," added Jon, using one of his new favorite words.

"And obligation," added Wes.

"Between love and obligation, I'm surrounded."

"Please don't feel that way," said Wes.

"Then don't make me."

"Well, what do you say?" Jon pressed on. "Do I have your permission?"

"Is that required ?"

"Preferred, but not required," said Wes.

"Either way I say no."

"Are you sure?" Jon said. "Really sure?"

"My answer is no."

"But Norman!"

"What's unclear about 'No'?"

"You don't want to give your father a chance at everlasting life?"

"He's already . . . living on in our memories, Wes. In Jon's and mine. For as long as the memories last, maybe not 'everlasting,' whatever that means, but, say, another thirty or fifty years. Not a bad run, he'd say. In fact I think about him a lot. I think about Paul more now that he's dead than when he was alive. What do you make of that?"

"Maybe *that's* precisely because he's *not* dead," said Oaks.

"Exactly," said Jon, with the tiniest note of glee entering his voice. It was as if they'd caught or somehow trapped me, finally. In what, I wasn't sure. So they thought. "That's because he's not dead. He's not."

"Saying it doesn't make it so. That's a little kid's way of thinking."

Wes knew exactly when to make his moves, and now interceded again: "Your memories of Paul and of your lives together, as beautiful as they are, and your father's everlasting life are very different things."

"Apples and oranges?"

"Yes, sort of. Your sentiments of love are worthy of praise, but are not enough. Our minds are trained to think in only one way, that death is final, but there is another realm. There can be more. So much more."

There was silence.

Then I broke it, but with words that seemed almost not my own, as if my voice were only a vessel for them. Still I said them. I heard myself say them: "You go this route, Jon, and it'll kill Ida. It'll make Paulene furious. Maybe kill her. Is that what you want?"

"Just listen to yourself, man."

"It's exactly what she'll say."

"Since when do you speak for them?" Jon said with a sudden calm, almost a remoteness, as if Wes had so much, Jon could borrow some. "That's what she might well *say*, at first. But that could change."

"That's right," Wes added, "because it's not . . . a taking away from your family, it's an adding on."

"Adding what? Another layer of bullshit!"

"An adding on that's a great treasure."

"We can do without the treasure, thank you."

"And how would you feel if someone says your Judaism is bullshit?" Jon came back at me.

"I say to them, right on! It *is* bullshit. I'm *the* expert on *that* branch of Jewish studies. Only it's *my* b.s.; it's our b.s. Let's keep ours, Jon. You don't need theirs."

"He's eloquent, isn't he?"

"But if it's such a treasure, such a fabulous thing, why not let it speak for itself? Why are you making such a flaming, agonizing fuss about converting Paul and about telling Paulene? Tell her! You don't need me. Let your treasure do the talking."

Jon, who had been pacing the kitchen, now re-perched himself beside Wes on the table's edge, and said, "I really need you to make an effort, man."

"I came here, didn't I?"

"You're not really here, man. Not at all."

"Don't get even more spooky on me. Please!"

"Gentlemen," said Western Oaks. "Look, would it help you, Norman, to see our baptismal font out in back? That's where we'd perform the ceremony for your father. You might find that very interesting, and not so, well, scary. One person standing by the pool reads the name of the person being offered the gospel. That might be me. That might be another. A second person, the proxy or substitute, is in white garments and standing nearby but not yet immersed in the pool. He would be a substitute for your father. Our font, by the way, is very unusual. It's a large basin supported by eight carved wooden oxen, to remind us of the flight from persecution to the desert Zion and how we kept to our faith in spite of so much anti-Mormon hatred. It's modeled after one Joseph Smith used himself."

Suddenly I felt myself being addressed as if by a tour guide.

"Just like the flight from Egypt. Like Passover," added Jon.

This was unbelievable, but, yes, it was happening.

"We don't normally show the font to Genti—to non-Mormons."

"It's a real honor." That was Jon again.

"We got permission from the bishop."

"Very nice of the bishop."

"He said he'd make an exception, given your rabbinic background, your training," added Wes.

"What the hell is with you guys?"

"We simply thought, you know, from a comparative religion point of view it would interest you," Jon tried again.

Oh, how my brother was trying.

"I'm sorry but I'm not going to let you just dismiss it. A shot at everlasting life for Paul. A long shot maybe, but he'd take it, Norman. You know he would. He's our father. We owe it to him. What did we ever do for him . . . in life? What did you ever do . . . to cheer him up? He was so . . . beaten down. He just lost and lost and lost. He lost all the time. He lost much. But not this. Now he'll have a chance to be a real winner. A winner in the biggest game of all. You know he'd take the shot."

"He's dead. D. E. A. D."

"Yes, and we didn't even bury him and mourn for him. Mourn for him the right way, did we?"

"Maybe we should leave it here, for now," Wes interceded.

"Amen to that," I said and, for a change, meant it.

My heart was beating rapidly. I was worked up, like Jon. I can't even remember how the encounter ended. I think Wes made some food for us and we talked about the Dodgers and maybe anti-war demonstrations.

I'd been around believers all my life. Wes's and all the Mormons' religious personalities were familiar to me. Weren't they? They were still evolving, a very young, nineteenth-century religion, whereas the Jews have forty centuries under their collective religious belt. Compared to us, including yours truly, and despite their vaunted historical claims, the Mormons are still babes in their spiritual development, in their dopey commentaries on their even dopier texts, and bereft of deep, honest readings.

Yessiree. That was it. I am way ahead of you in my spiritual sophistication, which is why I can afford to be, well, such an asshole.

So I told myself. Therefore, try to get it together. Try to behave about this stuff; be patient.

Because everyone knows there are no souls, no gauzy, bathed-in-white heaven of the Mormons. No Planet Kolob where little souls are incubated to travel to earth to pass their moral test in our bodies and then to go make the return trip to Kolob with a short stop in the heaven that has been earned. No anterooms of heaven, no spirit minimum-security prisons.

Oh, yes, before I left, I made it my business to tell Wes there is also no Jewish heaven either, no *shamayim* where the *k'doshim*, the holy creatures referred to in the daily morning prayers, hang out and sing to God about how great He is. Those were nice tunes, but in reality the creatures didn't exist.

Please! There was death. Period.

And that was it; beyond cheeseburgers one just could not be sure.

It wasn't the weirdo Mormon doctrines I heard then but Jon's and Wes's certainty that infuriated me. They had no more provable information about the afterlife than I did or the pope ever had or Adolf Hitler or Babe Ruth. Who were they flimflamming? Yes, they were just using words as a code for what amounted to no more than incoherent gobbledygook. Wes and Jon and the Mormons had, well, simply agreed to some kind of compact of understanding, such that they had decided that when they say "everlasting life" then they will agree it denotes XYZ and not LKM. "Spirit" means RSQ. And so forth. Sad, stupid conventions with no relation to *reality.* To what really is. A tasty Galleon burger with onion rings is. You eat it and then it's gone. What is disappears. What never was, never was. We know what our eyes and our sensations tell us: death, death, death.

After my tirade I wandered around the spacious Mormon industrial kitchen. Wes and Jon just waited on me, as if I were some kind of spiritual invalid, unconscious of the seriousness of my condition, a specimen they had been assisting and were now waiting for him to calm down, to emerge from his seizure.

Yet I wasn't going to give them the satisfaction.

I was tired from camp and especially exhausted from the charade of trying to be a good Jewish role model, which I now realized I had been doing at high octane to compensate for Jon's apostasy-in-progress, or so I had fashioned or rationalized the services I had begun to render at Camp Tikvah.

I reached up to one of the shelves by the freezer. I picked up a five-pound box of Sun-Maid Raisins. I shook the box. I studied the beautiful sun maid herself on the label, all aglow in her flouncy summer dress leaning sexily back on a swing made of vines in a perfect part of a green orchard and vineyard as groomed as the Garden of Eden on Ida's mortuary calendar.

By the way, the Garden of Eden is in rural Missouri, according to the Mormons. There were dozens of boxes of raisins on the shelf. Oh, sun maid, how I love you! I thought about the beautiful neck where Aviva's Star of David lay, above her cleavage. It dangled down in a sparkling crescent from a small cartouche with some Hebrew letters that she also wore. I had not yet deciphered or asked her about that.

Now *that* was the territory I was hoping to get to know this summer, not this world of loony ideas of the LDS. Why had I consented to this get-together, to this . . . consultation, whatever it was? I belonged with the angels, not with Western Oaks.

I was all tied up in, well, spiritual knots and I desperately needed to be untied. So, why didn't I just sign, give permission? Let them do their damn proxy baptism and get over it. Offer proxy baptism. See if Paul cares, wherever you find him. *If* you find him. What nonsense about souls. Shoot.

Then another part of me spoke, as if I had suddenly been possessed by two invisible lawyers who appeared at first polite inside my fevered cogitations, but now were losing it, like me, like Fredric March and Spencer Tracy mixing it up in *Inherit the Wind*. One had been eloquent for the cause of evolution—the ages of rocks—and the other ardent only for *Rock of Ages*. How I loved that movie. Who would prevail? They kept arguing between themselves, back and forth, slamming the table, appealing to one god and then to another god and then to some judge who sat higher than either the Jewish or the Mormon Gods.

And yet in the end my fractious attorneys were unable to reach a decision or offer me any sensible counsel.

I was prickly and confused, and despite a patina of prideful self-regard at my little spontaneous outbursts, peppered with a student of religion drop-out's half-baked erudition, still I knew some defense had been breached.

Western Oaks saw it. He was, as Paulene would later say, a very cool customer. Which is why he just lowered his gaze on me, like a beam from high above, reassuring yet at the same time far away.

I finished one last circumambulation and returned to the big table where the two of them, having washed our plates and silverware, were sitting and consulting amiably.

So I planted myself in front of Jon and Western Oaks with the kind of face-saving if callow defiance I thought I should have mustered for the rabbis but, alas, had not. Here it was now transferred, however inappropriately, from New York to LA, from the synagogue to the ward.

"I don't want to hurt anyone's feelings, but, gentlemen, this is really a load of crap." That was how my eloquent peroration began, and, alas, also ended.

"Like we said, just think it over, Norman? Just think on it a little more. That's all we ask," said Wes.

"For Dad's sake," Jon added, and my brother lowered his head when he said "Dad," and he spoke the word in a kind of hushed octave and with such unabashed true emotion of longing, it shamed me.

So I said I would.

"It's been a pleasure to meet you," Western Oaks concluded that first meeting. "A great pleasure."

And the marvel of it is, I think he actually meant it.

10

TWO more days went by at camp, and Jon and I barely spoke, apart from our necessary interactions with the kids. Despite my pip-squeak bravado before Western Oaks, I remained of split mind about Jon's Mormon turn—and whether I should fight it or just let him drift away. If I were lost—and was I ever!—what right did I have to deny Jon his own LDS drift?

If I could be said to have had a guiding light as this struggle grew, that callow formulation of fairness was it.

On the other hand, as emotionally true moments must be revisited to have effect or they just get lost and lose their punch in the flow and confusion of life, I found myself replaying what had just happened, and each time feeling more betrayed and furious.

I finally realized why: there *really was* this new element. It was not only Jon's dalliance or dash to the Mormons, but now also the disposition of Paul's soul. Paul's being pulled along in the flow of Jon's drift; that's what was most newly troubling about the revelations that came during those first weeks of camp and in the Mormons' kitchen.

Yet if I didn't even believe in souls, why was I allowing myself to become so exercised? Why should a flimsy, goofy, nonexistent thing like a "soul," *a pneuma*, as the Greeks called it, a foolish, silly little concept, concern the newly materialistic, cheeseburgering, Jewish dropout me?

Jon's soul or Paul's soul or any soul, were they not at heart airy little nothings!

Even Aristotle, who trafficked in *pneuma*, recognized it for what it was: a verbal construct, an idea.

Now, wait. Construct like a circle? They really didn't exist either, and yet you had to admit they were guiding abstractions, influencing so much that does, so didn't they have to be dealt with?

Either I was losing my mind, or my haphazard erudition suddenly was complicating the picture and taking me somewhere I could not have imagined back when I sat in Tom's Restaurant chewing that first cheeseburger.

My god! The soul of Paul Gould? Or just the wayward and mistaken *idea* of the soul of Paul Gould? No wonder I was an abstracted, lousy camp counselor.

All during the camp day I kept thinking thoughts like these. Like when a father is dead, can it still be said, in the present tense, that you still *have* a father? Is "soul" the linkage between having had and still having? Such a question, which would have sounded inane to me just months ago, began to feel urgent and, now and then, even on the verge of agonizing.

Of course I couldn't tolerate much of this shape-shifting thought without a little help from my friends. In fact, soul talk and pot seemed as natural a duo as milk and honey or a burger and fries. Between my wandering off from my duties for one or the other, I didn't know why the Foot didn't fire me; maybe because Aviva was always there covering for me, never complaining, never asking where I had gone.

If ever there were a time to locate another substantial stash of my brother's wine-soaked joints, the day after my visit with Wes was it. Jon wouldn't be needing them any more, so to locate and to put them to good use was not theft but a form of necessary liberation, as the phrase of the time had it.

A few days later, when Paulene had left for her shift and Jon had gone out to his Mormon beach party or whatever he and Wes were doing together, I ransacked the house. Like an addict, I went through every room and every drawer, but I came up empty handed. I couldn't find even a twig or seed of marijuana.

Still, while I looked so frantically, an alternative voice was also admonishing me: okay, soul. If the damn irritating thing does exist, then who should claim it? Then the other voice countered: Whoa! What is the point of claiming a lie?

Could any of this make sense?

I was still close enough to my pastoral psychology training to realize that something else, some other irritant, was continuing to gnaw away at me on the more earthly plane and in fact had been doing so since the first hour I had arrived home.

I could not locate it until, having searched the bedrooms without luck, I found myself in front of the drawers of the credenza. When I opened them, I found flowers, dried peonies, that, by the card, had been recently sent to Paulene by the Foot. The scent was that peculiar mix of the fabulously aromatic and the fetid.

THERE WERE so many things coming at me, it was hard to know what upset me more: how angry I was not only that Paul's soul was being snatched, but also amid that heist that Paulene could be dating the Foot when Paul's little *neshama*, his nonexistent soul, in which I still didn't believe, so that it couldn't possibly really be snatched, was in danger. Didn't she understand that by all these notions you had a full two months yet to transit to Jewish heaven—a district or concept to which I gave no credence at all.

Yet if there were indeed something out there, along these murky lines, his soul was in deep Mormon danger until the end of the traditional Jewish mourning period, at which point his little *neshama* would have completed the journey, dock in good old nonexistent Jewish heaven, order a coffee with Cremora and with a big fat glazed doughnut or tapioca pudding, or, hey, why not both, and get down to enjoying the afterlife.

That remaining time period was roughly the length of our Camp Tikvah summer gig.

Boy, did I ever need a joint now.

I was positively obsessing about Paul's little gambler's soul, which had not yet transited to the end of its yearlong Jewish journey to the golden casino or wherever it was destined to arrive.

Yes, I probably should have been saying another *kaddish* or two—yes, I had fallen down badly in that daily obligation to my dead dad. But that kind of thing was far behind me now. Wasn't it?

Paul, I am sure, would understand, I heard myself saying.

Yet what in the world did that sentence mean?

I was certain that, absent my visit to Wes, I never would have given any of this a thought. Sure, I had rushed back to New York after Paul's funeral, but hadn't I buried him? Officiated, said all the right words, intoned the prayer for the dead, escorted Paulene, with Jon on the other side of her, all wearing black, a perfect little conventional funeral?

And then I'd fled.

So think clearly, I told myself. What was the big deal? Hadn't Paulene been handed a bum deal all her life, and so, with Paul gone, who really should care if she were cutting the mourning period a little short? Hadn't I cut such corners all my winking religious life?

Shape up, Norman, I told myself. What do you care?

Problem was, I did care. I cared a whole lot, but I needed those angels to show me how much and what to do about it.

Still, after I searched our whole house and found no joints, I panicked a little. But I breathed deeply, I centered myself, as we used to say, and that's how I began to be able somehow to begin to drop my cerebral equivocations about souls, including the soul of one Paul Gould, just a notch.

What I mean is, how could I continue to deny absolutely that something exists and feel the need to fight against it or for it all at the same time, and mightily?

To sustain or to break through such a self-contradicting life back in 1967, you needed not only the occasional joint, preferably speckled with North African hashish, but also to fall in love with a Jewish angel, two if possible, at the same time.

It happened like this.

FRIDAY, AFTER the kids had gone home, we all four—Jon and I, Aviva and Tali—were hanging out beneath what had become "our" place, a small copse of ponderosa pine trees on the margin of the kids' lunch area. Jon was tossing a football high in the air and catching it himself. Tali lay beneath the bright sun with her sunglasses tilted up into her hair, and I as usual was ignoring my equipment breakdown duties as I tried to slip my hand around Aviva's fabulous waist.

As my fingers climbed around and up Aviva's slender but powerful back and approached near the envelope of the breast I'd had my eye on for what seemed the last seventy-two hours, she rolled away and jumped up in this gymnastic but also girlish way that also said: chase me and see where it gets you.

So I did.

My extra pounds made me so slow, of course, so that after she let me chase her once around the grass I was panting like an out-of-breath whale. Soon she had mercy on me and let me catch her back where we had begun.

That's when I asked her out Saturday and Sunday, two nights in a row.

"Those steps won't be necessary," she replied in that mysterious manner.

"What do you mean?"

"You haven't heard? I'll be seeing you tonight."

"How's that?"

"We're celebrating Shabbat with you. At your place."

"Really? Who says?"

"You must communicate in a more superior manner with your family. Your mother says. She invited us. We are to walk home with you, so we are."

"You are?"

"Very soon. There are only fifteen minutes of time I calculate before we should leave. So do your work, Norman."

"I don't believe this."

"If you don't want us to walk with you, we could take the bus."

I soon learned that Paulene and the Foot had arranged what would turn out to be a Sabbath meal like none other I'd ever experienced. For while we had been busy working with the kids, Paulene apparently had called the Foot and on an inspiration told him the Israelis absolutely must spend one of their Sabbaths in LA with us. In fact this very one.

The Foot had wanted to do the Sabbath honors at his poolside condo, but at the last moment was called to celebrate the day of rest elsewhere, with a donor, I believe. So Sabbath at the Orange Grove duplex was on.

Neither Jon nor I had heard about any of this until Aviva's revelation.

It's hard to describe how shocked I was. Yet as we finished up and parked the camp equipment back at the temple for the weekend and began walking home, it was clear that neither Jon nor I could avoid this occasion. It certainly wasn't the kind of first date I was hoping for. Yet as we ambled on down Olympic and across San Vicente to Crescent Heights, Jon walking alone ahead of us and I flirting with both of our marvelous girls, going to our dull home with two amazing creatures in tow did not seem like such a bad fate at all.

We climbed the steps, with Tali going up two at a time. There, on the landing, I hardly recognized Paulene as she greeted us at the flung-open screen door. She was dressed in her shined-up white waitress's shoes, trousers ironed to a knife-edge pleat, a Ghandi-esque tunic, and a white turban somewhere in between a Sikh's and a Carmen Miranda headdress.

"All my flower children," she exclaimed as we entered, and she handed individual pink carnations to Tali and to Aviva.

"What? None for us?" said Jon.

What *I* said was: "Mom! What in the world has happened to you?"

"Why, the Sabbath. Peace, love, the day and night off. What do you think? And on the seventh day God rested. He asked waitresses to join him. Come in, come in, children. Welcome all. *Shalom.*"

As we stepped into the house, all of the signs pointed to a Sabbath ritual repast of the kind we had not seen in years, if ever.

Tali withdrew from her army rucksack a small package wrapped in rustling blue and white tissue paper and presented it to Paulene. Our mother made a show of unwrapping what turned out to be an apron with a large State of Israel map.

Here was the blue Mediterranean, there the green and brown mighty cedars of Lebanon, and black dots signified the various cities of the Holy Land, Tali explained.

Paulene tied it right on and stepped here and there modeling it. "Wait till they get a load of this at work," she said as she hugged the girls.

Still holding on to my mother as if the two were, well, long-time sisters, one older and one younger, Tali extended her finger toward the apron very slowly, theatrically. She pointed to one of the black dots. "We live . . . right here. Sfad," she said. "Our holy city."

Paulene kissed both Tali and Aviva in extravagant gratitude. I had been trying to finagle affection like that from the girls for weeks now, from the instant I had laid eyes on them.

"If you found out . . . only this morning . . . at camp, how could you have bought a gift?" I asked.

"Listen to him," said Paulene, as she flipped the apron over, which side now featured Israel again, but with cities and towns of the ancient, biblical world.

"We have our ways," said Aviva.

They most certainly did, more and more.

Pleading that he was itchy with chlorine from his long camp day in the pool, my brother went straight in to shower. Then Paulene went back to her Sabbath preparations through the swinging door into the kitchen, through whose last sliver of an opening I caught a glimpse of the stove, with all of the burners firing away.

It was left to me to introduce the angels to Ida, whom Paulene had brought up from downstairs and placed by the picture window in the living room looking out onto the street. When I escorted them over to her, Ida turned her head from side to side, her skeptical Polish gaze trying to figure out just who these lovely creatures were, a challenge I well understood.

Instantly they were as familiar and affectionate with her as they had been with Paulene. They knelt down, one on each side of Ida's chair, and began to lavish attention on her. Never had I seen them so physical, so animated. Soon they were talking to Ida in melodious, low octaves of perfect Yiddish. Who knew they could speak that language?

Boy, did Ida perk up.

I watched as the angels, their heads almost cheek to cheek with Ida's, whispered into both her ears.

That's when the Relic pulled back slightly from them, a slow-motion elderly doubletake. That took maybe half a second, and now, like a wary bird, she was moving her head back close to Tali and to Aviva, her eyes opening wide, Ida's whole presence filling up with a kind of invisible revitalizing formula, as if the girls had been pouring into her a kind of fountain of youth made up of lovely, purring Yiddish phrases, none of which I understood.

I stepped close to listen, but I felt invisible to them as they utterly ignored me huddling up around Ida as if she were their prized new possession.

Feeling surrounded by what I was not understanding, I headed for what I expected to be a safe, known zone; I barged into the kitchen and and went right for the refrigerator. I reached for the quart of milk that had always stood right beside the ever-present Hebrew National salami. That was the next surprise.

"What gives? Where's the milk?"

"With a meat dinner? Don't we need to get a tad stricter, Norman? I'm sure you at least *try* to keep kosher in New York?"

I was dumbfounded. I just stared at this woman, my own mother, in a glittering white turban and wearing the flag of Israel over her abdomen—had a stranger walked in he would have thought, here is the world's first Zionist Sikh—while in the adjacent room two gorgeous girls were on their knees playing games with the Relic, asking her about Paul—I did hear some of that!—as if Ida were now the center of their world. What was happening?

"Mom?"

"Son?"

"Right, right. Kosher. I . . . try."

"So have a Coke, and see if our lovely guests would like a refreshment, until we bless the wine, of course."

"Love to bless that wine."

"There's a twelve-pack of Coke there in the back, untouched. Your brother used to drink four a night. Now he doesn't touch them. Why is that?"

"Dunno, Mom."

"Better for his teeth, I guess."

"That's true. Jon's teeth have never been whiter."

"Have you checked out the dining room table yet, Mr. Smarty Pants?"

"Just got here."

"Go tell me what you think. Go look. Look."

"I will. Don't be so . . . anxious about Tali and Aviva. They're Israelis. The Sabbath's . . . in their blood."

"Oh, really? You know so much?"

"Let me help you."

"Don't need it. The dining room's still through that door. Just go look."

"I'm going, I'm going."

When I entered and beheld our dark, ancient, elephant-footed table that we had inherited along with Ida and her other furniture from the gone world of Poland, I could not believe the transformation that had occurred. The various old, yellowing, discolored doilies and antimacassars, which usually lay helter-skelter over it, had been replaced by a single, ample tablecloth. It now fell in generous, knife-sharp folds on all four sides and was starched to a stiff, white brilliance.

And there was more: the large punch bowl.

It was Paul and Paulene's only wedding present still extant in the house, and it had always been filled with old bills and other mail, circulars, and racing forms with the almost-always-losing horses' names marked by the dashing red circle of our father's marking pen. It was always there, always, but this night that disorderly old bowl, the cracked, crystal symbol of our family life, such as it was, had also been removed.

The rarely used finest wine glasses Paulene possessed were also out and on glistening display, including the small ceremonial collectibles that Jon and I had received at our bar mitzvahs. Beside them on the credenza gleamed the third cup, more of a shot glass, that Paul used to like to have his whiskey in.

I detected Paulene's Jean Naté perfume floating toward me from behind. "Surprised?"

"You really did the whole thing, huh?"

"Norman, my darling, it's time your mother acted like the mother of a rabbi-to-be."

"Isn't it, well, a bit much? Tali and Aviva are hardly dressed up."

"I think you'll be surprised," she said as she straightened a large cloth cover decorated with Hebrew, an item I had never set eyes on, over the braided Sabbath ritual bread, the *challah*, at the center of the table.

Here my eyes and nose were struggling to adjust. We had enjoyed that traditional feature of the Sabbath table only a few times in the extremely short-lived observant periods of our family life right after our bar mitzvahs, but nothing remotely like this.

Although such a loaf struck my eye as being as foreign to our table as a bazooka, you had to admit it looked and smelled heavenly. This one was all browned on the outside, as perfect as an advertisement, with egg-yellow dough peeking out from its toasty crenallations.

"I'm even thinking of doing it permanently."

"Doing what?"

"What do you think, Mister! Keeping the Sabbath. Keeping kosher. *Challah* every week. What else? Keeping it right. The whole ballgame, honey. I want you always to feel comfortable when you're home."

"I'm comfortable."

"Pinocchio! Your nose is growing."

"Okay, most of the time, then, I'm comfortable." She was giving me the eye that was a distant cousin, but still related, to the evil eye. "Sometimes, sometimes I'm comfortable, and thanks, Mom. What a show."

"Anyway, the girls keep kosher. Mr. Footlick told me."

"Really? They hardly eat anything at all. Not even the snacks at camp."

"They don't look like dieters. In fact, have you ever seen such healthy, perfect-looking bodies! Well, you can be confident tonight it's going to be kosher, kosher, kosher. You can assure them. And so beautiful. You and your brother are certainly lucky ducks this summer."

"Yes, we are."

"You haven't mentioned a girlfriend in New York."

"I thought we had finished with this part of the interrogation."

"Me finish with this? Never. Are you keeping the biggest secret ever from a doting mother? Show your cards now."

"You're my only girlfriend, Mom."

"I'm sure. Now come with me," she said.

We reentered the kitchen, which was nearly foggy with Jewish cooking aromas rising in faint plumes above the hardworking stove. There were puddings and casseroles, plates of carrots, onions, and asparagus. I counted at least six bowls on the counter.

"Whisk this," Paulene commanded as she scooped up one and handed it to me, along with the appropriate tool.

Dutifully I stirred a dish of carrots and currants afloat in a kind of sweet glaze.

"Tali's a vegetarian."

"I didn't know."

"What else don't you know? Mr. Footlick told me, so I have all this," she said while removing the tops of two more gleaming white serving dishes. One had slightly browned cauliflowers, broccoli, and red peppers, the other strips of grilled eggplant. I lifted a third cover and here were noodles spotted with raisins, the traditional Sabbath pudding, or *kugel*.

"Mr. Footlick teaching you to cook ?"

"Norman. It's the Sabbath. Give it a real rest."

"You're showing off."

"Really? Believe you me, if I wanted to put on the dog this way, I'd know how to do that. I'm doing what I love and what I think my guests will love. Got it?"

" 'Putting on the dog'?" That had been one of Paul's signature expressions. I don't believe I'd ever heard Paulene use it before. The phrase struck my ear like an alarm.

"You really don't need to be doing all this. It's great, but, you know, how about you just be yourself."

"Norman, sometimes you make me crazy. Now, what next?" she said as she busied herself happily presiding over this novelty, a sort-of-kosher Sabbath extravaganza.

"And I just love this," Paulene said as she bounced from station to station in the kitchen and wiped her hands on her new State of Israel apron.

"Go make yourself useful and bring out the candles."

"Candles. Check."

Now Jon entered the kitchen; his was the next act of choreography in that strange and remarkable Sabbath. What was left of his hair was combed back with water and, I detected, a slick or two of Vitalis; over his dark brown hair sat a *yarmulke* like a cap of bright snow.

He was also wearing white jeans and a white shirt.

"Don't blame me. I'm just doing what I'm told by the boss here. She had them all laid out on the bed with marching orders."

"That's right," Paulene said. "Now your turn, Norman. Yours are on your bed, washed and bleached with love by Grandma." Paulene raised her red-fingernailed hand and magisterially directed me through the doorway toward my Sabbath whites.

At the threshold of the kitchen I paused. "Why are you doing all this?"

She put down her spatula, like a conductor exasperated with a player in a particular section of the orchestra. Namely me. "It's the Sabbath; you're going to be a rabbi; don't be a dope. Have you ever seen such beautiful girls? There must be something in the water in Israel. Any other questions?"

"Yes," said Jon. "Speaking of water, Tali and Aviva are in there showering now. You think the hot water will hold up?"

"You're acting like you need an assignment, Norman. Go check it, will you? Adjust the lever if you have to. Don't just stand there. Do *something*."

"Of course. I'll check."

I walked down the hall and peeked into the utility closet. I knelt down by the electric hot water heater. It seemed to be ticking away normally. This also felt like a fine place to hide because I felt not a little ashamed of all my raw behavior, and I was so deeply confused. After all, here was Jon all dressed up like a Mormon Sabbath cowboy but also playing along with Paulene, dissembling away as we had agreed we would, for now.

Yet I, the drama counselor no less, was balking at taking up my role. It was I who was cranky and petulant, suddenly wishing myself not here with Tali and Aviva but anywhere else with them, and preferably in a rented convertible racing along Mulholland Drive to make out at . . . and so here I was instead forcing these confrontations with Paulene who had worked so hard, who was, well, I didn't know who my own mother was any more.

At least I realized I was being an ass.

As I fiddled with the hot water lever at the base of the heater, my mind turned toward Jewish custom yet again. Even though our mother, technically, was still in mourning, as I've mentioned, tonight there was that satin outfit, the Carmen Miranda turban and more lipstick and more fingernail polish than I remembered her wearing. Ever. Boy, was that against the norms. Not a black or dark garment of mourning in sight. While you're supposed to keep celebrating the Sabbath during mourning, it's not supposed to look like what for us was a Vegas production.

So maybe she was in this outfit to impress our fantastic guests, but it felt, well, unseemly. I didn't expect Paulene to wear the sadness of mourning on her sleeve ten months after Paul had died, but where was Paul in this picture? True, the rabbinic laws say that even those who mourn must not refrain from observing the Sabbath, but the rabbis also ordained that even on the Sabbath someone in mourning shouldn't dress up like a chic model from *Vogue*.

I made my case very persuasively, even eloquently, I thought, and I didn't fail also to accuse myself of being suddenly a cranky, tradition-bound old Jewish fart to even have these feelings. It's bad my only audience was the thirty-gallon hot water tank; even it seemed to hiss back at me.

Returning from the closet where the heater now perked away just fine, I heard a little pop, pop, pop, and went back out to see the Relic in her chair in the living room. She was slapping the tennis ball into her glove. I sat down on the hassock beside her.

As we played a little pepper in our fashion, I heard through the walls phrases in Hebrew. They were too muffled for me to understand except for a word here and there. I leaned toward the hallway where the rapid-fire holy language got lost in the sounds of dishes, clattering, and girlish laughter.

"Play!" Ida suddenly demanded. "Curve ball. Low and avay."

So I pitched, low and away, high and tight, clipping the corners. The Relic cycled through her repertoire of baseball lingo Jon and I had taught her. She disagreed with my call on the third or fourth pitch. "Vos is vid you? Are you blind!"

I of course was, and somehow I think either I was so transparent—to all but myself because I sensed that even she saw through to what a massive car crash of emotions was piling up inside me. In her fashion she was trying to cheer me up.

When I placed the ball in the center of the glove to indicate the next pitch was right over the plate and very hittable, she called out, "Boom, over the vall. See ya. Bilko, Paulie. Bilko, bilko."

Wait a second! "You said, 'Paulie'?"

She gave me an odd look and slumped back into her chair, and the game was over as quickly as it had begun. Yet why had she just addressed me by my father's name? Just an old person's common mistake? I doubted that. Ida was still plenty sharp. Yet she had never done that. It had emerged for just an instant, between two Bilkos. Like Paulene's "putting on the dog."

These traces of Paul seemed everywhere. I wondered.

Our little seventh-inning stretch over, Ida perked up again and we played a few more minutes of fantasy Bilko ball, with many homers hit over her outstretched mitt.

That's when I detected a scent of lavender rippling in from the hallway to the bedroom, and followed by a smaller wave of green.

This could only mean Tali and Aviva were now emerging, showered, perfumed, and shampooed. I felt as though I were stoned, and the Sabbath wine I had nipped made its contribution as well, but as I imagined them dressing, there they were in my vision: every feather of their wings combed into brilliant, microscopic luster and folded with geometric perfection just so to look like fine, beautifully tanned skin.

Whoa! I jumped up from the hassock and turned and stuck my head into the hallway to catch a glimpse. They were just completing a quick and, for me, jaw-dropping seminaked dash down the hall.

That's when I swear I saw on Tali's back in the half-light of the overhead hall lamp not the glistening of water, but two tiny shimmering feathers folding down into the depression between her awesome shoulder blades.

Yes, it was 1967. Yes, I actually remember some of it. They were there. Truly.

The girls were now sealed and giggling behind the closed door and dressing in Paulene's bedroom.

I wheeled Ida into the kitchen. Then I went in and took my shower. As I dried off afterward, I sat on my bed wondering what had become of the two boys who had spent so many days and nights here. How had they become who we were now? And these incredible girls!

Nothing made any sense to me except to open the drawer between the beds again, where I made sure Jon's *Book of Mormon* was buried deep beneath folded white sweat socks.

Had I really seen wings?

Then I sucked in my fat belly, I stuffed myself into the white chinos, and prepared for my reluctant Sabbath.

11

WHAT I remember most about that dinner is whiteness: not only the smooth, shiny glow of linen napkins and tablecloths, but a kind of general dazzle as if everything and everyone were suddenly coated in a high heavenly gloss.

As I stood with my hands on the back of my chair before we recited the blessings, I felt both present and removed. I had the sensation that I was a theater hand or prop manager taking a quick inventory of everything needed for the scene about to begin: the white smock that Paulene was now slipping over her apron and Ida's painfully fragile chest, her abdomen like a tiny swelled cupcake, with an old, thin shift thrown over her bones.

What a blur it is: now Paulene dashes into the kitchen, and then out. Now Ida begins to hum some ancient melody. Paulene, quick as an arrow, quiets the creaky movement of the swinging kitchen door. Now she nods to Jon who understands immediately; he rises and obediently clicks off the dining room overhead light.

Now Paulene passes the matches for the blessing of the Sabbath candles into my hand. It's the hand of her son who she still, by all signs, expects will one day be a rabbi. I notice the images of Sarah, Rachel, Rebecca, and Leah, the mothers of Israel like a severe female Jewish Mount Rushmore, displayed on the pinafore Paulene is now smoothing around the Relic's ribs.

The four of us are awaiting the entrance of Tali and Aviva, who are still in the bedroom putting the finishing touches on their dressing. That expectation itself is like a pulse in the air that now grows when, with a thought-stopping susurrus and an aroma of new-mown grass, Tali slowly enters the dining room.

Here is the very Queen of the Sabbath herself, that is, if the Queen of the

Sabbath were also as tall and graceful and powerful as a broad-shouldered swimmer emerging victorious from the water after having won the race. She has put on high heels and rises now, I guess, to at least six-two or -three, and in a flowing dress. Her eyes, with more mascara than usual, are dark and volcanic. Yet as she rustles around the table to the place Paulene has designated, she casts her glance downward in a kind of embarrassed modesty.

Once she has arrived at her chair, she glances from each one of us to the other in a manner hard to describe, by turns seductive and challenging, like that of a lawyer at the jury box after a stunning summation, or a guide or coach or, yes, a camp counselor but, if so, it is the molten gaze of a counselor from a camp perched on the hillside of Mt. Vesuvius just before the eruption.

For something is about to happen here and now, and it will be much more than a Sabbath meal.

Next Aviva makes her entrance, also in a dress, but with spaghetti straps that show off shoulders smooth and brown, and powerful biceps. This is the first dress I have seen her wear this summer, and as she moves endearingly among us, she winks at me in that hoydenish way. She takes her place at the table beside me, and I notice her white tennis shoes peeking comically beneath the hem of her dress; she seems the little tomboy princess of the Sabbath to Tali's queen.

"Too much, Mrs. Gould?"

"No, Aviva dear. I always say, Never enough perfume. You look lovely. Doesn't she, boys? Don't they both!"

"Do they ever," Jon quietly said.

And as for me, the Israelis were just so overwhelming there was nothing this human throat of mine could produce. I simply was speechless. They had had that effect on me before, beginning with that first sighting at Ships; only this day, this Sabbath, it went far deeper.

When you see girls, even very pretty ones like these, whom you've known mainly in khaki shorts, T-shirts, and combat boots turned out suddenly in flowing dresses that are more like gowns worn by the stars on the night of the Academy Awards, and they are suddenly transformed into women and made up as if they had just stepped off the top of a seven-tiered cake, you are, I guess, entitled to a certain speechlessness.

Because Tali's skirts were so voluminous there was some uncertainty as to where she could find room to be comfortable around the table's elephantine legs. Finally, she placed herself, rustling, between Jon and Ida and across from Aviva, me, and Paulene. During all that rearranging the charged silence grew and grew, and I found myself riding off on it, to a memory of the last time I had marked a Sabbath in the clanging refectory of the Seminary, because there, during my first years in the East, I still had offered obeisance to the Queen of the Day of Rest, the Friday night service, and meal.

The Relic mumbled something *sotto voce* in Yiddish, and then Tali began to sway in place as she hummed a thrumming melody from deep within herself. "Yai did di dai di di, yai did di dai di di." We all joined or rather were swept up into the slow-moving wave of sounds that after a thrilling ride crescendoed into words: *Lchah dodi likrat kalah, pnai Shabbat nkablah,* "Come my beloved to greet your groom; let us behold your face, the presence of the Sabbath."

The glimmering Star of David at the base of Tali's long neck rose and fell with her singing like a tiny, glittering metronome.

Until this instant I'd never quite appreciated why women and men were separated in traditional synagogues not only by the symbolic orthodox partition but also by women often being acoustically exiled to a faraway corner balcony. Their voices—or in this instance Tali's soprano with its angelic tremolo combined with Aviva's alto—were irresistible.

Aviva and Tali's singing began to merge almost into a single shimmering sound. Paulene, who when we were kids was always mimicking songs from musicals like *Oklahoma*, and could carry a tune very well, skipped vocally slightly behind them. Jon was smiling but quiet and barely moving his lips. I was, well, dumbfounded. Now the Relic's sweet Polish croaking inserted itself into the chorus so that they all soon were harmonizing, and the sound they created together really did transport.

Men hearing voices like these in the synagogue, especially soft, callow men-yet-still-in-formation such as Jon and I were—so the rabbinic explanation or excuse for separation goes—could hardly be relied on to keep their minds on prayer, or on God.

I felt my funk begin to flutter away.

What's more, inside my too-tight chinos I detected the first stage of a blessed Sabbath erection.

Which is why, after the hymn of greeting to the Sabbath Bride subsided, Paulene practically had to elbow me out of my thrall.

"Now the candles," she commanded.

I handed the matches to Tali, who did not so much take as receive them from me as if in a slow motion into her outstretched open palm. After she lit the candles atop Ida's old silver holders that had survived the slings and arrows and the worst of Eastern European Jewish history, Tali spread her hands above the flames. She held her hands close and closer for the longest time.

"Careful there," Jon said when it seemed her fingers were nearly touching the blue tips of the fire.

Yet the expression of transport on Tali's face did not alter with the proximity, and her hands kept caressing the soft Sabbath lights until her polished fingernails appeared to glow.

Then she chanted the blessing over the candles.

Taking my cue yet again from Paulene, I followed with the blessing over the wine, and then over the bread. Although I have the voice of a frog, even my tunelessness seemed to be not half as bad as I feared, as if my voice belonged to another being inside the circle of beauty Tali and Aviva had created.

The Israelis had transformed our mundane realm so that what we now sat down to consume was no longer just chicken, casseroles, greens, and *challah*, but the bread of the earth and the fruit of the vine.

As we passed the food and chatted as if this were a normal meal, I began to notice something familiar about the dress, out of which Tali's smooth breasts swelled ever so slightly when she leaned my way across the table.

When she saw my eyes widen, Paulene said, "I should have wagered ten bucks on who would notice first."

"It isn't!"

"Yes it is."

"So it is! *Your* wedding dress!"

"Doesn't it look just perfect on her?"

"I had to take it in at the waist," said Aviva. "That's why we took long."

"And a beautiful job you did," said Paulene.

"Way to go. Very nice," said Jon.

Then in that serene, unperturbed, unaccusatory way of hers, as if she were reading my mind, Tali said, "Norman feels . . . something is wrong."

"I didn't say anything."

"If you don't like it, I could change."

"You'll do nothing of the sort. You look beautiful, and you," Paulene added with a nod to Aviva.

As usual, everyone was staring at me.

"Norman?" said Tali. I just stared at my place setting. "Norman?"

In that single word, my name, as Tali repeated it, I felt she had known me all my life.

I couldn't lie and I couldn't tell the truth. I couldn't speak.

"Norman?" Tali repeated for a third mesmerizing time.

"Oh, he's traveling very far away from us," Aviva said.

"Can I have a vote whether I should send Norman to his room?" my mother tried to ride to my rescue. "All in favor?" Only Jon raised his hand.

"What's wrong?" said Paulene.

"Not a thing."

"In that case, pass the carrots."

But sure enough I was remembering the dress in the formal photograph of our parents' wedding.

In it Paul is still sporting his pencil mustache. A raffish handkerchief the size of a dish towel is sprouting from near the breast pocket of his tuxedo jacket. Paulene's got the dress on, and a gardenia in her brushed-back hair, which was then thick as Tali's and all piled high. It's an odd pose for a wedding photo in that they are caught dancing, and Paulene is swaying, leaning over, allowing herself to drop at the last possible instant into Paul's athletic embrace.

That's how I imagined the moment, but now Tali seemed to be in it.

"Did you ever know your brother was so sentimental?" Paulene said.

"You know these rabbinic students, Mom. Tradition, tradition."

In the hour that followed, Paulene and Aviva chatted about camp and temple, and a little about Israel, but Tali said very little. She busied herself tasting the food, but, I noticed, forking only the tiniest morsel of each dish into her mouth, as if she were a food critic interested only in taste and not in consumption at all. "So delicious, so unusual," she said, as if she were tasting bread, carrots, and noodles for the first time in her life.

Aviva was more chatty, but you'd have to say it was pretty much one way from Paulene as Jon and I listened, as if from the back of the room, although we were right there among them.

There eventually was talk, of course, of the hills around Sfad and Jerusalem, but the Israel Aviva described, as I listened, seemed not the real geographic Israel I had read about, but a kind of deep, green Eden. Maybe it was the wine and the strange spirit that had descended on us. Aviva said she'd like to go back to school in Israel one day. Tali said after her visit to America she would be traveling more; she did not say where.

About the Six-Day War in which Tali and Aviva had served, they were especially reticent.

Then Paulene turned to me of course, and with the girls as prompts, I guess, she asked me about the seminary and about my studies. I knew Jon had not told my secret to her, so I took a page from the angels and I revealed as little as they did.

Yet my obfuscation was awfully close to lying, and you never felt any of that, or at least I didn't, when the girls spoke.

Not that Tali's mysterious ways were entirely unexpected. In camp she was always quiet, and not just with me. Whenever I saw her emerge from the water at the camp pool, I experienced her as this undersea diver living in a world of silence, rising from her depth with just so much oxygen in the tanks to expend on humans like us.

Each word she chose to utter to any of the members of the chatty Family Gould seemed like a breath expended from the limited supply she and Aviva possessed in order to accomplish their task with us.

How else to explain why they didn't engage in the usual boy-girl banter and even why their polite chatter here at the Sabbath table was so guarded and brief?

Who were these creatures? Maybe they were from an Israeli SEAL program at which top-secret training facility they had signed oaths of silence. Or maybe they were extraordinarily well-brought-up children of physician mystics in Sfad, sent to an unusual finishing school deep in the heart of Switzerland, some academy that trained extraordinary girls for extraordinary tasks— oh, I was making up all kinds of stories—when the simple truth was they were *our* girls, *our* angels and were already hard at work on our behalf.

When my thoughts returned to earth, there I was again looking between glowing Tali in my mother's wedding dress and Paulene.

Finally, I said, "What *is* this whole production about? Mom!"

"Norman, darling. It's the Sabbath, and it looks to me that a real Sabbath Queen has come to visit us. So we must treat her right! That's all."

"We didn't have anything, no dress to wear," said Tali. "Your mother, when we arrived, she says, 'Here, wear these.'"

"That's right," said Aviva as she gave me a sneakered kick that hit my calf beneath the table.

So moved the most unusual Sabbath dinner of my life toward its conclusion, and the Mormons' knock on the door had not yet even sounded.

12

AS the meal progressed, we poured a lot of expensive Israeli wine. If you believed the label, it was a Tekoa Earthquake Red, a pinot noir grown by pure fringe-wearing holy young men studying at a mystical academy on the same vine-covered hillsides around the ancient town of Tekoa where the prophet Amos had trod.

As Amos was one of my favorite prophets—due both to his wild sense of metaphor and to the brevity of his book—I drank quite a few glasses.

The two bottles, it turned out, were a gift from the Foot. Once I knew that, of course, I was disposed to revise my opinion, but they were good. Paul always said we were very much a Manischewitz family, and proud of it.

That night the Relic ate even less than usual, but she had her share and more of the prophet's wine. She raised her glass for refill after refill and toasted Tali and Aviva, she toasted *l'chaim*, and even toasted to Steve Bilko.

When she began to slip down in her chair, Jon rose from the table and carried her into Paulene's bedroom.

He returned via the kitchen, helping Paulene serve up tapioca pudding. That turned out to be yet another culinary surprise of the evening. Aviva, who loved sweets, pronounced it, in Hebrew, *tov meod*, "so good." Tali, who seemed never to squander a gesture or a breath, took a small dab of the dessert followed by a sip of wine, murmured that she concurred. I thought it would end there.

Then mysteriously she added, "I can see why your father loved this dish."

"How do you know that?" I asked, utterly surprised.

"Isn't it so?"

"Well, yes."

"Your mother must have mentioned it."

"Possibly. If you say so."

"Yes, in the kitchen when I was passing through. You don't remember?"

And there that mysterious interchange ended, at least for now. The sounds of eating, of utensils tapping on plates, and of slow sipping, subsided; soon the meal was done.

Everything fell quiet, and the whole room seemed to turn to me. I knew why. They were expecting me to lead the grace after meals. I was after all the older son, not that such status should have made any difference in our household where the only regularly observed after-meal ritual I ever could remember Paul leading had been a beeline to the credenza for a shot of Slivovitz and then to the radio to catch the late race results from Santa Anita.

I had led a grace once, maybe, at the seminary, in my first heady semester there.

That long, meandering set of blessings and psalms with all of those demanding tune changes? No, I felt very ungraceful in every sense. My hands went up in front of my face. "No, no, thank you."

"But, Norman," said my mother, "you know I've been looking forward to it."

Just then Ida erupted in a wave of snoring that rolled from the bedroom down the hall so loudly that even the girls laughed.

"She just said it for me," I said as I stood up.

"Where are you going, young man?"

"To check on her."

"Sit," said Paulene.

"She's fine," said Jon.

"Oh, really? Then you say the grace. Your Hebrew's good enough to handle that."

"I'd like to hear how it's sung at the seminary," Jon replied.

Then Tali and Aviva directed at me a collective glance, almost in unison, as if they knew exactly what was about to happen.

"Norman, I think you're up," said Paulene.

"Why not ask one of the girls?" I countered, and turned hopefully to them. "Then we can hear how it's done in the Land of Israel. What do you say?"

Tali smiled that enigmatic smile of hers that was like a seesaw, inviting you in with the upswing that what you have asked for is instantly understood and that you think you have been granted it, but then upending your desire coming down.

"You sing, Norman. You grace us," she said.

"It'll be practice for your career," added Paulene.

"Just hit it," said Jon, and losing no time he took his utensils as if they were drummer's sticks, and began a rhythmic beat on the tabletop.

"Aren't you grateful for all of this?" Aviva said, moving her arm about as if to take in the table, the room, the street, all of LA, and, for all I knew, the rest of America, planet Earth, the galaxy.

"Yes, but I just don't sing well is all."

"You will," said Tali.

"How's that?"

"Don't be concerned, Norman," Tali went on, her voice, calm and mellifluous and full of serenity and certainty.

"Just sing," said Aviva.

And so, with my escape routes shut down, I took a deep breath, I closed my eyes, and I opened my mouth.

What emerged was not as painful as I feared. Three-quarters of the way through my halting grace after meals, in the middle of a psalm about the Lord's glory evidenced in having made the hills run and the rivers race like young rams, the doorbell rang.

"Oh," said Paulene, rising expectantly from the table. "Please excuse me. Mr. Footlick said he would send flowers over. I'll go get them. *Shabbat shalom*. I just love saying that! You young people finish up. Carry on!"

When she disappeared down the hall to answer the front door, we young people did not carry on. Instead, Paulene's exit was as if the clapper had suddenly been removed from the bell, and my last off-key note fell into a deep well of nervous silence.

Tali rearranged the silverware in front of her, Aviva tugged up on the straps of her gown, and Jon bowed his head, his hands clasped prayerfully together on the table in front of him, just as he had done before his blessing at Ships.

Without knowing quite why—although I soon found out—I had begun to fold and unfold the Relic's napkin. In a flash I had straightened one edge and refolded another. My fingers seemed to be doing all of my thinking until the napkin had two small pointed knots at either end and a cap in the middle. Only then did I realize what I had been making.

"Our queen!" I declared as I leaned across the table and placed the cloth crown on Tali's head. "Long may she reign."

Tali's natural dignity immediately absorbed and transformed my silly gesture. She did not startle or resist. Instead, she lowered her eyes in a genuine regal thank you, as if such obeisance were not childish, inappropriate, or at all unexpected.

"All hail the queen," said Aviva.

"Here's to the queen," Jon said as he raised a mock glass. Then he tipped Tali's napkin crown back on the great wave of her hair. She *was* queen-like and ethereally beautiful. I could have put the *challah* or even a bowl of fruit on her head and she would have remained regal.

Suddenly Tali's eyes were bearing in on me with a gaze so disconcerting I had to look away. That's when I heard voices in the hallway, and here suddenly also was Paulene returned to the dining room.

She was completely emptied of the Sabbath light that had lit her features only a moment before.

"So where are the flowers?" I stupidly asked.

It was to Jon that Paulene addressed her ominous answer: "There's someone named Western Oaks and another young man at the door. They say they know you. They're wearing white shirts and black ties. They're dressed for the Sabbath, but I don't think it's ours."

Jon gave me a rapid glance, got up, and moved along the table's edge heading for the hall and front door.

Paulene's "Hey, Mister!" halted him. He stood, with his back to her and us, his hand resting near where the *challah* had ended up, near the edge of the table. "Are they who I think they are?"

Jon just stood there.

Then Paulene's prosecution shifted to me. "You're home a few weeks, and this happens!"

"What are you talking about?"

"Don't act dumb. You think I didn't have a hint of this?"

"Nobody thinks you're dumb, Mom," Jon said. He began to explain, but she cut him off.

"I'm not going to embarrass you. Not in front of our guests who are maybe wondering what goes on with Jewish families in Los Angeles. But for godsake on the Sabbath you told them they could come?"

"I did not."

"Why are they here, Jon?"

"I honestly don't know."

"They're not Fuller Brush men."

" Why don't you let me go find out?"

"Just tell me. Have you made any . . . commitments?"

"Commitments?"

"Yes. Have you . . ." and here Paulene looked at me for some kind of guidance or help, for words she couldn't seem to find. I couldn't either. She faltered, recovered, and said, "What I mean is, have you signed on the dotted line?"

"No, I haven't signed."

"Good then. Don't. Go to your friends, the missionaries. Invite them in. There's plenty left to eat."

"Come on, Mom." That was my dubious contribution.

"Well, do you want the Mormons to think Jews have bad manners? Whatever questions your brother has about our faith, you can answer for him. Here, now on the Sabbath, is a good time for learning. Right, Norman?"

"I'm not so sure, Mom."

While this was going on, Tali just looked from one of us to the other, and Aviva seemed to mimic her: left then right, Jon to Paulene, Paulene to Jon. As usual they conveyed no emotion. Just their presence. They observed. Occasionally they sent me a different, scrutinizing vibe.

"So go on. Here and now. In front of these girls from the Holy Land and your brother from the seminary—who sneaks cheeseburgers but still knows a thing or two. A regular Jewish brain trust we have here tonight. Let the debate begin, and offer them some *challah* while you're at it."

"We're at the grace after meals," I said.

"Fine, let the Mormons join in that," Paulene replied. "Why not!"

"You're a hoot, Mom," said Jon.

"But it's the Sabbath. Not good enough? You want to invite them over for the High Holidays?"

"I didn't ask anyone to come over. Not tonight. Not any night," said my brother. He stepped a half step, but no more, toward the hall.

"No, they just landed from Utah speaking your name."

"Someone must go the door," Tali finally said. "Shall I?"

"Why is that napkin on top of your head, young lady!"

"It's her crown, Mom. We made her Queen of the Sabbath."

"I hope you're good for something else beside joking. We'll see. Go on, Jon. Let them in."

"I'm not debating Mormons," I said. "And that's no joke."

As Paulene gave me the evil eye and as Tali slowly removed her crown and laid it on the table, Jon seized the instant to maneuver away, toward the front door.

But Paulene chased after him into the hallway. I was suddenly afraid of what would happen there, so I followed. I stood three paces away as she grabbed him by the sleeve. With muscles used to carrying an armful of heavy dishes, she drew his face down to hers until they were nose to nose.

"How could you do this!"

Both of us realized nothing he might say then would mollify her or staunch the tears welling up in her eyes.

"On the Sabbath, the day of rest, how could you! How could you!" she repeated, while still holding on.

Then she broke her grip. She whirled around, started down the hall to her bedroom, but then thought better of it and gave me a hard jab in the shoulder as she passed.

The punch to the spot where the bones meet at the shoulder hurt. I think she intended it to.

I can still summon the surprising quick blow today.

Paulene did not emerge from her bedroom for the rest of the evening, not even when Mr. Footlick came by later with those Sabbath flowers, a wild bunch of peonies, irises, and birds of paradise that he placed in a vase in the center of the table.

She wouldn't let him in the bedroom either. Then he drove Tali and Aviva back to his apartment.

After they left, I sat at the cluttered dinner table for a long time, alone. An hour went by, I nibbled at the remains of the eggplant and the carrots and the noodle casserole. I slowly cleaned up. Like a worried parent waiting for a kid out late on a date to return, I found one kitchen chore after another to fill the time as the flowers became more redolent.

I stayed awake thumbing through the grace-after-meals pamphlet, humming a line here and there, walking to the front room checking on Ida, scanning Orange Grove from the porch, and waiting for Jon to return.

Sitting there alone amid the empty chairs, I sang the last lines of the grace after meals. It wasn't half bad, yet no one heard it but me.

At two-thirty I finally was tired enough to go to sleep.

13

BY late afternoon Sunday when we still hadn't heard from Jon I was close to walking over to the Mormon ward building myself. Yet what in the world would I say to them? I pictured the scene as I barge in and declare: Wes, I've come to rescue my brother. What the hell have you done with him? Chained to the leg of one of your oxen over at the baptismal font?

In my crazy, jejune thinking, aided by one of the batch of oh-so-smooth joints Jon had fashioned and I had finally found, I now imagined the missionaries having wrought some Mormon miracle: having already scooped up my only brother, had they also already celestially teleported him away from aggravating, earthbound, sarcastic, backsliding Jewish me forever?

I thought he might not even show up to work at camp on Monday.

Our mother took a different tack. Not given to dire thoughts, or rather just refusing to succumb to what she feared or to such draconian imaginings as mine, from that Sabbath on, Paulene filled her every spare minute with synagogue activities.

When I awoke Saturday morning, she had already gone to services. She stayed for the afternoon service. She called to let me know, of course. She asked about Jon. I had no news for her. So she stayed for her sisterhood meeting that followed in the evening.

To the Mormon challenge Paulene brought the intensity of her busy new Jewish life along with this new status as the girlfriend of an important temple official; she also brought to bear on it a waitress's wisdom, and the hard-won practical lessons of having lived with us and with Paul.

On Sunday she accompanied the Foot to a men's club golfing "affair," as she had taken to characterizing such events. After that they went to a "gala" dinner for yet another new temple wing. Paul had once wisecracked that after they finished all the wings, the synagogue big shots were going to fundraise to put on new breasts; and afterwards maybe the building could even sport a gizzard as part of the ever-growing temple complex.

Now I also watched Paulene as she burrowed as far as she could into the heart of these Jewish routines; frankly I didn't know which was worse.

It all began to evoke in me, as I say, responses that did not feel like my own. Inside my head I began to hear condemnatory speeches that decidedly did not sound like my own self-lecturing. Could there be something to what the Mormons and even Tali and Aviva here and there already had been intimating? Could our dad, from beyond the grave, be somehow still out there in some fashion ranting away as well, and could I have become his vessel, audience, repository, and sounding board?

No, sheer nonsense. Yet if not, then what in the world was happening?

I should not have remained at the duplex, but Jon had dibs on the car and, anyway, it was my turn to take care of Ida. As I paced the rooms of our apartment and Ida and I watched TV for most of an overcast and lugubrious Sunday, Paul's presence seemed to grow palpable:

Did you know that at Chicago country clubs they recruited Negroes who were very obsequious to be the caddies? That's right. You're smart at book learning, but let me teach you a thing or two about the real world, son. You better believe it. They also had signs, Chicago, Wisconsin, all over the Midwest—I kid you not— Jews and Dogs Not Allowed.

"Yeah, Dad. So what," I said aloud.

When you "hear" voices such as these, are they your own masquerading as others'? How does one really know? Or are you hearing a transcription or legitimate dictation of another's voice that is expressing itself, with its own integrity, *through* you? Your own, sort of, but it also remains the sentiment of the other.

An *ibbur*? Paul's soul transmigrated to me? Ridiculous. Yet how to make these distinctions? How to be sure?

The question of course is as old as religion itself, as beautiful, thorny, and, yes, maybe as irresolvable. Yet they used to burn you at the stake—go ask Joan of Arc—or worse, if you provided the wrong answer to your interrogators about which "voice" you hear. If you were unconvincing in your argument, or if, in your desperation, you made false statements on purpose, well, lots of luck. You'd better hope the authorities let the little old ladies bring highly combustible kindling to your public burning.

After that Sabbath and after the Mormon visit, I was certain that none of this would be happening if Western Oaks and Jon would just keep their hands off Paul's soul. And where did Tali get off telling me that Paul liked tapioca pudding? How in the world did she really know *that*? I was surrounded by strangeness, pieces large and small that suddenly did not fit the puzzle frame, and all I wanted was to be left alone to my marijuana musings and to my adolescent indulgences.

As Sunday dragged on, I plunked Ida in front of a televised Pacific Coast League game—it was the Seattle Sea Dogs playing catch-up with the LA Angels—and I went out to the porch. Over the railing I leaned, surveying the block up and down, covering as far as my vantage would allow the route Jon and I had walked the day of my return, playing and replaying our conversation. Up and down I looked a half dozen times before I realized who I was on the lookout for: proselytizers and missionaries.

Never mind the Constitution that gave them a right to knock on any door they choose. Still you see a doorway with that oblong little thing the shape of a cartridge nailed on at the upper right? A *mezuzah*. Ladies and gentlemen, would you be good enough to skip those doors and to go on your merry way?

Was I saying that? The block was entirely deserted, not a car, not a walker. "Just skip on by, Mormons, Jehovah's Witnesses, troops of Father Divine, all of you!"

I'd rarely performed such monologues with myself before. This was not my form of cogitation. Who belonged to this ridiculous, Jewish superhero voice?

I stepped back into the living room. It was the fifth inning, and the Sea Dogs, down by eight runs already, did not appear to have a chance against the Angels. The Relic was watching with her eyes open but not seeing, not comprehending; I knew what she was going through.

I sat down near her and watched the next batter strike out; the next got a single, but was picked off. I tried to explain to her what happened. Then I paced around the room. Ida began to snore and was soon asleep in the middle of the claustrophobic space that seemed also to have become my life.

I turned off the TV.

This was beyond weird.

"Just get lost," I suddenly shouted. "Just get the hell out of here."

"*Vos?*" Ida startled awake.

"Nothing, Grandma. Go back to sleep."

"*Vu?*"

"Nothing. *Gornischt.*"

As she dozed off again, the imagined aroma of one of Paul's Lucky Strikes, smoky, robust, and warm, filled my nostrils. I was worried, and not only about my brother. These guys who were running around inside of me were not only talking; they were beginning to smoke.

I lay down on the couch near my dozing grandma for a nap.

These visions continued but gradually gave way to imagined vignettes of Mormon bliss: of my strong, muscular, sun-bronzed brother, now a woodman's axe over his shoulder, raising a barn in some desert Zion. Now there he stood in a straw hat by the Great Salt Lake, hacking away at the locusts attacking his crops; in another scene he's falling on his knees and praising Heavenly Father, as he now referred to God. In yet another he's carrying his plural wives, fabulous Mormon beauties with ravishing curling hair, their comely forms barely concealed in their small-waisted bodices and voluminous hoop skirts, dangling from Jon's powerful, outstretched arms. There he is bearing them over the threshold to his rustic farm house, and to his bed, piled high with homemade quilts. The wives' faces were not revealed to me, but their bodies were those of Tali and Aviva.

As I waited for Jon's return that night, I think I resented less what my brother was doing than how it had brought out all these anxieties and now all these stereotypes that were suddenly so alive and obsessive within me. That wasn't on his nickel; it was on mine, and I was not proud. It was a kind of running imaginary documentary movie full of clichés that I did not want to see but nevertheless kept viewing. No sooner had the whole seagull-eating-locust, Mormon Tabernacle Choir-singing saga concluded, than it began to unfold, run, and rerun, again.

Okay.

So the Mormon cat was now out of the Jewish bag, but the Jewish one, *my* story, what had just happened to *me* in New York and the new life that *I* craved, did anyone care about that? At least that secret was still secure. Wasn't it? I certainly hoped so.

Yet Paulene, as it now seemed, had already known something of my cheeseburgering as well as of Jon's sins. Yes, I felt guilty but I was also suspicious and in no small part angry that I might, to use a Paul Gould phrase, be being played.

Mormons didn't usually come calling on Friday nights. Exasperated with me, was it possible Jon had really given them instructions to show up just then, and to break it all wide open with one hurtful, transgressive gesture? Had he had time to lay out such a plan? He was so full of surprises and new ways of acting that I didn't recognize and could no longer "read" my own brother. Anything seemed possible. But, no. Absolutely not that. No, despite his zeal, he would not have forced the question in such a crude manner that obviously caused our mother such embarrassment and pain. No way.

Had I only done as Jon had asked, instead of delaying and malingering and belittling his new path, maybe none of this would have happened. In short, I began to feel more than a little contrite.

Still, at a Sabbath meal, and with Paulene and Tali and Aviva? Even in sin, dereliction, and apostasy there is room for moderation, compassion, and self-control. Or should be.

Sure! Look who was talking.

Whatever fraternal feeling we had cobbled together to protect Paulene through mutual if artless obfuscations was now fraying.

For all practical purposes, our cover-up, or at least Jon's, was now so totally exposed that not only could I now *not* reveal that I had left the seminary, but I felt an emerging and insistent obligation to counter in the exact opposite direction: to be the lead cowboy in circling the Jewish wagons against further Mormon attack.

I heard an engine outside, went out to the porch, and saw a car pull into the driveway. It was not Jon but the Foot dropping Paulene off.

I went into the bathroom—to hide, like a little kid, lest he come in with her and I have to make small talk about the seminary and Israel or camp.

But she entered alone and eventually we found each other in the breakfast nook off the kitchen. There we just sat over a yellow plate of Social Tea cookies and cups of Lipton tea that she made while I brought the Relic to her bed downstairs. Each of us sat there, our hands around the warm cups, and we began then to commiserate with the usual generalizations.

I mouthed the thin words of comfort that I thought were expected of me. Paulene spoke of our family crisis and that of the general intermarriage and thinning and diffusion of the tribe in conventional terms and with a mother's lament. Yet there was absolutely no misunderstanding the invigorated role she now cast for me as the older brother, eldest child, and even a kind of substitute for Paul. God help me; that latter was the character I least wanted to . . . inhabit.

The only arrow she did not pull from the maternal quiver was that I was a rabbinic student. That she did not remind me of this gave me much pause, and some relief, I don't know in what proportion.

"I know, I know. I'm just as upset as you are, Mom. Believe me."

"I'll believe you when your brother is back in the temple again. The right temple. Our temple, where he belongs."

She then began to emery board her nails rapidly and with an aggressive nervousness. When she looked up from her hands, it was to stare at me with a gaze so intense I had to break it off. I stood. I went to the sink for a glass of water although I was not thirsty at all. When I sat back down beside her, she was still sawing away.

"What?"

"What did we do wrong?"

"We didn't do anything wrong," I replied, with all of the cavalier assurance of a bluffer holding at best a pair of fives in a high-stakes game. "Things happen."

"Well, you're a very smart and capable boy. Make them *un*-happen."

"I will, Mom; I will."

"I'm going to bed."

"That's the best thing. You need your rest."

"Yes, and I need this," she said motioning about the room but meaning the unfolding LDS drama, "like a hole in the head."

"It'll work out. He'll come back to us."

"Are you sure?"

I said nothing.

"Maybe he'll send a postcard from Salt Lake City."

"He'll be home," I said.

"You don't stay up all night waiting either."

Then, without giving me even a peremptory goodnight kiss, she left the kitchen, walked wearily down the hall, didn't even use the bathroom, and went straight to bed.

I SUPPOSE if Tali and Aviva had interceded even a little more vigorously in those initial days, I would not have gone down the path I chose, but it's the style of angels, I came to learn later (and would like to impress upon you now), to let a person's free agency flourish right up to the point where he makes a complete ass of himself. Then decisiveness, or rescue, becomes imperative.

As it turned out, I did not have to call the LAPD's Missing Persons Bureau or drive over to the Mormons' ward or to break into the baptismal font behind, or to look up W. Oaks in the White Pages, although—no surprise by now—I considered each of those options.

Jon came home, by our glowing bedroom clock, at twenty minutes to midnight. I was in bed with my eyes shut but not asleep when he clicked the door open.

He disrobed quickly and, I believe, uttered a hushed prayer in the darkness of the bedroom. He was asleep almost instantly, his breathing an untroubled steady purr.

I lay there fitfully worrying and listening to Jon's quiet breathing as if it were some arcane Mormon code; if only I could discern a pattern, might that not reveal something essential? If Moses had his burning bush and Joseph Smith his golden tablets, hell, why couldn't I trade in revelations? Couldn't I declare a revelation just now to be deciphered from the gentle pattern of percolations emerging from my brother's fine Jewish nose? I decided to give it a shot.

"Where have you gone?" I all but whispered to Jon.

"Chhh, chhhh, chhhh" . . . came his snoring answer.

With Oaks or solo?

"Prr chk chhh."

I, of course, learned nothing except that I was desperate to know what was going on with him. It was all I could do to keep from reaching across the divide between our beds and poking him awake. I counted the little dimples of paint on the ceiling. Then I tried to put myself to sleep counting the sheep of my anxieties. I went through several flocks that had gathered, and then it was morning.

WE ROSE, peed, washed, and, without speaking, dutifully dressed in our Camp Tikvah T-shirts. We caught the bus to La Cienega and walked the balance of the blocks with a few perfunctory remarks about kids, about counselors, and about the weather. And then we were there, ready to go to work once again feigning the whole charade of advancing the traditions of the Jewish people.

It was as if all the air and the fun and the excitement Tali and Aviva had brought to the camp job had suddenly vanished. Hanging out with the kids went from okay to boring, to just barely tolerable. In front of the other counselors Jon and I acted out a barely sustained civility.

For days we said almost nothing to each other about the Mormons' Sabbath visit. Only the make-believe stuff I was doing with the kids and Noah's Ark gave me some relief from this other play or transaction Jon and I seemed to have entered into: acting as if nothing had happened.

We did so for the whole of the next week, not only at work but also at home. Neither of us budged. Our beds were as close again as in childhood. Yet there had never been such an abyss between us.

For some reason that week I also began to notice—or in memory I certainly associate that hard week with—The Mamas and the Papas' "California Dreamin'."

I began to hear the song everywhere, on the car radio when I was waiting to pick up Paulene at Canter's, from the kids singing it at camp or humming it during our warm-up exercises for the play, or while they waited on line for their morning snack. One of the junior counselors was even working with some of the ten-year-olds to translate the words into Hebrew to perform at the camp variety show.

When the Foot called me in to tell me blah blah how glad he was that I was at camp and to ask how things were going—blah blah, very fine—who would have thought that he would have the song on, pulsating slowly from the shiny maroon radio on the shelf behind him in his office? Even when I sneaked out for my cheeseburgers, the tune always seemed to be playing on one or two of the tabletop jukeboxes at Ships.

For those of you not up on your 1960s rock-and-roll history, the song is the anti- "White Christmas," as the lyric's narrator is snowbound and just yearning to be in sunny, surfboarding, wild-living LA.

Of course I had done just that, although not in the winter. Still, I had left New York and the crusty old world of Jews and observance and limitations and come home for just some of that good old California Dreamin' that

Mama Cass Elliot and the others were crooning night and day, the anthem of the summer I was losing my brother.

I think I was clinging to the song because it at least gave me some hope—thin as paper, but I'd take it—that Jon would just come to his senses and drop this fling with the Mormons and, please God, resume being the mellow, stoned guy I remembered, needed, and loved.

BUT HE was changing now it seemed almost physically, right before my eyes. Maybe it was the laps he swam before the kids arrived, but he appeared to be growing even more lean and muscular, as if the very pounds that I was putting on from my cheeseburgering at Ships had come directly off of him.

Sitting up on his lifeguard perch, shirtless and bronzed, and with that ever-present swatch of white cream on his nose against the sun, day by day Jon seemed like this future Olympian, and I increasingly a big blob. What was worse, he also avoided my eyes. That I could understand. But he continued to do the same to Tali, our fabulous Israeli in her tiny bikini. I was a spy, yes, and I swear I saw him almost turning away on his perch when she approached so that he wouldn't have to look at her, or inadvertently to gaze down into her cleavage when she stood directly below calling up to him with some question about a swimmer or about a float or about who knows what.

In short, to my eyes, Jon was definitely evolving into some new, no-longer-Jewish-but-not-quite-yet-other person, a reality I saw but didn't want to acknowledge.

On Thursday, with swimming cancelled because it was raining all day, the kids were sent home an hour early. I invited Jon again to go with me to Ships. Maybe he would say yes this time and, finally, we could talk there.

"I can live without all that grease, man. I really can," is how he greeted the proposal.

"Cutting out so much bad stuff all at once could be a shock to your system."

"Learning to live without it," he calmly stated. "Cleaning house, man," he added and set about rearranging the gear beneath the lifeguard stand by the pool. "Cleaning up in many, many ways."

We were the only two people on the pool deck. That's when I put my hand on his arm and practically begged him to accompany me. I don't know why it suddenly seemed to matter so much that my brother have a Galleon Burger and a side of onion rings with me. Yet he didn't get it, or, if he did, he refused to give me his old companionship that I somehow desperately needed then.

He was calm and serene, as if animated by what I feared to be a kind of new Mormon power-steering system. It was as if something had been installed within him, so that his refusal was now, I also saw, really resistant to the casual apologies I offered, the fraternal inquiries I made, as well as to my usual cajoling.

In fact, his new manner seemed eerie, even driven. Dare I say programmed?

"Anything at all you want? Anything on the menu. My treat, man."

"You go enjoy Ships," he replied, and lifted my hand, carefully but firmly, from his forearm. He added, almost as an afterthought, that he was going to use this newfound time to go turn in his Checker cab ID. He'd been driving still a little, occasional half shifts after camp, filling in for friends; that was now coming to an end.

That was another shocker because Jon had shown off a little by driving our Israeli angels about in the cab—one afternoon before the Sabbath debacle we'd taken a drive with the angels, a blaze of yellow Checker tearing up Cahuenga to the Sunset Strip, squealing around the curves into Laurel Canyon, and of course we drove the angels up to have a close-up of the Hollywood sign. I'd also been planning an elaborate make-out session with Aviva for the spacious back seat of the cab, but now?

Now all we had was our old oil-leaking Nash Rambler. How do you make out with an angel in an oil-smelling sedan?

"You sure you're turning it in?"

He just looked at me.

"You absolutely, positively sure?"

"Yup. Just the camp gig and . . . my studies. Afterward, after the summer I'm looking into a job in insurance."

"Insurance?"

"Life, health, auto. Wes has some contacts in the industry. The Mormons are big in insurance."

"I'll bet."

"You just go and enjoy your burger."

And that was the only exchange that we had all that week, apart from what had been necessary to negotiate the kids' activities.

It made me in equal parts sad and angry. I'm a physicist of those feelings, and I know that when two collide, there's a kind of cancellation. Yet the energy has to go somewhere, and it often transforms into an emptiness that in turn creates a vacuum, which clearly needs to be filled.

So I did go. I got that Galleon Burger, and a large order of rings, and a strawberry malted.

Then I ordered another because no matter what I ate, I still felt empty.

BY THREE and a half weeks into the summer, the waitress in the tangerine uniform knew my routine so well, all I had to say was hello and to sit down.

I rolled a quarter into the baby juke, and I played *my* song: "If I didn't tell her I could leave today" I hummed along with Mama Cass. I closed my eyes. I made believe. "California dreamin' . . . on a winter's da a a a a a y."

A few minutes later, as I sailed away eyes closed and absorbing the mellow chords, the feast was brought to me. It was as if my nose "saw" what was in front of me; I considered eating the meal with my eyes closed, but thought the better of it. I thanked the waitress and then, without even tasting beforehand, I salted, I peppered, and I slathered on a coating of Russian dressing on both sides of the bun.

Inexplicably—to me—I also quickly intoned the *hamotzi*, the blessing before breaking bread, and then I ate and ate and ate.

Midway through one particularly memorable pig-out, I heard news headlines from the static-y transistor radio the waitress had turned up beside the cash register, near where I was sitting: the National Guard was sending in more soldiers to Watts and to South Central because of the rioting. Three dozen had been arrested; three were dead. Crenshaw Boulevard was impassible with debris and still had several fires burning, one at the discount department store that had been looted. In other news, there was a pretty good body count of North Vietnamese regulars in several battles along the Mekong River in Vietnam.

Boy, my Jewish Problem and Jon's Mormon Problem seemed by comparison tiny. I promised myself I'd go out to the CORE demonstrations after work, over in Westwood by UCLA. A couple of our counselors had already. But, sad to report, not me.

No, I might have been a rabbinic dropout, but I remained a creature of some spiritual habits, albeit slovenly ones. I still must have held some of the belief in prayer's magic that had surrounded me in the first years in New York. I really did, because there in my booth I began praying for the war to end, for my draft number to be lost by the draft board, and for the riots to end. I couldn't recollect any rule against praying while eating, so on I went. I prayed. For Jon, for Paul Gould's restless soul, for Paulene, and for Paulene and the Foot to break up.

These were not elevating prayers and certainly light-years from the mainstream tradition of Jewish prayer at the heart of which is a practice not of personal solicitation but of awe and self-reflection. Definitely not qualifying was this Christmas list of personal intercessions, yet on I went. Another fry, another prayer: oh, boy. I especially prayed Tali and Aviva would continue, well, just to be there for us, or at least for me, despite what had happened, as they had been thus far. That they would not be offended by what was happening in our family, that they would not find better boyfriends elsewhere, as they so richly deserved.

And wouldn't you know it, when I looked up from my now-empty, ketchup-streaked plate, there Tali was, her long, tan beautiful thigh right beside my booth.

"Is this seat taken?"

"And this?" said Aviva, as she stepped out from behind her friend.

FINALLY!

My two great joys, food and these fabulous girls, had come together. Tali was still wearing her minuscule yellow bikini that I made out beneath her blouse and thin khaki shorts. Aviva was in a short-legged leotard with gym trunks over it. The angels, who always looked fabulous, were even more so.

Tali squeezed in beside me, with her great curving pelvis practically touching my leg. Aviva sat across the table, leaning my way. They were surrounding me; my prayers had been answered, at least a couple of them.

"I'd like to buy you . . . everything on the menu, and then some."

"Nothing for me, with thanks," said Tali.

"I've come to enjoy your chocolate malteds," said Aviva.

"Then you shall have three."

"One is good, with the straw and long spoon, please."

After I put in the order with my waitress-pal, I just sat and smiled at the angels. That's their effect sometimes. I just sat there and admired my great, unexpected good luck. I stared at their beautiful, fluted throats for a long minute and not once did either of them swallow. How strange. A whole fantasy summer opened up in my imagination: we'd split this place and drive up to San Francisco.

We'd spend the rest of the summer there, hanging out with the poets Lawrence Ferlinghetti, Allen Ginsberg, and Gary Snyder in North Beach; we'd drink coffee at Vesuvio's and read books that we'd shoplift, I mean liberate, from the rickety poetry racks at City Lights Bookstore. At sunset we'd head to Bolinas, where my one good seminary buddy had a cousin who was a professional pothead growing acres of weed by the bay. We could live rent-free on the beach, we could . . .

Talking suddenly a mile a minute, as if to make up for my aphasic break, I made the whole case to them at Ships.

Their response: they sat in their usual serene posture of intent, concentrated listening. I realize now that an outside observer passing the aisle in Ships where we sat that day, or seeing us from the window on La Cienega Boulevard as I held forth, might have seen ennui in their eyes. However, earth angels dealing with humans, especially such an undeveloped one as me, often can be, well, bored.

Never mind. The malted was brought, and on and on I went, now about how I needed more plaster of Paris for the props, now about the kids I found peculiar, and I don't remember what else.

After Aviva took a penultimate slurp on her malted, Tali said, "You do remember Jonah?"

At first I thought she might be referring to one of the kids in our camp production, Jonah Feinberg, a boy narrow in the head but already fat in the gut like me. I needed a kid who looked like he enjoyed a good meal. Maybe that's why he was one of the few I'd taken a liking to that summer. I had cast him as one of the two anacondas in the play.

"*Yonah*, in Hebrew, Norman. One of our minor prophets. You remember him."

"Oh, of course."

"Tell me what you remember," Tali said.

"Well, in Brief Books of the Bible 302, I earned a B minus. Jonah, Micah, Amos, and Habakkuk. I loved those short books. You know why?"

"Please tell me."

"Because they're only two, three pages of text, and that's it. You're in one moment and then you're out."

Now it was Aviva's turn. She balanced her chin on the rim of the tall frosted malted glass she had just drained and said, "Yes, of all of them, you resemble Jonah most. Same eyes."

"Same chin," Tali added.

"Excuse me?"

"But the main similarity is that you also keep trying to run away."

"I'm just suggesting a little vacation up in 'Frisco is all. Not a flight. We'll come back."

"Would you? Really?"

"Absolutely."

"When the captain asked Jonah who his god is, does he lie?"

"What!"

Tali put her hand on my forehead then, as if to take my temperature. As she did so, she said, "Norman, oh dear Norman." She spoke my name in a way I can't replicate ever, as if I'd never heard it before.

"Norman, Norman, Norman, dear Jonah, Jonah, Jonah, Jonah," Aviva said the same from across the table. Just my name intoned again and again and again.

It was as if they were somehow transformed into, well, beings who were performers, nurses, and spectacular potential girlfriends, yet also presences from somewhere else trying to speak to me in a new language.

One called my name; the other stroked my forehead as if I were a fever patient. The collective gesture thrilled, confused, but also angered me.

When she repeated my name for the umpteenth time, Tali added: "Everything suggests you're lying."

But the son of Paul Gould knew how to double down.

"We can live on the beach at Bolinas. Hitch down to Big Sur. That guy who wrote *Tropic of Cancer* is living there. Henry Miller. We'll drop by for lunch. Hello, Henry! A few days and then we'll return. I promise. My mother's in with the Foot. Substitute counselors can be arranged. You'll see . . ."

How I pushed my going-nowhere idea forward; I was making fun of it even while I was proposing it. That was typical of how I operated that confusing summer, moving in two directions at once. No wonder I was stuck, with the illusion of motion.

"We can be at the corner of Powell and Market Streets tonight. You'll love the cable cars."

"Norman?"

"Come on. You saved Israel and the Jewish People in the Six-Day War. I think you deserve a few days off. What do you say?"

"Maybe when camp is over," said Aviva.

"Can't wait that long."

"You have work to do."

That was Tali. Now Aviva came at me. "Jonah was desperate to run."

"Not that again!"

Aviva took a napkin and wiped chocolate from the side of her mouth. "What good will going to San Francisco do? It's just, what, a few hundred miles away?"

"Four hundred sixty-two Earth miles," said Tali. "To be precise."

"'Earth miles'?"

"Of course. What else?" she replied. "Tarshish for Jonah was much farther, the end of the world, as far as sailors had sailed at the time. Still didn't the Lord track him down there?"

"Stop with this already. The Lord is not interested in me or in Camp Tikvah."

"Wherever you are, there He is," Tali said quietly. She could have been commenting about what was going on out the window, a school bus passing.

"Girls, girls. This is getting heavy. I just want to go and to smoke some weed in Bolinas, not tell anyone to repent."

"We cannot forget your brother," said Aviva.

"I'm afraid he doesn't love you as much as I do."

That was when Tali reached over and undid the rubber band that I had taken to wearing to keep my unruly hair in place. When my mop fell onto my shoulders, she declared, "Hello, Jonah, ben Amitai."

Now Tali was caressing my hair. Whoa! Had there been a female instructor like this, I might never have left the seminary! I would have become an A student instead of a dropout. I would have said: Ordain me! Twice!

As they joked and fussed with me, trying to redo my ponytail as a French braid or as some other strange knot, it was as if they were treating me like a baby or like a girl, no, as both, as if none of the sex and dating vibes I was very obviously sending their way were getting through at all. That's, of course, exactly what angels are: genderless beings, although on the outside they take the forms we particular humans crave, and how I craved Tali and Aviva!

As a result of their ministrations, whatever my understanding at the time of their subtleties—their hints that were more than hints that I was falling down on the job of reeling Jon back to the tribe, and away from Western Oaks—despite all that, I was still experiencing a very nonangelic, concrete, nondualistic, big fat boner.

I took a deep breath. "How about if Jon will go with us ? A foursome?"

"He's hardly speaking to you."

"That's why," I countered.

"You do have fine, thick hair," Aviva said, as if she hadn't heard me at all. "Needs a wash."

"Definitely prophetic hair," Tali added.

"Knots and split ends."

"Only girls have split ends," I ventured.

"Wrong again, Norman. Jonah's hair was quite well kept. Even inside the great fish he kept a fragment of glass as a mirror. There he groomed. A minor and vain young man, like many of you," said Tali.

"I don't think I like myself compared to a minor prophet."

"Well, you're not a major."

"No, he's definitely not a major," added Aviva.

"Time out! Please stop talking as if you *know* Jonah! Jonah is a character in a book."

"And who are you?"

"She means the type, Norman. Like you."

"Now I'm a type?"

"Most definitely. You all are," Aviva said as she began to comb my hair with her fingers.

That's the way it was with the angels: flirting that felt playful and genuine but then meandered toward intimate hints of much more beyond. Oh, they were definitely flirting and horsing around, but then in an instant banter would pivot into portent and barely veiled admonition.

Still, I refused to believe that my long hair made me into a type or into a character from the Bible. Or my desire to go to San Francisco with them and play The Mamas and the Papas on the radio the whole way and to get away from a boring job made me a pusillanimous prophet.

We stood, and I placed enough money on the table to cover the check. I gathered my camp gear from the booth and, believe it or not, I began to walk away from the angels. Yup, I was fleeing.

Yet they followed and were at my side instantly. As we descended Ships's steps onto the boulevard, they came after me once again. No matter how fast I walked, they were there, talking between themselves, like a couple of gossips, and there was no getting away.

"Have you noticed how Jon cuts his hair short, like his Mormon friends?" said Aviva.

"As his grows shorter, Norman's grows longer and longer."

"Now he has hair for two," Tali added matter-of-factly.

We had arrived at the corner of Olympic and La Cienega waiting for the light to change when they addressed me directly once again.

"You won't keep him with you this way. It's bound to fail," said Aviva. "Steps must be taken." Then she added: "The uncut hair is also a sign of mourning of course."

To this I listened, half in wonder, half in dismay.

"And do you know who you are mourning for? Is it your brother?"

"Or your father?" Aviva did her part to tighten the screw.

"Maybe it's both," replied Tali, but casually, almost lightheartedly, as if she and Aviva were talking about how much they liked some sandals they had just seen in a store window.

Before I could reply to these wild remarks, *if* I could, the light turned green, and we crossed the boulevard heading back up to the park entrance on La Cienega.

On the far side they switched subjects yet again as Aviva thanked me for the malted and went on, in the same tone as she had about Jonah, about how remarkable the ice cream was mixed with bits of ice, which she called frozen waters. I could not believe these were the first malteds of her life, but it seemed they were.

That's the way it was as they insinuated their mission and themselves, inseparable from it, into the life of our family, both the living, and as you shall soon see, the dead.

We were late, and headed quickly back toward the park. The late afternoon light was intense and beautiful, an orange ball of the desert sun beginning to dip into the sea at Santa Monica, right over where the Mormons held their picnics.

As we made our way back to camp, their arms draped around my waist and occasionally inched up to massage the small of my back. Talk about being under the wings of angels! If this were the reward of flight, I was all for it. I felt I was being, well, swept off my feet, skipping steps, that is, literally being carried by these two immensely strong young women.

Why I deserved this and why they were doing it after their interrogation, I did not know and now did not care. All I knew was this lightness and now their breasts moved beneath their shirts on either side as they escorted me, a movement of such undulation and grace combined, lovely and inviting, well, it was so very easy only to look and not to hear what they were continuing to say about me and about my failings and about what I needed to do, and fast, to rescue my family.

That's how Tali and Aviva cast their spell.

We now were at the entrance to the park, where the angels and I resumed our camp roles and thanked our junior counselors for keeping an eye on the handful of kids who had not yet been picked up.

A few of these kids detoured to give Aviva and Tali hugs. One, a nine-year-old named Amber Weinstein, whose breath always smelled of peanut butter, raced down the sidewalk and leaped into Tali's waiting arms.

AVIVA KNELT down to give a tiny girl named Frieda a good-bye hug—we had just cast her as one of the antelopes in our Noah's flood drama—and Tali extended her arms around another of the little ones (revealing the fabulous envelope of her tanned, angelic breast in the process). I stood off by myself, leaning against the park's fence as the angels finished their good-byes.

As I watched, I wasn't sure what had just happened to me at Ships and during the walk back. All their talk and the challenges they had thrown down, all the angels' Jonah-ing of me seemed now as if it had not happened, or was only a reverberating echo from words spoken a long time ago.

But it was not so; it was not so at all.

I checked out Tali and Aviva as I stood there, these angels, these extraordinary creatures, and I determined that the only way to find out for sure, that is, for me, the next major front for evasion had to be to try just as soon as possible to get laid.

Precisely as I was experiencing that carnal thought, Tali walked boldly over to where I was standing and squared me to her. Now she put a hand under my chin and seemed to raise my face fully to behold hers. I wasn't aware that I had dropped my gaze, that I wasn't looking her in the eye. I was staring at my sneakers because I could not face her beautiful, dark, Brigitte Bardot eyes. I knew she could see right through me, to my heart, to my boner, to everything.

I felt her hand pulling at where my hair curled at the back of my neck. I felt almost like a baby, a tiny helpless thing, a homunculus inside a set of large hands. She touched me on the chin. She tilted up my head. She raised my eyes.

I dropped my gaze again, out of embarrassment, weakness, awe; I hardly could distinguish those things any more.

Aviva came over like the sheriff's deputy blocking the last exit from town. That was when Tali turned me to her in a manner that was both sensual and disciplinary, and spoke in a tone of command I had not heard before: "Norman, don't you see? You must see."

That's how the conversation, along with my intended flight, was ended. Just like that.

14

FLIGHT doesn't require you to go up to San Francisco or to travel halfway around the world or to alter geography even an inch, not if it's yourself you're fleeing from. It only calls for you *not* to pay attention. And in that specialized field of flight I had already earned my ordination, with distinction.

I continued to convince myself that Jon was not completely serious and that there would be plenty of openings, opportunities for me effectively to discredit Wes and the Mormons for the make-believe silliness of their ideas.

I became particularly obsessed with the Mormons' cartoon cosmology that centered on what they believe to be a real planet, named Kolob, from where all the little souls fly or teleport themselves down to earth to test their moral mettle by living good, clean Mormon lives.

Really! I made the mistake of going on about this one night to Paulene as I was driving her home from Canter's. When I'd finished my rant, she remained uncharacteristically quiet, and just smoked.

When we pulled into the duplex's driveway, she said a visit with Jon to Rabbi Joel was definitely in order, right?

Although she phrased it like a question, Paulene's suggestion was an order.

"He'll never go," I said as she opened the car door.

"Yes he will."

"Wanna bet?"

"He will because I'll ask him."

And of course she was right.

That didn't mean, however, our thirty-minute appointment with Temple Beth Ami's spiritual leader, which occurred after camp two days later, amounted to much more than a perfunctory formality for Jon.

Rabbi Joel was dressed in his usual light brown suit with a Hawaiian shirt with a pineapple design. He had been briefed, of course, by Paulene, but in a most general way, of a spiritual crisis going on with her younger son.

We met in the rabbi's library, a room I had loved, actually, a scene of various of my victories in Hebrew vowel identification contests and other such distinctions. Joel was kind enough, with a pastoral manner that did no damage but also didn't help much; he also always smelled not unpleasantly of the then very popular English Leather men's cologne.

He gave Jon a copy of a thin book called *Judaism: Frequently Asked Questions*, and another item, "How Judaism Differs." This was a small pamphlet dog-eared at the page ends, which I was also familiar with. Paul had a copy of it, which had been distributed to him during the war by Jewish chaplains, I believe, intent on arming the Jewish boys as they encountered other religions during their far-flung service in World War II.

Next, Rabbi Joel piled into Jon's arm Milton Steinberg's famous book, *As a Driven Leaf*; it's the one about the wayward rabbi from the days of the post-temple-destruction Roman period, Elisha ben Abuya. Elisha, Akiba, Hillel, and other big-name rabbis go on a journey, according to the Talmudic story, into a kind of metaphoric garden to confront or to meet God. Each has a different agenda. Elisha had demanded big things of the Lord, not merely revelation or even secret knowledge, but Total Transport or Compelling Proof; or, Thanks but no thanks, God, there would be no relationship.

Because of that he was deemed a heretic, and forever after drummed out of the inner circle of rabbis; naturally he was a hero of mine, I told Rabbi Joel.

Joel's response: "It's good to have heroes. Who's your hero?" the rabbi turned the question to Jon.

Jon replied: "Oh, I don't know what a hero is, or isn't, but I think it takes more courage to follow rules than to break them."

"That's very impressive," said Rabbi Joel.

Then, as Joel, his back turned to us, continued to rummage in his library for more books to lend to us, Jon took the opportunity actually to apologize, a decade after the incident, for having brought that large bag of Dolores Drive-In lard-soaked French fries to Hebrew school, the basis for one of his temporary expulsions.

"Not a problem, not a problem," Rabbi Joel said, distracted, as he couldn't

THE BOOK OF NORMAN

find what he was looking for. He piled onto Jon's arm a few other tomes, told us his office was always open, and that was that.

If Rabbi Joel knew, as was obvious to me by then, that Jon did not want a reading list or footnotes to the Talmud but a direct path to heaven, he didn't provide it; maybe he didn't know the way himself.

I thought we'd have better luck if I challenged Jon on Planet Kolob, and I could combine that with a sexy, romantic double date—I hoped and prayed—with the angels up to the Griffith Observatory on the observatory's late Thursday night.

Amazingly Jon agreed to come along, although he insisted on sitting up front in the Rambler with me, and not splitting up Tali to try to make out with in the back, while Aviva nuzzles with me, near the gear shift in front.

Still he came along, dutifully, I believe; I wonder if Paulene had read the riot act to him on this as well; I was never sure.

Even now I see us swinging up the winding road that night: from Franklin Avenue in the Ferndell section of the park, climbing the 350 feet or so of hairpin turns, past ponderosa pines, clumps of Spanish bayonets, and a few roadside cabins to the great observatory parking lot on the bluff overlooking the park and the smoggy lights of LA spread out below.

The angels really loved that trip. They couldn't get enough of the exhibits of the planets in our solar system and the other galaxies displayed on the observatory's sparkling ceiling. They ran like kids from exhibit to exhibit, giggling as if the whole place was some kind of mistake or joke; when I asked why, Tali rolled her eyes, Aviva broke out in more laughter, and they took off.

Outside they loved the telescopes, into which they popped the handfuls of quarters I had remembered to bring along, and they scanned the city and the heavens.

I couldn't get enough of the night sky, with them. After they oohed and aahed in front of the great pendulum at the observatory's main door, the device that marks the gravitational pull of the earth, I said to Jon, "If your planet Kolob is out there, would you mind pointing it out?"

He said nothing.

"It's supposed to be out there. Where do Wes and your leaders say it is? Between Pluto and Neptune, or what? Maybe the girls can help." The angels just stood off to the side, as if to say, what you're about to do is between you and your brother.

Jon refused to take any of my bait, but that was no reason not to press on: "You can't point to it or prove it's out there, can you?"

"Maybe not."

"But if that's the home of Heavenly Mother and Heavenly Father, you'd think that you'd have, you know, the coordinates, right?"

"I don't know, man," he replied.

"Not gotten to that lesson yet at the seminary?"

"There are a whole lot of lights out there. Stars and planets out there, many unnamed and untracked, so far. You can't *prove* it's *not* out there either," he said.

"No," I answered as I put my right arm around Tali and I draped my left about Aviva's smooth shoulders. "That's why these girls are so important, because down deep we know we may as well enjoy the loving down here because, well, like it or not, we are all alone in the universe."

"I don't feel alone. Not now. Not any more, and you don't have to either," he replied.

"You're doing it again."

"What?"

"That proselytizing thing. That's what I love about the Jews—maybe the only thing I still love about them—at least we leave other people alone."

We circumambulated the viewing area once again before we got back in the car and descended to the city below, but that interchange had pretty much ended the date.

I HAD told myself that when the appropriate time came I could lay Western Oaks out, despite his height, just knock the guy across his ward meeting room with an upper cut of my erudition to his oh-so-sure-of-himself jaw. Boy, would I ever show him the glaring self-contradictions of the faith he was foisting on my little brother. The comic-book bulb would illuminate above Jon's shorn head, and my Mormon problem would be solved.

Just to be sure, I decided it was time really to hit the books again, ours and *theirs*.

I'd already gone over representative passages in the *Book of Mormon*, many peeks of which I'd sneaked when Jon was out. Every other paragraph of Nephi's narration, for example, of the battles with the Lamanites (which word, unlike our Hebrew Bible's Moabites or Amalekites, always reminded me of plastics), was boring and ridiculous and to my ear rang very concocted and false.

On the other hand, the stories of the Hebrew Bible, especially the family tales, though likely not literarally true, seemed to derive from real events. You just get the feeling from how screwed up and complex the human relations are. I mean we're not called the *children* of Israel for nothing. All of the family jealousies, Joseph and his brothers, the fratricidal Jacob and Esau, and the infanticidal Abraham, with the father's knife raised over the heart of his child, whew! Even Adam and Eve were playing games with each other and ducking blame, or trying to, as far back as the Garden of Eden. Ah, my family members. Everywhere you look, such a mess of miscommunication; it just has to be true.

But not in the far-fetched Mormon tales. Here the world is only giants and ants, good guys and bad guys, darkness and light, God and Satan. Someone clearly passed down *our* biblical stories so maybe we could learn a thing or two about human relationships and not keep repeating the mistakes. On the other hand, *their* stories, the text of their new revelations, clearly show signs of having been cooked up, and by a not complex imagination at that.

For example, check out the style: Joseph Smith's text, allegedly translated from some ancient Egyptian script, has so many "And it came to pass" introductory phrases to each sentence or section—that's, by the way, a lazy translation of the Hebrew word *va-ye-hee*, which doesn't only suggest time passage but also causation and a true sense of before-and-after—well, all those repetitions, which are not the same as the Hebrew Bible's parallelisms, make the Mormon text feel like a high-school composition cribbed late at night, in a very rushed manner.

The cribber is also a creative plagiarizer who appears not even to care that much that he's been found out. Why else repeat the same old phrases and not have a character in sight who has a human dimension? Result: the entire reading experience is, as Thomas Jefferson said of the New Testament's Book of Revelation, "chloroform in print."

Far be it from me to overpsychologize, but maybe such was Joseph Smith's faith that he didn't care about dashing off all those "And it came to pass"-es. Maybe he *wanted* people to notice, to be caught on purpose in order to inflame, and to get attention among all the competing prophets in upstate

New York. There were so many of them preaching hellfire, damnation, and new worlds in the early 1800s, the prophet's hometown was in what a local wag termed the "burnt out" district.

But to just whom was I delivering these clever little sermons? Did I really expect that on the wings of my verbal distinctions Jon would come back to us? That on the literary style of the *Book of Mormon* or *Pearl of Great Price* the battle for my brother would be engaged and decided?

Yes, the power of self-denial was still very potent within me.

Jon had apologized profusely to Paulene for the Mormons' Sabbath intrusion, but his gesture had hardly mollified her. She saw how he was immersing himself in his early morning "seminary" and spending more and more time after camp and on weekends at Mormon social events. He didn't advertise it, but Jon clearly loved these after-work Mormon picnics and games down by Sorrento Beach at Santa Monica, and the more he went, the more Paulene appealed to me to stop him.

Yet how could I do that? By force? I will give it to the Mormons: What they lacked in sophistication and allure in cosmology they made up for in beach parties and in barbecuing.

Like me, Paulene could not help but notice all of the small changes that cumulatively were as alarming if not more so than Jon's new away-from-home schedule: the studiously maintained crewcut, the new preferences in his diet, the way he was cleaning up his vocabulary. Even the way Jon held himself was altering, with the slight introspective slouch of his shoulders somehow disappearing into something straighter, squarer, well, something more Mormon.

And there was more. I knew from hints that he was also studying, one on one, with Western Oaks over at the meeting house on Gregory Way. Yes, maybe conversion was coming faster than the timetable in my head.

And something else was in the offing. On one of the few nights we were home together I saw him sitting at the dining room table writing out, of all things, Hebrew.

From the hallway where I spied him, I could see he was well on his way to writing out the whole ancient alphabet, in block printing, several times. When I surprised him at this practice, he just leaned over and concealed his work.

Of course I had seen, and he had seen that I had seen. I think the angels were with me then because for a change I just transited on into the kitchen;

this time I made no comment, no joke, no snide remark. No words were even spoken, just a quick but charged stare. That's the way it had become between us, a summer of silent testing.

Yet in the days ahead, whatever he was up to, this little calligraphic pursuit really began to trouble me. I knew he was not doing it with the aim to re-enroll in Hebrew school.

No, a bar mitzvahed Jewish convert to Mormonism is a big catch, and I had the very uneasy feeling that Western Oaks was upping the ante, that he was exploiting Jon's knowledge of Hebrew; what's more, I suspected he also had something very special planned for him. My perfervid imagination saw Jon like some cross between a lifeguard and an LDS scribe, sitting with his stylus and tablet at the feet of the Mormon oxen's hooves at the baptismal font, with a bearded Joseph Smith dictating nearby.

The light began to hit the right place inside the dark, dark regions of my skull on another night when Jon pressed me once again about Paul's soul and offering him the Mormon gospel up in his celestial motel, and would I please think more about it, and did I mind?

"Of course I mind," I replied. "And Mom does, big time."

"But he didn't really belong to the temple, the Jewish temple. He belonged to . . . Santa Anita and to the Silver Dollar Casino over in Gardena and to . . . whatever casino he decided to go to."

"He was Jewish."

"He cared about gambling."

"He was a Jewish gambler then."

"All right, and it led him to a not very happy life."

"He's gone, Jon."

"No, he's not, and he deserves a chance at something better."

"You think they have casinos up there that you're going to save him from?"

"You know exactly what I mean."

In short, we were in deep trouble, and, to hear Paulene's version, the Jewish People were also in deep trouble as a result of Jon's percolating apostasy, and what was I, her big boy, her rabbi-to-be (!) really doing about it?

Despite what I had promised her—and with my own departure from professional Jewish life still a secret I could not bear telling her now—I felt morally unable either to justify what Jon was up to, or to condemn it with the ferocity she expected of me, or to confess to my mother why.

Under such circumstances what was such a flawed brother, son, member of the tribe and of the human species, such as myself, to do?

Naturally my next foolhardy gambit was—yes, once again, to go searching for as many of Jon's old joints as I could salvage from a stash that I was certain was still hidden in the garage behind the duplex. After all, how was my incipient Mormon brother going to dispose of that cool stuff? He certainly wasn't going to consume it now, or sell it. Turn it in to the LA cops? I guessed there were enough tightly packed joints there to support a rock band for several tours. No, I decided to help him through this problem by liberating all the Gould weed I could find for purposes of personal illumination.

It turned out that the carefully fashioned and neatly folded joints were well concealed inside several sixty-four-color Crayola Crayon boxes. I found every one of these delectable, mellow leftovers from Jon's fine pre-Saints life. If I could combine inhaling them with, as I have said, forgetting everything to do with religion and with God through wild Kama Sutra-esque sexual positions under the wings of the angels, I just might salvage a pretty good summer after all.

So, powered by a joint or two of Acapulco Gold before, during, and after camp, my denial still remained intact. I now harnessed it, however briefly, to sex. Well, to attempts at sex with the angels.

The strangest aspect of our early attempts at pairing up, Tali and Jon and Aviva and I, is that these strange girls, as I've intimated, found the whole exercise a little silly.

Take, for example, what used to happen at the Foot's condo. He was absent a lot—dating Mom, of course, or at the temple—so we had that place and no shortage of opportunity. And the angels had keys.

Irving Footlick's apartment featured a large sunken living room with shiny black-and-white floor tiles and gleaming black-and-white zebra-striped furniture upholstered in leather. By the furnishings you'd think the shul's capital campaign genius had had a previous career as a big-game hunter. There were also three bedrooms, if we were able to proceed beyond the perfect make-out den of the living room.

Yet Tali and Aviva seemed always to foil our, well, *my* plans, by arranging what we were doing—group activities and often with other counselors invited over as guests, always the darn group—so that what I was dreaming about with Aviva remained, at least for now, out of reach. Of course Jon liked it that way, the few times he joined us instead of going off to his usual after-work appointments with Wes, or off to the beach.

In addition to being like twins and always together, Tali and Aviva increasingly had this peculiar habit of chatting whenever I sat down next to either of them in private; it was as if they could read my dirty mind and that turned these otherwise quiet girls into sudden interrogators. They asked questions about the temple, our backgrounds, and particularly about our parents.

Paul and his gambling lifestyle were of special interest to them. Tali liked to hear me tell about Paul's snazzy suits and ties, about the greasy spoons our father had hung out at downtown, or about the Never Ending Bookstore on skid row off Pershing Square where he occasionally had picked up old poetry books for me and how I once made him stand on a chair and recite from one of those old tomes, Robert Browning's poem about Scotland's liberator, Robert Bruce. Or how he took us to the Pantry, a cavernous breakfast dive downtown, while he delivered to the owners their winnings from the track. Tali seemed to light up when I told her such stuff.

Aviva couldn't seem to get enough about Santa Anita, where the horses had so infrequently come in for Paul, or Gardena where he always just missed getting the one card he needed for that flush, or drawing to that full house over a big pot that would have subsidized a mink for Paulene and changed our lives.

" 'Full house!' I just love this word," Aviva said as if she were hearing it for the first time.

Why did those girls with fabulously smooth legs and dark eyes and . . . why did they seem so much more interested in stories of poker, horses, and of Paul than in us? That was the question.

Because Tali, Aviva, and Jon all just liked to keep it to sports and play it safe, they made me feel, well, like a predator. The marijuana of course contributed, but whenever I had an opportunity for, well, intimacy, I pursued it, and I frankly didn't care with which angel I might end up with on the couch.

Once when Jon and Aviva were playing badminton, Tali and I were sharing one large chaise longue together. Slowly, by gestures I sought not to seem as obvious and awkward as they were, I inched closer to her. I reached out and touched her beautiful clavicle where I asked her about the gold Star of David nestled there.

"May I examine it more closely?" I said in my jejune way.

She knew exactly what I was doing, dipped her gorgeous chest toward me, so there would be no misunderstanding, but then replied, "You do not wear one. Why is that?"

"Why are you so beautiful?"

"Jon doesn't wear one. No one in your family wears one. Why is that?"

"Do you know what I think is your most beautiful part?"

"Not even Ida, although she has one in her jewel box."

"How do you know that?"

"She wore it last in 1907, when the emperor Franz Josef rode by on his white horse."

"Really?"

"Yes, really, Norman."

"I'd say I love most where your jaw meets your . . ."

"Paul used to wear a Star of David."

"No, he didn't."

"Before you were born."

"How do you know *that*!"

"I know."

"You're a spy."

"Norman, do you know where *you* were before you were born?"

And that's how it went with the angels, splendid breasts and magnificent curving pelvises, and beautifully turned legs, and philosophy, and always the unexpected, increasingly having to do with our father.

Sometimes I felt Paul was actually sitting right there between Tali and me or between Aviva and me, and your father in that kind of situation is, well, a huge obstacle.

No, with Tali and Aviva there was never just harmless banter or goofing around, or easygoing teasing and taunting, horseplay, nuzzling, or unalloyed moments of frolic like you expect from normal girls. Their perfume and freshness, as if they were Eves just arrived from an Eden, made me crazy with desire, but there was always this complete absence of the small talk and kidding around that all the sex manuals said was the necessary prelude to love.

One evening while Jon and Tali were tossing the Frisbee out on the newly mown yard of the Foot's condo, I finally had managed to arrive at a moment of exciting making out, with Aviva.

My lips were a quarter inch from hers. Her mouth this night was shiny and Chapsticked and giving off a particularly inviting, sweet cherry flavor. Her lavender perfume had me swooning when I finally had the courage to press my lips against hers.

Instead of the fantastic experience I anticipated, I may well have been kissing a stop sign. Her shapely lips, opened to the size of a fascinating black pin hole, simply did not return my pressure; her mouth did not give, not even a puckering eighth of an inch. What's more, her eyes suggested that my attempt, the very gesture itself, was alien to her. Literally. In short, the whole experience gave little confidence to an insecure young man.

"Hey, what gives?"

"What do you mean?"

"What I just said: What gives!"

"Nothing."

"Yes, nothing. That's the problem. Am I doing it . . . wrong?"

"No. Well . . ."

"Let me try again."

"No."

"Out with it."

"It's just that . . . kissing is so . . . how do you say . . . weird."

"Maybe if you'll, you know, give it a try, you'll feel differently."

"Oh, I don't think so."

"I feel more warmth in a cup of coffee."

"I could brew you some. Mr. Footlick has an advanced Mr. Coffee with the latest fast-acting filtering technology. Based on that used in your space exploration program. Makes twelve cups in just a minute. Would you like a cup of coffee?"

"No, I would *not* like a cup of coffee!"

I was just so frustrated by how bizarre this was, and yet there had to be an explanation: they're Israelis, their English doesn't always say what they really mean, so, big deal, it's a little off, and they sound funny as if they are learning the language. And don't forget, I told myself further, they recently were involved in combat in the Six-Day War. Maybe something terrible happened, and that's why they're acting as they are, so strangely. Maybe they had a low-grade trauma-type injury that makes them like this. I'd show them softness and kissing again.

A child of the 1960s, I'd be love and peace personified. So I told myself.

I told myself a lot of things, and yet after another misfired and awkward attempt on the couch, when I felt I was nuzzling with a cool little marble statue, not a human female, Aviva put an arm's length between us and said, "Do you realize you're nibbling on my face?"

"That's what kissing is to you?"

"That's what it is to *you*."

"Well, what am I supposed to do?"

"Try closing your eyes."

"What?"

"Close your eyes. Now."

WHEN AVIVA commanded, especially in these physical matters, you'd better obey. And so I did.

Dear reader, nothing short of a spell followed. It began, almost immediately with a mixing of the senses of sound and smell and touch. It was like *Bolero*, that musical composition by Maurice Ravel whose notes begin far away, then grow and approach, and then it's excitingly resounding right in your ear and your heart's beating and it's all so irresistible.

I began to feel Aviva's presence, almost like a scent, not only in front of me but—it is hard to explain—all around, as if I were walking on a newly mown field of grass.

"I'm going to kiss you now, but your eyes must remain shut. That's the rule. Agreed?"

"Yes."

"I can tell you don't mean it."

"I do."

"You're peeking. You're a rule breaker."

"All right."

"Admit it."

"I do."

"Whenever you can get away with it."

"Yes. Whatever you say."

"Maybe now we're getting somewhere. You find me beautiful?"

"Very."

"Truth is also beautiful."

"Closed?"

When I finally complied and Aviva began to execute her kiss upon me, or at least I think she did, there was a touch so chaste and cherubic I barely felt anything, only a rustling and quiet breathing all around. The kiss was, well, more cerebral than physical; yet it also made me feel suddenly secure and warm and relaxed beyond measure. Had something happened?

"You may now open your eyes."

When I did, I heard the most remarkable thing I'd ever heard a girl or anyone say to me, after a kiss: "When humans were wet with their clay, they were kissed right here, each one."

She moved closer. She touched it again, the soft spot between the septum of the nose and the upper lip. "Right there. He touched."

"Who touched?"

"You know who."

I swear I didn't really know who she was talking about. I didn't know who the who she referred to was, but I was afraid I might know. Still I liked this game. Or I willed an ignorance. So I played on. "He kissed right here?"

"Exactly. The Lord God of Hosts."

"I don't remember that from school."

"Nevertheless, it's true."

"Let's try it again, so I can be sure."

"You're sure. You just don't want to admit it."

"Want to bet?"

"The Lord of all creation. Breathing in the breath of life. That's the sign of it, where His lips touched yours, the depression in the clay."

"Oh, of course. Excuse me for not catching your drift."

"You do now?"

"Because you're such a good teacher."

"And now you've got a job to do."

"A job? I'm staying right here. Kissing away."

"No, you're not."

"Come near me again."

Sitting, without moving, still as a human statue, she said, "Everyone has to do their part, Norman. Or it falls and it . . . crumbles."

"Yes, yes. Crumble right here, near me."

"Your father, your mother, your brother. Each person has a role to play. Or it all falls apart. And you're not even a very good counselor at camp. You think only of yourself. You have much to repair, and to understand. You could start there."

"Maybe tomorrow."

"There are forces at work."

"Yes, I know. I can barely contain myself. I'm going to explode."

"Not that, you silly boy. Talk to the kids more. Stop sneaking out for those hamburgers."

With that, the spell was definitely broken.

Aviva became, as suddenly as she had been transformed, just a girl again, and an irritating one at that. Telling me what to do, and where and when to eat. Sneaking out was my business.

An unexpected, peevish anger began to surface within me. I was surprised, but there it was: I'd had enough of this kind of talk in New York and I told her so. I ran through my whole litany of independence from theological gobbledygook, and mortals' responsibility to God, to . . . to whatever, to the whole bill of particulars. Breathing the breath of life into my clay. Really! She had to be kidding. I did not want Jonah or Lord God of Hosts—by the way, a military term—well, whoever the hell He was these days, to interfere with of all things my kissing this incredible female, or for His Honor to be in the room with us, or even in the house, in the county, or in the golden state of California, or in the entire west coast. God, go, please go somewhere else. Go to . . . Nevada or Salt Lake City, Utah, where you will please bother the Mormons, or to another part of the country, and leave Aviva and me, Tali and me, just the two of us, or the three of us, alone, together.

That was my thought. I didn't say it all aloud, maybe a part, or a big harrumph of it. Aviva nevertheless had heard it.

"Impossible."

"Not for me it isn't. You're an Israeli," I pleaded with her. "Look at what you've done in the war. By your own might, not by God's. This time not by some weird outstretched arm at the Red Sea, but by air power, courtesy of American-made jets. Oh, leave God out of it. Now I'd like to kiss you again. I know what to do now. You've taught me. How about we resume?"

She leaned slightly in my direction, as warm as the Leaning Tower of Pisa. "Give it a try then."

So I did.

In my fashion I kissed her. She let me linger longer this time, as I brushed her lips and inhaled her cherry-flavored scent, and her remoteness, wrapped in fabulous fantasies and promises unfulfilled but not yet outrightly denied. It all made my approach, well, perhaps sloppier than before. On the angel-kissing learning curve, I was still a C student, but unlike other educational venues I'd attended, I *wanted* to be here. Oh, most definitely. Nothing, no rabbi, no tribunal could get me away. I pulled her toward me, determined to topple over on the couch and to have the feel of Aviva's calves resting on the back of my legs, her fabulous pelvis beneath me, holding me like a bowl does fruit.

Of course that's when she pulled away as if she had just remembered she had an appointment at the hairdresser.

"Another time, perhaps, if you obey," and she nearly leaped up and skipped across the yard to join Tali and Jon at their game.

WHAT COULD I do, but follow?

So as Jon and Aviva hit the birdie high—they had now switched to playing badminton—catching it on their rackets and slamming it back at each other with fine skill on each side of the red mesh net, I took my seat beside Aviva on the verdant lawn. I let my knee just barely touch hers, still hopeful as a pet awaiting his supper, and watched my brother and Tali play.

Although Jon and Tali shared the pool duties and swam together often at camp and in the Foot's pool or challenged each other over and over again at sports events at camp, just like here on the badminton court, it was instantly clear that if Jon felt toward Tali the way I did toward Aviva, he certainly wasn't showing it. Again and again he was blowing this fabulous opportunity by not even trying.

They were with each other like a couple of friendly jocks. They sent the birdie high in the air and then even higher, and their display of skill was such that it didn't even occur to me to ask to play. I just wanted to sit there beside Aviva, and she didn't mind my leaning on her, grazing, as it were, on the cool beauty of her skin. Some minutes passed—I couldn't tell you if it was two or twenty—and for me they were a kind of sensual pleasure of time I have never experienced since.

Then Aviva announced that "The Price Is Right" or some such inane program about shopping was on TV. Just like that.

Tali dropped her racket, came over, and yanked Aviva up from the grass with a powerful hand-to-wrist life-saving-training grip, and they were gone. They were sprawled out—so I imagined it—on the Foot's black-and-white leather sofas in front of his huge TV—watching and laughing and expressing an interest in those proceedings with an enthusiasm I had hoped to engender in them for me, but I had obviously failed. Jon too had failed but by not even trying.

Boy, for angelic creatures, they were certainly into shopping and TV, and, if memory serves, the sillier the better. They particularly liked shows where the women jumped up and down and screamed mindlessly about the prizes they hoped to win.

With that, our "date" was definitely over. Jon and I said good-bye to the girls who now barely acknowledged us as they sat together, sharing the zebra-esque hassock only about now just a foot away from the TV screen. They waved distractedly good-bye back to us, as if they didn't want to miss a second of their program.

We closed the condo door and began to walk back across the wide green expanse of lawn to the street to where our old oil-guzzling Nash Rambler was parked; Paul had bought that tank of a car for one hundred fifty bucks years before.

Past a small bougainvillea-scented trellis at the corner of the property we walked, moving in that silence that you always worry is a preamble to some kind of blowup.

Jon looked back to the Foot's apartment complex, leaned against the front fender of our car, and said, "It's really something, isn't it, hanging out with the two of them!"

"I'll say."

"But I can't keep doing it."

"You ready to explode?"

"No, man. You're not getting it."

"No? What am I not getting?"

"They're very strange girls."

"They are. You think maybe they're old for us? Mature? That's what I've been thinking: How to get around that?"

"Not me."

"No?"

"That's not it. Not at all."

"So what is it?"

When he didn't answer immediately, and instead just looked dreamily away and back at the now sun-dappled condo complex, as if it were receding in the distance, I just ran on with my theories. "Maybe they've had all that experience, you know, in the war, battling the Arabs. They're warriors, man. They're like . . . a couple of Hebrew-speaking Amazons. I'd like to find out if they have only one fabulous, magical breast under there after all. Wouldn't you?"

He looked at me, not unlike Aviva had, as if I were crazy.

"I know they have two. Twice the fun, right? Come on, Norman."

"No, really. They're soldiers and they never talk about it. What they went through. I've asked, and they both refuse to say a word. Maybe they're, like, Green Berets, sworn to secrecy about their missions. That you must have noticed. Who knows the people they had to shoot . . . at close range . . . what they encountered and had to live through. It'd make anyone standoffish."

"You've been watching too many war movies."

"What then?"

"What they're saying to me is exactly what the Saints are: that the time has passed for thinking nonstop just about pawing girls."

"I was afraid you might say that."

"Well, I have, and it's true."

You could hear the insects buzzing and sniping at each other; maybe they had trouble in their families.

"You're in charge of your life," Jon said as he took off his glasses and cleaned them, as if to indicate that he was seeing clearly, and guess who wasn't? He put his glasses back on. "And, news flash, man: I'm in charge of mine."

"But in Tali don't you see what you've got. She's like a Playmate of the Month. No, better. A Miss January to Miss December all rolled into one fabulous Israeli babe, and you're throwing it all away?"

"Not what I'm about now. The Mormon way. In thought and in deed so your spirit is pure when it returns."

"Returns where?"

"To Dodger Stadium! Where do you think, Norman? To heaven. When the soul returns to where it was born, and messing around with these girls is not a stop along the way. I can't keep doubling with you like this. I'm sorry, man."

"Not as sorry as I am. It's depressing the way you turn everything into heaven talk."

"Never enough of heaven."

"Says who? You?"

Jon just stared at me.

"Oh, *them*."

"That's right, man. The point is the body is the temple of the soul, so like I said I've been cleaning up. First, the garage, then the kitchen with finally eating right, and the living room, and now I've gotten around to the bedroom. So that's it."

"What's it?"

"I'm not doing it anymore."

"It?"

"That's right."

"You mean 'It'? Screwing?"

"Don't act this way with me, don't . . . try to rub my face in it. I'm not a dog in need of training, man! So, yes. Not until I get sealed forever in marriage."

"Well, that's some of the saddest news I've heard in a very long time."

He took out a big blue handkerchief from the pocket of his jeans and almost ceremonially flapped it open. I could see it must have been very neatly folded, perhaps even ironed. With it he now began shining the top of the Rambler's hood.

I watched in growing dismay, my eyes focused on that handkerchief. Jon had never had folded handkerchiefs in his pocket, except maybe on the day of his bar mitzvah. Like me, like the rest of us in the messy world, the pocket had maybe balled up handkerchiefs or Kleenex. But now a handkerchief neat as a ritual cloth. The Mormons were now in Jon's back pocket?

As he shined the hood of the Rambler, he said, without looking directly at me, but as if he were talking to the engine of the car, "A little abstinence simplifies a lot in life. Unties knots, makes it far easier to look a girl in the eye instead of the chest. If I had a nickel for each time I saw you checking out Tali as if she were the next cheeseburger you wanted to devour, I'd . . ."

"Get out!"

"I'd be a rich man."

"Yes, and then stupid enough to give it all to your church."

"I'll just act as if you didn't say that."

After an interval that seemed torturous, Jon spoke again: "What's saddest is that you seem just to not *want* to know what this really means to me."

"Please don't go proselytizing. You're no Mormon yet."

"Soon enough."

"Not if I can help it. You're just running scared. You're scared and lost, like me. You feel you're drowning, you're flopping your arms around, and this spare tire of the Mormons happens to float by and you lunge for it."

"I'm a very good swimmer, if you haven't noticed."

"Not in these waters, pal."

"I don't want to fight with you, Norman."

"The Hare Krishnas. You've done it before. It'll blow over."

"It's not like that."

"Let's embrace doubt. I mean doubt is about as groovy as living gets. Love doubt!"

"How? By eating it every afternoon topped with bacon and cheese?"

"Doubt can be the basis of very good times, yes. And *that* I will help you with. Big time. Come on. You're just a little scared. I'll take care of you. You'll see."

"I'm not scared."

"Then you're lying to yourself. Everybody's scared. I mean, *that's* the basis of faith, isn't it? Religion's dirty little secret. The deeper the doubt the bigger the edifice that's built over it. The Catholics built the highest cathedrals, and now the Mormons outdo them. They build a cathedral right into the precincts of heaven. Go down to the basement with me, man. It's cool there. We can hide, real well. You'll see."

"Are you high?"

"Don't I wish. Everybody's scared and hiding. Mainly from Mr. Death. He's a very bad dude."

"Says you."

"Says Bob Dylan: '. . . The next time you see me comin', you better run. Well, Abe said, 'Where d'you want this killin' done?' God said, 'Out on Highway 61.'"

"I'm not hiding. Not me. Not any more. I'm not scared. I'm excited."

"First you turn in your brain, then your taste buds, and now your pecker. What do you have to do? Wrap it up in some official gear, a sacred Mormon codpiece sent to you by Wes and by the bishops? Then they unwrap it in a secret ceremony when you get married!"

"Dial it down, man. You're way out of line."

"Sure I am. But what's next? Oh, your money. Once you're official, they tithe you, which is a scam Dad would really have admired. Quite an operation. And, by the way, please leave Paul and his soul out of it. Congratulations on your new religion!"

By then Jon had rightly had enough of my mockery; he announced he was going to drive to Santa Monica where the Mormon crowd was having a cookout.

He neatly folded that handkerchief up again, replaced it in his pocket, and then offered to give me a ride home first.

"Hey, man, have a good time," I called, as I started walking down Olympic toward home alone. I didn't care if it took me two hours. I could use a good, long walk.

I wasn't proud about what I had said, but there it was. I hated what Jon was doing, but what right had I to stop it? So then why was I being such an asshole? I was missing something and I couldn't see it, let alone understand it. I paused; I took a few more steps. I heard my heart beating. Was I really walking away? From my only brother? Points of no return can be crossed very quietly, without your even knowing. I was on my guard; was this that moment? Maybe.

Yet what to do now? Apologize? My apologies were growing numerous, and thin.

No, I'd go home as usual. I was lousy company for everyone but a deaf old lady. I'd have a couple of grilled cheese sandwiches with Ida. The Angels, that is, the baseball team, were playing the Padres tonight; maybe the game would be on TV.

I had taken perhaps three more angry steps toward home when I felt an arm on my shoulder. Yes, it was my good brother. Jon just nodded back toward the car, whose passenger side door he had flung open.

"You're coming to the cookout with me. Go on. Get in."

15

THOUGH the Saints' theology and doctrines, their ceremonies and haberdashery, as I came to understand them, were woefully derivative (including lots borrowed from the Masons as well as from the Jews) and although these LDS notions were also, on the one hand, as bland and intellectually nonnutritious as a dollop of coleslaw, and as crazy as a banana split, still their appreciation of grilled meat was a different matter altogether.

We Jews know how to do *matzah* and corned beef, the food of people who remained for generations at the bottom of the food chain.

Not so the devotees of Joseph and Brigham. Though refugees like the Jews, the Mormons' sojourn in the American desert was far shorter than the two generations of Moses' wanderings—and, incidentally, I never bought the rabbinic gloss that the forty years of wanderings were part of God's plan so that old generations with the slave mentality of Egypt could die out and younger, freedom-loving, kick-ass Jewish warriors might emerge.

No way. Who were the rabbis kidding?

Here's what happened, and it's no Jewish joke: Moses just took one wrong turn after another. Then he asked his exasperated wife for corrective directions, and she got it wrong as well. Then it was Aaron's turn to get it wrong. The brothers fought as to who could be more wrong! This way, not that. No, that way, not this. God's mountain is there! Are you nuts? That little fog-covered midden?

They may as well have been on Mars, except they had air and could breathe. Result: another wrong turn and then another, forty years' worth. Yes, God had promised them the place, but no wonder when they arrived at the gates of the Canaanite cities, they were full of murderous rage and ready to conquer.

No, these Mormons were different. These were, after all, only Conestoga wagon refugees or handcart refugees for six months or so, or as long as it took to journey from Nauvoo in Illinois to the Great Salt Lake. Fleeing their Egypt in the Midwest to their nineteenth-century Zion, they had become pioneers whose profound heritage included all the ins and outs of hunting and cooking and surviving on the prairie. Thus they evolved a deep oral tradition, practically a Talmud's worth of direction and commentary on how to host a terrific barbecue.

London broil, spare ribs, empanadas, carne asada, burgers and dogs, of course, and meat in its many cuts and varieties—including an impressive palate of zesty marinades and sauces the Mormons had brought back from their missionarying around the globe—all that had created a cookery to me both novel and appealing.

It wasn't Ships, but it wasn't bad at all.

We didn't talk about it driving onto the freeway and cruising toward Santa Monica. I wasn't convinced that Jon's physical discomfort with the angels had to do only with his newfound Mormon abstinence. Maybe something else had happened between him and Tali, but he offered no clue. He just drove and let me direct my punches at the radio buttons until I found something I liked.

We had to pull over just past Sepulveda and get off to put two quarts of oil in the Rambler. We did that chore in silence and were soon flying west again on the Number 10 out toward the beach. Bob Dylan's "Mr. Tambourine Man" and "Like a Rolling Stone" accompanied us on the radio, and as we raced along we even sang a little together.

We both really didn't know that Tali and Aviva were just now huddling up to assert their influence once again.

We took the slow curving off-ramp onto the Pacific Coast Highway and soon we were pulling into a parking spot at the Sorrento Beach section of Santa Monica. As we walked across the still-warm sands, something made me stop and look up. Here were the high coastal bluffs where Wilshire Boulevard runs into an ocean-view park some two hundred feet above the beach. It was as if I had never truly seen these bluffs before, how the land could just, well, stop, and go ninety degrees straight down to the highway and the surf.

Nearby was a plaque commemorating the harbor's Spanish discovery that I suddenly remembered from a school trip. Near the plaque was a big polished black cannon beside a pile of cannon balls, with the whole artillery ensemble pointing menacingly out to sea.

When I was very little Paul once had sat me on top and said, "Ride that cannon ball, son. Ride it out to sea."

What a peculiar thing for him to have said, and for me to remember now.

As we walked toward the Mormon action, I could also see the white lights and even make out the musical tinklings of the merry-go-round on the Santa Monica Pier in the distance; that had been the destination of one of our rare outings when we still seemed to be a normal family.

"Just remember: behave yourself," Jon said, not as reprimand but as a lighthearted kind of joke. That was good. That was a good sign, and was I ever in need of it.

Then he took off jogging ahead of me eager to see his new Mormon friends.

When I arrived, they were busying themselves about several picnic tables all laid out in swaths of red and white checkered oilcloth; I noticed a cute girl planting herself in front of Jon to greet him. They chatted for an instant, he pointed me out to her, and the next thing I knew she was before me introducing herself.

From the way she treated me, it was instantly clear that once again and, to my great displeasure, Jon had spread the word that I was a rabbinic student. It was embarrassing how, well, deferential this girl was, as a result, as if I were this instant an honored guest.

The girl—Mary Anne Rogers was her name—had long sandy blonde hair tucked under a Dodgers baseball cap. Needlessly, she apologized for the pork that was cooking away and filling my nostrils with pleasurable aromas. Then she said she'd fill my plate with other stuff, and not to worry about going hungry for not wanting to violate the dietary laws.

Oh, I wasn't worried at all, I told her, as I had Western Oaks. I could eat anything and everything, and would.

I tapped my fat belly. "Here's the proof."

"Not bad," she said, as she tapped it back. "But you are a rabbi?"

"A new kind of rabbi."

"Meaning?"

"Oh, you know. New and improved. Like you Mormons are a new and improved version of Christianity."

Mary Anne tipped back her cap, as if deciding whether to take my bait. She did, and I liked that. "Mormons are new because they go way back to what's old and true, the original teachings that the fathers of the church let slip away in the early years. Our prophets rediscovered them."

"If you like going back to the original, you may as well just become a bunch of Jews."

"Jon warned us about arguing with you."

"What else did he say?"

"That you like to eat."

"Obviously."

She just laughed and escorted me toward the food tables.

What a contrast with Aviva and Tali was this amiable chatting. This was easy, this was no interrogation at all. This Mormon girl was direct and straightforward. She appeared to have no agenda, no guile. She talked about Jon and then about her brother, Tim, now a missionary in, of all places, Albania, and how she wished she could be in touch with him more than the single phone call at Christmastime, which was the only communication allowed the missionaries to their families. Whoa! She talked about how siblings are at the same time so different yet also so alike. Probably just like you and your brother, she said.

As Mary Anne introduced me around, I began to wonder if this girl really was, his protestations to the contrary, Jon's Mormon romantic interest. Had Paulene guessed right all along? That would explain a lot. And it would also just maybe give us both a strategy, something to *do* to stop Jon's Mormon drift; I couldn't be sure.

As we talked, I saw Jon standing a short distance away talking animatedly with Wes. They were chatting behind a line of blue coolers and beside a pile of driftwood that some of the other Mormon guys were adding to from along the beach. It was, I assumed, for a bonfire to come.

I noticed the guys tending to the grill and the wood and the girls to the tables as the Mormons tended to group by gender; but here, of course, Mary Anne was talking to me. Maybe I was her assignment. I didn't care. I was suddenly very relaxed, as she asked me, not about the seminary, but about how New York is different from LA, and, do I miss the Pacific coast. When I pointed out that New York has quite an ocean, well, she just smiled and said one day she hoped to go see it.

She stood with her strong stout hip thrust out, and her sunglasses raised now over the brown UCLA Bruin medallion on her cap, and darn if just about every dumb remark that came out of my mouth, no matter how loopy or banal, she just somehow took in and seemed to consider, as if I actually meant what I was saying.

What a remarkable take she had on my conversation. In no time I felt my edge of cantankerous irony, if not abate, then grow, as we used to say back then, a lot more mellow. Heck, I was thinking, maybe I should just get over the remote, standoffish, mysterious Tali and Aviva and find myself a Mormon girlfriend.

I set to work helping Mary Anne and the others lay out matching red-and-white-checked cloth napkins on several picnic tables. Then I helped in collecting more driftwood to add to the pile that was already becoming a nicely burning fire.

There were other tasks to do, and everyone pitched in with an easy camaraderie. As the sun dipped in the west, people slipped on sweaters or sweatshirts. When Mary Anne saw I had not brought one, she fished out a thick green flannel shirt from a nearby communal duffel and tossed it to me. It was just the right size and snug against the wind that was beginning to blow in off the harbor.

The Mormons were prepared, and we were soon warming ourselves in front of a crackling big bonfire. Over at the barbecue area orchestrating the disposition of the burgers, chicken wings, and sausages were Elder Oaks and that convert-in-training Jon Gould in animated talk.

Even while Mary Anne engaged me, I now wondered—a frisson of paranoia about the Saints was never far from my mind—if she had been specifically assigned to be with me and to *distract* me. If so, I could understand because, accidental guest though I was, I very much felt myself also on assignment. I was on a surveillance of another variety: I was not about to let my brother wander far from my field of vision.

As I caught glimpses of him in the firelight, what was most surprising was the big smile on Jon's face. It seemed to me that was the first genuine, relaxed smile I'd seen on him since he had greeted me at the airport a month ago; that smile was a kind of reproof that saddened me, and also made me troubled.

At a couple of other things I also marveled: first, how sociable and talkative Jon seemed here in a way he no longer was with us at home, or at camp. And then there was long tall Wes, whose nearness Jon seemed to be always seeking in the group of Saints and their friends.

When Wes walked over to begin working the grill, Jon followed. I followed at a distance but also watched closely.

How carefully and precisely Elder Oaks was lining up the sausages, wings, and patties across the large double-shelved barbecuing surfaces. The meat appeared organized into at least three different areas, which I took to be rare, medium, and well done. He was even-ing them into neat, equidistant rows and moving them around, spatula deployed and then raised above them like the baton of a choirmaster.

I was more nervous than I thought I was and suddenly felt, as I often had in school before delivering my student sermons, how we were taught in homiletics to go for the humor as an opening gambit. Yet it's dicey if you don't strike the right tone, and that happened often; it comes out only awkward, not amusing at all.

It actually crossed my mind now to say: Wes, I'm checking out the three quadrants on your grill there and I'm wondering if they reflect the three levels of heaven as you Mormons conceive them: rare heaven, medium, and a heaven that's so well done, it's downright the residence of God Himself. What do you think?

Thankfully, what came out was merely, "Why is it, Wes, that you and I always seem to meet around food?"

"And why not?"

"Why not indeed. Last time it was at our Sabbath meal, if I recall."

He just shrugged and shook his head at my taunt, as if to say, although he didn't actually say it, that others, and not he, had knocked on the door that Friday night. Then he invited me closer to see his handiwork at the grill. Wes extended the long barbecuing fork my way, and on its end was a delectable foretaste of the feast to come. I removed the sausage morsel he'd speared for me, and I bit.

"Beautiful," I said. "Crispy skin on the outside and moist inside, very much to my liking."

"Plenty more to come, Norman. We're glad you're here to join us."

"I'm here, but joining is not in the picture."

Wes continued to grill and to offer me little tastes of the chicken, and now a hot dog, a moist and beautifully seared portion of a burger, and I took them all. When Mary Anne handed me a napkin to wipe my fingertips I realized I was the only one in the entire group who had begun to eat.

The Mormons were refraining and waited for the formal meal to start with the blessing that was required before eating.

But not for me, not for this lapsed rabbi. For me the swallows of carne asada and London Broil, and, well, just about anything that they sent my way were fine just the unblessed way they came.

"You only say the Jewish blessing if you're actually sitting down at the table," I averred, making it all up as I went along. "*Noshing,* that is, nibbling, is blessing-free. Any of you folks can define the technical, religious term *nosh*? Please raise your hand."

"See what I mean," Jon said to his Mormon pals.

Blessed or unblessed, it was not long before my mouth was agreeably full of the tastes of broil and bake, a chicken and then a beef empanada, then a burger piled high with tomato, romaine, and blue cheese dressing.

My oh my, those first bites do live on in memory.

And I trust you also will not be surprised to hear that soon I was assisting Wes with the long-handled fork, spatula, and other tools of the barbecuing trade as I entered into my brief culinary life among the Mormons. Of course I had a good time as I stuffed myself—and yet, as you shall also see, there was a method to my gustatory madness.

"Wes," I said, as I looked up to him, "have you ever thought of the different ways history could have turned out if your predecessors had forbidden pork-eating, say, instead of coffee and similar stimulants? Then Mormons wouldn't be such calm, clean-cut fellows like yourself, but jittery Jews like me."

"You deal in many stereotypes, my friend. I don't think of you as either jittery or as a Jew."

"No?"

"But aren't these Hebrew National hot dogs you're grilling in *my* honor?"

That's the way it was. Each time I offered a barb or threw down the gauntlet, or tried to point out a silly contradiction or oversimplification, they, well, acknowledged it without a battle so that a tone of easy banter prevailed among us.

Mary Anne was also usually nearby to give me a friendly elbow in the ribs.

It was all too welcoming to be true. I thought maybe it was all part of their devious plan. Or, was it possible that this is the way it is among them all the time?

Because I was on guard, well fed, and enjoying my unopposed and immature cleverness, I stupidly upped the ante: "Tell me, Wes, you happen to know why the major Jewish communities around the world have developed in port cities like here in LA?"

"We're about to learn," said Jon.

"Is it because Jews are great mariners? No. Is it because they're great merchants, commercial geniuses? Maybe. In part. But the real reason is . . ."

"To make a quick escape, right?"

"Wes, you get an A in Jewish history."

"Are you already checking out the exits?"

"Have been for a while."

"Got his route carefully planned out," said Jon.

"I guess Jews just have it in their genes to feel threatened."

"You got that right, Wes."

"Can I offer you another burger before you flee?"

"Maybe he should have it 'to go,'" said Jon.

"I'm not going anywhere. Threaten me all you want. Who's got the mayo?"

"You know as far as being threatened and persecuted, that's the Mormon story," said Wes. "Big time. Although we settled not on coasts but inland, near a dead sea just like in the original Zion, a place where no one would be crazy enough to come to try to uproot us."

"Oh? What about the United States Cavalry?" I ranted on as Wes and I cooked and Jon hung out nearby with Mary Anne. "I'd like to point out that your Zion analogy with the Jews gets a little murky because the place you Mormons settled, Utah, wasn't a no-man's-land at the time. Nope. Not at all. It just happened to be territory that belonged to the United States of America, which the Mormons only recognized when it was convenient. Am I right or am I wrong, Wes?"

"You're always right, Norman. And always a little wrong," Wes replied as he jauntily flipped a patty. "Don't forget those Amorites, Perizzites, all the Canaanite guys you showed the exit to. Remember Joshua?"

"Oh, very well. But I'm sorry, man; it's not the same thing at all. You Mormons set up a kingdom, a theologically based *new* government right in the middle of your own country, in the middle of a United States-owned territory. You're telling me the feds don't have a right to be pissed off? To send in the cavalry?"

"Oh, it's much more complicated than that," Mary Anne said.

"I'm sure it is," I replied.

"But then came the locusts," Jon chimed in. "That's the most amazing part. They got to the crops, and a real miracle was needed. You know *that* story?" he directed his question my way but didn't trust me enough to wait for my concocted answer. "So God sends the gulls all the way from the sea to eat the locusts and to save those first crops. A thousand miles, man. That's a long way for a seagull to fly."

"Truly amazing," I said.

Of course, what was truly amazing wasn't so much the strange and unexpected arrival of the hungry gulls.

Rather, it was how my brother now sounded spouting such fairy tales. I could not recall, even when we as little kids were attending Hebrew school at Temple Beth Ami, that little Jonathan Gould had ever been nearly as fascinated by, oh, for example, Moses striking a rock and, lo and behold, water gushes forth. Or the sudden parting of the Red Sea before Moses fleeing the Egyptian charioteers. What was there about the Mormons and their magical sea gulls and Disneyland heaven that made him so susceptible to their silly theology?

"God of course already had practice sending the locusts to destroy the crops in Egypt," I said, with a big nod to Jon. "Remember Passover?" I ventured as I scored a small succulent pork chop from Wes's grill to keep my evil Jewish demons, at least for the moment, properly fed and at bay.

The moment did not last very long, like maybe two seconds, because I just kept running on: "All of Christianity—and the Mormons are Christians, are they not, Mr. Oaks?—from the very beginning liked to write up stories to make it seem as if they were already hinted at, prophesied in the Hebrew Bible. Prefiguration and all that. Gives a cool pedigree, right? The Mormons are no different."

"Hold on there, buddy," countered Wes from beneath the tall chef's toque that Mary Anne had just handed to him. "Because in America you find not the new and improved but a whole new ball game, a totally new revelation, a brand-new story that caught all the early Christian errors."

"He forgot his first lesson already," said Mary Anne.

Pointing his fork heavenward for extra emphasis, Wes added, "I'd also say, as regards Jewish teachings, the new doesn't invalidate the old. It's just new."

"Then why not let people alone and not try to convert them?" I mumbled with a mouth full of pork.

Have I mentioned that in the interval between talking with Mary Anne and watching Wes from a distance fire up his grill, I had surreptitiously fired up another of Jon's joints kept in my pocket for just such socially demanding occasions?

Well, I did.

Maybe that explains what a poke-holes-in-Mormon-doctrine rant I was now on, and, alas, like the waves crashing on the beach, I just kept slamming away.

"All right, brother," I said to my very own true brother, "I see your gulls and your insects, and I'll raise you by their souls. All of them. That's right. What about the souls of the locusts that those gulls ate? And for that matter, the souls of the gulls ? 'And God created all of the flying creatures, all those quick with life that fly in the heavens and crawl on the earth.' Says so in the first chapter of Genesis. Wes, do Mormons believe animals have souls? Insects? Give it some thought and pass along the suggestion to the Quorum of Twelve and the Prophet, man."

I was getting that look again from the both of them, and I surely deserved it. But who cared? As they paused—I felt as if they were getting ready to send me to the principal—yet on I went.

"See what your big guys think if you can't make up your mind yourself. You could grab millions of souls and do it really efficiently if you included, you know, bugs and birds. Hey, man, why not algae, bacteria, amoebas! Think of it: a whole new offshoot, a Mormon Church of One-Celled Creatures. There's a lot of target populations out there."

"That's about enough, Norman," my brother said. "More than enough."

And of course he was right.

Yet here was Wes coming to my side, sort of. "No, no, no," he chided Jon, but gently as if he were in so doing really trying to deliver a lesson on how to deal with a Gentile's obnoxious behavior.

"We're never fearful of challenges. The teaching is that only beings capable of moral action have souls," Wes said as he turned and now repositioned a well-marbled New York flank steak to the corner of the grill.

"And, my friend, I believe you already knew that."

"You got me again, Wes."

"Nobody is trying to 'get' you."

"You sure?"

"Thing is, we revere the Jews."

"That again! You *revere* us? Aren't you, uh, gilding the lily a bit, Mr. Oaks?"

"If it weren't for the gumption and daring of those original Hebrew refugees fleeing the Babylonians' destruction of the temple back in 586 BC, and crossing to the Americas, well, where would the Mormons be?"

"I don't know. Maybe Mars? Tahiti?"

"Always joking," said my brother ruefully.

"Right," replied Wes. "Without them, we might all be Methodists or something."

THIS BANTER had its point because, as I've reported, all its skating around super-sensitive edges kept the tone polite enough and also disguised my deep indecisiveness about God, the Jews, and just about everything except cheeseburgers. Hell, for all I knew maybe I should succumb and try out a little simple-minded Mormonism myself. First you consume their pork chops, then fall on bended knee in front of one of their women, then you consume their ideas. Isn't that always the way it happens?

After an hour of enjoyable hanging out and good eats I tried a little more to suss out whether Mary Anne or one of the other Mormon babes really had her eye on Jon, or he on any of the half dozen wholesome, clean-cut, demurely dressed females at this beach party.

Maybe because my mouth was so full, my eyes just didn't see. That wouldn't have been surprising.

By about eight o'clock, I decided I'd had enough. I was going to leave and take the Rambler home as Jon said Wes could easily drive him back to Orange Grove.

Maybe if I hadn't been such a pork pig I would have left five minutes sooner. But the aroma of the meat simmering beneath the stars and the rhythm of the waves landing were so delicious, so hypnotic. There was always one more bite to taste, and then one more, and one more.

I stayed on, and as a result our lives that night changed forever.

Wes handed his barbecuing tools to Mary Anne, and he and Jon walked me over to the bonfire, whose flames now were leaping into the night sky several yards from the grilling. I guess they figured I needed, well, some kind of companionship, and they weren't wrong at all.

There beside the fire the three of us sat down, enjoying the warmth for a long, silent interval. After two, maybe three, minutes, it began to feel like a contest: which of us two talky folks, Wes or yours truly, would open his yap first.

None of the other Mormons and their friends or conversion prospects or whoever the party consisted of that night, was by the fire, just us.

This was curious and made me wonder if something planned were indeed unfolding, if the other Mormon shoe—make that a boot—were about to fall. I sat between Jon and Wes reclining comfortably in a roomy blue-and-white-striped beach chair, but I was anything but comfortable. The waves seemed to be hitting the beach with more thunder than usual; the sparks flew off the logs, flitted about, and then extinguished against the darkening sky.

I was ripped.

Now Jon shifted in his chair and removed a sheet of white paper from the back pocket of his Bermudas.

It looked like *that* sheet.

He unfolded it, rather solemnly, and handed it to me.

I took a glance. It was. Just like the one I'd noticed on Wes's table at the stake building. I braced myself.

"You sure you want to be handing this to me?"

"Please read."

There at the top of the form in English was Paul's name. At the bottom, to my consternation, was Paul's name in tall, awkward, letters in black ink in Jon's handwriting, and placed in a rectangular space. And they were block-printed in Hebrew.

It looked like a motor vehicle registration form. Yet it wasn't. The document was the ordinance, the Mormons' official document naming Paul Gould's soul as one to whom they would like to offer the gospel in telestial heaven or in the heaven above or below that. Or maybe it was to echo up in the anteroom to heaven in southeastern Missouri hard by the Garden of Eden, or wherever they had located our fugacious dad's evanescent essence, or however they defined the frisky little corpuscle they called his soul.

That is, it was the document to trigger Paul's proxy baptism.

Jon had intimated about this document before, how it required, optimally, two close blood relatives to sign it, thereby giving permission for the proxy baptism.

Now here he was coming back again looking for my signature.

"First you feed me, and then you present the check? Is this the price of a burger and a couple of pork chops and some empanadas?"

I held the ordinance loosely between my fingertips. It reminded me of the form I'd filed when I registered to get a flu shot.

I refolded it and handed the form back to Jon.

"You sure, man?" he asked.

"I'm sure."

"Rejected out of hand?"

"Out of hand."

"You didn't even read it."

"That's right."

"Won't you at least give it that much respect?"

"I perused it," I told my brother. "That's enough."

Wes looked on. Solemn is not the word I'd use to describe his face. Intense, game-faced, a little gaunt even, like a fighter getting psychologically prepared before a match.

"Do you have any questions about the . . . process?" Wes asked.

"Nope."

"It's all voluntary."

"Feels like some kind of ambush to me."

"Why do you reduce everything to something . . . ugly?" said Jon.

"I can't emphasize enough how very very important this is to your brother," said Wes.

"I can't emphasize enough how very important for me it is *not* to do this."

"It can't wait. Dad can't wait," said Jon.

"You keep dragging Dad into this, but you're one thing, he's another. Go do what *you* have to do, for yourself, although I don't get the rush. Let our father and his 'soul' alone."

"You don't credit souls, Jon tells me; you don't believe in them. So why put a road block in front of something you don't believe in?"

"Good question. I guess I'm covering my bets. Like our father."

"You see?" said Jon, again with a nod to Wes.

"Your brother can always get another signature," said the elder.

"Whose? Which close relative? Paulene? Ida? Lots of luck."

"The point is, we want his only brother, his closest relative, to do the endorsing. Don't you want to give this to your father? It's a very precious gift."

"Come on, guys! I don't think we're speaking the same language. "

"Well, you might be right there," Wes said. "People, outsiders, often tell us they don't understand, at first blush."

"You explained it before. Very well. I get it. And I don't want it."

"Won't you at least think on it, sleep on it some more?"

"Why?"

"It's different with your father."

"Why's that?" I asked.

"Because there's no time," Jon repeated.

The two of them now stood up from the beach chairs, a simple action I would have been hard put to emulate I was so zonked.

Leaving me alone by the fire, they walked away a few paces toward where the tide was breaking along the beach. They were conferring—the way the rabbis had conferred before they threw me out in New York. I couldn't hear what they were saying, but I didn't like it, and their chumminess set me off, so that now I made what turned out to be one of the most stupid moves of the summer.

I took out one more of Jon's stash, this one a really thick joint that I had rehabilitated and had been keeping all these weeks nestled neatly in my wallet, for just such moments of surprise and moral emergency.

I plucked a small piece of wood from the fire, turned my back fully on the little impromptu tribunal of two, this time conspiring against me, and I lit up. I inhaled deeply and I held the smoke in, swirling around the lungs.

In no time I was feeling, as we used to say, no pain. Soon enough I was buoyant again and I rose, clumsily perhaps, but began to walk with my renewed energy along the noisy margin of the shore, kicking my feet in the arriving and receding surf, and moving away from Jon and Wes. If I kept going, maybe I could get up to Big Sur in a week or two.

With each step my anxiety began to subside and I felt I wanted to throw off all these constraints in my life. So naturally I took off another piece of restraining clothing, and another, one shoe and one sock at a time, and, with a very satisfying grunt of "good-bye!" I heaved each into the Pacific.

I must tell you that Jon had outdone himself with this particular joint, or maybe it was just the X factor of the marvelous compression my tush had wrought on the weed. Because through the wallet over the days of sitting I must have been exerting an intense melding of the cannabis and the morsels of hashish. Jon, Wes, and the Mormons not twenty-five yards away by now might be debating about Paul's soul, but I was already traveling off into a zone that left Mormon heaven and the flights of souls far behind.

"Bye-bye, Heavenly Mom and Heavenly Dad. Bye-bye, you twinkly residents of Kolob," I waved gently as they flew by.

I inhaled a few more times and held the smoke deep in the lungs, and, well, "mellow" was now my middle name. No, my first name. Mellow Gould. With a name like that I could become, well, a jazz singer of some kind.

I thought again of that champion smoke-holder and smoke-ring blower, Paul Gould, and how he could, I had firmly believed, propel and direct the smoke down anywhere in his body so that I would not have been surprised if little plumes had arisen from his toes.

So I inhaled again.

By the time I exhaled, I was walking out into the water toward Catalina Island. The Pacific surf on my feet was feeling like a wash of cold, golden honey.

You better believe I was fleeing; yes indeed, I was Jonah just as Aviva and Tali had said.

I heard Jon and Wes calling my name, and here they were coming splashing after me and I called back, "Hey, I'm just practicing walking on the water."

By the time they had me sandwiched between them and were taking me to dry off by the fire, I was both deeply stoned and also oddly clear-headed once again. Or thought I was.

I heard the bounce of a basketball from the court adjacent to the parking lot where we had pulled in what seemed like days ago. Whoa, was it this late already? I noticed the tall lamppost lights had turned on, illuminating a friendly game of basketball that had gotten under way at the nearby court.

As I babbled on, they pulled off my shirt and here now was pretty Mary Anne with a green T-shirt and another large, dry, hooded sweatshirt that they put over me. I began to shake. I thought it might be another California tremor rumbling up from the earth, but it was only Mary Anne rubbing my hair dry with a towel.

I thought again of Paul, my easygoing dad, who believed not in souls and heavens, but in aces and kings and queens and jokers wild and fifty-two cards and randomness and luck. I thought to myself, in that cannabis sort of free association way of joy that now bathed and eased my weary Jewish synapses: wait a minute! It's all part of the big picture, it's all good, it's all connected, it's all well. I won't deny Jon any longer. If this is what he wants, just my signature, well, why not? What the hell! It won't be me, but just an impersonation of me who signs. I could keep my fingers crossed or write so illegibly that Wes and the higher-up elders might disqualify the ordinance, like a bum name on a voter petition list.

I took a look up into the Santa Monica sky. Between the streaks of haze there were whole gauzy constellations of stars, rivers of constellations, scarves of blinking lights, and might those more stable pinpoints be planets? Was one of them Kolob? If so, excuse me, dear Kolobites, for my aforementioned rudeness and planetary slur. Is that other cluster near you one of the Mormon heavens? And over there heaven above heaven or the *elyonim*, a region of the heavens that the Hebrew morning prayers referred to in at least two spots in the liturgy? Oh, my god, I heard myself saying, that psalm-writing guy was so cool, so absolutely right, and right on: the heavens do proclaim the glory, the . . .

FINALLY THEY sat me down at a picnic table by the basketball court.

At what appeared to be my brother's urging, Wes was the first one to talk: "Offering proxy baptism for the dead, especially for one's parents, how to put it, is just about as important as observing the Sabbath in your faith. I mean among the Jews. It's a very big deal for us, and now for Jon. Are we getting through, Norman?"

"You are. You made the spiel before. You are, you are! Through and through. In one ear and out the other."

"He's ripped," said Jon, but Wes nevertheless kept at me.

"In short, it's a *mitzvah* to offer your father the gospel of Jesus Christ."

"That's well put, Wes," I said, "and congratualtions on your Hebrew pronunciation."

"Well?" said Jon, and I could tell he wanted this business to be as brief as possible because I was embarrassing him.

"Don't stress, guys. It's all very cool. Go on. Take him. Take Paul's soul. Ta ta, little thing. Good-bye, little *ibbur*, or *neshama*, little *pneuma* of Paul, little pal, wherever you are. I'll sign. Where's your paper? I've consented."

"You have?"

"Absolutely. *Absolument.* Gimme the goddamn paper."

Then he surprised me. Jon didn't accept my acceptance.

He walked away and stood with his back to Wes and to me. Now I saw him dig a little depression in the sand with one foot. He walked around it. He deepened it, and then he filled it with more sand that he slid in with the toe of his shoe. Wes joined him. Where there had been a hole in the sand, there was now no hole. I found his excavation fascinating. They were deliberating again. What was there about me that aroused deliberation in other people? Absolutely fascinating. I was really stoned.

Then they returned.

"Why aren't you guys jumping up and down? You've won."

"Tomorrow you'll just say you consented 'under the influence.' You said you wouldn't do this, man. You said you'd respect my friends," Jon voiced his complaint, and he had every right to.

"We understand," said Western Oaks.

In my chemical expansiveness I felt I could decide both ways, make everyone happy, and party on. In short I felt I wanted to make it up to my brother, give him what he obviously dearly wanted, and at the same time not feel I'd betrayed myself, my family, Paul, and my Stoned People Israel, all at the same time.

I guess Jon just couldn't see it that way.

The remarkable thing was, the bouncing of the basketball nearby had just given me precisely that opportunity, to concede and not to concede at the same time, or the first glimmer of how to do it.

"No, no, no, Jon. Hear me out. I just got a great idea. I mean a wisp of an idea, a notion; no, no, no, this is very good. And if you go for it, yes, take Paul's soul. Take it. I'll sign. No questions asked, no, no. And no going back. I swear."

Wes knelt down on one knee on the sand in front of me and held up his hand with not all digits outstretched. "How many fingers?"

"I count three."

"Who's the president of the United States?"

"Brigham Young."

"Try again."

"Joseph Smith."

"Last chance, Norman."

"Oh, okay. Boring old Lyndon Baines Johnson."

"You really mean it? No shenanigans?"

"Why is shenanigans always plural, Wes? Will you allow me one little shenani*gan*?"

"See what I mean?" said Jon.

"No, I think he understands exactly what he's saying."

"I most certainly do. You and my one and only brother can have your paper, no shenanigans, but on one condition. And one condition only."

"You see!" Jon said to Wes.

"Which is?" Wes kept his gaze lasered in on me. "What's the condition?"

"We play for it."

"Excuse me?" said Jon.

"We play for Paul's soul."

Silence.

Except for, on the one side of the beach, the bouncing of the ball on the court and on the other the crashing of the waves. Maybe Wes and Jon were as astonished as, frankly, I was, by the idea that had just popped into my head.

"You're nuts," said my brother, and he began to walk away from me with that I'm-not-coming-back gait. Wes, however, brought him back.

They both stood looking down at me. I guess they both were wondering whether I'd puke, or shout something crazy. The odd thing was, I suddenly felt really clear-headed, without fogginess or conflict, as if what I'd just proposed was a kind of elixir, the first right, honest, appropriate, clarifying gesture I'd made since I'd come home. The truth is like that sometimes, very heady.

"The thing is," I went on, "we play a little, say, three on three. You two guys pick someone else for your team, and I'll take two of your awesome Mormon players, and, presto, we'll play twenty-one buckets. Let's say you need to win by two. Whoever gets there first wins Paul's soul, gets to have Paul's soul in their very own heaven."

"You're nuts," said Jon.

"No, I'm not."

"And insulting."

Wes wasn't so sure. "Tell us more."

"Well, wouldn't this be, you know, in keeping with who our dad really was? I mean we could play poker. Paul would like that more than anything. That'd be his real spirit. That'd be his game of choice. Anyone sneak in a deck of cards to the picnic? But you folks here wouldn't approve, would you?"

Oaks didn't answer. No one said a word, so, naturally, I talked on.

"So it's a game of b-ball, the perfect substitute! Instead of for money, it's for his soul. We shoot hoops. You guys win, then I fill out your ordinance. I win, and it's back to the celestial drawing board for you. What do you say?"

"Just sign it, man," said Jon.

"Where's the fun or sentiment in that? What do you have to worry about? I mean . . . look at the condition I'm in. I've got a buzz bigger than a queen bee's. And look at this gut. You'll win. How could you not? That's about 99.999 percent certain, right? But it'll be more fun this way. We'll make ourselves a real Paul Gould Invitational Basketball Tournament. The first and the last."

"So just sign it then," he repeated.

"No, no, no. It's like something he would enjoy. The gamble, man. Paul Gould's boys playing for his eternal soul. You see the smile on his face already, don't you, Jon? We all know the Mormons are great at basketball. And then you can offer him the gospel fair and square. Your treasure, your trophy, call it what you want. And Paul would maybe even say yes because you won him fair and square, Wes. What do you say?"

"I don't think so," said Jon.

I opened my mouth wide. "What are you doing now?" You're looking a gift horse in the mouth, man! You can have Wilt here on your team if you want. I don't care. You got game, don't you, Wes?"

The Mormon nodded. He most certainly did.

"So that's it. Let's say the game is only a way of shaking hands on the matter. Does that remove the gambling for you, brother Jon? Does that make it more, what? More acceptable?"

"I just don't know," said Wes. "Never happened before."

"In all the annals of Mormons! Well, I always like to be part of a precedent."

"Not every precedent is a good one," Jon said.

"But have you folks ever gone to convert the soul of a rabbi's father?"

"I'm sure we have," said Oaks.

"What rabbi?" Jon said.

"A future rabbi. A future rabbi of, hell, all Israel. The world. The universe."

"Just a game? A friendly way to seal the deal? A sort of formality?" said Wes.

"Exactly right. We'll just end it, Jon and I, this whole thing, this struggle. We'll just end it in a way that feels good."

"You're up to your old ways," said my brother.

"Meaning?"

"Some trick," Jon said.

"You mean I win? How could that possibly be? Even when I was in shape, I was mediocre at best compared with you. I bet Wes can dunk just by standing on his tippy toes. I'm carrying an extra twenty pounds with each step. I can barely move. What could be the trick?"

"Who's going to be on your team?"

"I have no idea. I don't care who the others are. You choose them, or whoever shows up."

"Maybe you should really consider," Wes said to Jon. "You'll be giving Norman something he wants and values, a gesture, a meaningful symbol, or something for your dad. Sounds bizarre, but just may be equitable."

"That's right. That's being a real wise elder, Mr. Elder. You two and another against fat old me and two more Mormon bro's. All that matters is, you know, you and I, Jon, we're playing for Dad's soul. What a story he'll have to tell up in your good ol' telestial tea room, or wherever."

Jon remained skeptical, but Wes gave him an encouraging tap on the shoulder and then, showing the right discretion, he excused himself and walked back to the barbecuing so that the final decision would be left to us alone, to the Brothers Gould.

"Come on, man."

"I was trying to be a good guy. I shouldn't have asked you here."

"Admit it, Jon, don't you think Dad would have loved the idea?"

My brother looked into my eyes—as if he wanted to see something there he had never seen before. I doubt he found it. Then he turned to where Wes had gone, and indeed Oaks had paused, turned, and was looking our way. Maybe it wasn't a full nod, and more of an incremental dip of his long neck.

Maybe I was seeing what wasn't there. If so, it would not have been the first false sighting during that fabulous stoned time so many summers ago. No, I was fairly certain Wes was communicating his encouragement once again, his blessing.

"Dad would not only love it, he'd adore it."

"You're so sure?"

"Yes I am. I even think he'd want to bet on us himself."

"Maybe."

"I know he would."

"But where would he put his money? On which one of us would he bet, Norman? You or me?"

"I don't know, man. Maybe both of us."

"You're darn right on both!"

"Then it's settled. I've got a pair of Keds in the car. Choose up."

16

A few minutes later I was crossing the sand from the parking lot where I'd just fetched my sneakers from the trunk of our car. I was suddenly so zonked again, I mean tripping away in a mellow sort of way that made me think how elaborate and beautiful each lifting up of a leg is before each step. Since such thoughts are not conducive to playing a fast game of hoops, I thought the moment had arrived maybe to find a substitute among the Mormons to play for me against Jon and his team.

I was just about to look for a giant among the Saints when, as I zigzagged my way toward the margin of the basketball court, I was stunned to see a figure standing there, both statuesque and familiar.

"Tali?"

Her back was to me, her long arms raised to the sky. I know I was high, but could it be as she turned to face me she also held a basketball over her chest?

"We meet again."

I closed my eyes. I took a deep breath. I looked again. She was still there and indeed the ball was there, like a globe in the hands of a female Atlas. She threw me the ball, a chest pass. It nearly knocked me over, but I caught it. Now she did some jumping jacks, and as I peered, nearly gawking, under the windmill action of her arms I thought I now saw Aviva dribbling away in the half-court behind her. How zonked was I! Aviva in red shoes and gym shorts was taking turns shooting with Mary Anne; the scene had all the signs that they were warming up.

"How did you know we were here?"

"Was this a secret?"

"No, but I . . ."

"We know."

I glanced over at the parking lot. There were the same three or four sedans of the Mormon picnickers that had been parked there when we arrived, and, of course, our Rambler. There were no other cars beyond what were there when I'd put on my shoes moments ago.

"How'd you get here?"

"What does the mode of transportation matter?"

"You take the blue bus?"

"Bus transportation in your city is lightyears slow, man," she said, her talk as strange if not stranger than ever, as if she were stringing together words and phrases in a new language she was learning.

"Well?" she continued.

"Well what?"

"As you see."

"See what?"

"Here we are. We're your team."

What, I wondered, was in that joint!

How had they known we'd be at the beach, and at this very spot? Neither of them had an international driver's license, Tali had told me. I don't think that either of them could even drive, although, as I was soon to find out, could they ever fly.

Hadn't she also just said "team"? How had she known what had just transpired between me and the Mormons?

My surprise turned into, well, a kind of low-grade elation, as I took a step toward her, and carefully touched her powerful forearm. She *was* there.

Tali did not move or flinch but held her ground, without a blink, as if she knew exactly what would happen next, as if such fumbling human touches had come her way, had simply had to be endured, as they had a thousand times before in her angelic career.

Very slowly I raised my right arm and moved it toward her back. I felt an absolute need to touch her, and precisely *there*. I was tentative, but she didn't resist. I had to see if there were signs of, well, sprouting. I lowered my hand and let my fingers graze the awesome blade of her shoulder. I was like some kind of boy playing doctor exploring for a scar or a contusion or a secret raised area. She didn't budge. Tanned, unmarked, no pimpling, not a perforation, or deep fossa or sign of an opening, this back felt and looked like cool marble flesh tanned and glistening in the starlight.

"Don't tell me! You flew here! That's the only way."

"Silly boy. Okay. I won't tell you."

It was as if I were in a trance and just coming out of it, because only now did it really hit me that she was wearing the yellow bikini, the one that drove me nuts at the Camp Tikvah pool; it now had the same effect, but double. As she almost operatically lowered the basketball I saw she was also wearing over the bikini top a thin, nearly diaphanous jersey that bore calligraphic Hebrew letters. I couldn't keep my eyes off her like the callow myopic boy that I was.

And I was not alone because even here among the sedate, far more covered-up, one-piece-bathing-suited Mormon girls and future missionary boys, there were lots of other stares in addition to my own at this six-foot-two-inch beauty.

"That's right, " Tali said as she now commenced some leg stretches and I continued to, well, gawk. "Study the Hebrew," she laughed. "You'll figure it out."

At first I thought the letters formed the abbreviated name of a school or maybe an Israeli army team she had recently played on during the Six-Day War. How wrong I was.

As if to make my next essay easier, she struck a pose like a model rotating her torso my way and with a bold sensuality brought the letters closer to my gaze.

With deliberation I sounded them out: *aleph, mem, toph.*

When one of the many little cannabis clouds obscuring my vision lifted, I saw it. A midrashic lesson, some nonsense of numerology, floated into my consciousness, and I instantly knew: the letters spelled *emet*, the Hebrew word for "truth."

If you reordered the letters with just a little hermeneutical razzle dazzle, and jiggled a vowel, you ended up with similar letters spelling another word, *mavet*, whose numerical value is identical to that of "truth." Yet this word, *mavet*, means "death."

Then, as if Tali grasped precisely what I was thinking, she turned around and there it was: *that* other word—*mavet*—on the back of her shirt. Forwards and backwards. Truth and Death surrounding the most fabulous breasts on the entire California coast.

I was dumbfounded, randy, elated, and still pretty much stoned. Yet for the first time in my so-called spiritual life, I also was in the state the religious theorists term *radical amazement.*

"Close your mouth, Norman," she said. "The flies will get in."

"Very, very heavy."

"What did you expect?"

"Who are you? What are you doing here!"

"You know."

"Remind me."

"The letters. The letters live. *Aleph, mem, toph,* the first, middle, and the last letters of the alphabet. The whole world is in them."

Oddly, neither Wes nor Jon nor Mary Anne, who continued to trade jump shots with Aviva, nor the other Mormons seemed shocked, as I was, by the angels' arrival. Maybe they had rented a car and had stashed it somewhere on the Pacific Coast Highway beyond the beach. Or maybe they had hitchhiked, as Israelis often did. Sure, that must be it. Who wouldn't slam on the brakes to pick up these two girls!

Still how had they known?

With her right arm at the small of my back, Tali now guided me onto the court.

I came to a stoned sort of stop beneath the basket, which was now illuminated, along with most of the half-court, by the floodlights that had come on. A cone of light thrown by one of them near the parking lot's edge bore down on us. Yes, the cannabis contributed, but I saw it again: that look in her eye, that mysterious aura, just like the one she had about her when she had donned Paulene's wedding dress and had revealed a secret self to me for the first time at Sabbath dinner.

"You look fabulous."

"I have a pretty good jump shot."

"I'll bet."

"It's going to be you, Aviva, and me."

"No!"

"Of course. Their team is Western Oaks, Jonathan, and Mary Anne Rogers," she said matter-of-factly.

"You're kidding."

"Isn't this what you wanted?"

"*They* were supposed to choose . . ."

"They have. Mary Anne and Aviva have talked it over. Mary Anne says the teams are fine. She and Aviva are well matched. Just a friendly game. Right, Norman?"

"Oh, yeah."

"So?"

"It's game time. Are you ready to play?"

AS IF the angels' arrival weren't a surprising enough development, I also could not believe the change that had occurred in Western Oaks after he laid down his fork and toque, slipped into his shorts, and was now tying on his Converse All Star high tops.

Yes, he was tall, but does a costume ever make a difference! As I stood on the edge of the court and saw him begin to stretch and limber, Wes seemed to me also to have been transformed, all length and acute angles, into an athletic center big enough to play on an NBA team. Now as he bent and pressed his chest against his knees to tighten his laces and stretch his hamstrings, well, Wes's legs seemed to just go on and on . . . for miles! He stood up, like a ladder being lifted against the side of a house for a high-up paint job. He took a bounce pass of a ball tossed in from one of the Mormons on the sidelines, and now Wes began taking practice shots. Tali soon joined him, and, of course, I just stood there, and watched.

It wasn't bad at all, Tali's one-handed set-shot form, I mean, yet Wes was sinking them from everywhere. He clearly was four, maybe even five, inches taller than Tali and all his shots seemed to be traveling *down* as soon as they left his fingers.

"Don't you worry," Tali said, with the usual clairvoyance—or maybe I just imagined her saying it—as she dribbled over to reluctant me. "I'll be guarding him. Aviva's on that girl, and you take Jon."

On cue, my brother now came dribbling near for his warm-ups. "Nice stutter step," I said, but who was I fooling? At nearly six feet, Jon was easily three inches taller than I and a far superior athlete. Plus I was still so stoned my sneakers felt glued to the cement.

I joined the others on the court. Here now was Mary Anne taking a shot, retrieving the rebound off the rim, and now offering me the ball. Physically, yes, she was built very much like Aviva, with powerful, stoutly calfed legs, and a low center of gravity. Unless she was also, secretly, an Olympian in training—and that evening anything seemed possible—Aviva would at least likely have the advantage there.

"You're not going to take a few before we start?" Jon said to me as, instead of going for the ball, which now bounced my way, I just grabbed a few old towels and swept away some wind-blown sand that had gathered into a mound at the base of the steel pole that held the basket and backboard.

"I don't need any practice."

"You're that good?"

"No, I'm just . . . beyond practice. Way beyond. In fact, maybe I'll just do the housekeeping and ref. Someone else can play."

"Oh, no, he's playing," said Aviva, who, right on cue, was dribbling by. "No subs in this game allowed. Norman is definitely playing."

As Jon lofted an aerial from the corner, I wondered what, with my fat collection flopping over the band of my bermudas, did I think I really might contribute to my team by trying to guard my brother. The only way I could prevent him from dashing by me was perhaps by simply collapsing in front of him, and that very well could happen. Were there age limits to getting a heart attack? I wondered. From a basketball point of view, the cannabis was making me feel about eighty.

I closed my eyes. I opened them. I was still pretty buzzed. I began to regret the deal I had proposed, but here was now yet another twist. When next Tali cruised by dribbling the ball, rising up for a two-handed shot from the corner, and it dropped in, all net, *whoosh,* that's when I heard it, the word, for the first time.

Maybe not the word itself but a sound awfully close to it, a *whoosh* of a perfect shot that goes through, all net, leaving the knotted strands of string rippling in the wind, a *whoosh* with an additional syllable of sound before and after it, and definitely different from the sound of Jon's rimless hoop of a moment before.

What it added up to, was that I thought what I'd heard was not *whoosh* but an elongated *whoosh-a-ma* that had elided into *ne-shaaaa-ma,* the Hebrew word for soul. Was this possible?

At first, as I say, I thought it was merely the acoustics of the ball making that marvelous sound of whooshing or *swishing* through the strings and a faint reverberation and ping of the rim and backboard to follow. Yes, maybe that was the source; I was sure I'd misheard. Maybe it was all cannabis-distorted noise, softened and distorted by the slow roar of waves arriving and receding.

Neshama.

Tali came dribbling by, niftily changing hands and bouncing the ball between her powerful and lovely haunches. I looked at Wes, a dominating tree at the half-court, ready for the game to begin.

"What's going on?"

"You know," Tali whispered back.

Not surprisingly, as the game began, Wes played like quite the gentleman. He kept his distance to avoid even brushing the breasts of the angels.

Instead of trying to score much himself, he passed frequently to Mary Anne and then to Jon. Naturally Jon eluded the slow-footed blob that was me and then dribbled back toward the half-court line. There he flipped back to Wes, who faked a drive, and then shot it over to Mary Anne at the top of the key. She made a short underhanded pass to Jon, who promptly decided to test me.

He went up for a short jumper that once—maybe when I was nine years old—I may have come close to blocking with my outstretched fingers. But burdened now not only by so much extra weight but also by motor responses more attuned to chewing cheeseburgers and passing the ranch dressing than playing a perimeter defense, my feet barely left the ground.

I didn't even come close. Jon's shot hit the backboard at just the sweet spot and angled into the basket.

Two to zip, and we had decided to play to twenty-one baskets, win by two. That seemed like an Everest of hoops. I knew I would die before we got half-way. How could I possibly last?

In short order, Aviva had determined that Mary Anne could not move equally well to her left as her right. Taking advantage in the next series, she proceeded to scoot by her, and in two steps she elevated to the basket and I swear seemed to sail through the air like an athletic Mary Poppins in shorts, first beneath and then above Wes's skinny-armed defense.

Aviva's ball fell into the basket like an egg into the nest.

We backpedaled and waited for Wes, who now huddled up briefly with Jon and Mary Anne. I noticed a few of the Mormon picnickers placing their dinner plates on the tables and meandering their way over to check out our game. Who could blame them? There really was a kind of energy rising from the asphalt.

It had to do with more than basketball, and we had only begun.

Jon made the inbound pass to Wes. I sensed from the way he bent from the waist with his back low over the ball as he dribbled that he had sized up the opposition and was now thinking about jettisoning some of his laid-back ways. With her muscular arms outstretched—and I mean outstretched like the wings of an eagle—Tali tracked the Mormon and confronted him at the top of the key.

He moved left, but she countered right, and blocked him. He tried to pass her on the right with a feigned, hesitating stutter step, but she was there. In a half second she had shifted. No, a quarter second. She would not allow him to dribble any farther down the lane.

Where had Tali learned to play this way? In the Israeli army? Or in pick-up games among the descendants of mystical, basketball-playing rabbis on the hilly streets of her hometown? Not likely.

Jon and Wes conferred, and on the next series they sent Mary Anne across the middle as a kind of decoy. Naturally I fell for it, and left my position, which took me out of the play altogether. Wes passed to my brother, who set up a pick against Tali who crossed over when Jon flipped the ball back to him.

Yet when Tali, having avoided the pick, or, as it seemed to me, neutralized it like water through a sieve, there was no path there either for Wes to make for the basket. So he pivoted and lofted one of those sky hooks from the far corner of the court. The ball hit the front of the rim and bounced high and straight up, at least three feet, yet it fell right in.

What was even more impressive is that when we failed to score in our next run at the basket, Wes performed this feat, in their next offensive series, from the other side of the lane as well, left-handed.

Now it was Tali's turn to respond.

On our next two chances, I inbounded to Aviva, who faked that run down the lane again. She did it well enough not only to get Mary Anne to commit, but also to convince Wes that he needed to slide over to help. As soon as he left his position, Aviva passed the ball niftily around her back. Tali caught it, stopped, squared to the basket, and jumped, all in this fabulous single motion. So doing, she launched a ten-footer. Wes reached to block it, but he was late. When it angled in, he gave her a much deserved high five.

Tali's shot had hit in that interval right after the waves had crashed onto the Santa Monica shoreline and before the noisy roiling of their receding; once again it had sounded like a *neshama* whispered softly right into my ear.

And she did that again, twice more.

I didn't understand what was going on, except that now I knew Tali could score on Wes. That was enough for me to give in to an impulse that I had felt growing within me from the moment I'd set foot at the picnic. I wasn't proud of it, but here it was: after all the superficial warmth, the chops, empanadas, burgers, and the sauces with which the Mormons had tried to seduce me, even within this silly game I had concocted and they had agreed to. In the end I just wanted to take a shot at Wes, to hurt him a little, to push and to elbow the missionary and this whole oh-so-friendly enemy who were abducting my only brother.

So when the next series began, I tried.

I stuck my foot and hip out to set a pick. It was not a bad pick, but in the tangle, it was not Wes but Jon whom it targeted, and he stumbled badly, losing the ball.

"Way to go," Aviva said as she retrieved it and sped by, with Mary Anne after her.

"For a game that's not supposed to matter much, that's pretty aggressive," said Jon.

"Just play."

Having picked up Jon's ball, Aviva now scored over Mary Anne. As Jon walked the ball back to half-court for the take-out, he said, "Don't forget, man. You agreed!"

"Maybe my fingers were crossed."

We played on.

For the next five or ten minutes, we exchanged baskets, more or less evenly, although none was cheap or easy. There were many passes to get someone open, each side looking for weaknesses, probing, retreating, trying again and then again. If it were baseball, each at-bat would have taken eight or nine pitches. It really was good basketball, and—another surprise, given all of the dope and food in my system—I was acquitting myself fairly well.

Even more surprises were on the way.

Having faked that she was going to make a move on Wes, Tali now reversed and dribbled in a small circle behind me. I didn't understand her move. Aviva then made a sudden cut to the basket. Tali, dribbling the opposite way as a decoy, flicked me the ball, and as she did so, brushing close to me, I heard her say, "Give her, give her."

She meant she didn't want me to take the next shot but to pass, to *give* the ball to Aviva. Give her! That made a lot of sense: Give her. Yet I swear what I also heard, or, in retrospect, heard instead was not "give her," but *ibbur*.

Ibbur, you will recall, or learn here, as I soon did in some detail, is the Hebrew word for the form the fragile little soul takes when it returns inside a living person in order to finish up its business back here on earth. *Neshama* is the breath of life, if you will, the physical emanation of the soul, particularly palpable around a body that has just died, the exiting action.

But *ibbur,* that's the energy of the soul getting ready to make amends and to clarify itself for the return trip. The root in Hebrew is not unrelated to *ivri,* which means in Hebrew, "those who cross over." In the case of our ancestors, it was the Jordan River to the Promised Land they crossed over; in the case of this basketball game, I couldn't help but think it was, thanks to my teammates, Paul's soul crossing back to where some contact might be made.

Or something like that.

Even without souls hanging around the court, one hell of a ball game was unfolding. I was in the midst of it. Funny thing was, I was hardly out of breath.

I now retrieved an errant pass from Mary Anne and bounced the ball to Aviva. She immediately dished back to Tali. Yet Wes recovered and ran up head-to-head with her and gave Tali no space to shoot. Tali now reversed, made a wide arc getting herself out of Wes's reach, and lofted a ten-footer; this one missed.

As he dribbled back with, this time, an easy grab of the rebound over Aviva, Wes said to Tali, "You're human after all."

It was as if she hadn't heard him or didn't want to, so I answered for her: "I wouldn't be so sure."

Tali now began to guard Wes so closely during the next series he couldn't find any daylight to shoot. After three forays toward the basket, he passed to Jon.

Jon faked me out pretty quickly and hit one, then Wes did, but on our next run, Tali passed the ball to Aviva, who had dazzled Mary Anne with a fake and was open. She sent up a floater, underhanded, and it rolled in.

Twelve to twelve.

Tali came right up to me and whispered in my ear: "Next time give her the ball, right? Give her, give her."

As we lined up our defense and Jon took the ball out at center court, I whispered back to Tali, "Why do you keep saying that? '*Ibbur*'?"

"Norman," she replied, "just watch your brother doesn't make another run down the side."

But before she took off down the lane, she whispered, "Yes! Of course! Now for godsake, play!"

The game went on, and to say I was being swept up in something larger than myself is a cliché; yet a cliché is a truth by a threadbare formulation, but a truth nevertheless. Something big had me in its thrall.

Here came Wes right at me, loping like a kind of human crane, dribbling slyly at the top of the key, hoping I'd lunge for the high-bouncing ball and he would go easily around me. I kept my separation pretty well, I didn't commit, and as our little contretemps played out, I noticed the now-thick throng of future Mormon homemakers and future missionaries who were now gathered at the sides of the court. Suddenly they didn't seem so benign, but more like members of the other squad cheering on Wes to steal away not only the ball, but also Paul's soul.

When the score reached fourteen for their side and twelve for us, my brother came up to me and said with some urgency, "Maybe we should ratchet this down?"

"But why?"

"Because you agreed to a *friendly* game. Your word. Wouldn't be a bad idea if you kept it. Now and then."

"Didn't know they could play this way, did you?"

"Did you?"

"Pretty amazing, huh?"

"What's going on, Norman?"

"Dunno."

"Yes you do."

"Dunno. Ask Tali."

"She ignores me. Anyway, it's you I'm asking. You cut the bargain. Not them."

"Yes, but she's got the hot hand and she's in the zone and she's floating, and she . . . is fabulous, isn't she and . . ."

Jon shook his head and gave me one of those looks that the saved and the certain offer to the lost and to the still suffering and questing; then away he dribbled.

By now I *was* rethinking my ceding so easily of Paul Gould's immortal soul to Jon and to Wes. Never mind that, despite the signs, I still didn't truly in my heart believe in souls. I also began to feel something new. Maybe it had just required this blood-pumping game to clear my head, but I sensed that my half-felt cranky objections, my half-baked jokes, and all of my sarcastic erudition were begining to fall away. I mean through this sport or gamble or whatever we were engaged in that I had so cavalierly concocted, here suddenly coursing through me was instead a righteous anger at Jon and at Wes. What's more, the feeling suddenly was unadulterated by my own equivocation.

I mean I was craving a triumph.

So, despite my lousy physical shape, I asked Tali to switch with me so that I could guard Wes and help deliver it.

When we next huddled on the court, my gorgeous and mysterious teammate whispered, "Are you sure you can handle him?"

"No."

"Then we can't risk it. Don't you understand?"

"I thought I did. It all comes in and out of focus."

"Just stay on your brother," she said, "and we can win."

We each had two more inconclusive runs. Then we stopped for a swig of water, although I was the only one on my team who drank. I noticed how the angels were barely sweating. Tali's mouth was puckered open a little and she seemed to be breathing a little harder than usual through it, perhaps like a canine that has just had a relaxing jaunt, but otherwise her face and arms were dry, and she may as well have been at an air-conditioned tea party. There was at best a thin film of perspiration on Aviva's forehead, and she tucked her ponytail up a little higher as we stood watching Jon, Mary Anne, and Wes, all pouring with sweat as I was, gulp water and make their plans.

As the game resumed, Tali began to guard Wes ever more closely, relentlessly.

Wes first backed off. The basketball player in him, which had seemed at loggerheads with the gentleman Mormon and with his desire to avoid, most especially, a brushing against Tali's Truth-and-Death-framed breasts, now gave way to the competitor.

The Mormons like to think of life, at least on this planet, as a kind of test of their moral mettle. Well, this game had become a huge test for Western Oaks, because he had never seen a woman play like this, and he didn't know who he really was up against in Tali and Aviva.

Angels on the job are so single-minded that they sometimes lose sight of the human context in which they are operating. The result is a fierce intensity that sometimes crosses our notions of decorum, manners, and modesty. I'm trying to say that Tali now began to come at Wes like Jayne Mansfield in a bikini and wet T-shirt single-handedly leading an Israeli armored division.

He was a terrific player, but move by move and score by score, Tali answered him.

The other four of us were in the game, of course, but as the two dominant forces now truly engaged, even Jon began to miss many of our shots. By now, after seesawing, we were tied at twenty-two baskets each.

On their next run Mary Anne managed to fake out Aviva, but she stalled on her own drive and sent Wes a pass that he caught two feet from the mid-court line. Even though he was not within scoring range, Tali ran up to him, stretched out her long, windmill arms, and nearly smothered him.

"Hey, what are you doing?" he called out.

Despite all of her defensive exertions, you heard not a single panting breath from her, not a word, not a curse, not an exclamation. Not a grunt or other human sound. There was not even a rustle of clothing from her as Tali's arms paddled the air in front of Wes. She was a player silent as a magician performing a great trick.

"What gives?"

"Play," she urged him on in a loud whisper. "Just play."

Wes finally had to lean aggressively into Tali to make some daylight, but then he thought otherwise and deftly passed to Mary Anne, who dribbled back out to half-court, killing some time so that Wes, after all of his evasive yet fruitless dribbling, might recover.

His face and Jon's were by now streaming with sweat, and I looked as if I had just stepped out of a hot shower. Tali and Aviva both remained remarkably cool, almost glistening like brass, as if they were people without glands.

When Tali in guarding Wes on his next run took an odd lunge at him, Wes looked at me for some sort of understanding of what was going on. I only shrugged. What explanation could I offer? I knew no more than he did.

Finally I decided that physically I had really reached the end of my capacity; it was time for a blow.

At twenty-eight baskets to twenty-seven, I called a time-out and the angels and I huddled up at mid-court; Jon, Wes, and Mary Anne convened under the basket.

Tali's complexion had become roseate during the game, and her red hair had curled up a little about the nape of her neck and around her ears, making her look even more beautiful.

As she stared off into the distance toward the ocean's horizon, I swear she had the look of a goddess in a painting. I don't know which goddess or which painting. Maybe all of them. Yes, I was on Tali and Aviva's team, but some intuition told me I would not be needed any more, and soon. In absolutely every sense I was out of my league.

Standing beside Tali during the time out, Aviva leaned forward. Her arms rested on her knees, her legs seemed, despite all the running, fresh and relaxed. Not a cramp or a tremble in sight. The angels could have been talking about game strategy, or about going shopping after the game at May Company or up to Century City. Neither of them made eye contact with me, as if that would distract them from their business. I felt invisible even as I began to wonder if their expressionless faces, bent next to each other, with lips barely moving, as if in prayer, might even be whispering "Holy, holy, holy" or reciting a roster of divine names, or calling on the gods of basketball. Whatever they were up to, it was absolutely clear it was not for me to approach them.

When I could take it no more, I finally found the courage to say something, and this came out: "My tank's close to empty. Mind telling me what in the world is going on here?"

Tali barely turned her head to acknowledge I was there. She just kept looking out toward the sea as if she were connected to some current rolling in on the night waves.

"Just let her operate," Aviva answered on Tali's behalf. "Let her play her game. Give her room."

"I have, haven't I?"

"Keep it that way," Aviva said.

In the first few minutes after the time out, Tali strangely eased up on the fierceness and maneuvered in a far more gingerly way around the opposition. For our side, Tali did almost all of the ball handling, and it was Wes for the competition. Both sides were holding fire. We were waiting for the next moment, the next sign, for something to turn. It didn't, and then it did.

I looked at Jon and he at me. Mary Anne and Aviva exchanged a similar glance. Aviva was the one who called the time out, and then the four of us in a kind of acknowledgment, in unison walked off the court. Wes and Tali would finish the game one-on-one.

It seemed, well, inevitable.

And, oh, to watch the two of them play now, as a spectator.

Never in all my meteoric days as one of the rising and soon-enough-to-fall stars of the LA Jewish diaspora, 1959 to 1963, or even during those first hopeful years of study at the seminary before my Jewish lightbulb went all dim, had I ever been so proud of Our People Israel as I now was. For they, we, had somehow produced this basketball-playing bombshell, this kabalistic phenom, this ex-commando from Sfad, this Tali, this woman without a last name, this angel, this messenger who had the most unerring jumpshot with a gravity-defying backspin and the most quick-footed defense I had ever seen.

In my measureless admiration I was not alone.

The sidelines around the court were by now nearly completely lined with the Mormon picnickers who, for all their bewildering (for me, anyway) intricate cosmological fantasies, still knew and appreciated the swift subtleties of a good game of hoops.

I don't think they'd ever seen a woman play with as much skill, power, and relentless drive as Tali. With an elbow to the ribs or a flick of her great curving pelvis, she made Wes pay for every rebound he got. Her defense wasn't flagrant, but for those who were there that day and really knew the game, it was close, which is to say somewhere between vigorous and awesome.

Again and again she came at Wes as if precisely to force contact, but with our departure from the court, and all eyes following the one-on-one unfolding before us, Wes's tentativeness on defense oddly seemed to return. He backed off, surrendering ground to Tali on a few drives, as she stutter-stepped trying to fake him out.

Again and again he avoided brushing her fabulous angelic chest, which, of course, had the effect of creating space for Tali to shoot; call it a distinct natural advantage that compensated for Wes's height. After ten furious minutes they were playing even, basket for basket, and the score was thirty-two each.

Back and forth they continued to battle. Wes's hair and forehead were slicked with sweat that he now wiped regularly away from his eyes with the soaked hem of his gray T-shirt, gone all dark with perspiration.

Tali, on the other hand, continued to seem hardly winded at all, her face cool and composed beneath the flying waves of her long red hair. I wondered if at some point, in a very non-Mormon gesture, Wes might try to reach out and grab a handful of her luxurious mop as if it were a rope and just fling her down, just to put an end to the storm of basketball prowess that was gathering around him.

Or maybe that's just what I would have been thinking if I were in his sneakers. Yet I wasn't, and I was thrilled with every minute of the balance of this game—whose moves all these decades later I can still reconstruct as if they were unfolding again in front of me right now.

At thirty-six baskets each, Tali paused briefly before dribbling back in from the backcourt. Dropping the ball to the asphalt beside her, she stilled it beneath one foot. Tali's gaze now found Aviva, who instantly and wordlessly knew what was being asked of her. She skipped over and produced a hair band, golden in color, that the court lights bounced off of.

Aviva banded Tali's hair back. It took all of fifteen seconds, but Wes needed every single one of them; you could see he needed air. I wasn't playing any more, but when I now saw that golden hair band amid her red curls and all her limbs glistening in the court light, I had to catch my breath.

When the game resumed, Tali's powerful legs seemed so fresh it was as if she could go on forever. Once again I sensed Wes's frustration; he would have liked to reach out and grab her and hurl the Israeli to the ground.

Yet, eyeing her with a new wariness, Wes somehow was able now to elevate his game. Twice he started his drives from the top of the key with a lowered shoulder and with the spring of a football lineman at the snap. It had the effect of backing Tali off.

She adjusted.

When Wes did that a third time, he hit the ground hard, smacked there by Tali who suddenly was in front of him blocking his path. A groan of disapproval at her play went up from among the Mormons gathered by the court. It was as if she had moved with the speed of light that took her from one position to the next. She was suddenly there. Then she was not, and Wes was blocked.

"Time, time," Jon called out, and leaped up to assist Wes, who was like a bundle of angles on the ground, but already getting up under his own power. Mary Anne threw a towel over his shoulders and jumped up to wipe away the sweat from his neck.

During this pause in the action, Tali did not come over to Aviva and me on the sideline. Although we were still her team, she chose to stand apart. She remained there on the court, alone. The ball was under her control, still and immobile, beside her ankle.

In a kind of peace-making gesture, Mary Anne came over with a bottle of lemonade and a bottle of water. I hadn't been playing for twenty minutes, still I drank and drank. Aviva sipped a little just for the taste, and then Mary Anne checked out Tali; her formidable posture said, keep away. Mary Anne did, but asked Aviva, "Do you think she wants something?"

"No."

"Everyone needs liquids."

"Not her," Aviva replied matter-of-factly.

Only when I'd finished gulping did I look around and become aware that the courtside was lined not only with the Mormons picknickers but, it appeared, also by people from other beach parties adjacent to ours who had drifted over.

They were now two or three deep along the out-of-bounds line. There were even a few people over in the parking lot standing up on the back seats of their cars not to miss any of the action.

I could have sold tickets.

Then something unexpected occurred. Tali suddenly walked off the court to the sideline; the little sea of spectators quieted down and parted, giving her space.

There was some kind of communication I sensed but didn't understand between them, as Aviva, having huddled briefly with her, now commenced a circumambulation of the half-court line, down the sides, under the basket, and then back up to where she had started. It was a gesture of demarcating in some enigmatic way. I thought she might have been looking for something, like a lost contact lens, but that wasn't it at all.

When Aviva finished, Wes stepped back on the court, but Tali did not, not right away. I don't want to make a bigger deal out of this than it was, but Tali just stood there, eyeing him, looking around, it seemed, at the sea, at the horizon, and at the bluffs overlooking the highway, taking it all in before she

THE BOOK OF NORMAN

resumed. Yes, as if she were a visitor or a tourist getting her last looks, preparing to finish her business and to move on to the next destination.

None of this took very long, only seconds Then Tali stepped back onto the court, and the game was about to resume.

As they neared each other at the top of the key, where the ball still lay, Tali began saying something to Wes. I leaned toward them desperate to hear but in the buzz of the crowd and the crash of the waves, it was inaudible. Then she reached out her hand and drew him to her. He didn't have a choice, he couldn't resist, because she now gave him, of all things, a kiss on the cheek. It was, well, a nano-kiss, very brief, very quick, over before Wes knew what hit him, and yet exactly the caress I had been craving all these weeks and had been denied. Was I the only one who saw this? Was the cannabis kicking in again? It can't be, but then, without a comment or a murmur from anyone, the game resumed.

With her left foot Tali tapped the ball over to Wes. As it slowly rolled, she followed it to where it came to a stop, like a perfect putt, at Wes's feet.

When he knelt to pick it up to restart play, however, she did something else strange again. This time she gripped Wes's wrist and pulled him up and toward her, very close. Despite his size he seemed almost a puppet in her hands. That's the way I felt with her all the time. Then she as quickly released him.

Wes was clearly confused by these enigmatic gestures, and he wasn't ready to resume.

"She's amazing, isn't she?" said Aviva, who, while all this was happening, had been on her own mysterious travels around the court.

No sooner had she knelt down beside me when Jon came up from behind and now placed his hands around Aviva's neck. It was sporting enough, but also firm, but with a touch of real threat. "I smell a big rat. What's your pal up to?"

"My *pal*?" Aviva said. "If you only knew."

"So tell."

"For me to know, for you to find out."

"Tell more or I squeeze it out of you. No, really. She's playing hard, she's playing crazy."

"Squeeze all you want," Aviva replied insouciantly. She wasn't flirting or being coy. As always, the angels spoke the truth; we had only to see it.

Jon swung around to block Aviva's view of the court and studied her like a frustrated interrogator; he also made the mistake of keeping his hands resting on her neck.

He shouldn't have.

"What gives?"

"These give," Aviva said as she lifted Jon's considerable paws off her shoulders as if they were two snowflakes. "You boys are a hoot."

"You're sandbagging us. Just who is she? Who?"

"The sixty-four-thousand-dollar question," I said.

"Worth a lot more than that," Aviva added as she retied the laces of her sneakers.

"Why don't we just call this a tie, and you go on home?" Jon persisted. "Let's get this over with. Let's stop the game right now."

"No can do," said Aviva.

"Why not?"

"How do you say? See? The lines are drawn."

We followed her eyes to center court where Tali was standing quietly beside a second basketball, which someone had rolled out to her, so she could take some warm-ups too, while Wes shot his. Yet it lay under her left foot, and she towered above it as if it were a little brown apple. She was ready. She was always ready. Her right hand was on her hip, and she was waiting for Wes to finish his shots. She was studying him now, intently. It was as if she had been ready to finish this game since the beginning of time.

"See? " Aviva said.

"See what?"

"It won't take much longer, but it needs to be decided."

"You've got to be kidding."

"Your brother made a wager. Remember?"

"It was a joke, like everything he does. Anyway, you weren't there. How do you know? You tell them?"

"Not me."

"Did you?" he repeated.

"Nope. They just knew."

"Of course we knew," Aviva said. "How could we not? Now why don't you go back to your side of the court?"

With that dismissal, Jon loped over across the court to Wes. I'm not sure what he told him but they and Mary Anne came together and huddled up. Then with the score remaining tied, the game resumed.

Tali now began to guard Wes extremely closely once again. However, he was a brilliant player, and now really showed it. He had husbanded his energy or found it anew, and he also had picked up his game. Although her stamina continued to be indefatigable, and Wes's thin frame, especially in such a protracted contest, was an increasingly poor match for Tali's, still the Mormon found creative ways to score.

She answered his high-arcing hook shots by lofting fall-aways over Wes's fingertips. Then momentum shifted, and shifted again, but Tali really elevated; she was drawing on her military fitness or, more likely, on a new energy source, which I will leave to others far more cosmically versed than I to explain.

Her drives took on an agility, speed, and urgency that surpassed what she had shown in the first half. Some players are like that. He scored, she scored, the seesawing just continued.

When Wes tried a twenty-footer from the far corner, with his back practically against the Pacific Coast Highway, and barely missed, with the ball swirling around the bucket like a top, you could hear Jon and the congregation of Mormons exhale in unison.

On the next drive that Tali attempted, he stole the ball from her cleanly, retreated a step, and this time deftly used his left arm to scoop around her defense and to score. That was his fortieth basket, and the score was tied again.

Now Tali took the ball out at half-court, and dribbled up to Wes, squaring herself to him. As she switched hands, dribbling now left and now right, back and forth in a brilliant show of technical skill, she also never took her eyes off him. No matter how close she got, how she tempted him, and no matter how many times Wes darted his hand out to grab the tantalizingly close ball, it was never there for the taking; it was as if the ball had become as invisible as the air.

Finally he took a quick swipe, stabbing at the ball, which was when Tali, accelerating her trickery, transferred the ball between her legs and around her right foot with such withering alacrity that Wes lunged, but missed, and stumbled.

Jon raced over to us again. "She's trying to embarrass him."

"The stakes are far higher than that."

"Tell her to stop," he demanded of Aviva.

"No can do."

Jon stormed off to rejoin Mary Anne who was now ministering to Wes, placing a large Band-Aid over a bleeding scrape on his leg.

On the far side of the court, the Mormons grew subdued.

On her next run, Wes refused to go for Tali's fake. When he held his ground, she tried a different tactic. She feigned left, then whirled around in a full 360-degree pivot move that razzle-dazzle Knicks guard Earl Monroe would have admired.

Her fake was successful, and she raced straight for the basket.

However, with three or four huge steps, as if he had suddenly channeled the leaping ability of an antelope, Wes caught up to her. Her drive for the open lay-up might have dead-ended right there. With his outspread fingers over the ball and she in an awkward position trying to protect it from his effective reach-in, there was no way she could launch except if she managed to switch the ball to her other hand—which was precisely what she did. With a finger-flick the ball went up and in.

This time *I* couldn't keep myself from applauding.

On his next run, Wes was able to take the ball from her, dribble to the side of the key, and put in an easy jumper.

"You're hotter than the grill," Jon shouted, and high-fived Wes and then Mary Anne.

Wes tried that move again on the next series, but this time Tali not only blocked the shot, she positioned herself so close that when Wes landed, it was nearly on the laces of her sneakers.

The dangerous awkwardness of the landing made him nearly topple. A few of the more vociferous Mormons roared foul, but Tali reached out and clasped Wes so powerfully it was as if her arm had just reached around his entire torso, and she yanked him up. It was to steady him, but for the briefest instant it was also like an embrace in a strange dance.

For a moment Wes seemed mesmerized by her aid, and Tali capitalized; she took the ball out at the half-court and made an uncontested short jumper for a score.

The game was now tied yet again, forty-two to forty-two.

After Wes sank another shot, Tali lofted one to answer. However, this time, the ball misfired. She'd released it with no backspin, yet the ball, a deep orange-brown globe, courtesy of the Spalding Company, still somehow began to spin upwards when it rolled off her hand, and appeared to be arcing out to sea. Yet there was an aerodynamic power attached to the ball almost as though a string were attached, one that Tali controlled. Of course it could have been an optical illusion or just my angle of vision into the dark sky over the court— anyway, the ball was arrested in air so that, almost contrary to gravity and to the rest of nature, the ball vectored back toward the backboard. The ball hit with authority, banged onto the rim, whirled around rapidly four times, and then spiralled in.

Now it was forty-four to forty-four.

A baseball game can go on for an infinite number of innings, on into the deep hours of the night, and so, theoretically, could a win-by-two basketball game. I never before had enjoyed a game so much in my life. I wish it had gone on for that kind of eternity.

But now the action, especially Tali's defensive work, took on a whole new character for which the sports-commentary terms *intensity* and *covering him like his shadow* are completely inadequate.

Tali was all over Wes. He gathered himself, protecting the ball with his body as he tried to maneuver by her. Now he turned and, dribbling at an angle to her right, he collided with her, not head on, but at the shoulder. The impact or maybe this time it was a push—it was hard to deduce intention amid all that flurry of outstretched arms and legs between them—had its effect: Tali backpedaled, and then began to fall.

Yet this tumble was not ordinary either; nothing with Tali was. As she began to fall back, the Israeli seemed almost parallel with the ground, the fall that seemed imminent in the next second or the next, the fall that absolutely had to occur if gravity still meant anything. Yet it just didn't happen. Because each time, almost as if in a cartoon, her feet raced backward beneath her.

Then from that nearly unsustainable position, she reached back with one hand, like a gymnast making a quick correction in her floor exercise, touched the asphalt and somehow not only broke the fall, but righted herself. She did all that almost gracefully.

She and Wes now circled each other. At the first approach, she went back to shadow-guarding him. This time he remained closer and didn't resist. For a long interval they continued to block and to neutralize each other. Neither backed down; neither gave ground down the key or in the corners; neither was able to get an open lane, or even a clear glance at the basket to score.

"What in the world is she doing?" I finally said to Aviva, and in a tone that would not this time take the usual coy evasiveness for an answer.

"She's looking for it, dumb-dumb."

"For what?"

"Norman!"

"Aviva!"

"For your father's soul."

"But that's crazy."

"How quickly they forget."

"You're kidding!"

And then she laughed. That's all. A laugh that said it all because suddenly I was up on my feet and cheering for this gorgeous Israeli and with an abandon I didn't know I possessed.

If fans can be dangerous, I was becoming one. The basketball game had become like a prize fight. It's true, as Jon had said, that I was a guest at the Mormons' seaside picnic and I must behave, but I no longer cared about how partisan or even unseemly my behavior had become. I was filled up with that infectious, furious fan's energy, a compound of loyalty, hysteria, and, yes, I confess it, the impulse to violence as well, if that were necessary for my side to prevail.

With sports as my metaphor and my camouflage, let me admit that the darker side also emerged, as I have been reporting: I was in the thrall of a resurgent anger at the theft the Mormons were attempting to commit in trying to glom onto and to claim access to a soul to which they were utterly not entitled. Jon's own living soul was one thing. If he wanted to hand it over like a free will offering . . . like an organ donation . . . and wrap it up with a ribbon and leave it on the ward's doorstep, all right, go ahead. He had free will, he was entitled.

But Paul's postmortem gambling soul? For better or for worse we Jews had from the beginning of Hebrew time collectively produced that thing and whatever it was, wherever it was, it was now our obligation to hold onto it, even in death.

No matter that I had become a marijuana-addled, cheeseburger-eating seminary dropout. To even consider letting them offer him their gospel! All my jumping up and down and cheering on Tali's play had cleared my head.

I was her number one fan, and I began to scream for blood.

And Tali delivered.

Because when the score was tied at forty-eight baskets for Wes and forty-eight for Tali, it happened, the climax to which this contest had been building.

Wes extricated himself from her defense, stutter-stepped to make some space, rose, and somehow converted his next shot—a short, wheeling underhanded drop over the rim.

Tali wasn't able to reply on her next run, and she also lost control of the ball. He recovered it and beat her out for the next rebound.

One more basket and the game would be over.

He now was protecting the ball extremely well from her repeated reach-in attempts to steal. Yet he was committing a blunder for which he can be forgiven: he thought he was playing merely a game of basketball.

A sizable van had pulled over into the parking lot—its bearded driver and a bunch of his kids, I presumed, were sitting on the top to watch the game, to catch a glimpse of this greatest interfaith, Judeo-Mormon one-on-one game in the entire history of hoops.

Wes knew his tank was on empty, and he was now going to make one last, extraordinary effort to win the game. All he needed was one more basket. He dribbled away from Tali, but slowly, in an almost leisurely loop near the half-court line as if he were husbanding his energy for the shot of his life. If he sank it, the game would be over; and the picnic, along with normality, might resume.

The court was silent; even the waves seemed to have become muted.

Now down toward the lane, starting from the half-court line, Wes began his drive, with Tali matching him step for step. If the drive for a lay-up continued, she certainly knew that his height and ability to extend would put her again at a critical disadvantage, so she had to force him to stop and make a short- or medium-range jumper; she needed him to alter his course, and therefore his shot; that would give her a chance to tie yet again, but how?

These many years later, I'm still not sure I trust merely the evidence of the eyes.

It unfolded mysteriously, both slowly and also swiftly, like still frames that accelerated into action, as she now stutter-stepped or stumbled, I'm not sure which, but with the result that Wes now had a crucial half step on her. Tali's effort appeared to have failed. He strained to gain another half step on her—even a half of a half would do it to complete the drive and to give him just the opening needed for the lay-up.

Yet suddenly there she was in front of him, as if there were two Talis, as if a copy of her, having leaped out, without the first Tali leaving her space or moving her feet, were suddenly there.

Wes put on the brakes. Big time. He had to. He couldn't plow through her. So he circled back to the top of the key. He would try again. From here he considered briefly, and then again advanced toward the basket, but in a manner that was almost a leap after a single great step toward the hoop.

Yet Tali somehow recovered and with a burst of power from her legs, like a broad jumper's initial lift, she rocketed up and caught him.

The collision occurred while Wes was in the air, and in the millisecond the ball was leaving his fingertips. Tali's formidable hip had also caught him at the thigh, upending him so that he toppled over, awkwardly and also lunged forward at the same time to break his fall.

Wes's body hit the surface of the court with a disturbing thud followed by a snapping noise as his head cracked against the metal base in which the pole of the basket was planted. He groaned, then rolled to his right, his mouth opening wide like a fish caught up on land and trying to catch an impossible breath. Then he went limp and silent.

The shot did not drop.

17

JON and Mary Anne were the first to reach Wes, who lay alarmingly still beneath the backboard; a trickle of blood meandered out the side of his mouth.

The angels stood intently watching within the ring of concerned Mormon onlookers who moved inch by inch forward, peering over my brother and Mary Anne to see how seriously Wes was injured.

Mary Anne's cousin, a small, thin Mormon from rural Utah, as it turned out, and a third-year pre-med student at Brigham Young University in town for a visit, now joined them, leaning over Wes to take a pulse. Now he lowered his head above Wes's nose to check for breathing. He seemed uncertain of himself, and nervous as Wes tried to raise himself from the asphalt and to speak; only garbled, incoherent sounds emerged. He fell back down in a scary sagging way and his eyes turned glassy and radiated an eerie, non-responding stare.

When Wes's body suddenly spasmed, Tali and Aviva stepped forward, and the Mormon lines parted to make way for them.

From where I stood, shocked beyond immediate comprehension, it was difficult to see exactly how they proceeded. Yet it was clear that they exuded a calm and confidence that the moment required, because Wes began to shake or spasm. Aviva tapped at his forehead with her index finger and carefully examined the back of his neck. She withdraw a very white handkerchief from the back of her shorts and dabbed the blood on Wes's face.

Tali put one arm under him and with the other tapped his temple, gave his face a soft slap, and performed some other manipulations that seemed to me to come out of nobody's Red Cross emergency manual I knew of.

Yet the result was that Wes seemed to calm down. Tali touched the side of his mouth from which he was bleeding and the flow of blood slowed, and eventually stopped. Remarkably, Wes startled awake, and tried to sit up again. Tali cradled him in her arm. Having done the damage, the angels now—or so it seemed—were providing the repair.

Wes looked around with eyes somewhere between not seeing anything and looking beyond to a horizon invisible to us. He tried to communicate again, but a groan swallowed his first syllables, and his face crumpled again into pain.

That's when the angels really took charge. Tali examined him further and conferred with Aviva. Then she called out specifically what materials were needed. Mary Anne took charge of that aspect of patient care, and soon it was as if Tali and Aviva were transformed into battlefield medics. Now, they were fashioning a splint from the handles of two wooden spatulas to prevent Wes's jaw from moving.

Although the angels were completely unknown to the Mormons, they permitted Tali and Aviva to minister to Wes; even the pre-med and nursing students among them deferred, because the girls exhibited such authority and effectiveness. Now they checked Wes's pulse again, wiped his forehead with ice-water compresses that Mary Anne had brought over, and kept him if not calm, then still, and stabilized.

By then Jon had run over to the phone booth by the parking lot and had called for an ambulance.

In the interval of perhaps ten or twelve minutes, before the ambulance siren was first heard wailing along the Pacific Coast Highway, Jon gave me withering looks whose message was unmistakable: the delicate balance we had been managing had altered; the unspoken makeshift truce of brothers was broken.

ON MONDAY our lives returned to a version of normal, but only at camp where decorum and the eyes of the director and a visiting Mr. Footlick and visiting parents forced Jon and me to put on a charade of civility.

As to the angels, they said nothing; they revealed nothing. It was more than that they simply had no comment. It was as if that dangerous game had not even occurred. Their conduct remained consistent, that peculiar combination of the quotidian and the quietly strange that I never could get quite used to.

They did their jobs with the usual efficiency and aplomb. Jon went out of his way to avoid them, but during at least my interactions they didn't once even ask after Western Oaks or refer to the picnic, the remarkable basketball game, or the accident.

When the day was done and the campers sent home, I told Tali and Aviva that Jon and I were going to visit Wes at the hospital.

They expressed no interest in joining. They just stood by the car, where we had walked together, silent, like two shy girls with no social skills at all, waiting for us to say the next thing, whatever that might be. It was extraordinary; it wasn't the way normal human beings react, especially after what had happened, unless they were, well, in a kind of low-grade shock themselves, or aftershock at the accident; or maybe it was because they were just from a different realm altogether.

"I'll give him your best wishes," Jon finally spoke up as he stood in front of the passenger door as if to block the angels' potential entry. "You two are dangerous."

They neither laughed nor smiled at Jon's barbed irony, neither argued nor questioned him, nor answered, or even reacted in any way.

They just stood there, as if waiting for us to get on with it, to cycle through our necessary formulations, our litany of silly human sounds.

Finally, Tali announced she was going up to Century City, and that Aviva would join her. They were going shopping; their target this time: to select materials to make rubberized swim caps with crests, antlers, and other animal-designating detail for the costumes for the Noah's Ark play, she explained.

"You could go some other time," I tried.

"Dress rehearsal tomorrow. Remember?" said Aviva.

"Don't you love all these animals!" Tali exclaimed.

It was as if they were reciting lines—actually maybe even flubbing them—from a play, but an awkward one not appropriate at all for that moment. As always, the awkwardness is hard to explain.

"You should come with us," I tried again.

"But the sale ends today," said Aviva. "Half off."

"Half off, half off, half off," Tali repeated with a kind of mechanical giggle, an inappropriate glee at the sound of the phrase as if she had never heard it before. Or it was as if she had not been listening, as if she were not there at all.

"Let's just go, man," Jon finally said.

"Yes, go," said Aviva. "Go, go."

"Go, go," Tali repeated. "Go, go, girls," she giggled. "Go, go, boys."

Then they did that laugh again, stifling it slowly as Aviva pulled up her white socks. Tali checked the bus schedule that she pulled out of her left front pocket. Then she hoisted her rucksack, high on her shoulder.

With that, they gave us a wave, like the little kids from camp, and the two of them headed out toward the bus shelter across La Cienega Boulevard. That's where the Century City, west-bound bus soon was due.

Not a word or thought or emotion for the condition of the guy Tali had almost decapitated. It was as if they had not even been at the beach with us when the accident occurred, which, as it turned out, had broken Wes's jaw. The docs out at UCLA Medical Center, where we were headed, had determined that mandible surgery was going to be required before Wes reclaimed full ability to speak.

We had told the angels this, of course, but obviously none of it had deterred them from their sale and from their half-off shopping spree.

I was really dumbfounded, but now, after they loped off, another surprise awaited me. I guess I shouldn't have been surprised but I was: Jon said he preferred to visit Wes alone, without me.

"From the minute you met him, you've wanted to shut Wes up. Don't you think I know that? So, congratulations, rabbi. Now you have. But not for long. Mormons are used to attack. They rehabilitate fast. I need to get going." He walked over to the Rambler, and I followed as he got in behind the wheel and slammed the door in front of me. "Wes doesn't need a visit from you either. Believe me. Go and have a cheeseburger. I'll talk to you later."

I leaned into the window with my arms. Jon pushed me away, but I grasped the door again, I held onto the car, I didn't want it to go.

Then, for the first time I could remember since we had tussled as kids, he used his size and strength to intimidate me. He slowly, almost theatrically, I would say, extended his arm out the window. He placed his hand, all five fingers spread out over my chest. There's a way to push a person that says, You're blocking my path. Jon's gesture said more. It said, You're blocking my life.

Then as he put on a pair of sunglasses, so I couldn't see his eyes, he added, "You provoked those girls."

"Now wait a second."

"You deny it!" He got out of the car. He towered over me. "I told you to stop it."

"They were my . . . teammates. I cheered them on."

"I know what you did. I know what you wished."

"How come everybody thinks they know what I think?"

"Just lay off what I'm doing with the church. You got that?"

He slid back into the car and turned on the ignition. The engine kicked over, but had a second thought and died.

"Maybe it's telling you to let me come along."

"It's telling you to get lost."

He keyed the engine once, then twice; finally, it turned over. He put the car in gear and gave it a little gas; it began to move away from the curb. I kept my hands on the window near him. I refused to let go. He pushed me away. I jogged alongside.

"Why are you doing this? Are you high again? Someone's going to get hurt. Someone already has. Get away, man."

Some urge then possessed me and I ran around, in front of the car. I was daring Jon to keep going. For all I knew in that crazy instant, I wanted him to keep going, because I did feel bad, very bad, for what had happened. I liked Wes, yet, mea culpa; I was also elated they had not won that game. On the horns of my usual dilemma, a step forward, a step back. It was all so serious and yet also so flat-out stupid. Had he kept rolling and pancaked me, it would have been a kind of solution, but I knew of course that he wouldn't. Still I stood there, now in front of the Rambler, by the left head lamp, and I dared him.

"You're nuts."

"All right, I am." So I inched in front of the hood a little more, maybe a shoe length, a shoe length and a half. Had he moved forward, my foot would have never been the same.

"Get out of the way."

I stood my ground. He honked the horn loudly, once, twice. I stood there. Jon pulled slowly back into the parking lane, turned off the engine, and got out of the car.

"Listen, you maniac, I still don't think you have any idea how you were acting. You were like her insane coach storming up and down the sideline. An out-of-control character that they should eject from a game! Yes, you, pal, signaling, egging her on to play like an animal out there."

"I signaled to her?"

"Of course you did, and boy, did she ever respond. There's something strange here. I don't get it, and I don't want to get it. I just want it to stop."

So I told him, more clearly than ever, that they were angels sent to stop him from stealing our father's soul. Plain and simple. There it was.

Jon would have none of it. "You're high. They're not angels, man. If anything, they're devils. You and them! Both of you, all of you, please stay away. Now I don't want to be late for visiting hours."

With that, he got back in the car, reached across for the handle, and pulled the door toward him.

I held onto it.

"Come on, man. Take a nap. You need it."

Then he slapped my hands away, and pulled the door shut.

"At least tell him I'm sorry."

"Send flowers! And go home."

I DIDN'T go home. I turned back toward the park. Through the slats of the fence I saw some of the junior counselors collecting the orange cones we used for the kick ball and soccer drills. It was their turn to close down, and they were doing just fine collapsing the small trampoline, stowing the other equipment. I decided to do something useful if only to stop thinking about Western Oaks and the angels and what had happened, so I pitched in.

I carefully folded up a mini volleyball set we used for the eight-year-olds; I stacked plastic milk crates we used for the snacks. It was good to work at tasks where the thinking side of the brain took a rest; boy, did mine ever need a long sabbatical.

Yet when I was through, twenty minutes later, with all of the camp gear stored, including our growing collection of rubberized antlers, snouts, and tails for my Noah's Ark extravaganza, my feet began to guide me somewhere totally unexpected.

From the perspective of all of these decades since, it was to a destination no longer avoidable, even inevitable.

I was walking the usual route along Olympic Boulevard toward Orange

Grove and home, but at La Cienega Boulevard, near Ships's aromatic corner, I paused. I thought about what Jon had said. I thought hard about it. It's not as if I didn't feel that I possessed free will. I felt something like that within, a warm familiar sense that I was just who I thought I was, and, God knows, I was exercising it all the time if generally in unattractive ways.

Yet on this occasion it was as if that free will, like a doppelganger of myself, stepped right out of me like a dance partner or like my own shadow that simply had had enough. He gave me a polite tip of his cap, like Mr. Peanut in the advertisements, as if to say thanks for the memories, pal, and then he began to walk home alone, a choice I could have made, while I now headed to another fate.

As if guided by, yes, some new vectoring power from outside of myself, a slight wind at the back, so it felt once again, I turned and entered the precincts of Temple Beth Ami.

From what I knew of the Foot's schedule, he'd be gone. Now, if the building were still open, I felt I could fulfill some business I apparently had here, although on the steps, as I mounted them, I didn't yet know precisely what that business was.

I first tried the sanctuary doors at the top of the grand steps where you entered all dressed up for the Sabbath or for the holidays. But today was an ordinary day and growing gray with threatening rain, last I'd looked up. Either I'd get in this place, or get drenched trying to make my way home.

I tried all three sets of redoubtable double doors—the first with the crossing of the Red Sea sculpted in dark and shiny wood panel reliefs; the second depicting Moses loping down the mountain cradling the Ten Commandments with a hopeful expression on his bearded face; on the third door a bird was flying just out of reach of pointing fingers in a crowded tabernacle, an avian scene which I could never place or figure out. No doubt I had been sleeping in class at the seminary when that lesson had been taught.

Every one of the imposing doors was locked tight. But the side door, the school entrance, which I now tried, was open, and when I stepped in, there was the old Negro janitor, Solomon, sweeping away.

We had always called him only Solomon. I'd like to think that back then it might have occurred to me to wonder why we had just lopped off the man's last name, but it had not.

He was sweeping the hallway now, his eyes on the neat line of dirt he was pushing along on the otherwise shiny floor; he was intent on his job. Since camp had begun, I'd waved casual hellos, but we had never talked or reminisced until now.

"What you doin' here?" he said when he spotted me.

Now he paused, seemed to clench the handle of his broom, and turned to face me from beneath the black, boxy, fez-like skullcap that he always wore and that had made him, obviously a non-Jew, look a little, well, ridiculous; his eyes appeared bloodshot and not a little alarmed as he looked over my shoulder to see who else—like my whole camp group!—might be coming in at this irregular hour to ruin his just-swept floor.

I well remembered Solomon from when I was a star in Hebrew School fifteen years before, and he was still sweeping in precisely this same methodical manner. I had liked him, his plain talking, without the frills of inane compliments that I'd been receiving much of at the time from every teacher, parent, and Hebrew-school secretary in sight.

Solomon didn't treat me like some junior Hebrew prodigy. I'd felt early on that I was a kind of fake prodigy, and I was silently deeply grateful to Solomon; his ignoring of me confirmed that here was at least one person in the building—maybe in the whole wide world—who could see the truth of things.

I also liked the precise way he set up the folding chairs for our little holiday or academic award assemblies. I liked how he took the big industrial broom that spanned half the width of the corridor and swept out after we'd spilled potato pancakes and apple sauce, dropped our grape juice cups and squashed Milk Duds, and in general had messed up his shiny floor at our Hanukkah party.

His stolid face and voice had an edge of suppressed anger, not unlike Paul's when he stopped the wisecracking, that to me seemed a perfectly normal way to be in the world.

"I hope I'm not getting in your way."

"No one gets in my way. What you want, son?"

"I'm not sure."

"Then why you here?"

Paul had said to me ten years before when we had watched on TV President Dwight D. Eisenhower announce he was sending the army to help integrate the high school in Little Rock—and I was hearing it again right there in the corridor with Solomon—"There's got to be someone lower than you on the human totem pole, even for the Negroes there's got to be someone lower. No man likes to feel he's at the bottom," Paul used to say. "No one."

Solomon and I now said a few banal words of reacquaintance. Dialogue's not the right word. It was mainly me yammering on and Solomon staring back at me with an occasional, "Uh huh."

"Mind if I look around?"

"I don't know. At this hour maybe I do."

Then he just resumed his work, pushing the line of dirt a few more inches down the corridor; I took that as a green light, and he didn't stop me.

I felt like a sleepwalker stumbling into the past as I peeked into the nondescript classrooms with their green metal doors, behind which I had spent so much of my life.

I guess Solomon's very presence at the temple had always made me feel, yes, a little guilty, as if my being one of the young stars of the LA Jewish diaspora had somehow contributed directly to his status in life and to the lousy work he had to do. Sure it had given him a job, but quite a crappy one.

He was still wearing his uniform, heavy-duty blue work pants and matching shirt, and the hallways smelled of that slightly astringent chemical that he still was using. In the silence all about the empty classrooms, except for the smooth sounds of the sweeping, I could hear the teachers I now remembered—Rosner, Yaroslavsky, Slomovic—asking the class their questions; here now was the chair-on-floor scraping sound of my obnoxious little self popping up from my desk, always with the right answer, especially on trick questions dealing with arcane points of Hebrew grammar. Never mind that the day before, as my friends had been out playing Little League ball and having a good time, I had been studying at my desk at home for hours just to achieve my puny distinctions.

I stuck my head into another room, and here I practically could hear every word of my Hebrew recitation as if it still lingered on the molecules of air: "Hear O Israel the Lord our God, the Lord is One," that fundamental declaration of the faith, and its accompanying paragraph, that I used to utter at night, in the morning, and several times a day for practice in the run-up to our annual *Shema* speed-reciting contest: "And thou shalt love the Lord your God with all your heart, with all your soul, and with all your might. And these words, which I command you this day, shall be in thy heart."

Whoa! It was as if the words had never gone out into the endless near vacuums of space. They were still here like motes of dust that I'd just stirred up by entering; maybe that was part of Solomon's job: to guard them, to clean daily but without sweeping the memories away.

Now he paused, moving closer to me, stepping into a shaft of light that was coming through a transom window. I could see now that his hair had really turned a speckled gray.

He put his chin on the nub of his broom, and finally took his measure of me. "What you want now?"

As if my destination only now came into focus, I asked to be let into the temple's library.

I had lost all track of time, but Solomon hadn't; he always knew the time, precisely, without even checking his watch. "It's near to closin' and anyway, that's private for the rabbi."

"I know, but all I want to do is check some books."

"I got to get home to my wife. She's makin' chicken dinner."

"Fifteen minutes?"

"What books?"

"I'll know them when I see them."

"You sure are bigger than you were before."

"That's what happens."

"And nosier. And fatter. What you been eatin', son?"

"Nothing good."

"What you need the books for?"

"I'm going to look up stuff. About souls."

"Souls?"

"Jewish souls."

"Really? Well, I'll be."

"Solomon, you think there's a difference between, say, a Jewish soul and anybody else's soul? Say, a Negro soul?"

"I couldn't say."

Still I could see by the way he looked off down the hallway that he was in his way ruminating if not the metaphysics, maybe the balance of his chores that I was interrupting, or maybe his thoughts were just of the fried chicken.

"Any difference between your soul and mine?"

Solomon thought a long time before answering your questions. I liked that about him. Wes and the Mormons, and now even my former doper brother, also seemed to have this deliberative quality of mind. On the other hand, my teachers and especially my erstwhile seminary pals had always been, like me, quick hand-raisers, eager to beat the others to the answers of tough questions, and right away. Compared to the Mormons we certainly were an argumentative bunch.

"I just do the cleanin'."

"Well, what's it mean, for example, when people say James Brown has 'soul'?"

"Where you comin' from, son?"

"I mean does he, James Brown, the King of Soul, have something, say, that's different from you? From your soul?"

"Well James Brown can dance and sing a lot better than me."

"Is that all? Your souls, yours and James Brown's, will go to the same heaven?"

"How can a person know any of *that*? Wherever he go, he be dancin' and singin'."

"And you?"

"Me? What you think? *I'll* be sweepin'!"

"In heaven? You don't believe that."

"What you say, boy? Someone's got to do it."

"Doesn't sound right to me. That's why I need the library. Rabbi Joel won't mind."

"How you know he won't?"

"Just twenty minutes."

"Twenty minutes?" He checked his watch.

"I'll be fast. I promise."

"You said fifteen."

"Thank you!"

"You be quick. Hear?"

SOLOMON JANGLED his ring of keys as he led me up the service stairs and then down a back hallway that opened into the brown-carpeted office area where behind double glass doors Rabbi Joel's study beckoned. Book-lined on three sides, this had been among my favorite rooms in the temple, and I actually still remembered quite well the placement of the books.

I had been here several times for those inane little competitions I've mentioned before—Rabbi Joel called the *Shema* speed reading his Hebrew Olympics!—and to receive my pins for excellence in junior congregation attendance, another pin for my services handing out skullcaps by the door at junior congregation, and for winning a prize in identifying biblical quotations and Key Dates in Jewish History.

I can still recite details of the dour event that occurred in Europe in 1290. That's when Jews were expelled from France.

I passed over the many-volumed Talmud, an oversize group of tall sentinels that lined the top shelves as if monitoring the less imposing books below. For a guy who spoke in clichés and in banalities, Rabbi Joel had assembled a surprisingly vivid and eclectic collection. Now I let my fingers walk with familiar pleasure up and down the spines. Every tenth book or so I had formerly owned, and had sold to fly home.

Now here I was scanning them once again.

Soon I found what I was looking for: the small but, as it turned out, sufficient section with books on Jewish folkways, legends, myths, and, I hoped, the lowdown on Jewish souls.

I had to wade through tales of the *Chasidim*; here was a shelf on the eighteenth-century movement of Eastern European Jews who had scandalized the rabbis by putting the emotions, especially in response to prayer and God, above erudition. Their heirs had given us Shalom Aleichem's *Fiddler on the Roof*, and the cozy practices and superstitions that are part of the holidays. These, along with collections of Jewish jokes, toasts, cookbooks, and detective fiction I quickly picked up, and put down.

In short order, I found several I was looking for: one, an old volume about angels, souls, and those troubled demon-like souls gone awry, the *dybbuk*s. It suddenly occurred to me that maybe one of them had lodged within me or had been trying to enter ever since I arrived home in LA. That would explain . . . no, there was plenty else to explain my crazy ups and downs without looking for a *dybbuk*.

Here was another with a mottled spine and with a medley of smells I will associate forever with old Jewish books: leather and old men's loving if bad breath and something vaguely agricultural, like bushels of hay or some tall, wavy grain crop you could hide in from the taskmaster. This little volume was kind of an everyman's encyclopedia of Jewish populist theology, folk beliefs, and tall tales, and in English no less.

Having finally tracked down in print what I'd heard from the angels on the basketball court—because it could no longer be denied—I settled in to read: technically, "breath" or *neshama*, it turns out, is the word that describes the aspect of the soul that, like glue, links or adheres the fragile, death-defying consciousness to the mortal, physical body. It's the substance or energy that somehow leaves the body at precisely the point of death, like a gaseous evaporation of water, which characterizes the soul's departure.

By contrast, the *ibbur* is something very different, I confirmed. It is seen as the filmier, gauzy emanation of the soul on its return journey, the flighty, flimsy thing that, according to this source, travels back to this earthly realm in order to find a person to inhabit as a kind of spiritual headquarters; from there the *ibbur* tries to finish its person's unfinished business on earth.

Who even knew the sophisticated Jews engaged in such stuff?

Among the categories or types of scores needing the *ibbur* to intercede for settlement, the text went on, are the financial, including debt payments; finishing acts of charity contemplated but not quite undertaken; cleaning up nasty, envious thoughts; saying things that were left unsaid to loved ones; and other outstanding matters.

The *ultimate* goal: the punch list is shortened with those blemishes eliminated or at least diminished, so that the soul can enter heaven and be all polished and set to shine.

Absolutely amazing, I thought. They hadn't taught any of this at the seminary in New York.

The *ibbur* is then, yes, a kind of residence of a "living" soul of a departed person inside the body of another living person, and presumably a person with whom the business is to be conducted. But not always. There, of course, is the rub.

You can't help the *ibbur* in any dramatic, detailed fashion until you've located where it is and then can make an effort to communicate.

I read fast, and then faster.

Another key point: the *ibbur* is the opposite of a *dybbuk*. A *dybbuk* is a nasty, unhappy, angry spirit that refuses to accept its condition of death, namely, that the body it was originally attached to is, well, gone. It's in a post-death denial of the highest order. It is desperately unhappy with the result and is now in headlong rampage. Like a criminal on the run, the *dybbuk* chooses its resident body not because of a connection to its person's business, but at random, like a man at his wit's end taking as hostage a body that just happens to be at the wrong place at the wrong time.

Or there *is* a kind of connection, but the *dybbuk's* spiritual stuff is still so flawed with the crap of earthly existence that the result is a terrible misfit, and torment.

On the other hand, our good little *ibbur* is always trying to obey the laws of souls. A good citizen of the afterlife, it is being polite and just going about its soul business; it just needs here and there the helping hand of the living to journey to completion.

That's why, in part, after a person's death Jewish tradition dictates that you're supposed to give money to charity. Which charity? Well, if you don't know those places the departed cared about, if to do this work you haven't located the *ibbur* within the allotted time—those twelve months after death I've referred to earlier—you just cover all bets by spreading little contributions all around and hope for the best that something critical sticks.

As Paul would say, a kind of Jewish crap shoot.

I looked up and around. I was still in the library. I didn't know how much time had passed, and I felt the presence of the angels.

If I had read the texts assigned to me with the intensity I was poring over these, they never would have kicked me out. I felt my heart beating very fast; I checked out the clock on the rabbi's desk. It sat beside a picture of Rabbi Joel's family, his pretty, long-haired wife Rebecca and the kids, Tova and Tamar, who both wore black glasses as thick as mine. The clock was the only sound in the room; it was ticking away loudly the minutes I had left.

I sat down in the spacious, Naugahyde desk chair and, as I read, I began to swivel, but slowly, as if my revolutions in the rabbi's chair were keeping pace with new insights being born. I closed my eyes. Like a kid, I whirled myself around once, then slowed down, then once again more slowly I swiveled.

I was locked in. I was riveted. The Jewish soul business was far more subtle than I had given it credit for. And the kicker, as Paul used to say, in one of his many poker-is-like-life metaphors, is what had happened on the basketball court. I now understood: they *are* angels. They are, I heard myself repeating, as I swiveled slowly around like a guy sitting on the hand of a turning clock. They are. Out in Santa Monica, on that court, they were fighting for Paul's soul, and so should you, man. So should you, dammit. I swiveled, I turned again. So should you!

On the other hand, wasn't this completely crazy? Paul Gould certainly had plenty of unfinished business, but looking for his soul, battling for it, as Tali had, against a Mormon missionary?

Unless . . . of course. . . . Yes, another way to interpret the action: Paul Gould's soul, his *ibbur*, had also been there precisely because he was fighting Western Oaks. If he were alive, in body, he certainly would be going nuts at how Wes was trying to, in effect, appropriate Jon's soul, his own boy's soul as well as his own.

Look, he would say, how they are sandbagging you, son. They are using all these friendly beach-party means to conceal a spiritual crime. The Mormons suddenly seemed nefarious, but scary, like street kids lifting valuable souls out of the many people they encounter, like pickpockets at Times Square or on the subway. And to counter this, Tali and Aviva were grabbing at the offending hand. No wonder Tali had played with such abandon. They took my wager seriously as I hadn't. Their lesson to me: souls live!

I was suddenly proud of my wayward father. Through the Israelis, who were his substitutes, he was fighting Wes. He was pouring it on. Of course, of course!

Suddenly the library door opened and there was Solomon. "You find the souls you was lookin' for?"

He eyed with irritation all the books I had scattered in disarray across the desk. I felt my forehead covered with sweat, as if I had just returned from playing that half-court game once again. I found a tissue on the rabbi's desk, and wiped the perspiration. Solomon surveyed me and stayed silent. I stood up and carefully closed several of the open books. I began to replace them on the shelf under the janitor's supervision.

"You put it right back, *exactly* where you took it from."

"I am."

"Exactly?"

"Exactly. Look. I'm doing it."

"To the inch? Rabbi will notice if it's off. He'll be checkin' it in the mornin'. Always does."

"That's okay. You be my witness. I'm putting back all of the books precisely where I found them."

"Lemme check."

"Okay."

When he had, Solomon half-murmured, half-grunted his okay. "If Rabbi notices something and asks, what do I tell him? Boy dropped by lookin' for souls?"

"Sure. Tell him that."

"I gave you more time than you ask for."

"You're a generous man."

"Because you lost your daddy."

"You remember."

"I remember. What was it . . . about a year ago?"

"Yes. Not quite. Ten months."

"That whose soul you lookin' for?"

I didn't answer. When he draped his arm over my shoulder and said, almost as an afterthought, "Let's go home now, son," I could barely keep from sobbing.

18

IN the days following Wes's injury Jon began to spend even more time away from us. He said he was helping his new best friend with the facial exercises that were part of his rehab; he was pitching in at the ward; he was serving as a driver for local missionaries; he was away, and always bound for some LDS destination.

"Why aren't *you* spending more time with your brother?" Paulene asked me over a dinner of stuffed green peppers that we scooped out of a Canter's take-out container.

"Because he doesn't want me to."

"You don't try hard enough."

"I do, I do."

"Liar."

"It's not easy."

Paulene sensed, rightly, that the ante had been upped, and big time. She could have interrogated me further, but on this occasion I lucked out. I was fortunate that she was tired and depressed by it all and had even turned down an evening with Mr. Footlick—I liked that part—because I wasn't quite ready yet to talk to her about *neshama*s and *ibbur*s.

I was still doubting the evidence of my eyes, and my heart. I was retreating from my insight about the angels as the spell of the game and the library became more diffuse.

It was just as well, because I sensed if I began talking about souls, right around the corner could be a teary confession about the seminary. Jon's Mormon wanderings were making our mother's craving for a rabbi-soon-to-be in the family more acute by the day. The very last thing she needed now was to find out her other son had become a draft-card-burning, dope-smoking, soul-and-angel-chasing rabbinic-school dropout.

I can't recollect what we talked about as the evening wore on and what we both had been silently hoping and listening for—the rattle of the screen door and for Jon to appear—did not happen. The best thing either of us could do would be simply to go to bed and to hope for a better day tomorrow. Then, however, Paulene did something very uncharacteristic: she fell into a rare fit of remorse and began to berate herself.

As she talked on, it dawned on me that she must still think that this abstracted, newly fat-bellied and self-indulgent elder son of hers could actually still listen and pay attention. To my slowly percolating consternation, she was unburdening herself as if, God help me, she were asking for a kind of—how I hated the word but it applied—pastoral guidance!

At least this told me that my brother had not yet spilled any of the beans about New York, or even hinted at it, that she thought me still capable of, and even interested in, offering not only a son's but a chubby chaplain's ear. That's what she really liked about the rabbi-ing profession that she had long urged me to embrace: for some bizarre reason it had gotten into her head that, compared with other more distracted human beings who share the planet with us, rabbis are superior listeners.

Of course my behavior that summer was not exactly proof of this dubious contention.

Yet I tried, as Paulene began to unburden herself: had she accepted too many extra shifts during our growing up? Is that why Jon had taken this awful turn? Had she made a mistake not being home more for him, especially when Paul went missing on his mysterious one- and two-day excursions away from us—"on business" to the casinos—just like Jon was doing now but instead of going to the slot machines, *his* business was the Mormons!

"You were little kids, and you had a right to expect at least one of us to be around."

"It was fine with Ida. It was fine, Mom."

"No! One of us should have been with you there, all the time. More than we were. She can hardly speak English. Could she help him with his fractions? Not even arithmetic. Could she help him with his Hebrew? No. I think I made a terrible mistake."

"Don't do this."

"First he drops out of Hebrew school. Now he's dropping out of the Jewish People altogether," she said as tiny streaks of her mascara trickled down from her left eye, leaving a sad trail down her cheek.

"Please don't do this to yourself!"

She barely heard.

Yet even if she had unearthed some parental path not taken, what good would it do to dwell on it now?

At bottom what Paulene craved was simple assurance that she had been a good mother. I tried to provide it, and yet I also had Paul's bad habit, the insecure poker player's invariably bad bluffing habit, of straining to make yet another lame wisecrack and then another, giving an impression I could hardly support, neither with money nor with cards, nor, in this case, by telling the truth.

A FEW days passed, but not without each containing a reminder, a nudge, a serious lobbying of me to push, to rescue, and to save my brother, and each always accompanied by these terrible child-rearing recriminations that continued to assail her. One night, a week after the game as I clicked open the door for her in the parking lot of Canter's, Paulene said, "So are you finally getting through to your brother?"

"Oh, yes."

"Be serious," she said as she folded herself into the seat, and looked straight ahead, not at me.

"I am."

"He's your only brother," she said as we drove slowly home. " He's—" and then whatever sentence she was forming just stopped saying itself, snapped itself right in half. I could almost hear unspoken words crumble in her mouth like an old, brittle cracker. I reached out to touch her shoulder, still in its Canter's white uniform, but my mother pulled away. Her recoil wasn't much. A ruler might not have been able to measure it, but I had.

We were stopped at the light at Crescent Heights Boulevard. By now she knew that the Mormons were down that street, just a few blocks away, behind the last ball fields of the park, in their stout little ward building, and that Jon and Wes likely were there. Even as we sat waiting for the signal to change, Jon may have been answering the phone for Wes, the new eager Mormon intern fetching him tea with a straw, or jello, or a malted, or double-checking the addresses of the newest street full of proselytizing prospects, doing who-knew-what as the missionary got back to his duties.

"You want to go storm the place with me?"

No reply.

"Throw bagels at the windows? Till they break?"

No reply.

"With cream cheese? Make a big mess?"

When the light changed to green she said, "Ah, what's the use?"

It wasn't so much to me and my nonsense that she'd spoken as to, well, who knew? Maybe to the Mormons, or was it to the whole listening or unlistening world?

Then she fished out the pack of Lucky Strikes from her purse, and lit up, and smoked in silence.

As we headed down Fairfax, I drove at maybe fifteen miles an hour, letting cars pass. I kept it very slow as if not talking would slow down the trip because neither of us wanted to arrive at the duplex; delay was good; delay meant avoiding further confessions that seemed to be in the offing.

I caught troubling raw glances of her in the passing cars' brash head lamps. For the first time since my return, Paulene appeared to me really older. I didn't think it had anything to do with the caking of her makeup, which she very occasionally let happen. It was rather as if on this one night all her years of waitressing had suddenly crashed down on her. It was not a wrinkled kind of old, but as if a sodden heaviness were sagging on her and pulling her down from within. Although this vision of her exhaustion was brief, it stayed with me.

As we turned onto Pico she blew a stream of smoke out the window. Then, as Paulene rolled up the glass, she emitted a sigh that trailed off into an agonized, "Why, why, why, why?"

It was a cry I now recognize, all these years later, that had contained an entire disquisition on frustration and dismay not just for herself and her family but for her generation: that here in the Los Angeles of the 1950s and 1960s, in this golden postwar land, bathed in the kosher-style sunlight of Conservative Judaism's gentle and loosening grip, and so far removed from Jew-murdering Europe where, okay, back there in Ida's Poland, you could forgive people for changing their names and for even becoming Christians to avoid the pogrom or the gas chamber. . . . But here in LA? In Santa Monica? In Hollywood and in Beverly Hills? Near Rodeo Drive? Here, where it was so completely *easy* to be a Jew, what possible reason could there be for your child to want to join the Mormons?

Why was he insulting us, the living and the dead? It was inconceivable. Yet it was happening.

I was fortunately by now at a calmer pitch than Paulene. I can't explain why or how it had happened. Yet since the basketball game and the angels' intercession, augmented by my new studies, the gauntlet had been thrown down. And, in my on-again-off-again fashion, drifting in and out of my sense of commitment, I had picked it up.

And there was something more; in the taking up of the task before me, this new, miraculous thing was sweeping over me: an actual sense of purpose, direction, and, dare I employ a Mormon term, mission.

I mean all these souls flitting about all these different levels of heaven, Mormon souls and now Jewish souls, *neshama*s and *ibbur*s, Muslim souls and Negro souls and who knew what else! Other people's souls were out there in the invisible but palpable world that existed all along Pico Boulevard, moving up and down the chutes and ladders of the heavens, looking for matches and for places to reside and carrying on their quests as frantically as mortals trying to mate on earth. They were moving, well, like all this traffic navigating Olympic, Fairfax, and Pico.

Now I wanted to tell Paulene everything! Fortunately I held my peace, for now.

Some jerk ran a red light just before our turn. I slammed on the brakes as Paulene called out, "Jesus Christ, look where you're going!"

"I'm just tired. Sorry. Almost home."

I drove on, but my brain *was* full up with visions of all these souls, the Jews and the Mormons, the Mormons with their premortal lives out in space, little homunculi in space suits is how I saw them traveling, and then they come to earth, and after giving it their best shot, they take off again for a postmortal return flight . . . and suddenly my brain filled up with images of them colliding with these Jewish souls.

Why, it was like where the Harbor, Hollywood, and Santa Monica freeways all intersect, a downtown Interchange of Souls, a layer cake of freeways just full of souls, bumper to bumper and honking at each other, and this one skitters along the shoulder pissing off that one, a Jewish soul curses a Mormon soul, and then they get back on their way . . . yet what if it weren't a joke?

What if through the Mormons Jon had indeed found a way to navigate all of this? What if he had all of the secret signs and the tokens, all of the keys and the garments and passwords and whatnot that good Mormons hope to have to open all those celestial doors? In that case, he'd be like a motorcycle cop or an ambulance tearing through all the soul traffic toward God, while the rest of us Gentiles have to inch along, braking and cursing our frustrating way.

As our house loomed, Paulene, no mincer of words, said, "That skinny one, whose jaw got broken?"

"Wes. You can say his name."

"It just goes to show."

"Show what, Mom?"

She didn't answer right away. She just dragged on her cigarette and let my question dangle and disappear like a smoke ring. We parked in the driveway, and walked slowly across our patch of lawn.

The air was fresh. A few bugs zoomed around the globe of the street lamp. Mom slipped out of her heels and scrunched her red-toenailed feet into the cool grass.

Maybe it was for my sake, maybe it was the nicotine rush, or maybe it was just something she had seen during the ride in *my* face, but she went on: "It just goes to show there's some Mormon girl after your brother. That's the way I still see it."

"No."

"The tall one, Tali, you don't think she gets jealous! What girl wouldn't?"

"I don't get you, Mom."

"So she goes out there and she floors what's his name, their leader. The head of their cult."

"Wes."

"If your brother had been paying attention to Tali, do you think he would have been lured in? Do you think any of this would have happened?"

"What have you been smoking?"

"It's not the first time such things have happened. You don't think cults use sex and . . ."

"Mom! It's not a cult, it's . . . a religion . . . sort of . . . I guess."

"Call it what you want; it's a girl."

In an instant it was all replaying in my mind how Jon and Mary Anne had huddled up during the game before it had devolved to the one-on-one and the accident had happened. And she had been so warm to me. Why? Was she eyeing me already as a future brother-in-law? Could Paulene be right? Mary Anne? It had of course crossed my mind, but then the game had happened, and I dismissed it.

Yes, was she the *one?*

Had I looked but perhaps not really seen, not taken in what was going on between them during Tali's fabulous play? Had her arms gone around Jon during one of the many intervals I had zoned out?

Or was it some other hot Mormon babe, whom Jon was concealing from us, who was luring my brother to her calico and gingham Zion? Not Wes or the highest rung of heaven and eternal family life but a Mary Anne who was the draw? Could my down-to-earth mother be right?

Yes, I was now powerfully tempted to backburner not only the insights of my new soul research, but also the implications of my new sense of mission. Why not instead just give Paulene the benefit of the doubt? I wanted to offer her what she seemed to want, or at least to bluff my way into exaggerating even a seed of the particular view she seemed desperately to need confirmed.

So why not? Why not go along? Or if not that, then tell her about the Battle of Souls going on invisibly all around us. What would she make of that?

We sat on the steps now and smoked, and we talked, finally, not the language of *neshama*s and *ibbur*s and flying Mormon angels or basketball-playing Jewish ones, or the particular soul of Paul Gould, whom Paulene had no clue yet that Jon was after. Instead we talked of sexual attraction and Mormon romance.

I really had never gone for Jon's abstinence line one bit either. Tali and my brother really were a perfect match. Their height, their body types, their athleticism. Paulene pointed it all out. So why in the world wasn't Jon being drawn to our incredible and powerful Sabbath Queen except that he had a hidden Mormon Queen?

I checked on Ida downstairs and climbed back up to the apartment, where Paulene had gone. I noticed how she was stepping quickly, powered by what seemed like new conviction.

Then I followed her outside onto our porch. There, as she lit up again, I took in a long, slow un-nicotined breath of the atmosphere of Orange Grove Drive. This night the air seemed tinged with the particular sweetness of the jasmine in our driveway, or maybe it was from the lemon tree next door, or the perfume of souls flying by.

She pulled another Lucky Strike out of her purse, and held it exactly as Paul used to do. When she said, "Gimme a light, honey," like a starlet who may have made one appearance in an old movie and then disappeared, I realized, as I leaned in toward her face with the match, that the sweetness, almost cloying now, was her perfume, still verdant but left over from the long shift at Canter's where it had gone mixing with Paulene's perspiration, pastrami, corned beef, and pickles.

"I wish you would lay off the smokes, Mom."

"I wish for a lot of things."

"I never see you without one."

"Can't help it these days. So you think I'm right?"

I said nothing.

"I'll talk to Tali, woman to woman."

"Okay."

"You think it'll work?"

"Maybe. Maybe Jon'll come 'round," I lied.

"Sure he will. He has to."

"I hope so."

"Do your part, older brother. Do your part."

"We'll go on some more dates. How 'bout that? Tali and Aviva, Jon and yours truly. I'll fix it up. Jon and Tali in the back seat. Making out like mad. You'll see."

"I sure hope so."

"I know so."

"You're a real *pisher*, you know that, Norman?"

"If you say so."

"I knew a few Mormons in high school. They were all home-ec majors. Made the best pies and cakes in the class. Maybe your brother just wants someone who's, you know, real domestic, around all the time to take care of him. That's not Tali, is it?"

"I bet she could bake if you asked her."

"I suppose," Paulene said almost languidly as she continued to look out into the night sky. "I'll tell you this, though. If she stays in town after camp— and don't think Mr. Footlick isn't trying to make some arrangements—she won't stay single for long. Someone's going to discover her sitting on a stool at the Rexall Drugs like they did with Marilyn Monroe and make her a star."

"She's a star already in my book."

"So?"

"So what, Mom? So what?"

"I should have done a lot more with your brother."

"Stop already."

"Well, you can't make a nickel on the day shift. What else did I know how to do? I thought of going back to school to design clothes, but at my age? And your father didn't make it any easier. A man with two growing boys shouldn't have his income depend on a horse's ankles or drawing an ace. Working shifts at night at least I could make a steady living. One of us had to. Who do you think put milk and bread on the table? Elijah the Prophet?"

"Mom!"

She blew a ring that floated big as a doughnut out over the lawn.

"You know, when you boys were very little, I got your father to stop gambling for a year. One whole year. Boy, did I ever work on him for that. He promised he would go into business, and he did. His tie business? You remember that?"

I didn't.

"He made fat ones exactly when the style began to change to thin. And thin ones including those skinny little lariat cowboy things when the style went back to broad. I'm telling you the man had a gift. And then came his investment in the lawn-furniture business. Another beauty. In a showroom next to that beautiful public pool out at Rancho Park by Cheviot Hills. Who's going to sit on their lawn when the pool is around the corner, and a free public pool! A business genius he wasn't."

"He struggled."

"He certainly did."

"You did the best you could."

She took a drag and kept the smoke deep inside her as long as she could. Now it seemed it wasn't only smoke she was holding in.

"It's going to get better, Mom."

"You've been to a few of those functions with him," she said. She meant the beach parties. "So tell me what this girl looks like."

"Who?"

"Norman! The girl, the love interest, who's pushing Tali away."

"I'll tell you when I set eyes on her."

"You have no idea?"

I was up against it, so I played a card: "There was one. Maybe. Who was playing basketball with them. On their team."

"An athlete? What's she look like?"

"Oh, Mom, can't we shelve it for now?"

"You're some detective. What can any boy want in a girl that Tali doesn't have? She's . . . a goddess."

"That's true."

"Your brother never cared for girls with large breasts. Maybe that's it."

"Mom!"

"Well, then, take Aviva. What's wrong with her? Her boobs are smaller. One of this kind, one of that. He could choose."

"Will you stop!"

"Too much for you?"

"It's you who's too much, Mom."

"You, I think, are destined for a more at-home type too, if you asked me."

"I haven't."

"A mother can dream."

"Just because they're pretty and Israeli. . . . I mean you can't *force* one person to like another person. To love them."

"Stranger things have been known to happen. What do either of you little smart alecks know about love anyway? Look at me and Mr. Footlick."

"I'm trying not to."

"There you go. It's not as if I'm not aware of that, from the both of you. You don't have to *say* anything to me. He treats me with a great deal of respect, and sometimes respect is more important than looks, money, anything."

I was very uncomfortable with this turn of the conversation. We were discussing Jon and his secret Mormon love; that was enough. I didn't like it when she talked about the Foot, and she talked about him far more than she talked about Paul. When she did mention Paul, she seemed only to be highlighting his faults, and he was always in the past tense.

Come to think of it, even though Paul was gone, dead, wasn't she, Paulene, well, still married to him?

If she were a Mormon, she would certainly think so. Death, move over! To hell with "till death do us part." Matrimony has it all on you, Mister Death. For Mormons anyway, marriage holds four aces.

"Norman!"

"What?"

"You're drifting. And please don't be mean to Mr. Footlick."

"Sorry."

"You'll help your brother. You promise?"

"To undermine his Mormon love, whoever she is? Absolutely."

"Don't keep joking."

"I'm not. I mean I will."

"You're certain?"

"Is the Pope Catholic?"

"You're so peculiar this visit!"

"Okay, Mom, okay."

That's all I was good at, making light of stuff. The more serious, the more I joked. I even now began to pull a few exegetical tricks out of my facile sleeve: if the Mormons aren't even technically Christians, I told her, as Bishop Sheen and other local LA prelates had often accused, then maybe Mary Anne or Jon's secret, yet-to-be-discovered Mormon amour would technically not even qualify as a *shiksa*. Was every female non-Jew a *shiksa*? Or only when she becomes a marriage threat?

For a few moments there, I was really cooking. Maybe this yet-to-be-revealed babe could legitimately therefore be termed only *shiksa*-esque? So things weren't so bad after all.

Paulene indulged me, and she just puffed on. In the smoking silence I fancied I could see the shape of Paul's profile, Paul's *ibbur*, the blur of his evanescent soul. But what in the world had she meant a moment ago, that the Foot respected her in a way Paul never had?

How I wanted to ask her, but it was so raw a subject and I couldn't find an opening.

Anyway, my marching orders had been delivered: I would keep searching for the Mormon princess, and with the vague but exciting feeling that souls were all about me and Tali and Aviva my guides in searching for them as well, I kissed my mother good night on her rouged and nicotened cheek. I left her out on the porch, where she said she wanted one more Lucky Strike.

19

AFTER a few days at a rehab facility near Santa Monica and San Vicente Boulevard, Western Oaks had been released to his house, a small bungalow not far from the ward building on Gregory Way. He wore a mandible apparatus, a partial cage that looked a little like a catcher's mask, fashioned of straps with wire and hinges to secure his jaw. The device was also very uncomfortable and sweaty, made worse by the very hot July weather. He was required to eat mostly jello and malteds through a straw.

It escaped none of us—but of course I went on the most about it—that Wes's was the perfect injury to have inflicted on a garrulous missionary whose job is to offer the gospel to souls in this life and the next.

Jon, who reported the news of Wes's condition to us, didn't find my irony very amusing. No one did. I wasn't even amusing myself. Yet that was no reason to stop, not quite yet. How could I, on the one hand, make such thoughtless remarks, Jon asked, and then, on the other, bring Wes a cool and refreshing black-and-white malted from Ships, as I had?

The real conundrum for me was that both gestures, the sarcastic jibe and the guilty peace offering, felt oddly sincere, two sides of the cracked coin I was that summer.

During these days what was especially remarkable was the behavior of the angels. They acted as if, well, nothing out of the ordinary had happened. After camp they usually rushed off by bus to shop at Century City, the May Company at Wilshire and Fairfax, or up to Hollywood, all around town. Neither Tali nor Aviva asked about Wes, or mentioned the game or the accident. It was beyond not exhibiting remorse; it was as if Wes were somehow no longer part of the angels' world; he'd been investigated and silenced, and he was off their list.

It wasn't suprising that Jon not only expressed no interest in double-dating the angels with me, he also stopped speaking to them.

What was most disturbing was that he began to shun me as well. It's a terrible thing when your only brother avoids your eyes, or refuses to look up from a swimming lesson he's giving to a kid, or even dives in the water when he sees you approaching across the deck.

Yet that's what now began to happen. The only silver lining of the accident was that with Wes on the injury list, Jon at least was refraining from more talk of the ordinance to offer Paul the gospel in heaven. As it turned out, that was more my hope than fact.

Jon kept going off so regularly to his seminary in the morning, and now in the evenings to his new assignment, to be Wes's assistant for the ward; each hour Jon spent with them felt like an hour's worth of repudiation. With the angels having become shopaholics, and Paulene working more and more night shifts and dating the Foot, there was only me and Ida. Which is to say I felt more and more alone.

I'm embarrassed these decades later to admit it, but I found company in smoking—not Paul's old Luckys but the remainder of Jon's mellow stash. And that summer I found a lot. One nice hefty bag was labeled "Acapulco Gold" and a second, hidden, of all places, at the bottom of a Hadassah thrift-shop bag, he had labeled "Baja Blue."

When I'd inhaled my way through all that, I had to figure out where I might safely buy more. Twice I cruised an anti-war demonstration, once at UCLA, another time downtown near the federal building. It was well known you could always find some cool anti-war dope, make your purchase, and support the cause in the process.

Once, when I saw a transaction on the border of the picketers where I thought I might nab a nickel bag, I got ready to get out of the car to make my approach. The seller was a ponytailed fellow, fat like myself, and I got ready to offer him my high five of support and my V-sign for peace, and to make my buy. Yet when an LAPD cop in jodphurs and sunglasses cruised by on his motorcycle, I just drove on.

Another time I was cruising the streets down in South Central, where some recent rioting had left blocks of Crenshaw smelling of burn and of wet fireplaces. This turned out to be a very bad idea. I got lost, and the street vibe felt so dangerous I stayed in the car.

I drove and drove, looking for weed and feeling lost between fleeing from, and yet also hurtling toward, this soul business.

It was only one early Thursday evening when I'd I tucked Ida in, and the silence of the house became too much for me that I found myself driving downtown toward Pershing Square, where Paul used to hang out.

I parked and locked the Rambler, then walked the intersections Paul had walked, and waited. I wasn't sure what I was waiting for, maybe just some moment, some breakthrough in the white noise, maybe a lifting of the smoggy haze, and there suddenly would emerge, yes, a flash of *ibbur*, a hasty glance, or some physical vestige, some evidence of Paul's soul.

I now noticed, beneath the waving fronds of the tall, bottle-washer palms that lined the square, two street-corner saviors going at each other on opposite sides of a bed of spikey Spanish bayonets. They both had gathered sparse but enthusiastically listening crowds around themselves not twenty yards apart. They seemed to be trying to outshout and outcompete each other in their apocalyptic predictions, like boxers punching each other out debating which signs are truly markers for the impending end of the world, and which, like this day's heavy, yellow smoggy blanket of air pollution, were only false positives.

Yes, Paul would have loved to be here now listening to these entertaining, logorrheic talkers. Just as Paulene used to remember to bring home lots of chapter and verse from Rabbi Joel's dull sermons and even from the Foot's financial messages at the temple, Paul—was it to counter all of that?—would recount these downtown spiels to Jon and me with absolute glee, sometimes in large sections, and nearly verbatim.

As the preachers ranted, the sidewalks grew busier with pedestrians, lots of desperate-looking types to be sure, zigzagging alcoholics, panhandlers, and the occasional hurrying "normal"-looking guy in a suit. Unlike on Orange Grove Drive, this neighborhood was well peopled, and had a New York feeling that nicely balanced vitality and menace. I felt strangely at home.

One of the preachers, a brown-skinned man in a shiny suit, cited all of the recent racial rioting, the parents turning against their kids about the Vietnam War, and a few other phenomena as definite harbingers of the End Times. He wore a baseball cap and those Cool Hand Luke reflecting shades and hardly took a breath, it seemed, as he prophesied a flood that would leave our LA basin with water so high it will cover the spire atop city hall so that fish from out at Santa Monica will have swum all the way in and now will be flopping on the tiles of the roof of the library.

The other guy, a lanky, white Western Oaks-looking character, but not nearly as tall, offered a massive earthquake on the San Andreas Fault as his preferred method of destruction. He painted a vivid picture of the rides at Disneyland plummeting into a gaping abyss, even the mountain of the massive Matterhorn Bobsled ride would crumble, falling onto the nearby Santa Ana Freeway, precisely at Exit 66.

One more 6 in that number and you'd have the well-known sign of the Antichrist, he pointed out.

I'd loved the Matterhorn Bobsled, and this prediction, despite its preposterousness, made me feel oddly sad.

The other preacher countered by advancing an argument that we shouldn't need the end of the world to motivate us to give up the bottle and the weed and to live virtuous lives. It was a pretty challenging argument to make to this crowd, among whom I now felt a sense of desperate brotherhood. *Sotto voce* I mumbled, "amen."

Now the preacher with the baseball cap waved for me to come closer to him. I hesitated, of course, but I was giving myself up to events and flows and powers, if you will, that I didn't understand. If Paul's *ibbur* were not inside Wes, or no longer there, then was it possible it had migrated right here, to one among this wounded throng where Paul had obviously felt so comfortable?

So I approached. I stopped a foot or so from his soapbox—well, it was an Adhor Dairy milk crate, on which he stood beside the pigeon-poop-encrusted statue of Gen. John "Blackjack" Pershing.

The preacher paused, he gave me an enigmatic smile, and then he said, "You're on a mission, aren't you? I see it in your eyes."

"What?"

"A thirst. A need."

I couldn't deny that, but this was no mindreading, no clairvoyance. What he had said to me could be applied to everyone in the ragged circle around him. Then came the kicker. "You're on the way to the library, aren't you?"

That was when I realized, for the first time, that, yes, that's precisely it, the task that without knowing had been impelling me to drive downtown. First, the rabbi's library. Now this place. This is where I'd been headed all along. I'd left the Jews, but apparently, at least when I wasn't stoned, not my bookish ways.

"Go on, young brother. Don't let us keep you. All of the books you want are right over there, Fifth and Olive. Go on now."

LIKE A sleepwalker, I climbed the steps and entered the cavernous corridors of the main branch of the LA Public Library building, which, lucky for me, was open late this evening.

On the cool marble main desk I renewed my card that had lapsed a decade before. Then I found the religion section, in the basement, and lost no time in locating and quickly checking out three volumes on the Latter-day Saints. Then I left.

Had that preacher ever been right.

I found an available stone bench where I had once brown-bagged it with Paul when I couldn't have been more than nine or ten. I settled in to read beneath a lamppost. I lit up a cigarette, distinctly aware that the gesture, complete with a nod to Humphrey Bogart's thumb-flick-of-the-match style and a first deep inhalation accompanied by a tilt of the head skyward, as if to draw the smoke down to his toes, well, they were also all the gestures of one lost soul named Paul Gould.

I smoked and I waited for something more; a sign, or even a glittery cinema ghost's appearance would not have completely surprised me. I don't know how much time had passed when I suddenly imagined one of these preachers coming over to me and saying, Paul Gould, that bastard. You're his kid, aren't you? I knew it as soon as I laid eyes on you. He still owes me twenty bucks. Still arguing about it! Look no further. He's right here inside of me.

When I pay the debt, he opens his mouth wide, I reach in, and pull the ghost of my father niftily right out of his throat.

I read and smoked, smoked and read.

Nothing happened.

BACK AT the duplex, I stayed up half the night reading about Mormon souls and about Jewish souls, and yet the next day I felt I had to return to the temple library.

The rabbi and the Foot were both out at meetings, and this time, with

Solomon's silent consent once again, I took a small stack of books home for a few days.

Like a real researcher, I spread out my haul from the two libraries on both of our beds. Here finally I felt I could do justice to all sides of the soul question.

It turns out the Mormons have these premortal-mortal and post-postmortal worlds, as they term them, even more vast and busy than I had guessed, all populated by souls coming and going from earth to the outer planets. Science fiction, to be sure, but when the soul enters a body for its test on earth, we are animated to live moral lives. That was a riff that was, well, sort of part of the Jewish mystical tradition as well.

I flipped through the pages as if I were cramming for a test. What I didn't grasp was how the formal reciting of the ordinance and the offering of their gospel, occurring as it does on earth, how that transaction floats on up to the aerial locale where, according to Wes and Jon, Paul would be waiting in spirit prison. If I could understand that, I figured that even if I couldn't prevent an ordinance ceremony, maybe I could nab the news so it never gets up there.

Yet the exact pipeline for that communication was left undescribed in the books I read. So I read on.

It seems a Mormon's performing of these ordinances for the dead is pretty serious stuff, just as Wes had said, roughly akin to a Catholic sacrament, or a Jew reciting the *Shema*, the credo of the faith, or maybe even observing the dietary laws or the Sabbath.

In short, messing with this intergalactic filing system of ordinances might seem silly, like a kind of cosmic telemarketing call that just arrives on a recording asked for or not. And yet it was playing with Mormon fire.

There seemed to be no one in spirit prison available to argue with you or to listen or to chat with. Before converting, even in heaven, where was the ceremony or instrument for discussion? Shouldn't a gambling and wandering Jewish soul like Paul's at least be able to give as much attention to the truth of Mormon gospels as he gave to the racing forms?

At least with an *ibbur,* a Jewish-style soul in residence down here on earth, in a living body, there is a chance that, at least technically, you could have a chat, and some meaningful communication. That was assuming, of course— and, boy, this was the biggest assumption of all—that the wandering soul can be identified, located in the right body, and "spoken" to.

I took a deep breath. I smelled a faint scent of the bougainvillea drifting in from the driveway. Paulene was working a double shift, and then she had said she was going to catch a movie up on Hollywood Boulevard with the Foot.

That couldn't be her scent—or could it?

Jon was out with the Mormons, as usual, and here I was bringing a Talmudic style of close reading to Mormon soul texts.

I set the books aside for a moment and checked on the Relic. Could Paul's soul be now residing in her? Of course everyone has unfinished business with their mother. He had more or less ignored her as she got really old, and once or twice I'd read between the parental lines that Paul had taken a portion of her small pension to cover some of his bets. But *ibbur* business?

Ida was as usual dozing. I waved my hand over her puckering mouth and her dark nostrils. I whispered Paul's name to her. Once softly and then louder. She didn't stir.

Then I went out to the wall phone in the kitchen. I leaned against the fridge, feeling its reassuring warm hum as I tried calling the angels over at the Foot's apartment. I let the phone ring four, six, eight rings.

The angels were likely out shopping yet again or doing whatever these earth angels were up to. On the other hand, I felt—although I couldn't explain it as I pondered this far-out stuff—that they were also somehow here with me.

What a way to spend an evening in LA.

To read even more closely I took off my glasses. I arranged the set of Mormon books lower on the bed, and inched the Jewish volumes up to where I lay on my elbow, by the headboard. I spread out a little on Jon's bed too. With all of the texts open, nearly surrounding me, I could absorb this stuff not only by reading, but by nearness, by osmosis, like a human sponge.

In Rabbi Joel's copy of *Handbook to Jewish Mystical Practices,* published in Prague in 1826, I read that Jewish souls are apparently yappy as can be. They have no patience to spend time in any ethereal waiting zone. No, except for the major saintly Jew who enters the divine presence immediately after death, most souls are back here on earth right after death just as soon as possible to mop up the problems they've created. The assumption is that no one, even the saintly, is perfect. Everyone has made something of a mess in their life. I liked this realistic approach to life and to our failures, and I felt, as I turned page after page of Rabbi Joel's book, that I was reading a bit about myself, and about my father.

But the Jews set a practical limit on mourning and remorse and on this whole fixing business, and that's of course why we are supposed to say *kaddish*, the prayer for the dead, daily, for only a year. Those wandering souls have but one year more or less—ten months being short and the full twelve months of mourning much—to take care of business. After that, the book's closed.

Aha! Now I truly began to understand why Jon was in a rush to nab Paul's precious little soul . . . oh, but that was ridiculous, that as a nascent Mormon he should nevertheless still have his eye on the limits for a soul on a Jewish calendar!

Crazy! Or was it?

Whoa! If I were a cartoon rabbi, and maybe I was, the bubble over my head now told me that maybe this was the very reason why the rabbis had kicked me out of the seminary. Could it be?

Was this my destiny, to become a Jewish soul warrior in LA, the city of angels?

If you're astonished at this prospect, imagine me lying there—exhausted, elated, maybe still powered by a bit of marijuana buzz and buried in books, and yet now rising phoenix-like from them with a new and liberating notion! My God, it *was* astonishing, a kind of bizarre calling. What had happened to me in, what was it, the six short weeks I'd been home?

Yet that is where, precisely, the matter lay.

So where *was* Paul's soul?

I kept reading.

The rabbi's books were not so detailed on the matter as the Mormon books. They were at best okay but in a folkloristic sort of way, and so I now gave them the Hebrew Olympics treatment, perusal by the first sentence of paragraphs, and then fast in and fast out. Jews didn't seem to take their soulology as scientifically as the Mormons.

Still I kept turning the pages.

Although the *neshama* and the *ibbur* as concepts remained murky for me as I read on, I was transfixed by descriptions of the various groupings of Jewish angels. As I read avidly about one group and then about the next, I tried to place Tali and Aviva. Here were the *seraphim*, the fiery creatures, like Janis

Joplin and Jimi Hendrix, if they were angels, tearing up the stage, only their stage was up there, the firmament.

Nearby check out the *chayot,* which translates as the "wild and crazy ones." If Ram Das or Timothy Leary were Jewish angels, those guys would definitely be *chayot.*

Then there were the *ophanim,* who are like great disembodied voices of praise, wheeling—an *ophan* is a wheel in Hebrew—and roaring doxology after doxology through the cosmos. I imagined this category to be outsize athletes, creatures so in love with God, but nonverbal, expressing themselves best in a kind of silent celestial choreography, touchdown dances as loud as a thunderstorm and choreographed by Busby Berkeley. I mean they can't constrain themselves from doing cartwheels of praise.

I thought of Aviva, of course, but somehow she didn't fit into that group.

I took some time with the *ophanim.* I checked cross-references. Apparently repetition becomes these creatures and doesn't bore them as it would us. They are Johnny one-notes, of course, as their only song is praise of God and of His creations, with small variations only in the over-the-top adjectives used in the language of praise, traces of this heavenly chorus comprising many sections of the psalms and of the morning liturgy.

Ah, now here was something: taken together, all of these categories are the "hosts" of heaven and are the angels that serve God. Their focus is not on us humans. No, not us at all. They are but the divine one's private army of over-the-top admirers—that's what *tzvah* translated as "host" means in Hebrew: cohorts, brigades, endless columns of praisers.

Yet why would the Lord need such flattery?

Interestingly, the commentaries do suggest, however, that God is not satisfied with angels' praise, because they *must* offer it; it is their job, their assignment from the beginning of the beginning. Their praise is essentially a divine form of self-publishing.

And that's why He invented humans—those of us who *choose* to praise, well, that's the kind God really favors. The problem is, unlike angels, we mess up the voice of praise with all of the sour notes of our doubt, skepticism, complaint, all the grousing and murmuring, the cranky tunes sung by our free will.

Still, if you study the morning prayer text, when we get into it, we're supposed to leave all that human quibbling behind. We pray and we try to emu-late, so says the tradition, the voices of the holy creatures in wild praise, unadulterated and undiluted by questions.

Lots of luck.

I BELIEVE I heard Ida moan from downstairs but judged it a sound not of alarm but of dreams. Then there was the distant wail of a police or fire engine or ambulance racing through the streets. I kept listening. The floor of the duplex creaked slightly. A few crickets were signaling each other from across the street. Otherwise the night was silent. I stayed put. I continued to read.

It turns out the smallest chapter of all in the angelic reference works I was consulting, the subject receiving scantest attention, dealt with the likes of *my* angels of that summer. Yes, I recognized Tali and Aviva almost instantly as members of the group called the *malachim*, or, in English, the messengers.

That's the great democratic group of angels dedicated to helping us humans, one on one, with our seemingly impossible tasks here on earth like choosing what work to do in life, or finding the right partner or, in my case that summer, coming to terms with Paul—his life and his death.

Still, there was absolutely nothing in these old texts to indicate that angels could play basketball like Tali or do a handstand like Aviva, or kiss and thrill the small of the back like the both of them, or talk about the prophet Jonah as if he were some stoned hippie longhair they had once dated and dropped, or shriek and giggle as we drove fast along the Sunset Strip, or become shopa-holics, or be such first-rate counselors in a camp for spoiled Beverly Hills kids.

So many essential aspects of Jewish souls' and angels' behavior remained unclear. It was as if the whole tradition came down to saying: What! You think we *alte cocker* rabbis have all of the answers? We barely know the ques-tions, and, anyway, it's verging on the idolatrous. The Torah's not enough? What's wrong with you, son? Let the Gentiles have the angels. You say you want more of this esoteric stuff? Solution: Just keep reading, pal, because in this territory you're pretty much on your own.

Something impelled me to locate a pamphlet with the daily prayers from the top drawer of the desk—it clearly hadn't been touched since my bar mitz-vah—and I read and haltingly translated aloud what you're supposed to recite at the first instant of waking up. In translation that would be: "Thanks to you, God, you ever-lasting ruler, who has returned *my soul* inside of me with mercy, *a sign* of your great faithfulness."

Whoa! This suggested that Jewish souls, of the living anyway, fly out of you and scatter off during the night. But by what aperture or means do they exit? There aren't that many available orifices in a human body. Right, rabbis? On the breath? Carried along by, say, a moan? Had Ida just let loose her wandering soul for its nocturnal voyage?

And where do they go? Do the angels function as, er, travel agents, helping the flimsy souls on their journeying? Do they help them to book temporary nocturnal residences until you need them to return and to restore your very consciousness and personality on waking? In New York I knew people—and they included my so-called colleagues and even a few venerable professors—who came to those early morning lectures seemingly without a personality, and maybe not even with consciousness, and stayed that way until about noon. Had a few lost souls missed the return trip?

Yes, the key question: just how might angels help in our life's tasks?

Or was I conflating two problems, each complex enough on its own? I mean do the souls themselves carry on without angelic assistance? Do they have a kind of navigational system of their own, say, like a migrating bird? Possibly. If that were so, could you somehow break into it to program a new mission or to alter its course? Or is the soul somehow preprogrammed to reside where it will nightly and then, in the morning, return, like a carrier pigeon to its roost?

I knew Paul had plenty of places to visit during the night as he always had the other bookies, the poker buddies, the coffee shops and waitresses he patronized by Pershing Square.

Now what if Paul's wandering soul just happened to have come to reside during the day—I almost shouted it out in the bedroom—in me? His son. Night was one thing, but as long as the sun shone? Where else could he go? I sat up in bed. I thumped my chest. I practically knocked to say, Hello in there!

As fire often but not inevitably follows smoke, here came questions and of course doubts fast on the heels of this novel notion.

I had never thought much about my own soul, but now I sure was. Would my own living soul and Paul's liberated one, his *ibbur*, be in conflict? It was hard not to think of your body in physical terms even for these immaterial entities, and so I wondered just how much room was in there. Would the souls have to negotiate a small residential zone within me, like be on two beds the way I was crammed in sharing this bedroom with Jon?

Was I my father's crash pad? If you were like me when I was young, who thought—unless you got sick—about your interior? About your organs that crowd around the internal cavity? Now I conceived my insides like this vast new space, not jammed like a tenement, but a kind of communal hall or dormitory for souls. Why, there might be room there, in each of us, for a busful of traveling *ibburs*, along with Paul, room for a score of our cousins who were never in touch, all the family members, Ida's Family *Tot*, our Holocaust dead. Everyone. Yes, welcome, welcome, one and all!

I heard a kind of voice within me. Was it truly emanating from within, or was I manufacturing it? Did the voice belong to me? To Paul? To another? I held my breath as if trying to make out the scraping of furniture in a room at the corner of a large house. I closed my eyes. I could almost hear my heartbeat, but, no, no longer a voice, nothing that echoed like a soul.

So many questions, and the angels hadn't helped address any of them. Not yet.

Setting aside the soul overcrowding issue for a moment, for example, when your soul returns to you in the morning, as the prayer suggests, what precisely happens? I'm speaking here not of an *ibbur* but of my very own soul, not a transient.

Does it become one with your personality? Is your soul the same as your personality? No, that wouldn't be the case, because a baby has not yet developed a personality, yet it still has a soul. Right?

Well, maybe not. Then that fantastic look of the newborn is not personality but just the effects of chemistry? I never liked that conclusion.

And here was another doozie: how is a soul different from the experience of consciousness?

Soul, personality, consciousness—are these three separate or interrelated phenomena? When you think you "hear" the voice of conscience, not consciousness, who's sending that? Is that yet a fourth internal item to contend with?

And if souls linger on beyond death and communicate, doesn't the communication over the generations and the transmigrations get confusing, like a vast choir with voices from the various sections maybe not in sync or at times trying to drown out each other?

What a mess.

Paul's father, the Relic's husband, whose name was Michael and who died in Chicago before they came to sunny California, had been in a coma before he died. How did that affect the exiting of his soul? Where indeed was Grandpa Michael's soul these days? Hovering about somewhere here in LA, checking out where his wife and kids ended up living? Or lost and trying to figure things out, like me? Or back in Chicago?

So many unanswered questions.

I CLOSED the books, then my eyes.

I heard a kind of remote din drift in from the driveway-side window. It was a distant, rhythmic, pulsating that was coming from the southwest, out by the Pacific, perhaps from Sorrento Beach. Why did I think it *was* from Sorrento Beach, where that miraculous basketball game had unfolded?

I went to the porch and listened. No, it was more from the south, from the direction of Culver City where the talkies first were made.

Or was this a kind of intergalactic murmur arriving from the Mormon planet in the far-off universe, where good people were busily evolving into gods and their deified speech into mysterious Morse code-like patterns that I couldn't yet decipher? Was that now reaching me down here on little old Orange Grove Drive?

Where was my Rosetta stone? Where were my code breakers? Where were my deciphering sticks like those Joseph Smith used to read the Golden Plates and to translate his Mormon book from the ancient Egyptian? Maybe that's all I needed now.

I wasn't even high. Yet I had to lie down.

I put my hands together behind my head at the nape of the neck, and closing my eyes felt suddenly very comfortable, and relaxed. Paul used to lie like this in his bed as well, except he had been surrounded not by books on souls but by scratch sheets and horseracing forms.

I was still in a murky, dozing state when the bedroom door suddenly opened. I pulled on the rope of my will power, but very slowly. I raised myself up. I said hello or something; whatever it was, it was like talking on the tape recorder at the wrong speed. I made out the shape of a head silhouetted against the dim light in the hall.

The familiarity startled me. I reached for my glasses on the bedside table. I pushed up on my elbows. The shape of the head was his. I felt my heart racing. Had I really summoned Paul?

"What are you doing on my bed?"

"Jon?"

"What's all this?"

"What time is it? Where are you coming from?"

"Why should I tell you? You'll just send those girls to tail me."

"What?"

"I'm telling you. They're popping up everywhere. Even on Gregory Way. A ward member saw them. They're stalking me, man. Walking with a bouquet of flowers."

"For Wes?"

"How do I know? I guess. Yes. They left it at the door."

"I'd say that's very nice of them."

"And then they came to his house, while I was there, just this evening."

"Double nice. What'd they bring this time?"

"Funny you should ask. Get this. A huge stuffed thing. A bear."

"Really?"

"They said they got it at Pacific Ocean Park."

"That's nice, I guess."

"Why bring a stuffed animal to a man you practically killed?"

"Well, they're unusual, Jon. We know that. They do what they do."

"I'll say."

He began to pace the bedroom now, checking out the books I'd been reading, opening and closing a few of them with interest, as if he were gathering evidence.

"How'd they know?"

"Know what?"

"Where he lives. Wes's home address."

I hadn't a clue.

"You know it?"

"I don't."

"So you didn't tell them?"

"I told you. Maybe they looked it up."

"Except he's unlisted. So how'd they know?"

"Got me."

"You sent them, didn't you?"

"Hey, it's easy to find an address. Remember: they were in intelligence. What can I tell you?"

"What *can* you tell me? First they almost kill him and now these . . . sick visits. I think they're your spies. That's what I think. Somehow, some way you're pranking me . . . us, with them. You're sending them."

"Please."

"I can see in your eyes that you are."

"I wouldn't know how!"

Yet, even as the formulations of my hollow denial left my mouth, I felt my excitement growing. "Maybe tell me what happened. When they came to his house."

"They just walked in and handed that thing to Wes. Exactly as they played basketball, without a word. Acting like zombies. They didn't apologize. They didn't ask him how he felt, or chat with him, or with me. They didn't talk about what happened like normal people."

"What did they do?"

"Tali leaned over him in this weird way, nose to nose, as if she were still guarding him."

"That's strange."

"You haven't heard anything yet. Then Aviva began to open drawers in the table by the bed. Unasked. Like it was her room or something. Can you believe that?"

"Actually I can."

"Then they opened his closet where Tali started to sniff around. Without permission. What were they doing?"

"Maybe looking for Paul's soul."

"Are you nuts?"

"Please go on."

"Aviva then practically crawled under the bed. I was ready to call the cops."

"But you didn't."

"The whole thing took maybe ten minutes. They were out as quickly as they came in. I swear I will get them arrested next time. What are they look-ing for?"

"I told you. Maybe Dad's soul. You believe in souls now, don't you?"

Jon just stared at me, but he also cleared a space of books on the bed and sat down.

So I told him. I told him what I had been reading. I told him about my visits to Rabbi Joel's library, about my cruises downtown where Paul had hung out. Wasn't he a Mormon-in-training? He didn't have to be self-taught about souls. So I told it all to Jon because I thought, well, it was making more and more sense, and if he would believe me, maybe this strange soul-ology and angel-ology might heal the rift growing between us, be a kind of rope bridge across the abyss of losing each other.

But he didn't buy it. Not at all.

He stood up, he padded some more around the bedroom, he went out into the hall, he checked his watch. I knew what he was thinking: that he should go downstairs to check on the Relic, even though he'd done that on the way up. Any excuse to get away from me.

Yet he didn't go this time; he stayed on the threshold, his shoulders filling up the doorway. "They're no more angels than you or me, man. They're girls, humans. Israeli females, camp counselors. The Foot hired them and some-how . . ."

"Somehow what?"

"I don't know . . . your little evil helpers. Under your control. Somehow."

"How?"

"I don't know, but you're in control."

"Really! Then how come I can't get a date with either one of them? What control?"

"Why would Jewish angels take an interest in someone who has just been kicked out of the Jewish Theological Seminary? Someone who's doing all the nasty stuff you're up to?"

"That's the best point you've made so far."

"Someone who goes out of his way *not* to be Jewish? Why would they want to help someone like you?"

"Maybe they want me back."

"Good riddance, man. Just stay out of my life."

"Let's just say for argument's sake that they are just beautiful counselors, gorgeous girls, right? Then suddenly there's this change. They sprout these wings, these . . . powers that make them act this way. Suddenly they go into action. What prompted that?"

Jon didn't answer, but he wasn't leaving either.

"What's the trigger?"

"Trigger?"

"The cause, Jon. Didn't they go all strange precisely when you announced your plans to file the ordinance for Paul's soul? Remember that little inconvenient fact?"

He said nothing.

"Wasn't that the exact timing? As long as you're dealing with your own conversion, keeping yourself busy with your own soul's business, they just, well, did their job. And my leaving the seminary, that's not their business either. But Paul's soul, his Jewish soul, that is. As soon as you threaten to file that ordinance, or have Wes do it; because I've been doing a little homework, I know now that you have to be a Mormon in good standing for a year before you yourself can do it. Am I wrong?"

"Go on."

"With pleasure. So Wes is getting ready to have your little ceremony at your Mormon *mikvah*, to speak the words, so guess what it is they now do? They appear at the beach out of nowhere and break Wes's jaw. Makes perfect sense to me."

"Ridiculous! And now they bring a stuffed bear! What's the significance of that?"

"I can't say."

"You're just so full of it."

"Maybe you leave Dad's soul alone, and we'll see who's full of it. We'll see what happens. Back off, and maybe they will."

"You believe that?"

"Maybe Wes's jaw will heal overnight, like in a miracle, if you take your hands off Dad's soul. Try it."

"I don't have 'my hands' on his soul. He'll be *offered* the Gospel. How many times do I have to explain? No force, no coercion. Get it out of your head. A choice. That's all."

"What's the Mormon doctrine on tithing the dead? After you convert him, you go after all that celestial spending cash too?"

"Screw you."

"I thought you'd given up talking like that."

"In your case I make an exception."

"I return the sentiment."

"I won't let you ruin this. You have no right. You're just carping, and finding fault. You don't even believe in the existence of the soul."

"Maybe I do now."

"Just back off. You and those girls!"

I don't know why, maybe to lance the tension, I broke into singing Johnny Tillotson's "Earth Angel, earth angel, will you be mah-ine . . ." It was a stupid, off-the-wall gesture, and I didn't sing it very well.

"Shut up."

I kept singing.

"Are you high again?"

I sang some more.

"Nothing matters to you, does it?"

"Dad matters. Dad's soul happens to matter to me. A lot."

"From the beginning you've wanted to torpedo me. From the very first day you came back and I told you, you've been treating me as if I'd been infected, as if I've got some kind of snake bite, and I need an antidote. You've got to get me an injection before the Mormon toxins travel far in my system. That's the way you make me feel. You and Mom both. Those two girls are the Jewish antidote. Am I right?"

"Well, you need something."

"What you don't get, Norman, is that I've found it. The church is the antidote."

"To what?"

"To death."

"You should be so lucky."

"See? Sarcasm is your only religion. You make fun of everything, but you can disprove nothing."

"Is that your argument?"

"You going to send them to break my jaw now?"

"I'm just pointing out that . . . just because you've got questions you can't answer, that's no reason to change your religion."

"What should I do instead? Follow your example? Smoke dope and eat myself to death? You're the one playing a game and fleeing from what you need. You're suffering, you're doing nothing about beating death while you can, while you have the chance, while you're alive on this earth. Instead you ridicule the Mormons, you ridicule the Jews. As long as you're in that mode, you'll always think I'm a sucker, so what more is there to discuss?"

"What's to discuss is Paul's soul."

"That's being taken care of."

I stood up from the bed, and the books, Jewish and Mormon, all tumbled onto the floor beside me.

As I bent to pick them up, I began to declaim, in Hebrew: "*Elohai, ha neshama she natata bee, tehora hee. Atah barata, atah yatzarta, atah nefachta bee, v-ata meshamrah b'kirbi, v-atah atid litlah memeni, o-lhachzira bee l-atid lavoh. . . .* Shall I translate?"

"I don't care what you do."

" 'My God, the soul that you placed within me is pure. You created it, you fashioned it, you breathed life into it, and you will guard it within me. In the future you will take it from me but then return it when the time comes. . . . ' From the daily Jewish morning prayers. So don't let anyone tell you Jews don't believe in souls."

"Who you trying to convince? You just keep those girls away from me."

"What's going on, man? Why the express and not the local? Why are you rushing to baptize Paul?"

"I have just as much right to act on my beliefs as you do."

"How about you letting your god be your god and my god be my god, like in the Book of Ruth?"

Jon didn't answer.

"You at least remember that, from Hebrew school?"

He removed his belt and hung it over the knob. He slipped out of his jeans and hung them on the rack behind the bedroom door, folded and creased so they'd be neat for tomorrow. He reached into the pile of our clothes, still after all this time haphazardly ditched there, behind the door. He found his pajamas.

So it had almost landed, then and there, that mystery of the summer and why Tali and Aviva had been sent.

But not quite.

He went down the hall, brushed his teeth, and then returned without saying another word. That night he did not read from the *Book of Mormon*. He slipped under the covers, and as he did, another of the books I had borrowed from Rabbi Joel, this one on the transmigration of Jewish souls, fell off the foot of the bed and plunked onto the floor with a kind of finality, as if a gavel had sounded.

I picked it up and added it to the small pile on the desk.

As I turned the light out, I noticed how Jon, now lying on his back and staring up at the ceiling, had placed his hands, fingers intertwined, behind and at the base of his neck, as I was doing, as Paul used to do.

The silence was deep and thick, and soon Jon was snoring.

Still he had not answered my question: Why the rush to convert Paul's soul?

The answer was hiding in plain sight, the proof of it, and yet it took a command visit, ordered by Paulene at the temple, our temple, the Jewish temple, to discover what it really was.

20

CAMP the next day was one of what had become those perfectly normal yet totally abnormal days: we worked on my absurd Noah's Ark play, with my acquiescing to one of the kids' ideas that our ark, which was morphing to be more and more like the *Titanic* every day, should have an outboard motor and life rafts.

"Why life rafts, *haverim*?" I asked the kids, dropping in a little Hebrew, which I had refrained from doing at the beginning of the summer, but now did to impress Tali, who had come loping by in a long T-shirt over her yellow bathing suit. She hardly noticed me.

"You don't need life rafts if there aren't going to be survivors. Everybody drowns in our play, right, kids?"

They all stared at me as if I were crazy, which maybe I was in that moment.

"None will be left, none at all, and life can just start anew from amoebas, protoplasms, and stuff like that. You'll learn about it next year in science. Whatever."

"We'll name the amoebas 'Noah and Mrs. Noah,'" said the apple-polishing Amber Weinstein, who I am sure always got A's and great report cards in science and in all of her classes.

Soon enough Aviva was reading my warning signs and wisely gathered the kids and took them away from me to practice the drowning gymnastics moves or some such activity she had been fashioning to accommodate my nonsense.

So I wandered over to the pool area.

There Tali was busy with a group of about a dozen older kids teaching them the backstroke. Again, she was too busy to notice me. Jon, who did, averted his eyes immediately, as if the traveling dentist had just arrived to pull his teeth.

I waited for her campers to begin swimming their laps, and then I summoned the courage to ask Tali about the flowers, the strange bear, and her visits to Wes and what had happened.

"Personal matters are not to be discussed at work," she said, quoting verbatim from the camp manual that the Foot had written. My own question made me feel instantly uncomfortable, insubstantial, seen by the angel through and through as the craven little nothing of a human that I was."Especially in the presence of campers."

"But they're in the water. They can't hear," I went on. She just threw her beautiful head back, her wild hair catching the wind.

Then she did answer. "We find bears just so cute!"

"But why?"

"Just like you."

When an angel says that to you, what is there to do but shut up?

When I did, she just laughed; there wasn't cruelty in her laugh, but criticism of something that I knew I could not fix in myself, at least not then, not yet.

I wandered back to my duties, fulfilled them in a kind of dream state, and then the day was over.

When I sought the angels out after the kids went home, in their mysterious fashion they had already vanished from the park.

When the camp gear was stowed for the day, without as much as a wave so long, Jon walked across the putting green and over by the baseball courts, taking his shortcut over to the Mormons behind the park. There I was then, alone again, and standing on the steps of the park at the La Cienega Boulevard entrance, wanly waving to some last departing nine-year-old wearing a Davy Crockett T-shirt.

At least I had the car.

I slid in and found myself driving out to the Sorrento Beach basketball court in Santa Monica where Wes and Tali had played their game. This despite the fact that Paulene had asked Jon and me to be home by 6:30.

"Family meeting," she had pronounced in the morning, with unusual formality.

Still it was a beautiful late afternoon with a bright warm sun, a cooling breeze, and I had time. I could make it. I drove, thinking about everything and about nothing, and then suddenly the air had an astringent scent and I descended from Highway 101, and I now beheld the rippling white spume of the waves all along the Santa Monica shoreline.

Just as I had cruised downtown yesterday, with a purpose uncertain, to Paul's haunts and to the library, I wasn't quite sure what I was looking for out by the beach. Yet suddenly here I was pulling into the sandy Sorrento Beach lot, in fact into the very same parking slot we'd used that day the angels had performed their basketball magic.

On the very same court two young teenagers were shooting hoops. Like some paranormal detective, like some salmon guided back to a native ground, or—come on!—like some lost soul, I just stood at the perimeter of the court and watched the kids play one-on-one; they weren't very good at all.

On impulse I asked if I could take just one try. They were friendlier to me than some of my campers had been that day, and the taller of the two soon bounced the ball over to me in one hop.

I scooped it up and walked around the court wondering just where Tali had taken some of her more amazing long shots. Nowadays it would be beyond the three-point line, and at the very far corner; I found the spot where I remembered she had launched a few of her aerial wonders.

Barely aiming, I heaved the ball high in the air. The spinning brown globe of a Spalding made a beautiful ascending arc, and, to my utter surprise, dropped straight in, not touching the rim at all.

"Whoa! Bombs away!" said the kid. He retrieved the ball and bounced it back to me.

So I shot again. Same spot. Same result. I tried a third, and, yes, a fourth. All net all the time. I asked the kid to shoot from the same spot, and he did, missing all three times. It was amazing.

I took out a five-dollar bill—as if to celebrate having proven something to myself, but exactly what I wasn't sure—and gave it to him.

I got in the car, and headed home.

As I drove I felt as if I were floating on yet more strange evidence of a force that had truly entered my life; it was there, it was real, and yet it seemed so odd, diffuse, and quixotic that only by opposing it further, and by questioning it, did it manifest at all.

At three miles or so from the beach, traffic began to slow into fits and starts until near the intersection where Olympic narrows into Westwood, it halted. Whatever the power I was in touch with did not enable me to leapfrog LA traffic congestion.

When I finally got through the next light I could see the cause: a half dozen police cars were blocking the two left lanes north going onto the Avenue of the Stars as it rises toward Century City. I concentrated and thought I was hearing one of those distant muffled roars you get when you stick a sea shell next to your ear. I leaned toward the noise coming from up the hill toward Century City, and now the amorphous sounds shaped themselves into a din of what I thought were calls of protest.

Sure enough, when I rolled the window down all the way, and leaned as far out as I could, there the chant was: "Hey, hey, LBJ, how many kids did you kill today? One, two, three four, who we fightin' for! Hey, hey, LBJ . . ."

I next heard myself formulating one of my finer self-accusations: Wake up, man! Souls aren't real. Lucky hoops prove nothing. This nasty war is real. Provoked by us. Drop this nonsense about souls and about impossible basketball shots and about angels and about all of your regret about Paul. What's done is done. Let Jon live his own life. Remember what you did. Pull over and park. Sneak through the police barricades. All these weeks have been one long interruption of what you intended to do that day in Central Park. . . . What's Judaism worth if not to oppose immoral wars, if not to. . . . Hey, man, I lectured myself, pull over. How long can you be an idiotic drama counselor? Really do it! Make this a real summer of love, as in loving your neighbor as yourself. Join the demonstrators at the top of the hill. Now!

Yet the light changed, and stole my resolve.

If shame could be translated into reckless speed, I broke the limit because when the traffic cleared, I gunned it, passing through at least two intersections beneath red lights, and now I was pulling into the driveway on Orange Grove barely ten minutes later.

I'm certain that had all the laws of the physical world not been slightly altered for me—or, sure, you can call it just dumb random luck—the Rambler should have been T-boned. What's certain is that I was driving as if I really *wanted* to die of shame. I was completely reckless, and yet here I was. No accident, not a ticket, alive and at home. This soul nonsense was cradling me in its thrall.

When I stuck my head into the kitchen, I saw Paulene filling the yellow kettle. Nearby the Relic was waiting for her tea in the breakfast nook. The radio, perched on top of the refrigerator, was broadcasting a bulletin about that very demonstration that I'd just driven by.

When she saw me lingering at the threshold, Paulene pointedly walked over to the radio and raised the volume.

It turned out President Johnson had tried to make a completely surprise visit to town and was staying at the International Hotel in Century City. Students from the Congress of Racial Equality chapter at UCLA had been tipped and surprised him there. They were surrounding the place trying to block his exit unless he responded to their demands. The LAPD had rushed patrol cars over to deal with a spontaneous demonstration against the war.

"I was just there."

"Shoosh!"

That's when the announcer got to what was for all of us the real bombshell news of the war that really affected us, then and there, the details of what Johnson had said. It was not about the day's body count from the Mekong Delta or a reaffirmation of confidence in the always stone-faced General Westmoreland but, at the president's request, Congress had asked to fast-track a revised Selective Service Act, and a lottery. Divinity school deferments, such as I possessed, or had possessed, would be continued, at least for now.

"They'll let you finish the seminary, I'm sure."

"Maybe," I lied.

"Always comes in clusters," said Paulene.

"What?"

"Bad news."

"What else? You need at least three for a cluster."

"This, plus your grandma had a bad day. But the real problem is in the living room. Go on in and talk to him. I'll be after I give her tea."

I half-expected to see Western Oaks reclining with his mandible device in Paul's easy chair, but when I walked in, Jon was sitting on the hassock at its foot. He was fiddling with the rabbit ears of the TV to get rid of the snow on a channel he was searching for. He glanced up briefly at me as if a polio epidemic had just entered.

He was wearing, I now noticed, Paul's old cardigan, the thin gray one with the too-shiny, cheesy-looking gold buttons and the frayed ribbing. Now he thrust his hands into the sweater's roomy pockets. It looked ridiculous over his white T-shirt. I was just about to ask him why he was wearing it—it wasn't cold at all—but I didn't. I felt so full of things to say—none very delicate or useful or wise—but for a change I said nothing.

Soon Paulene joined us to conduct the family meeting she had convened. Although she'd made it clear our attendance was mandatory, she seemed in no great rush to begin. We moved nervously around the room, the three of us, thinking our thoughts, and as comfortable as three people, all of whom would like to be anywhere but there, could be.

"Can't get the demonstration. Lousy reception, Mom," said Jon, back again on bended knee before the Muntz TV.

"Blame your father, not me. He bought it."

We got the voice of the reporter covering the demonstration now a little more clearly against a still-white, scratchy, snowy background.

"A lottery! If something happened to either of you, I don't know what I'd do," said Paulene. "This war is terrible, and now this."

"Bummer," said Jon.

"Turn it off," she said, and sank onto the hassock. She removed her white waitress shoes. Her toes, usually painted red, now were golden. I don't know why I kept noticing such things.

First item was her usual description of her waitress's weariness, how her "dogs" were barking, and how the tips lately had been, well, just okay, and how she didn't want to waitress the rest of her life, and maybe soon wouldn't have to.

There she paused, waiting, and added, almost casually, that this coming Saturday morning, this coming Sabbath, tomorrow, at nine sharp, she expected the both of us to join her at temple.

I'd been avoiding that chore for a month, with every excuse I could think of. Paulene was no longer interested in my excuses.

"Temple. Right, Jon?"

My brother nodded.

"How about you?"

"How about me what?"

"Smart aleck!"

While Jon and I played this game of religious chicken with each other, she nonchalantly reached down for the *Life* on the floor beside the hassock. The magazine cover showed what looked like a spread of pictures of soldiers scrambling out of a helicopter. It was the "Summer of Love," but it was also a summer of Vietnam and of daily reports of military casualties, that is, death, just barely disguised, that was everywhere in the magazines, in papers, and in the headlines.

She riffled through the pages briefly and then looked at us. "And, please . . ." she stated oddly, without quite finishing her sentence, "please."

"Please what?" Jon said.

"Please, I know you're exploring; you're trying to find yourself. It's normal. But am I right that no one outside of this family knows?"

" 'Knows'?"

"You know *exactly* what I'm referring to."

"He's not taking an ad out in the paper, if that's what you're worried about," I said.

"Is your name Jon?"

I kept on being a smartass, and an evasive one at that. I guessed if I stuck with it long enough, that might delay the next wedge driving deeper into our so-called family life. As usual, I was wrong.

"I don't hear a resounding yes from either of you."

My brother kept on fiddling with the TV.

"What is going on, son?"

"You're ashamed of me!" he shot back at her.

The much-avoided word from that summer finally was out, and its sudden utterance silenced Paulene, but not for long.

"That's not true."

"It is."

"It's not *you*. I'm never ashamed of my own flesh and blood. Embarrassed is more like it. Ashamed of your choice, but not of you. I know you haven't made any final . . . decision. You haven't, have you?"

"If you *know*, why ask?"

"So tell me. Have you, or haven't you?"

"How can you be ashamed of my choice, but not of me when *I* make the choice?"

"He's got you there, Mom."

"That's what you think."

Then she stood, went rapidly into the kitchen, turned off the radio, and returned standing over Jon like a Mother Colossus.

"Norman, if he has to serve, will maybe be a chaplain if this god-awful war goes on. They don't put chaplains in helicopters, but what about you, Mister?"

"What about me?"

"At least maybe you could choose a religion that has chaplains!"

"Stop it, will you?"

"The Mormons don't have chaplains, do they?"

"No, Mom. Everyone's a kind of priest. Just like with Jewish people."

"Not the same," I said.

"Of course not," Paulene added, with a hopeful look my way that finally now I'd pitch in with a mini-sermon on the matter. Yet I had nothing to add. Paulene's dating the Foot also seemed to have given her a kind of new borrowed authority to say what Jews do and don't believe. I was liberating myself of such talk. What did I care? So I let her say it.

"You've got to be a *kohane.* That means priest in Jewish, I mean, in Hebrew. So if you're named Kahn or Kahane or Cohen, then you're a priest in the Jewish religion. But not everyone. Then there's two other categories, the priestly helpers, and the rest of you. Right, Norman?"

"I don't know, Mom. Yes. Probably."

"What do you mean 'probably'? Is anybody in this room named Cohen? Of course it's right. You think the draft board or lottery will give a deferment to someone named Cohen if he says he's a Jewish priest?"

"Well, that would be nice," I said.

"Think again."

"Technically, all Jews are priests, a nation of priests, each person required to fulfill the 613 commandments to make yourself holy in your daily life," said Jon.

"Well, what good does that do you down the road you're going?"

"I'm impressed," I mumbled, and for a change I meant it.

"Ask the rabbi," said Jon.

"The 'rabbi' is not in a mood to offer an opinon."

"And why not?" pressed Paulene. "What's wrong with our 613 commandments? That should keep both you boys plenty busy."

I had no idea of Jon's state of mind any more, and I pretty much did not trust my own. He could blackmail me if he wanted. What would he next utter about the Jews, priesthood, or me and the seminary? I decided not to mix it up any more.

"What games are going on?" Paulene said. "What's going on with you two boys?"

"Nothing," said Jon.

"Nothing. You see, we agree on that."

That's when Paulene had had enough of us both. "I wasn't born yesterday. Lots of young people do what you're doing," she said as she rose and walked across the room, touching Jon's hair in her stride. It was a gesture with more anger in her fingers than affection, I thought. Then she made her way to the window that looked out to the street. She stood there for a brief interval, rearranging the long, purple drapes, looking out, pushing the heavy pleated drapes open wide, deciding, it seemed to me, how much to say and how much to censor; I knew the condition well.

"So you're exploring. Like you've done before. It's all right especially at your age. Look at the news. We're all explorers of one thing or another. Taking chances. And when you do that, sometimes you end up . . . colliding with each other, like we do now and then at the restaurant, one waitress coming out of the kitchen at the same time that I'm going in. When they had to throw away enough pastrami to feed an army, finally they put in the little window on the door, so you can look. Problem solved. You can see what's coming."

"So what's coming?" Jon asked.

"Listen, young man, I know your brother's trying to help you answer all these questions about being Jewish. Am I right?"

"Night and day, Mom, I'm helping. You bet."

"Night and day, is it?"

"Yes, Mom. Night and day, day and night."

"Good, then. So, *this* coming *shabbes* you'll join me, the both of you. You'll come to Sabbath services for a change and you'll ask all the questions you want. After services Mr. Footlick has arranged for the rabbi to linger, to take a little time from his busy schedule so he can talk to you boys. It's an honor that Rabbi Joel is making time for you. Our faith is not afraid of questions. Is it, Norman?"

"I don't think so."

"You don't sound convinced."

Now she gave me a quick glance that was twenty-six percent evil eye. "To ask a question is Judaism's middle name. Right?"

"Right," I said.

"So it's settled then?"

We both nodded. Yes, it was settled.

"So shake on it."

Neither of us was eager to do that, but as she stood between us, we reluctantly did, to please her, if it did at all. That's how much things were settled. That's the way it was in our family of bluffers.

Yet Paulene still had more cards to play. "You teach acting at the camp, so perform a little if you have to, Norman. At the temple. I'm sure you know how."

"Right."

"And you, young man," she came right back at Jon, planting herself in front of him again, as if he were not only a son but a difficult customer, arrived just before the kitchen of her patience had all but closed for the night: "Listen, Mister, as long as you haven't signed on the dotted line with this conversion *mishagas*, you're still a Jew!"

"Always," Jon said, without looking up.

"And don't forget it."

"I won't, Mom."

"And where does a Jew belong on Saturday morning?"

This time her interrogatory eyes were searching for mine, and I, the drama counselor taking up her challenge after all, did not miss my cue: "At temple."

" 'At temple,' exactly, from the rabbi-to-be."

"Jon, let me hear you say it."

His answer this time was to rise from the sofa where he'd been sitting during the interrogation, and to walk silently into the dining room. He quietly closed the swinging door behind him.

Paulene and I exchanged a glance, then looked away from each other as if returning to our corners in the ring of our family life; without exchanging another word, we both followed Jon in.

We found him standing at the Relic's old credenza peering at the pictures arrayed there in several rows like a miniature photo cemetery.

We watched as he now began to lift up and to rearrange all the dead relatives from Europe, the sepia ones that I'd liked best, those with their small glass frames slightly cracked, and a few that lay unframed, in a kind of curled repose, on ancient, fringed, yellowed doilies.

You don't interrupt someone communing or meditating or paying respects at the cemetery, and that's really what this felt like. Paulene and I exchanged a glance. We just stood there, and waited.

Now Jon lifted up these images of the Family *Tot*—had they survived Hitler they would have been our granduncles and grandaunts and great-grandparents, Ida's parents, from Poland or from Austria-Hungary—the border kept shifting every decade or so depending how the most recent war had turned out. Except for Ida's brother Albert, who had emigrated to Palestine in the 1930s, and wrote her letters signed with his new name, Aaron or sometimes Aharon, all of the people in the photos were, as Ida always put it, *tot*. Dead at the hands of the Nazis.

Once, I remembered, we had played an eight-year-old's game trying to imagine how the Nazis had killed the Family *Tot*. But we had changed the scenario. We fought back big time, in our imaginations. We lined the photos up, each of us taking half of them, and set them up facing each other on opposite sides of the living room. Then we hid the relatives behind the tangles of wires or peeking out from the feet of Ida's elephantine furniture. We divided up Paulene's bag of clothespins, designating each one a different kind of weapon. Machine guns, machetes, mine sweepers, flame throwers, bombers to fight the Nazis, and Davy Crockett's musket, Old Betsy. Never mind that we were throwing the clothespins at the Family *Tot* picture frames trying to knock *them* down. There was some little kids' logic there that now eludes me. Last picture that remains standing wins the game and beats the crap out of the Nazis.

Here and now, however, Jon was treating them in a manner—what turned out to be a Mormon manner—neither Paulene nor I expected.

He peered at each photo, bringing it close to his face, examining the black-and-white or purpling images in their frames, and then lightly kissing each of them. Then he replaced them lovingly back on the credenza but in new, different kinds of rows, as if—this was my thought at least as I beheld this odd ceremony—as if he were setting tombstones in place. What was going on? Was he also *sotto voce* reciting some sort of Mormon *bracha*, a blessing? We were mystified.

"There's something you should understand, Mom."

"Surprise me, my darling son."

"I never felt so Jewish as I have since I began spending time with Mormons."

"God in heaven," Paulene declared.

"But it's true," he protested.

"That's why you're playing around with leaving the Jewish people? Because you suddenly feel so Jewish? Am I crazy? You understand this?"

"Don't ask me. Ask him."

"No," Jon relieved me of trying to explain what I didn't understand or refused yet to accept myself. "The Mormons are picked on all the time, just like the Jews. Persecution is a big part of their history. I don't think either of you has any idea how much they love and identify with the Jewish people."

"Well, that's just hunky-dory," Paulene said, as she extracted her rumpled pack of smokes from her purse, and lit up. "What's he talking about?"

"I'm right here, Mom. Right here."

"Okay, okay."

"Look, as a Jew, nobody ever has really picked on me. Or Norman. Right? You remember how Dad would say he got picked on plenty as a kid, and we should be on guard. And, well, you remember how we would argue with him and he would go on about it? Now, finally, I understand what he was talking about."

"So you're tired of all this namby-pamby theoretical persecution. You want the real thing?" I joked.

I shouldn't have.

"Now I'm getting picked on a lot. Starting right here. Where I live."

"My children have gone crazy."

But Jon was on a roll now and he wouldn't let up. "You remember how Dad used to do it?" With that he moved back into the living room and claimed the La-Z-Boy. We followed. He opened the side table drawer and grabbed a cigarette from one of the many packs Paul had left behind; Paulene was the opposite of sentimental, but she couldn't throw these smokes out.

Now Jon picked up our father's favorite lighter, the globe with a dim, dying green light inside.

Jon feigned lighting the Lucky, almost a perfect imitation, I thought. "Now, listen up, boys," he said, echoing Paul.

"Now listen up, boys," I spontaneously joined in—I don't know why, echoing our father's strange, mocking tone on this subject. It always had combined a forced, awkward, lackluster foray into parental seriousness that often came out sounding more like Edward G. Robinson or an FDR lilt of gravity that died into self-mockery. Jon was much better at capturing it than I.

"Watch out for those signs: No Jews Wanted. You remember? Jews, Dogs, and Negroes Not Allowed. You better believe we saw plenty of those signs. In Chicago, Wisconsin, all over the Midwest, right? Am I right, boys?"

"If you say so, Pop."

"Right?"

"Right."

When the mimicry ended, Jon added: "I just wish he'd lived long enough for me to tell him about the Mormons."

"Why?" said Paulene, who had been stoically listening to Jon's star turn as Paul. "So your father could die twice?"

"No! Don't you see? With the Mormons, I can still tell him all about it. I can still reach him, and them," he added with a glance toward Ida's pictures on the credenza. "All of them."

He meant, of course, all of the relatives dead in Auschwitz and in Bergen-Belsen and in other concentration camps, all of those people whose names she had always refused to utter in front of us. "I can be with them. All of them. They're family," he said, weighting that word with a long elongation of the first syllable, a new accent, dare I say, of love, which I had never before heard him utter. "They're family for all eternity."

Paulene slowly flicked away a dot of ash that had fallen on her blouse. Then she said to Jon simply, "You're forgetting who you are."

"What! Eternity isn't for the Jews?"

"Of course it is. Why do you think they call it the 'eternal light,' the *ner tamid*, hanging above the ark at temple? At temple, where you're both going to be on Saturday."

"I'm not talking about bulbs, Mom, but about their souls, about their essence, about just who they were in this life as they were going on in the next life. Their immortal souls in a kind of . . . evolving new life without end."

"Norman?" she turned to me.

"Mom," I replied.

"I'm already feeling closer to Dad than I ever did. What it must have been like to be . . . him. I'm feeling what it must have been like growing up like Ida with all that hating and . . . and with that anti-Semitism."

"Would someone please get me two aspirin and a ginger ale?" Paulene asked.

"Well, if you want to get your ass kicked," I finally spoke up if only to Jon's disappearing back as he went into the kitchen to fetch our mother's antidote, "That's a piss-poor reason to become a Mormon."

But he was out of the room and the water in the kitchen was already on loudly.

"If you want persecution," I called out, or maybe I was already shouting, "I can get it for you wholesale!"

"Enough," said Paulene. "Shhh."

But it was not enough.

"Hey, Jon," I raised my voice toward him. "I probably can arrange for you to get your ass kicked as a Jew today. No problem. I can think of at least one or two locations. Let's drive downtown. Then you won't need the Mormons. Just say the word."

I thought he was going to leave the apartment then, fleeing from my ridicule, from all the various forms of our concern that he now saw as persecution, descending by the outdoor emergency stairway down from the kitchen on the outside of the duplex to the driveway, and then off to the Mormons, the Mormons who now alone, in this terrible, war-torn world, truly loved him.

Boy, was I wrong.

Jon returned and handed Paulene the two tablets and the Ginger Ale in its pale green bottle, and an empty glass.

"Shall I pour for you?"

"No, that's okay, dear."

"By the way, that's the last of them. The aspirin's empty."

"The way you're going, you know I'll need more."

Then as Paulene took down the two white pills, Jon added, "And I don't think Norman takes *any* faith seriously. I don't think he takes *anything* seriously."

"He's going to be a rabbi," said Paulene after her first long sip. "That speaks for itself."

She had a talent for putting doubt and anxiety to rest, even though down deep she knew the fix was only temporary and sat on the hopeful sands of a belief or resolution so shifting it might not endure an hour, let alone to the Sabbath.

"Norman?"

"I said I was going, didn't I!"

"And you'll talk this over with the rabbi? The three of you? Civilly. Like the gentlemen you are?"

"Right, Mom."

"And you?"

"I'll be there," he said.

"It's settled then," said Paulene. "Done and done."

AND SO the following Saturday morning, with Jon in an understated black suit, white shirt, and skinny tie that struck me as Mormonesque, and I a little more sartorially daring, in brown striped bell bottoms that I could barely stuff myself into, and an old blazer, we climbed up the steep temple steps.

With our mom between us, the sons of Paulene Gould and her late husband Paul entered through the center set of three ornate doors whose decorated brass panels the Foot had raised money for; he had dunned Paul many times to pitch in. I don't think he ever had, or could.

The imposing doors depicted equally Large Moments of Jewish History. The ones we passed through were Moses receiving the decalogue on the right and God splitting the Red Sea on the left.

Our shoes sank soundlessly onto the deep brown pile carpet of the lobby area. As we entered the sanctuary itself, I placed my hand dutifully on Paulene's elbow. She, Jon, and I walked alongside row after row of green upholstered seats that fell in a steep, terraced decline ttoward a mighty mahogany dais.

When I close my eyes, this is an interior whose features, even all these years later, I feel I know as well as my own face. Right there, years before, both Jon and I had been bar mitzvahed. Here we had formally joined the Jewish community.

Now, precisely what were we doing here? The seminary dropout and the Mormon-in-training? We were here to pray to a god we didn't either of us believe in and to talk to a man whom neither of us respected. Act, I told myself. Smile, and act.

As we greeted a few couples and several widowed ladies, now Paulene's closer pals than ever since Paul had died, I felt a gushing wave of congregational pride surround me. It was as if the ladies' Sabbath greetings meant something far more than the words: they meant, specifically, look how the Sons of Paulene Gould are supporting their widowed mom in her grief. Just check them out: one big handsome boy on each side of that still-pretty lady, and, look, so devoted and helping to buck her up in her time of sorrow.

As we inched down a row toward the front, to seats Paulene had selected,

I heard an unusual rustle of clothing, a susurrus arising from somewhere in the temple. At first I ignored it, but when the rustling, like great crickets, I imagined, sounded again, I elbowed Jon; he did not respond.

As I turned my head toward the sound, there at the back of the sanctuary I saw it, a flash of red hair up in the balcony. I knew that hair. It could belong only to Tali. I looked again, and there she was, and beside her Aviva smiling impishly down on us from behind the railing.

Why was I not surprised that the angels were here worshipping this Sabbath morning?

"Tali and Aviva are here, Mom."

"Of course," said Paulene. "Why wouldn't they be? They're wonderful Jewish girls."

"Would you mind if I joined them upstairs?"

"Stay put."

I didn't understand her firmness until I noticed Mr. Footlick sending an excruciatingly warm and friendly beam of welcome down on us from the dais where he sat; it felt like the heat of a tanning lamp. He sat up there, a small man lost in one of the high-backed, outsize ornamental chairs of honor right beside our immense holy ark, which held the Torah scrolls.

Something was coming our way, thanks to the Foot, but I didn't know what.

I looked up at the balcony, but the angels weren't immediately visible now. Still I was certain they hadn't flown away. I riffled the pages of the morning service in the *siddur*, the prayer book, which we were about to begin.

There were, I estimated, ten minutes or so before the service would start. I kept turning, hoping to see my two angels looking down on me. Yet each time I peeked, no faces were visible above the railing.

Instead, here was the Foot beaming down at me yet again, or was it Paulene to whom he was sending the love vibe? Or at all three of us?—as if he were proud of this new trio in his life. I didn't like it. He was not part of this family, not yet. And I didn't like the way she gave him a cute wave of her gloved hand.

I wish I'd known what Jon was making of all this; what he was thinking about, and especially if he'd noticed the angels. Yet he sat impassively, it seemed to me, eyes forward, waiting for the service to start, and, if he were like me, hoping it would be over as soon as possible. For all I knew, he was thinking about Western Oaks and about the Mormons, or about Joseph Smith's teaching on how you're supposed to conduct yourself when you're in the Gentiles', that is, the non-Mormons' house of worship.

Now the Foot's peculiar scrutiny made me think again of the tribunal in New York, the old men in their pince-nez and three-piece suits, those guys who had kicked me out.

What would they, those rabbis, have made of Temple Beth Ami's four-ply carpet, its cavernous architecture, its outsize holy ark, its efficient air conditioning, its plush upholstery, its congregants checking out each other's shiny suits and snazzy Rodeo Drive Sabbath dresses? Where was Torah love and Torah study amid all of this? Where was social justice? Where was Rabbi Joel's charge to oppose the war in Vietnam? Whatever the subject of his sermon, it would not be that.

Then I wondered why our Torah ark was so big you could practically walk into it, like the meat freezer at Ships.

I kept peering at the ark, with its two immense convex doors and sculptural handles at the top and bottom of each door. The intent of course was to mimic a giant Torah scroll and its handles. Then there was a kind of odd, yellowish gold lamé that kept nudging me at the margin of my attention: Just what did this color remind me of?

To distract myself from my growing irritation, I concentrated on the prayerbook that I now repositioned on my lap. That was when I felt a finger in the ribs.

With her glance Paulene was motioning me to please raise my eyes and to acknowledge Mr. Footlick, from whom I was apparently not so secretly trying to hide.

It was at this very instant that I saw it! The Foot came into focus as a kissing cousin of Porky Pig. I mean almost a caricature, with his round face and his pate illuminated down to his eyebrows by the lights above the dais. Indeed, the half dome of his head, augmented by the sheen of his large, boxy, white skullcap, positively gleamed beneath the dull glow of the Eternal Light.

Oy.

Despite all of this, I was struck by how Paulene was also, well, shining. How pretty she looked this morning, by far the prettiest of all these temple ladies, in her white gloves and blue dress, with a periwinkle scarf wrapped raffishly over one shoulder. Was it all because of the Foot's attentions? And how could she be so, well, sexy even while Paul's maybe nonexistent soul was roiling about and the allotted time of mourning had, technically, not yet ended?

The world, or at least your own personal world, is supposed to make more sense, is supposed to sort itself out a bit, when you go into a house of prayer. Yet it was working in the opposite way with me, and powerfully so this morning. Everything felt familiar, yet off-center and wrong.

Paulene asked me to shake Mrs. Greenblat's hand behind us, and I did. I said hi to Mrs. Gordon sitting in the row in front of us; she said her kid Howard always remembered me as the genius of his class *daled* at Hebrew school. Howard was now clerking for a federal judge.

"Terrific," I said. "That's just great."

God help me, I didn't want to be presented like some accessory to Paulene's new post-Paul temple life. Still, I did what I had promised. I continued to act the role.

Yet what of my brother? I was fascinated by his posture. I had never seen him sitting so erect, so still and intense. It all seemed to be a harbinger of some alarm to come.

I now saw the Foot turning to Rabbi Joel and amiably chatting with him on the dais; I might be a dropout, but I could still read the rabbinic clues the way a hunter can follow a trail. They were waiting for the latecomers to have found parking, for the sanctuary to fill up a bit more. The signs all meant there would be still be a slight delay before the rabbi would rise, arrange his long black robe squarely over his shoulders, grab the sides of the lectern with his very large hands, as he always did, and start our services.

"Jon?" I tapped his shoulder. "What's up, brother?" The sidewise gaze he sent my way was almost chilling.

At that fragile moment, I once again heard that rustle of clothing. I looked up at the balcony. I didn't see them, but there was the unmistakable verdant scent floating down toward me. I closed my eyes, and I felt I was suddenly at the perfume counter, but not at Rexall Drugs or at the Broadway, where Paulene once or twice had taken me, but at the perfume counter in Eden.

My senses were swooning. How could no one else be affected? I turned again and I saw Tali and Aviva this time fully standing up, each in a beautiful, shapely white sweater. They seemed to lean toward me, their waists against the railing in the first row of the balcony.

That's when the service began.

We rose, we sat, we stood, we rose, and sat and stood again; we sang some psalms, and the next thing I knew we were already headlong into the prayers, and Rabbi Joel and the Foot were standing on each side of the ark and opening it to remove the scroll.

Yet just as I had screwed my resolve to the sticking place to rule my thoughts and to conduct myself appropriately on this day that seemed such a red-letter Sabbath in my mother's life, my backsliding had already begun. Because I saw it! I got it! The ark. Paul had been right!

The few times, like at our bar mitzvahs, that Paulene had gotten him to temple, Paul had always called our ark something that belonged in a Hollywood show. "Where are the chorus girls dancing around it?" he used to say, before Paulene got him to shut up and warned us to ignore him.

And yet he had been prophetic. The huge ark over which I had been puzzling and been especially irritated this morning and all of the previous Sabbaths of my life, thanks to Paul, well, this day, nearly a year after his death, for the first time it all suddenly came into sharp focus.

The two large doors of the ark now revealed themselves to my eyes to resemble nothing less than a couple of giant seven-foot-long, golden brown and glistening hot dogs hinged together at the top and bottom and opening in the middle. And the ark's paint was a color that could have come directly out of a jar of Gulden's Mustard, our perennial condiment.

Our ark was nothing less, or more, than a kosher version of Oscar Meyer's Wienermobile, sanctified, and upended.

I was just about to share my giddy revelation with my brother when I stopped myself. Instead, an urgent communication arrived: Forget the ark! It's a distraction. What's at stake is your father's soul, and it's no joking matter. The voice was inside my head and it cried: Jonah! For god's sake, souls live. It's you who has to wake up!

I TURNED toward my brother, and now was able to discern that he wasn't asleep or frozen or immobile at all, as I had thought, but rather in a kind of deep, almost meditative state. He had taken out the prayer book but not opened it; his head was bowed over some pages, and his lips were moving. I leaned toward him. I was certain that here, in the midst of the service, he was praying his own prayer that I now heard in whispered words—invoking Jesus Christ—his Mormon prayer in the synagogue.

I felt my pulse pumping and my breath grow a little shorter.

"Honey, wake up!" Paulene's whisper interrupted my fevered eavesdropping.

"What now?"

"Look."

When I did look up to where she was pointing, sure enough, the Foot was energetically motioning me toward him. This time it was not a mere wave but a directional hand signal to approach the dais. What's more, it appeared his signalling was intended not for me alone.

Horror of horrors, it instantly became clear that both Jon and I were being recruited to participate in some public fashion in the unfolding Torah-reading service. Could it be?

I heard myself thinking: which will it be, the bathroom or the exits?

"Neither," replied the voice of the angels.

"No, no, no," I muttered.

"Yes, yes, yes," Paulene countered.

Now Jon gave my jacket cuff a yank. "What does he want?"

"Go up and find out, the both of you," Paulene said.

This time her whisper carried a tone of urgency and anticipated pleasure; she knew exactly what was unfolding.

The short journey we now undertook, with Jon walking mechanically beside me, from row to aisle, across the front of the echoing sanctuary, then up the steps to the dais by the Foot and the Wienermobile ark, well, it felt as if it took not a quarter minute but a quarter hour.

If I kept walking more and more slowly, taking half steps and halves of half steps, like a tie game still going in the fortieth inning in baseball, technically I would never arrive.

"You will," said the voice of the angels.

Suddenly we were up on the dais and to my anxious astonishment the Foot and Rabbi Joel really were tapping Jon and me for two honorific, yet thankfully non-singing, roles in the Torah-reading service now drawing to completion.

We were being summoned, I to re-wrap the scroll in its little felt dress cover and silvery finials, and Jon to carry it in the concluding procession of the service. This procession's purpose is to promenade about the sanctuary holding the holy scrolls out for congregants to kiss with the tassels of their shawls or with the corners of their prayer books, and to raise the Torah high aloft for all to see and to admire.

Paulene, of course, had known about it all along.

"*Ya-a-mod ha-magbiah, ya-a-mod ha-gogellel,*" called out the cantor in his robust baritone. That is, "Let the scroll-raiser rise and and let the holy-roller join him."

What a show my incipient Mormon brother then put on at Temple Beth Ami. Jon seized the handles of the still-open scroll and hoisted it up until, straight-armed. I thought he might power it right through the skylighted ceiling of Temple Beth Ami and straight to heaven.

To whose heaven? That, of course, was the question.

He did more than merely raise the Torah from the reading table the way the old men usually did it, their arms quivering with the ungainly weight of Moses' words. No, Jon grabbed onto the Torah's two handles as if he were teaching them the Australian crawl and they needed reassurance.

He practically launched the Torah, which must never be allowed to touch the ground, way high into the air as if to give the old Pentateuch a little thrill.

If the congregants only knew what this was about. If only I did!

And now, after I dressed the scroll in its coverlet and put on its tinkling finials and other jewelry, we could begin the final procession.

JON, THE Torah, and I led Rabbi Joel, the cantor, and the Foot in front of the Wienermobile ark, down the dais steps and through the aisles of the sanctuary. At every row we paused so that congregants could shower the Torah with respect and affection, and scrutinize the Gould boys in the process. Finally, on the final leg of the circumambulation, we approached the row where our mother was sitting.

Here Paulene sidled into the aisle and very publicly gave the scroll its required peck and her sons big ceremonial hugs. She practically took a bow before she returned to her seat. Was I ever relieved that we had only a small jog that remained before we arrived back to the dais to place the Torah back in the Wienermobile.

Right before we ascended the short flight of steps to the dais and to the end of our ordeal, the cantor signaled for Jon to raise the scroll up once more. He gestured this time toward the balcony, where Jon was to raise the scroll symbolically toward those worshippers there who had not been able to come down to bestow their kisses, that they might now offer reverential smooches from afar.

Suddenly, there the Israelis were again, Tali and Aviva, rising in all of their radiance in the first row of the balcony, like angelic creatures swimming up from the bottom of the picture frame formed by the balcony rail. They were aglow with the wild beauty of their flowing hair and their form-fitting Sabbath whites, Angora sweaters, fuzzy and wispy with elegant feathery borders at the shoulders and along the sides.

As she leaned steeply over the railing, Tali extended her arm so regally toward us that her elegant fingers seemed to span the gap and to actually touch the Torah Jon carried.

Then the ripple of sweet approbation that had been coursing through the congregation crescendoed even more when Aviva, beside Tali, threw a kiss so loving and gentle it might have alighted on the scroll like a butterfly; then it caromed off and landed right on my cheek.

I know this may sound like exaggerated nonsense, but this is the way it was.

The circumambulation complete, Jon and I stepped up, returned the Torah to its resting place, and then ourselves to our seats on either side of Paulene.

Yet if she or the Foot actually thought that the modest commandments just fulfilled in doing these ceremonial chores or the admiring eyes of congregants were going to deter Jon from his incipient Mormon path, what happened next—the real surprise of the service—disabused them.

It centered, not surprisingly, not on the Torah at all, but on the *kaddish*, the prayer for the dead.

The *kaddish* was the real reason why Paulene had been so eager for us to be there with her on this Sabbath, for that's how a family shows public respect for their dead.

The recitation of the *kaddish* was about to begin. For Paul, and for his soul. That page number was about to be announced by Rabbi Joel, the beginning of the end of the service—and my struggle with my angels—to which we now raced.

21

IN the *kaddish*, you don't just intone the Lord's praises, you belt them out and up toward the rafters of the temple like Aretha Franklin. No matter how broken up you are; no matter how unfathomable death might be in general or the death of your loved one in particular, you're supposed to keep your mouth untainted by the sour taste of remorse or by particular complaints. Instead, you must extol the Lord most high.

That's the Jewish way of grief.

Because this approach seemed so counterintuitive and, well, dead wrong, I had always rather liked this prayer.

That's right: no grief, no complaint, no bitching about the incomprehensibility or the unfairness of it all, about injustice, and about the untimeliness of being yanked away. Only praise, praise, praise God. For He rules, He is magnified, He is sovereign, He's the one and the only, no one else. He's the government, all three branches, He's the alpha and the omega, the up and the down, the in and the out, the coffee and the cream. So praise Cole Porter, and praise, praise, you pip-squeak Norman Gould, who has neither sufficiently mourned his father nor praised his Lord.

Oops. That's exactly what you're supposed to avoid. No irony, no sarcasm. Only praise, praise, praise.

We stood up, we sat down, and now we stayed standing as Rabbi Joel and the cantor were cruising efficiently through the balance of the service; the *kaddish*, like the car right before the caboose of the service, is just now rounding the curve and coming toward us.

Paulene leaned toward her sons and on her perfumed whisper to Jon were these simple instructions: "Page 113, dear."

"I know where it is," he said, but it did not bode well that he refused to look at her.

I didn't either, because suddenly I felt deeply ashamed. I had left quickly after the funeral service at Mt. Eden; I had not stayed to say the *kaddish* even a full seven days, and, after that, in New York, I prayed the *kaddish* barely at all.

A page or two away from our required recitation, the scene of Paul's death began to flicker and then to play in the little one-person, one-car drive-in of my mind. How I'd picked up the phone in New York to hear Jon describe how someone who was there had said it had happened: how Paul was playing seven-card stud in Gardena at the Silver Dollar Casino when the huge heart attack struck, so powerful he closed his eyes in a swoon of pain, how his body, with the cards still upright in his hand, tilted him left into a kind of slump in his chair. How quiet the heart attack had been, fatal and huge but soundless as it swept him away.

See why the *kaddish*? Praise sweeps away such guilty memories. Praise cures you. Reciting it will give the soul of Paul Gould a nudge in the direction of heaven. Like a gentle wind to your gossamer spirit, Paul, the words of praise will blow you this way, Dad, and not that; they'll enable you to take that turn right at the curve of that cloud bank, yes, because if you go left you'll end up, well, elsewhere, where you don't belong. Take that, Mormons, I was thinking. I'll see your ordinance and I'll raise you with a *kaddish*.

Was it possible that after all these months of my ratiocination, after all of the books and my comparative soul-ology it could it be this simple?

Now here came the moment.

"Please rise," intoned Rabbi Joel.

Paulene stood. I stood. With a collective rustle of dresses and petticoats and a few brittle joint sounds of the elderly rising, perhaps a third of the congregation collectively got to its feet.

Yet Jon remained sitting.

I tapped his shoulder.

No response.

"Get up, man," I whispered.

Rabbi Joel stepped out from behind the shiny wooden lectern, and glanced our way. He took a concerned step toward the edge of the platform. The Foot followed. "All those reciting the prayer for the dead, may I ask you please now to rise?"

"*Kaddish* again, darling. For your father!" Paulene whispered urgently. Her eyes implored me to do something, but what?

"If the Mormons love the Jews so much," I whispered, "show some of it now."

"Please, son."

He did not stir.

"This is a hell of a time for a sit-in. We'll discuss it later. Get up!"

He didn't.

I leaned across and poked him at the armpit. Jon looked at me as if I'd inserted not my hand, but a knife, into the side of his body.

And yet he didn't stand. "I said the *kaddish* when you skipped out of town, man. And when you were at work and busy. And when the rabbi wasn't around either."

"I know," Paulene whispered.

"No, you don't. Every morning, I parked the cab out front. Right on La Cienega. I got tickets. Eight of them. You want to see them?"

"Now's not a good time for that. Why didn't you tell me, son?"

"I was here; I was always here when neither of you were."

"I know, darling. All right, so one more time? Finally with all of us together?"

"I prayed for two of us. I prayed for the three of us."

"So I owe you a *kaddish*. I'll make it up to you," I said.

"Not now. It's over," he said as he now removed his *yarmulke* and stepped, at first hesitatingly, but then with a kind of resolution, out into the aisle.

Silence, thick and audible, as he turned away and began to walk toward the exit.

"You get back in here!"

Paulene's voice stopped him. Jon's feet sank into the thick pile rug. He grasped the curving corner of one of the pews. "Please, son."

"You know where I'm going and you still want me to stay?"

"Of course. Stay," she said.

So Jon did return, but neither put his skullcap back on, nor stood with the rest of us. He sat himself and even moved a few inches away from us.

Now Rabbi Joel leaned into the microphone: "Is the family of the bereaved finally ready? If one of the boys has, or is having a . . . physical . . . problem, he can certainly pray from his seat. People in wheelchairs do so all the time."

Now the cantor, with the Foot musically following right behind, lanced the tension by beginning to chant the prayer: May He be glorified! May He be sanctified, the Great Name, God. "*Yit-ga-dal, v'yitka-a-dash, shemay raba.*"

Paulene now joined them in her quavering soprano and with an awkward, long-suffering maternal half smile at her embarrassment before the onlookers. I added my own raspy voice. I usually just mouthed or whispered the words, but not now. Bad as I sing, I sang it louder; I sang it to double up for the one who was sitting and not singing. Then, with a collective exhalation of relief, the rabbi and the congregation joined in.

The chanting cascaded throughout the sanctuary, everyone belting away to help out Paulene and me to compensate for whatever peculiar affliction had struck the other son.

When there was no stopping the rolling and growing *kaddish*, and it was safe to detach my voice from the communal crescendo, I leaned down and whispered to my stolid brother. "However badly I acted then, however I offended you," I said, the words sounding to my ear like the very liturgy of the Day of Atonement, "please forgive me, and absolve me. I'll make it up to you. Just please stand the hell up!"

He still didn't.

So on the *kaddish* went, with Paulene gamely chanting and looking imploringly down at Jon; but each time he avoided her eyes, and mine, and stayed seated, solid as a stone in his anti-*kaddish*.

While he sat, the doxology sounded like the slowest-prayed prayer for the dead ever intoned in the history of Jewish mourning.

Yet now Paulene's tenacity was rewarded, and Jon relented. Slowly he rose from the seat. Yet as he did so he said to her and to me, "I don't want him in heaven, *your* heaven. This is no game. I only wish I could *un*-say all of the previous *kaddishes*, every last one of them."

As if in a kind of response, the *kaddish* we were singing grew louder, and continued to glorify and to thunder about us.

Now Paulene wrapped her arm around my brother's waist as if to reel him in. She sang right beside him, as if she were singing a lullaby or a kid's song and teaching him. But, my god, it's not "Itsy bitsy spider climbed up the water spout." It's the *kaddish*! Her face was cheek by jowl with his, her eye on him; yet his lips remained closed.

That's when I heard Aviva's alto and then Tali's angelic soprano sailing out from the balcony. Their voices seemed to detach from the general song and now found ours and entwined with my own and with Paulene's, as if a kind of musical bandage were being applied to the deep and now visible wound in the body of our family. "*Yit-ga-dal, v'yitka-a-dash, shemay raba.*" May it be elevated and made holy, the name of the Lord. "*D'almah dvra chirutey, vyamlich malchutey, vchaiyachaw uvyomaicha, d'chaiyeh d'chol bay't yisroel . . .*"

Right before the ending, having himself studiously not sung a word, Jon disengaged from Paulene. Without a remark he stepped into the aisle again but this time bolted toward the rear of the sanctuary, heading directly for the spot at the balcony overhang above which the angels sang, and the nearby exit door.

What could either of us have done? Paulene stopped chanting. She dropped her head as if it had just doubled its weight. Now she moved closer to me and grasped my arm. Hard. She held me as though she thought maybe I was about to head for the exits.

She did not look back. I did. Jon's eyes met mine, and then he left the temple.

"Did he go?"

I nodded to my mother.

As if in a kind of compensatory refrain to Jon's flight, the intensity of the remaining notes of the *kaddish*, which had momentarily flagged, now surged. I heard the cantor and Rabbi Joel's and Mr. Footlick's voices lashing the tired vocal horses of Temple Beth Ami.

With the home stables at least now in sight, we galloped on gamely, praising the Lord whose glory no words of praise could touch or even approximate.

"I'm going to wring his neck," Paulene whispered. "After you finish with him."

22

I FOUND Jon not at the ward and in the embrace of Western Oaks, where I raced first only to find a closed and locked door. Instead, he was stretched out on a chair beside our grandmother watching an LA Angels baseball game. In her deaf and silent acceptance, she was his friend. She slept, he watched, and they both ignored me when I righteously charged in.

I was used to delivering sermons to people who paid scant attention, and so I threw myself down on the rug at their feet and rolled onto my back like a tipped over bug. I shook my raised hands and legs in the air. My feigned tantrum was as much to amuse Ida as to lambast Jon, maybe more so. Still his behavior had shocked me.

I righted myself, and launched: "All you had to do was stand up! Mouth a few words! You couldn't bring yourself to do such a small thing?"

" No matter how many times I've explained, you still don't get it."

"Oh, you got through this time. Right through to her heart. You broke it."

"She'll be fine."

"You couldn't fake it?"

"Then I'd be like you? No thanks."

He stepped over me and adjusted the knobs on the TV.

"Do you have any idea how many times I said it with her and with Foot-lick? The *kaddish*, man. After you left? I've out-*kaddish*ed you by dozens, hundreds, of times."

"I said I'll make it up to you."

"There's only one way you can do that."

"I'm not going to sign."

"Then what's more to discuss? Shut up. Watch the game."

So I did shut up, but strangely this time it was he who went on. "Ten months, eleven months along in Dad's journey. . . . Believe me, had I known I'd been moving Paul along, helping . . . lock him in there along that path, do you think I would have said even *one*?"

"What 'path'?"

"You know exactly. Heaven, Jewish heaven, man. *That* path."

This was beyond strange. He was a Mormon now, or 90 percent of the way there, yet he was also still a believer in the *kaddish*'s power? He was such a heaven-believer. How many other heavens up there were, by his lights, also competing for Paul's soul? How had this brother of mine become like an all-faiths engineer of heavenly vectoring, and Mormonism his mission control?

He was about to leave few details to my further surmise. "I want him out, and, yes, the Mormons will allow me to rescue him and to bring him to a better place. I can do it without you. Wes is going to help me de-*kaddish* our father."

"'De-*kaddish*' him?"

"That's right."

"Jesus!"

"Yes."

"De-*kaddish*? What's that? Like some kind of . . . spiritual tonsillectomy?"

"Maybe it is."

"And what about the others? Her, for example?" I said indicating Ida. "On the highway to heaven ?"

"I told you."

"Ordinances all around?"

"Eventually. After I'm settled. Give it a rest, Norman. Please. It's not so horrible."

And yet it felt precisely that way.

"The way I figure we have about a month left—well, three weeks, four days to be precise—before the end of the eleventh month since Dad's death. Before that happens I intend to redirect him back, to reach him before the Jewish heavenly door is shut, and the *mezuzah* shakes, and the lock is turned, and he's in there forever."

"That's not the way it is."

"Yes it is."

"You're addressing a problem that doesn't exist."

"No? To have to hang with all of the dead Mr. Footlicks isn't a problem?"

"But, Jon, they don't fundraise in Jewish heaven."

"You really don't know that, do you? Heaven's not a dramatic rupture, but a continuance."

"Okay, okay," I said, "all right," ceding theological points I knew we couldn't settle then, if ever. "Apart from going on a *kaddish* strike, just what is it you and Wes plan to do besides the paperwork?"

"Look," he said, "I really want us not to hate each other. It's not paperwork. It's a symbol, a metaphor, a reflection—you understand those things, don't you?—for what's happening in the other realm. The ceremony will seal it."

"Unbelievable."

Jon, to his eternal credit, kept trying, and he slowly withdrew the ordinance yet again from his back pocket. I noticed the paper appeared different this time. Not only white, but a high glossy white that caught a sparkle of the refracted light from the TV screen.

Across Ida's rising and falling abdomen, he offered it to me. This time I didn't shun it, reject it out of hand, or even flinch.

This time, because of what he had done at the synagogue, I acknowledged its power.

The document this time appeared to be half an application from the motor vehicle department, half a genealogy chart.

"You've got Dad's name down here, in Hebrew."

"Did I get it right?"

"You did."

"Good. I wanted to be sure. Maybe the Hebrew will help. I don't want him to be a loser in heaven."

"I never considered him a loser."

"Why do you keep lying to yourself? Of course you did. I know what you felt. We know who he was. You have got to stop faking it. Isn't the prospect of heaven a good time to start?"

This talk had shaken me. It was true of course, it was very true. And he knew that he had gotten to me. Yet what I said surprised me and Jon as well: "I happen to like the *kaddish*, and I intend to go to *shul* and say it until the end of the eleventh month. You weren't anticipating that, were you?"

"We have a little problem, then."

"Only if you make it so."

"Would Paul himself care about the *kaddish* being said on his behalf? Would he? I never thought so. When did you ever hear *him* say it? For Grandpa? For Uncle Dan? I never heard it from his lips. Never. When did you ever see him go to the synagogue except for when Paulene forced him? He no more belongs in Jewish heaven than Steve Bilko belongs in the Majors."

"Well, surprise," I said to my brother, "but our father was, despite his spotty synagogue attendance record, a very Jewish guy. I'll tell you how. In his *luftmensch*-y employment, he was Jewish. In his sense of humor, he was Jewish. In his choice of lousy heart-attack food, he was Jewish. In his bad luck, he was Jewish. In his gambling and in all of his failures, he was Jewish. So maybe, yes, in the fifty-cent bleacher seats, but in Jewish heaven nevertheless, thank you very much."

I was about to qualify that with "in Jewish heaven *whatever that is*," but I caught myself. Still, Jon somehow had read my panicky mind.

"You see, that's just it. You really have no idea of heaven, and you don't care about it. You belittle it even as you defend it. What gives with you? No matter how much you *read* about them, you have no respect for a spirit or for a soul. Unless something is material and comes on a bun with fries and onion rings, it's not real and it's just meaningless to you."

"The angels are not meaningless."

"What angels? Come off it! If you want to send his soul to the place of all places where more crap is sure to come his way, then what kind of love is that?"

"I think they've brainwashed you."

"If that's what thinking for yourself is, then, yes, I'm brainwashed."

"You can't really be doing this."

"Look, you went away from here, and you didn't see what he went through in business and with Paulene. You have no idea. They say it was a heart attack at the poker table, but it was his soul. His soul and spirit had a heart attack from not enough love and from much bad luck. I think that happened a long time ago. And only then did the bodily organs follow. I really believe that I was at fault. So was Mom. So are you. I never told him I loved him. Just, did ya win, Dad? How were the nags tonight, Dad? Sideways, stupid talk. Now you want it repeated into all eternity? I guarantee you that if Paul gets into Jewish heaven, where he's headed, within weeks, maybe within days—"

"—What days! There is no *time* after you die, there's no . . . heaven is not some continuation, some . . . help, please!"

"—Within days," Jon calmly continued, "he'll have another heart attack, a heavenly Jewish heart attack. And that could really be fatal. No, he needs a new beginning, a fresh start, a new place. I know it, and what's more, I'm going to provide it for him."

"How did you ever get this way? Look, here's what I really *know*: when you die, the body decays, becomes . . . soil. Your atoms live on that way. In the ground, migrating out, becoming, I don't know, air and food for turtles, bees, sharks, a loaf of *challah*, a new TV, how do I know. Eternity is the way people live on in the memories of those who follow. You and I are Paul's life after death."

"That's it? Really? And when we die and no longer is there anyone on earth who has even a passing thought of him and Paulene, or Ida or you or me, then what? The curtain falls for the final time? Darkness? Extinction?"

"Look, man, I don't have all of the answers but this I know: there is no pastrami Jewish heaven any more than there's a Mormon-basketball-beach-and-barbecue-party-apple-cobbler heaven."

"Just listen to the way you sound."

"What's wrong with the way I sound?"

"So angry and cold at the same time. So detached and sarcastic. Didn't you love him?"

"Of course I did, you . . ." and then I caught myself, because, God, yes, God help me, maybe I never truly did. Unless love and shame are somehow related, like terrible kissing cousins of each other. In that case I had loved him a lot.

Jon let me cry for a moment, and I did cry, but he would not back down.

". . . Then I just don't understand how could you want *that* for him. Again?"

"It's not up to me for chrissakes!"

"Aha," he said, "QED, man! That's exactly it. I have a way, and you don't."

"Look, did you ever ask Paul? Ask him about this?"

"About the Mormons? How could I? No."

"You know he would never want this."

"I know no such thing. We've explained and explained it to you, man. He can review it and study and then decide. He can turn it down if he wants."

I was still holding the ordinance in my hand.

"It's preferable if next of kin signs. Yes. It would be nice if you entered your name."

I peered at the sheet. "It asks for Hebrew? For my name?"

"As well as English. Yes. They're interested in languages. Don't be a jerk."

"If the Jews disappointed him, the Mormons will, all religions would. Paulene told you the only soul he ever cared about was filet of sole, with lots of butter and lemon. He wasn't a heaven-and-hell kind of guy, Jon. He should be left alone, in his Jewish grave."

"I think we're right back where we started."

Then he took back the document, folded it, and replaced it in his pocket. He wrapped his long arms around himself at the chest, a gesture that reminded me of Paulene. "It takes a lot out of me to talk to you about this. But I felt bad about what happened. At the temple. And Wes said to try until the very end, to try."

"You tell Wes everything?"

"About this? Absolutely."

"You make a new family, you lose an old one."

He heard, but he said nothing.

The Relic sighed. Jon fidgeted with the shawl around her shoulders. Her eyes opened, she looked at the both of us, and I thought she was about to say something. Paul's mother, after all. Maybe she was the repository of his soul, and Paul would now make a pronouncement right out of her. I waited. I think in his own Mormon way Jon was waiting, but the Relic just sighed, and if that was Paul's soul, it sputtered and it petered out, without any drama whatsoever.

"I'm going to get her to lie down," Jon said, turning suddenly away from me, flicking off the TV, and picking up the Relic and cradling her in his arms.

"I just know what Paul would say if you pitched him this line of bull. And you do."

"Don't be so sure. And what hurts most is that you don't respect him even enough to give him his own shot. You turn heaven and hell into a basketball game to bet on. It was violent and demeaning and stupid, and I'm embarrassed. You were so high and so hot to do that, so we accommodated. I never agreed. Dad was beaten up by this life. And I'm going to rescue him from repetition. Period."

"Don't file it."

"If you don't believe in any of this stuff, why does it upset you? If it's nonsense, why are you making such a big deal out of it? Why don't you just let me have my fun, my illusions, my third-grade-level nonsense as you call it. By the way, I loved the third grade. Hey, you're a dropout, so drop out already!"

I let him go on, standing there in the doorway with Ida in his arms, like some old Polish, Jewish pietà.

"And what will you do about it? It's not as if I'm going to stick the ordinance in a mailbox, and you can go break it open and intercept it. And even if you did and tore it up and burned it, so what? It's going to happen, Norman. In fact it's happening right now. Arrangements are being made. Just what do you intend to do about it?"

It was an excellent question.

23

THE next day, Monday, I lived in a fog that all these decades later still obscures my memory, but I do recall I was up at 5:45 by the clock and it was only just getting light. Jon was not in the bed beside me. Maybe he'd stayed downstairs with the Relic, maybe with the Mormons. Either way, I knew I was losing him. I dressed, skipped eating, and was soon angling across La Cienega Boulevard.

My destination was not camp, because I felt I couldn't go to work that day without making a stop beforehand. I was suddenly missing my father, and in a new way that was no longer cerebral in that I was thinking about him or trying to analyze just how I missed him or the experience of missing him. It was something different; it hurt.

I don't mean to dress up my state in more psychological complexity than it deserves, but Jon's naked emotion—call it a strange potion of love and yearning taking the form of his Mormon journey—now shamed me deeply. What I mean is that for the first time that summer I felt a real ache—not for food or for dope or for the embrace of the angels—but a longing for Paul's company. Oh, there's so much guilt involved in mourning, you never know where that ends, and the purer stuff, the inexplicable sadness of rupture and departure, begins.

I pulled open the double doors, took the stairs immediately to the right in the corner of the lobby, and descended to the small subterranean room where the temple's orthodox-leaning *minyan* gathered for daily services before work. The timing was just about perfect.

As I raced down, I felt another self within me as if it were slowly perforating and then seprating from my "self," so that the self I was now bearing downstairs was somehow pulling a faint outline of my shadowy double behind me.

Still we seemed to be functioning together, at least for now, as I joined the quorum of about eleven others for morning prayers.

I knew every seat, corner, and vantage in this musty, always-in-agreeable-disarray little makeshift sanctuary, for it also served as the headquarters of the Junior Congregation in which I had starred.

With prayer shawls not properly folded and dangling out of a humble cardboard liquor box by the door, and piles of books on various chairs as if the previous users had left in haste or been evacuated, in short, in its humble messiness, the room was everything the Hollywoodish sanctuary above, with its Wienermobile ark and its neon eternal light, was not.

I chose a threadbare *talit*, a prayer shawl whose odd markings made me think I might have used it myself more than a dozen years before. Then a quick dip and turn of the shoulders and a susurration of the tassels and knots—a silken sound I associated with that made by angels when they slowly extend their wings. I wrapped myself tightly in the shawl and began, yes, to pray.

My fellow worshippers included Dr. Waterman, a pencil-mustachioed dentist I had gone to as a small child with precociously bad teeth that I felt challenged his skills. I now recalled how his hand used to tremble when he approached with the hypo of Novocaine and its two-inch needle.

This morning he approached me with a hug, and I returned it.

I recognized none of the others, but I sensed they all knew who I was: the bookie's son and formerly the pride of the LA Jewish diaspora whose brother had just dissed God on the Sabbath, insulted the rabbi and congregation as his dad used to do, and dishonored his widow and his family.

The service proceeded very quickly with these men. Without a real leader in prayer, they moved on their own like an uncoached and senescent soccer team, sometimes streaking alone down the sidelines of the *Amidah*, the Eighteen Benedictions, occasionally coming together when necessary toward the common goal of worship.

In this cozy hive, they buzzed so swiftly through the Hebrew prayers that even I had to pay close attention to know where in the order of the service we were. I was eventually able to lose myself in the words in a manner that never occurred upstairs.

Barely ten minutes after my entry, and still feeling as if my cover in some Jewish witness protection program had been blown, the proceedings arrived at the *kaddish* and I with them. This was the vocal solo that I, as the mourning older son, had to lead, and the part I deeply dreaded because of my awful voice.

Upstairs, despite the damage Jon had caused through his reticence and through his dramatic exit, we at least had a dozen of my mother's sisterly friends from the hospitality committee, with their nurturing voices, who had clustered about us, along with the Foot, Rabbi Joel, and the cantor.

Even if one of these old guys joined in, which was always possible, I would still be counted on actually to lead the prayerful pack in the *kaddish*, and I well might be chanting alone.

My dry mouth grew drier. I had to sing it right, to sing it beautifully, to sing it—this was the minimum duty one must perform—at least in tune, to send Paul's soul, on the wings of my song of praise, blowing along a Hebraic trajectory toward its resting place. God, after all, was used to magnificent choirs, was He not? It felt as if it were me alone against the Mormon Tabernacle hundreds.

Moreover, was it possible to have a voice so terrible and so unfit for prayer as my own that, whatever the efficacy of my new intention—and there was still much to question in that department—its croaking tunelessness might entirely undermine my enterprise?

You bet it could.

And now it came. I stood and saw that I was indeed alone.

"*Yitgadal,*" I cried out. "*Yitgadal, vyitkadash, shmey rabbah,*" I called, with fervor, and with an unexpected force, belting my *kaddish* out so that it seemed to rattle the three small transom windows of the little Junior Congregation room on their tilted hinges.

Immediately I knew it was awful.

I knew there was no tone or pitch to it. It sounded like something Herman's Hermits might have sung had they been compelled to rise from throat surgery off their sickbeds in the intensive care unit. I mean I was off, way off, and I imagined God, like a music teacher insulted and long-suffering, painfully averting His celestial face from my hideous offering.

Dr. Waterman, not much of a singer himself, gamely tried to help me out, but since I didn't know where I was going musically, he soon gave up accompanying me.

The fear that had gripped me earlier now found my throat, and the more I tried, the more musically misshapen my solo prayer became. I was not only off-key, I was off everything. Suddenly I was giving birth to a monster of a *kaddish*.

I imagined the hosts of heaven reaching for their white earplugs. The revered prayer for the dead was beginning to sound like some vocal mishmash more akin to "Take Me Out to the Ballgame."

I thought of stopping, but wouldn't that be tantamount to fleeing like my brother? No, that was impossible. I would go on, I had to finish it, and croak my way to the bitter end of these words of praise.

In my perfervid imagination, Jon now appeared; I could make him out listening just outside the temple wall at one of the small transom windows. Bent on one knee with a kind of black *kaddish*-catching butterfly net balanced over his shoulder, he was wearing, beneath the Camp Tikvah outfit, his new white Mormon undergarments, modeled on the biblical *ephod*. His mission, received directly from Western Oaks and from the bishops, was clear: he must intercept my prayer before it could ascend heavenward as reinforcement at the field of the Great Battle of Kaddish versus Ordinance in which we were engaged.

Now, as I continued haltingly to chant, he rose and backed away from the transom, and there it finally appeared for him: my *kaddish* emerged, and it was a wounded butterfly or bird of a *kaddish*, a fledgling with possibly still undetermined birth defects somehow now escaping from the transom's opening. It was so limp and fragile, a *kaddish* so poorly performed, it fluttered on an injured wing, this prayer for the dead practically DOA itself, so that it fell of its own weight, with hardly a sound, right into his net. *Plop*.

"*Ba-agalah uvizman karive*," I persevered, all effort, all volume, all strain, no tune, and no result.

Then I heard *their* sweet and soaring voices.

As I turned, there they were, Tali and Aviva for some reason both back in their military shorts, boldly rolled up on their thighs, as they had been the first day of Camp Tikvah. They swayed gently in their musical assist to me, their hair bouncing like the coiffures of the girls in the Breck Shampoo ads as they emerged from the women's section behind the separation curtain beyond the back row of seats.

It was all I could do not to fling myself into their arms. Yet that wasn't necessary, for with a fine defiance of custom, out they now walked amid the astonished old men as they planted themselves, one on either side of me, my very own choral rescue squad.

"Pray," Tali whispered her mysterious command as if she'd known me all my life, with all of my hypocrisies and fears and fakeries. "Pray, Norman, like it finally really did matter."

And pray we did, together, as our threesome engendered a sound, to which the old men's voices, now aroused, conjoined, so that a chorus, as opposed to a pick-up group of bedraggled, separate, and Wandering Jewish Tones, was genuinely brought together, many voices as one.

Then this new aural phenomenon gathered momentum, began to rise, and seemed ready to break out onto the boulevard, float over Ships and over the waterworks, over the parent-tousled heads of the arriving campers, over all of La Cienega Boulevard, and across all of Los Angeles from Santa Monica to the mountain passes of the Angeles Crest to the Mojave.

Boy, if this didn't move my father's soul along, nothing could.

The doxological yearning of the old blended with the craving of the young to become a single extended note of praise that lifted up my sorry, hurt little voice as if on the perfect white stretcher of their harmonies—I know I'm overdoing it, but it really was wonderfully beyond words—and they carried me and my *kaddish* for Paul, my poor father, into whose ear, yes, I had never once said, "I love you," bearing it high and aloft, and to its conclusion.

24

WILL it surprise you to hear that from that day forward for the balance of the summer I began to pray the *kaddish*? And not just early in the a.m. with my new elderly friends, but also at the end of lunch break at camp?

I explained to the kids what I was doing, of course, as I separated myself from them and skipped to a place of some privacy under the nearest pine or eucalyptus. I say "skipped" because I was eager. Suddenly to say this prayer was like drinking a cool glass of water after a long exertion.

And there I stood. I took a deep breath. I closed my eyes and, with no need of a text because I knew the prayers by heart, I began to chant, and, darn, if the melodies didn't begin to sound better and better.

After my first few solos, a personal style also seemed to evolve as I began to unglue my feet from their stationary position on the grass and instead to bob and sway in the traditional manner of Jewish prayer. In New York I had found this movement silly, embarrassingly anachronistic, a *shtetl* throwback, and counterproductive; I thought it only broke concentration. But no longer. Now I began to experience it for what it is: a smooth, undulating, oceanic way to somehow break through, to insinuate yourself outside of the prison of your solitude and, in a larger sense, the space-time continuum to which we are all sentenced by virtue of being alive. You step out into the universe, you step back into yourself, you pray.

Whoa! Was I ever launched, and I wasn't even high.

I even began to walk a few paces this way and that, and to nod hello to someone riding by on their bike or to a parent who once waved hello as she picked up her sick kid from camp; their curiosity rarely disturbed me or my concentration as I always returned to the words of praise as I prayed the prayer for the dead for Paul.

Naturally I performed this ritual facing east. In that direction not only Jerusalem lay in the great distance, but closer to me the baseball field and its green scoreboard, the dugout with its chain link fence, the dense copse of trees at the edge of the bleachers down the wavily chalked left field line, and, right beyond that terminus, Gregory Way and the Mormon ward and stake building.

My prayer didn't take long—all of ten or twelve minutes at most—and the angels, of course, always covered for me with the campers.

Finally, when camp concluded, at the end of each of the remaining dozen days or so when I was back home, at sunset, I also never failed to pray the prayer once again, my third *kaddish* of the day, the evening's prayer for the dead. Usually I did this one out on our upstairs porch overlooking Orange Grove, sometimes downstairs with Ida nearby awake or dozing, it didn't matter. Now and then she recognized a phrase or two and sang along with me.

At none of the three daily prayers, not even the midday *kaddish* at camp, did Tali or Aviva ever join me again. I was now truly on my own.

The angels treated my new regime as if it were a natural part of the camp day, like a snack. They didn't talk about it or inquire about what I was experiencing, or how it all was going. They treated it like the injury to Western Oaks, something that had just happened and required no more comment than the weather.

Nor did they comment on Jon's reaction—how my brother, who had been keeping such a painful distance, now curiously seemed to approach and to observe me each time I prayed. Once or twice I found out from Tali that he had even given himself an errand to run so he could stand nearby like a kind of sentinel no more than ten or twenty yards away from where I *daven*ed.

Or I might catch a glimpse of Jon, his head above the pool deck barrier or standing up on his lifeguard's perch, stretching and rotating toward me with an intense gaze from behind his shades.

When I returned from my afternoon *kaddish* one day, and I must have given in to a shrug of frustration or pointed to my throat or somehow indicated that on that particular day my *kaddish* had sounded like the old me, when all I could do was expel the words like so many pits caught in my throat, Tali inclined toward me and enveloped me in her verdant scent. Then she whispered, "Not to worry. A pure heart will eventually find the right key."

I prayed not only as law and custom demanded, I did it in the Jewish uniform of mourning, wearing almost all black or dark colors every day. That look I now pursued with fervor. I found a pair of black bermuda shorts behind our bedroom door, and then black socks, and I even located deep in our closet a pair of all-black Converse All Stars.

The camp director and the Foot, of course, gave me a wide berth to don the colors of mourning instead of the standard camp T-shirt. How could they not?

Each day of the first week of this new regime I also ripped some of the bottom of the T-shirt a bit before the morning or afternoon *kaddish* because rending your clothing is another of our customs; after a week or so my T-shirt's hem showed a line of tatters, and I was proud of it.

Not shaving is also an orthodox expression of mourning, and I embraced that as well. Within a week I had the makings of a real beard. One of the parents, on picking up her kid and noticing the facial change, asked me if the goal of my new look was Herman Melville or Moses the Lawgiver.

"Both," I replied.

And I wasn't through yet.

I drove out to Sorrento Beach, where so much of the magic had occurred, and I scooped up some ash from the barbecuing pit and then another small brown bag full from the depression in the sand where the bonfire had been a short distance from the basketball court. I didn't know if it was still Mormons' ash or by now if it belonged to some other beach picnickers. That wasn't the point. The ash was. I took a small pinch, and smudged it on my forehead, because this too is a Jewish mourning custom, dating all the way back to the biblical days when the bereaved took up "sackcloth and ashes."

During those last two weeks of camp, if you happened to have been walking by, your gaze may have lingered on me longer than usual—as the kids' increasingly did—and you might conclude I had forgotten to wash my face that day; or I was troubled and growing unkempt and in need of help. This was an interpretation I could understand.

But it wasn't true. I was feeling better and better. And the more I performed all the mourning rites and rituals, the better I felt. After the healing of the *kaddish*, I especially loved the feel of the ash, the grittiness of it on my skin, the source of the stuff and its closeness to earth, wind, and fire.

I should not omit that I also flushed down the toilet what remained of Jon's stash of marijuana, I stopped eating my Ships burgers and pork of all

kinds, and began to dine happily and mainly on Ida's grilled-cheese sandwiches at night and on whatever the camp offered during the day. Food and
dope both lost their allure; in my black sneakers, I became, yes, a kind of All
Star of grieving, an athlete of Jewish mourning.

I was full up with prayer and with praise, and I wasn't hungry any more
and I spent my free hours walking the neighborhood and taking the bus
downtown, retracing Paul's footsteps, not looking for a soul, but feeling a
presence, and all the time in my dark clothes and shoes.

And Paulene? At first she was not a little embarrassed by my excesses. Well
shocked is more like it. Yet what could she do? I had a lot of *kaddish*es to
make up, I told her, just as Jon had said. And there was no arguing that I was
doing it for the both us. What's more, I was the talk of the end of summer,
the rabbinic student come home to be a role model of filial piety, Jewish style.
Paulene reported that one of her friends, Mrs. Greenberg, had seen me praying away at the temple early one morning, and said to her: "What are they
teaching them back in New York?"

The remarkable thing was that I felt it, I meant it, and everyone sensed my
passion and sincerity; no one at the temple had ever seen anything like it.

As I prayed, and even during the long intervals between, I tried not to
think how what I was doing would affect the flight of Paul's soul. If I indeed
through these efforts was wafting him toward the right ethereal destination,
well and good. Or if Jon through his efforts was trying for the intercept we
had been battling over, well and good.

I no longer obsessed about it. The battle seemed beside the point because
the *kaddish* was the point: to pray it over and over again, to explore the words,
to hear the rumble of the praise, the elision between untranslatable sounds, to
have joined the ancient and never-ending chorus. All I did was pray and con-
centrate on the prayer.

Yet as I did so Jon moved inexorably toward the weekend when he planned
his baptism and conversion.

Nothing was a secret any longer. The Foot even told me that he and Paulene had known of my dismissal from the seminary. Somehow I wasn't surprised that Leifman had called him from New York, as the Foot was fairly
well-known at the seminary as a man who assembled scholarship money,
including the fund that paid my tuition, and that had made my journey to
New York possible.

I was not happy to hear this of course, but my praying had steadied me, and I began to understand why he and Paulene then took the steps they did.

"I talked to your mother, who naturally was very upset, and she agreed that you'd come and work for us. But there was more, and this was all Paulene."

"The girls?"

"Yes."

"I knew it," I said as he and I stood together late one day at pick-up time, and Tali and Aviva were doing their magic, escorting the kids to their waiting cars, giving and receiving hugs, and exchanging small talk about the food the kids had eaten or the activities they'd liked best with the interested parents.

"That's right," the Foot went on. "Your mother devised the plan. 'If my sons are going to work at camp,' she said, 'how about making it really, really interesting?' I got her drift, and a day or so later I was on the phone with the Jewish Agency."

"That's where they come from?"

"We use the agency to recruit staff from abroad. This time, I said to them, as your mom instructed, 'Send us the most beautiful and talented Jewish girls you have.'"

"They really fit the bill," I said. "And then some."

"They are lookers."

When the Foot said that phrase, I was astonished. He didn't talk that way, Paul did! That was one of Paul's favorite words; in fact every waitress who served him, except Paulene, was a "looker."

Suddenly I was on the hunt again. "Would you repeat that, Mr. Footlick?"

"Look, I was just speaking about the girls. You'll look them up in Israel one day. You'll hike with them. You'll have adventures. You'll have a life different from your father. Norman, don't take that the wrong way. He had game, but you have something else. You have . . ."

"Mr. Footlick, say *that* again. Please!"

"He had game."

That was one of Paul's favorite phrases too.

"Amazing."

"What's amazing? What's happening to you now, son?"

I now walked around the Foot; I peered at him. I tried to pick up vibrations of Paul's soul. In my backsliding now, I was excited. It made perfect sense. Paul's unfinished business would be mostly with the Foot, whom he had hated and who now was about to sweep away his wife. It had been right before my eyes all this time, and I had never noticed. Was it possible? I felt practically like opening Foot's mouth to examine him closely, like the proverbial gift horse to see if Paul was there.

"Do you know what an *ibbur* is, Mr. Footlick?"

"Can't say I do."

Then I explained it all to him, and while he listened patiently, at the end of my peroration about souls, all he said was, "That's very, very interesting."

I let my insight or vision or delusion or hope, or whatever it was, pass, like a residual pain from an illness cured, and I was glad for it.

Then, however, the Foot sat down on the railing nearby. As he did so, he crossed his legs, the right over the left with a little lift that, yes, yet again reminded me of Paul. My god, why was I still seeing clues everywhere?

Now I studied the way he sat there and now shifted his whole body in a kind of little *tuchus* lift after crossing the legs. Boy, was that ever like Paul, raising his trousers and torquing slightly so that the back pocket on the left, often lumpy with a wad of winnings—mainly one-dollar bills wrapped by a fifty, if he had it—and held together by the ever-present rubber band, wouldn't bother him.

"You feel okay, Mr. Footlick?"

"Your behavior is making me a little on edge, but that's all. Yes."

"Would you mind just walking around a bit for me?"

"Your father's what is it, again?"

"*Ibbur.*"

"Well . . ."

"I know I sound crazy, but I mean for just a second, like in a beauty contest, just a few steps."

"Sure. Maybe I should call your mother and tell her I'll let you lie down in my office to rest up a bit before you go home? What do you say?"

"Just turn a bit, walk, please."

So the Foot obliged me, and as he walked I looked and looked. His gait had a little hitch in it, and Paul's never did. The Foot didn't say anything else that reminded me of Paul. Lots of people use those phrases, I decided. My evidence was scant, and who needed it any more?

The Foot patiently finished his circumambulation and stood in front of me awaiting my judgment, just as Tali and Aviva raced by with some campers.

That gave him a chance to change the subject, which was an excellent idea because I knew now that he was the Foot and Paul wasn't there, not within him, not anywhere close.

"Your mother would like you to marry one of those girls, you know."

"Is that part of their contract?"

"No, it isn't."

We had a manly laugh together, and then he added: "As to you and the seminary, she and I decided to make believe it didn't happen. Just like you. Now you don't have to talk with me or with her about it either, if you don't want. I've worked with rabbis all my life. It's a hard career, and there are peaks and valleys of enthusiasm and commitment. Some leave, some return. Like marrying, then divorcing, then remarrying but the same woman. No one's consistent in this life. Your mother prefers to think that you're not throwing in the towel, that you're in one of those troughs or valleys of faith. A hiatus."

"Hiatus. Sounds very relaxing. Like a condition."

"Take your time."

"Oh, I am. I'm just praying the *kaddish*. I think it has a lot of power."

He nodded, and let me go off and do precisely that.

Still, even if I were letting Jon go, he and Paulene had not given up, not quite yet. The next day, early in the morning as we went off to work, in one last attempt to change Jon's mind, Paulene prevailed on me to do what I had promised to do when I'd arrived home: simply to visit Paul's grave at Mt. Eden Cemetery.

Amazingly, I hadn't done it yet.

She asked Jon, of course, to drive up there with me. "Talk to him. Directly. It's a summer full of surprises. Who knows, maybe you'll get through. Look what Houdini could do. Stranger things have happened. See what your father has to say about what his boys are up to. All of you be crazy together."

Jon was reluctant, but he could not say no, and did not.

Inexplicably, Tali and Aviva asked if they could join us.

AND SO, on the second day of the second-to-last week of camp, when the kids were all accounted for, we climbed into the Rambler and began the trip to Mt. Eden.

The girls were in the back seat, as usual, and Jon was behind the wheel. It was immediately obvious the girls weren't interested in visiting Paul's grave. That was our business. They each had bought a new Brownie camera because they'd never been to the San Fernando Valley and wanted to take some pictures of sites they'd heard about: orange groves, earthquake-damaged overpasses, and a drive-in restaurant that attracted customers by having on its roof a thirty-foot-high sculpture of a pickle. Could we oblige them?

We drove down Fairfax, hopped onto the Santa Monica Freeway, and then merged with the 495 north toward the San Fernando Valley. All the while Jon drove slowly, reluctantly, with maximum safety and obeisance to the rules, not like the former cabdriver but like the future Mormon. Although he took his time, as if he did not want to arrive, he knew the route well.

Soon enough we were on the 118, making its long, lazy curve into the residential neighborhood of middle-class tract homes where the cemetery was located.

Within minutes the small, gentle slopes of Mt. Eden loomed into view, a series of terraced and rolling hummocks green as the infield at Dodger Stadium; picture a diamond not with white bases but studded with gray, brown, and black stones.

Maybe it was just the vantage from the highway as we descended toward the necropolis, but the cemetery seemed huge, far larger than I remembered. For some reason I thought of several other of the cemeteries in LA that I'd been to now and then as a kid: the one in Hollywood where the movie stars were buried and where Paulene once took us along as part of a tour she'd signed up for; then there was Forest Lawn where the rich moguls are buried; and the little cemetery in Boyle Heights, in East LA, the old Jewish part of town where we buried Uncle Dan and where the Relic had her spot and was destined to be placed in the ground. I thought of all the cemeteries like these in LA, in California, and then their counterpart locations in all of the cities and towns of America, and of the whole world.

As we looked for the parking lot, I was assailed by one of those simple thoughts, so obvious it hardly bears mention and yet also cannot go unsaid; namely, just how many dead people there are all around us. If you add in all the lost cemeteries, those now beneath buildings, malls, shopping centers, and very likely beneath so many highways and roads, including the very roads we had been driving on, the dead are around us always, and are almost always very near.

The whole of this bracing thought went by so quickly, and yet I remember it, and it just filled me up with a kind of preternatural contentment, as we idled for the light at Balboa and Rinaldi Streets.

We stopped at one more intersection, where the gas stations on all the four corners competed with each other, cheaper gas for longer trips, for more travel, for more enjoyment, for more life: Go Royal 76! Go Shell. Go Union Carbide!

By the time we pulled into the parking lot of Mt. Eden, with its hill after hill of surrounding gravestones, it was clear that if the dead were everywhere, outnumbering the living by great degrees, didn't the dead, despite their muteness, in effect rule? Democracy demanded it. And wasn't their silence not silence, but the laughing and the carrying-on of the victorious dead below?

As if they had read my mind, the angels now fairly leaped out of the Rambler and began taking pictures of the cemetery. They were photographing the whole place, as if it were all a kind of panorama full of action they saw and I was only just beginning to glimpse, like a picture emerging on the paper, out of the chemical bath, from the developing tray. I felt exhilarated.

We walked up to the main gate, and all four of us just stood there for a moment. I remembered that as kids when we had driven past graveyards, we always held our breath. Our reason had something to do with ghosts and not wanting somehow to inhale their invisible plumes or traces.

Now I really understood: the dead have real strength, presence, and perseverance, and over the aeons of time, oh, what an army of them have gathered beneath and all about us. They really could sweep us away if we let our breath entwine with theirs.

Made perfect sense.

And there was more. It was growing on me that those dead then, and these stretching out before us, all Paul's neighbors at Mt. Eden, didn't need to have God, the Jews, the Mormons, or any organized religious organizations helping them out. Or speaking for them. Just look around! Just look at this vast place, I thought. Just listen!

By themselves, the dead are a huge part of the very picture of our daily lives. Only we don't like to admit it. Why search for and agonize about souls, as I had been doing, when the dead, the rock solid, bone solid dead, are so close by and are exerting their profound ossified influence already?

From beneath and all over the earth, are the dead not pressing *up* at us just as surely as the atmosphere of the air presses *down* on us from above? Up and down, up and down, we split the difference every day, in our every waking second, and we are as a result balanced and steadied.

At least that's the goal.

Under the earth as well as on it, in the mausoleums and in the vast necropolises that fill in every gap between the freeways and the housing developments that we had whizzed by today and almost every day, there the dead truly live.

These were the cities and the burgs of the dead. If you extrapolated how many dead have been interred in the earth from the beginnings of human habitation, they clearly far outnumber us, the living.

So, yes, I might say the convenient word, God, in all of its forms in my *kaddish*es, and use it to orient my prayer, but it now dawned on me that it was not God but the dead in whom I truly believed.

Now we stepped into the cemetery proper. Well, Jon and I did. Tali and Aviva had spotted a winding street that led away from Mt. Eden and down toward the old San Fernando Mission. The angels chose the mission as the next destination to go to take more pictures. We agreed to meet right here in the parking lot in thirty minutes.

That left Jon and me slowly to climb the rising hillside and head to section 140, quadrant 18, grave bed 8b, there to find Paul and his marker on the place designated Shalom Hill, the Temple Beth Ami portion of the cemetery.

As we walked, no funeral procession, gravedigger, gardener, or groundskeeper emerged. From the small white stucco chapel and from its adjoining administrative office, which we passed and where I remembered rabbinically signing the official papers after Paul's service, no one came out. Not another car was parked nearby. There were no visitors, living visitors, that is, but us.

Then we finally arrived and stood in front of Paul's resting place, a green rectangle slightly raised at the end of which his stone stood, a modest gray piece of granite curved at the top and low to the ground: Paul Gould, 1901–1966.

That was all. No image and no words about his being a good husband, father, okay horseplayer, or having been very, very good at Texas Hold 'Em.

We both stood there. Waiting and listening. There was no more arguing between us. We were just doing as our mother had asked of us: to stand and to wait.

Maybe it was only the wind that now swirled up and swept in from the freeways that encircled the green precincts, but I did begin to detect a kind of shape to all of the white noise. It was as if the din formed itself into discrete, distinct units of sound, of the dead speaking to each other, notes and patterns among rolling voices and choruses across their grounds.

Then this was the most remarkable thing: in the midst of all of this I *did* hear the clear voice of Paul. I don't think it was my rendition of Paul, but Paul's are-you-kidding-me-little-guy voice sounding in my ears.

I didn't startle or move or turn to my brother. I just stood there and listened in the silence.

Paul didn't berate me for not having said sufficient *kaddishes* for him; nor was he about to get on Jon's case for hitting the Mormon trail; and he made no mention of Paulene or the Foot.

No, Paul's bombastic entrance to the yammering chorus in the cemetery, his solo voice, was nothing less than a recitation of some lines from Thomas Gray's "Elegy in a Country Churchyard." He had recited that long poem to me by heart once, long ago. Now I heard it. It was here and it was him:

> The curfew tolls the knell of parting day,
> The lowing herd wind slowly o'er the lea,
> The plowman homeward plods his weary way,
> And leaves the world to darkness and to me.
>
> . . . .
>
> The boast of heraldry, the pomp of power,
> And all that beauty and wealth e're gave,
> Awaits alike the inevitable hour,
> The paths of glory lead but to the grave.

I didn't know these lines well, if at all, and certainly not by heart. It could not have been me reciting them. Was Jon hearing it? He stood silent, respectful, head down, his thumbs thrust into the front small pockets of his jeans.

No, this was our father's pleasant baritone, and with an earnestness that knows that underground, from where it arose, the bluff is truly over. In short, it was eloquent and beautiful, and it was all I could do to keep from poking Jon in the arm, and crying, Did you hear it? Hey, man, did you hear that!

But of course I did not.

And yet I knew something had happened.

I knew significance had planted a flag in the heart of that moment. I wanted to shout, but I restrained myself, because I knew I was the recipient of new and utterly believable proofs from beyond. I now knew that the dead and their unadorned lifestyle in the dirt should be acknowledged and celebrated precisely for what it was, for what it is, no more and no less.

That is, forget heaven and forget hell. And forget rotting away. No, rather the dead were to be viewed as genuine denizens of neither a Jewish afterlife nor a Mormon one, but simply as citizens of the most secular locale in the world: the ground. Everyone shared it, everyone trod on it.

Should it therefore not be said that the dead, including Paul, were utterly unconnected with God as we conceive Him? Contrary to popular idea, the dead were even farther removed from God than the living, way far away. Paul recited that poem because it was true: we are born to die; we are destined for the ground. So that's what they speak of, not God or heaven or angels, but what they know best, what they know intimately: the coolness and the moistness of the dirt; its occasional rankness when something goes awry, say, with the plumbing at Mt. Eden or the runoff after a storm; or of how in the earthquake of 1953, they feared a whole hillside might move beneath them; but now, in these later more secure years, of how a few clods of dirt might shift around them, and how when that happened the clump of dirt might sound like a knock on the door.

That's what the white noise was all about, a discussion of dirt in its various qualities; the way the living speak of the weather is perhaps the closest analogy.

They would speak of their quietness in the dirt occasionally disturbed by noise from above; of car crashes just beyond the cemetery gates; of the pneumatic drilling Jon and I now heard in the near distance where new construction was unfolding so that the still living or the pre-dead, as I now saw them, could fill up new tract homes in San Fernando's and in Granada Hills's newest communities.

And then the dead might speak of the building collapses that occurred just above them in 1964, and the shifting foundations and the tectonic plates, all the interesting auditory action and the eyewitness news from the world below all mediated and translated to them through the dirt, which, after all, is the air the dead breathe.

I was so excited by this kind of communication that I began to wonder if there might be a grave-digging position available here at Mt. Eden. Perhaps I could apply for it when camp was over.

"Time's up, I guess," Jon said. Then he added, with humility, "And I didn't hear anything. You?"

"No, not really."

We met up with the angels in the parking lot, and then drove back down to the city, but fast this time, very fast, with all of the speed of young people who want to flee death and the dead, with that headlongness to which we were entitled by virtue of our youth.

As we approached the center of the city, Jon's cabdriver speed and daring returned to him once more. It was as if he too knew this was the last trip with the angels and, maybe, the last ever with his brother. We were racing past everyone, no cops stopped us, we were in a zone of our own, and we were out at Santa Monica and the beach in record time.

What I'm saying is that as we approached land's end again, the long way home, I rolled down the window and the wind whipped my hair and the wisps of my beard, and whooshed by my ears making a salutary comforting sound. And in that sound I began to hear it again.

The voices of the dead were still audible out here. They were not confined to the environs of Mt. Eden or of any particular locale. They prevail, and they speak in the voices of the winds' and the highways' reverberations, especially to the young as they pass cemeteries, and occasionally you can hear them as you fall asleep and wake up.

The trick is to discern the individual voice. I was lucky. I had heard Paul. Maybe all the *kaddish*es had prepared me to listen in a new way; maybe they had earned me his evocative recitation. I did not think I was going to hear him again, and in any event, as I reported to Paulene, he offered no opinon on the living matter at hand: Jon's conversion.

It in fact occurred very quietly—we found out many months later—just a few days after the visit to the cemetery.

My Noah's Ark play turned out to be not the disaster all had feared, because once I'd gotten into my *kaddish* groove, my concentration on whatever other task was at hand had grown.

There was even some applause from the audience, and compliments from the anaconda's father. He had just finished co-producing one of those *Planet of the Apes* movies and said I'd done an inventive job.

Yet neither my assistant, Aviva, nor Tali was there that day to see the play performed and to take the bows they deeply deserved—for the play, for the summer, and for changing my life.

The day before the performance they didn't appear at camp. The Foot reported that a midnight message had arrived for them at the condo. It was Jerusalem calling. They had been summoned back to Israel by the Jewish Agency on behalf of the IDF. Some military crisis was emerging, the Foot guessed, but the angels of course were not permitted to tell him the reason they were being summoned home.

They packed quickly, he reported, and he drove them to LAX early in the morning. At the airport he noticed other Israelis that the angels seemed to recognize. He gleaned there were post-Six-Day War rumblings on the border with Jordan or with Syria, and they, as well as the many other elite reservists who had been deployed to Jewish communities around the world, were being called home and back to duty.

"We're lucky we had them with us as long as we did," he said.

Then the Foot and I discussed the ordinance that Jon was going to file not only for Paul, but for the rest of the family, and for the Family *Tot*. He knew all about this. Paulene, who had observed it all—but not let on to me—had discussed all of it with him. He said the Jewish community was aware of the Mormon practice, and there was even talk among temple executives of the community as a whole of suing the Mormon Church in a class action for their practice of offering their gospel to Holocaust victims randomly if they had Jewish-sounding names. He said we could sue the Mormon Church specifically on behalf of Paul if I wanted and if Paulene wanted.

We never did, and, frankly, I'm not even sure Jon ever filed the ordinances. I never heard about it again, and I never asked. Anyway, I had my *kaddish*es to say then, and every year since, on the anniversary of his death, for the rest of my life.

Jon's decision to convert, as I have said, turned out to be the right one for him. Western Oaks recovered quickly enough to preside over Jon's marriage to Mary Anne, which occurred about six months later. Neither of us had our lottery numbers called. Neither of us went to Vietnam. His marriage has been a happy one, and they have three kids. The firstborn, a boy, he called Paul.

Jon and his family came to the Foot and Paulene's marriage, which, yes, I officiated at shortly after I was ordained at the seminary, to which I did return.

I also officiated at the Relic's funeral, where Jon had the beautiful idea to bury her with the baseball glove, and Paulene said to throw in Paul's lighter and ashtray.

At the ceremony I told how we tried to teach her the infield-fly rule in Yiddish, and Jon spoke movingly about that ball game where he tried to tell her about the Latter-day Saints concepts in Yiddish, the nurturing mother tongue of our East European forebears. I never knew my brother knew so much Yiddish, and he loved to use it. I heard he was even offering an adult ed class in Yiddish and elementary Hebrew at his church.

I have not had a terribly distinguished career as a rabbi. I failed at the two pulpits I decided to try after my ordination. One was in Iowa and another in Nevada, where the temple's executive director's complaints about families not paying their dues made me sound off.

I liked the emptiness of Nevada, and have stayed. It's a place where big things yet might happen, and I found Moon Lake, a small town that has a big casino, and a total of about thirteen regular resident Jews. Their obsession with gambling appealed to me and I enjoyed looking at their faces when I ran into them at the casino, where I too hung out regularly to play a little stud and blackjack, but never, absolutely never on the Sabbath or on any of the major Jewish holidays.

I've managed to make a living teaching courses at various community colleges on basic Judaism and mysticism, and I also tutor the many Mormons in the area who have a passion for learning Hebrew, including bishops and high-ranking leaders of the church. One was referred to me by Western Oaks, who went on to become a major leader in the church and a vice president of Ralph's Supermarkets. One of my students told me he believes, as did the Puritans, that when God speaks, His chosen language is ancient Hebrew. What can it hurt?

I'm working now, as I have been for many years, on a book about Jewish angels and how they figure in our tradition. I'm in the midst of a chapter on

Sandalphon, the great angel who arose in the Middle Ages, at the height of persecutions, and the stories of this huge angel's redemptive powers and how he bestrides the world like a Jewish Colossus to save it.

My book has many other chapters, but until these pages I have not gotten personal. I have until now made no mention of Tali and Aviva or of that summer of 1967.

Nor did I ever see or hear of them again.

I've had numerous opportunities to go to Israel, but I have always found a reason to back out, often at the last minute. If I were to go, this is how it would happen: I would arrange transportation to Sfad the moment my plane lands. I would find the phone book in the lobby of my hotel. I would not even go up to the room. My bag would rest right there beside me in the corner, near the phone. I would try to look up Tali and Aviva, even though I know there will be no listing; I mean I don't even know their surnames! Still, I would try and I would fail. I would become desperate, obsessed to see what became of them, to see if they married, if they had families, or if they vanished into thin air.

No, I'd end up walking the hilly streets of that holy and mystical city hour after hour looking at the faces of women as they pass me. I'd tap someone on the shoulder whose long red hair reminded me of Tali; she'd turn but not be her. I'd find a soccer field somewhere between the Torah academies where young women are playing. Maybe. I'd rush up to a girl racing down the sideline, but she would not be Aviva.

For all I know, the police will be called, and what would I be able to explain to them?

No, I prefer to think of the angels as having been there that summer in LA for me, and for Jon, and for Paulene, and for my father and for my family alone. And that that was their mission, their entire reason for being.

I want to think of them only in LA, their hair flying as they ride in the Rambler with us, their bodies soaring in the air in the twilight at Sorrento Beach. I still smell their perfume. I still hear their voices and their whisperings for me not to forget that while we are, like them, nobody in particular in the eyes of heaven, we are everything to each other here on earth and always must try to act that way.

ABOUT THE AUTHOR

ALLAN APPEL, born in Chicago and raised in Los Angeles, is a prize-winning novelist and playwright whose books include *Club Revelation*; *High Holiday Sutra*, winner of a Barnes and Noble Discover Great New Writers Award; and *The Rabbi of Casino Boulevard*, a finalist for the National Jewish Book Award. His work has appeared in the *National Jewish Monthly*, the *Progressive, National Lampoon,* and *Tablet,* and his plays have been produced in New York, Chicago, New Haven, and Provincetown. *The Excommunication of Mrs. Eaton,* about Puritan theocracy in early New Haven, won the Connecticut Heritage Productions full-length play award in 2011. He has published 14 books, including eight novels. His most recent novel, *The Hebrew Tutor of Bel Air* (Coffee House Press, 2010) is being optioned for television. The winner of two fellowships in fiction from the Connecticut State Office of Arts and Tourism, Appel lives in New Haven, where for the last decade he has been a staff writer for the online *New Haven Independent.*